THE PERFECT GENTLEMAN

"Perhaps the perfect Lord Andrew has a longing to kiss someone like you. . . ."

He lowered his mouth and kissed her neck, and she buried her fingers in his hair. He lifted her onto his knees and pulled her even more tightly against him. The wine they had drunk at dinner, combined with their fatigue, had deafened them to proprieties. Penelope felt her body becoming loose and wanton under his caressing hands and mouth. . . .

THE PAPER PRINCESS

"Look at me, my princess," he said softly. His arms were tightly round her. The effect of holding her so close was making his head swim. Felicity turned bewildered eyes up to his face and saw a light burning in those black eyes that made her tremble.

He suddenly held her very tightly against him, smelling the light scent she wore and feeling the trembling of her body. . . .

Also by Marion Chesney
Published by Fawcett Books:

QUADRILLE
THE GHOST AND LADY ALICE
LADY LUCY'S LOVER
THE FLIRT
DAPHNE
THE FIRST REBELLION
SILKEN BONDS
THE LOVE MATCH
THE SCANDALOUS LADY WRIGHT
HIS LORDSHIP'S PLEASURE
HER GRACE'S PASSION
THE SCANDALOUS MARRIAGE
A MARRIAGE OF INCONVENIENCE
A GOVERNESS OF DISTINCTION
THE DESIRABLE DUCHESS
THE GLITTER AND THE GOLD
MISS DAVENPORT'S CHRISTMAS
THE SINS OF LADY DACEY

THE
PERFECT
GENTLEMAN

THE
PAPER
PRINCESS

Marion Chesney

FAWCETT CREST • NEW YORK

A Fawcett Crest Book
Published by Ballantine Books

THE PAPER PRINCESS copyright © 1987 by Marion Chesney
THE PERFECT GENTLEMAN copyright © 1988 by Marion
Chesney

Library of Congress Catalog Card Number: 94-94268

ISBN 0-449-22307-8

Printed in Canada

First Ballantine Books Edition: September 1994

10 9 8 7 6 5 4 3 2 1

Contents

Contents

THE PERFECT GENTLEMAN

Chapter One

The marriage proposal of Lord Andrew Childe, younger son of the Duke and Duchess of Parkworth, was everything it should have been.

For Lord Andrew did everything well. He was handsome and faultlessly dressed. He was a famous whip, he boxed with Gentleman Jackson, he read ancient Greek easily, and he wrote witty poems in Latin.

He saw no reason to trouble himself by pursuing some debutante at the London Season. Some time before it had begun, before the leaves were yet on the trees, he had singled out Miss Ann Worthy as his future bride.

Lord Andrew was thirty-two and considered young misses insipid. Miss Worthy was twenty-eight and hailed from the untitled aristocracy. From her long, aristocratic nose to her long, narrow feet, she was every inch a lady. She never betrayed any vulgar excess of emotion or committed any common faux pas.

Only an admirer of Lord Byron or some such woolly headed creature would have criticized Lord Andrew's proposal, might have pointed out that the very passionless chilliness of it showed a sad flaw

3

in the character of the Perfect Gentleman—Lord Andrew's nickname.

He had broached the matter to her parents first and had been accepted by them.

He was left alone with Miss Worthy for a short space of time in the blue saloon of the Worthys' town house in Curzon Street.

Miss Worthy was sitting in front of a tambour frame, neatly putting stitches into a design of bluebells. She affected not to know what was in the air.

He stood in the doorway for a moment, watching her.

She was attired in an expensive morning gown of tucked and ruched white muslin. A cap of pleated muslin almost hid the thick tresses of her red hair. Her nose was long and straight, and her mouth small enough to please the highest stickler. Her pale green eyes veiled by red and gold lashes might have been thought to be a trifle too close-set. Her hands were very long and white.

Although she knew very well Lord Andrew was standing there, and why he had come, she continued to stitch for that short minute before turning her head and affecting a start of surprise.

"Lord Andrew!" she exclaimed. She rose with a graceful movement and went to sit on a backless sofa in front of the cold fireplace—for the Worthys did not light fires after the first of March, no matter what the weather.

"Good afternoon, Miss Worthy," said Lord Andrew. "I trust I find you well?"

"Very well, my lord. Pray be seated."

He was carrying his hat, cane, and gloves—that traditional sign that a gentleman did not intend to stay very long. He laid them down on a small table, approached the sofa, and fell to one knee in front of her.

"Miss Worthy," he said, "I have leave from your parents to pay my addresses to you. I wish to marry you. Will you accept me?"

"Yes, my lord."

He stood up and took her hand and drew her to her feet. He bent his head and kissed her on the mouth. The day was cold. Icy lips met icy lips in a chaste embrace.

Right on cue, Mr. and Mrs. Worthy made their entrance. The happy couple stood hand in hand, gracefully accepting congratulations. Mr. Worthy, thin and ascetic and longing to get back to his beloved books, called for champagne after having been nudged in the ribs by his small, dumpy wife.

Lord Andrew took a glass, toasted his fiancée, toasted his future in-laws, and then took his leave.

All just as it should have been.

With the long, easy stride of a practiced athlete, he walked to his parents' house in Park Lane— although it, like the neighboring houses, still faced onto Park Street. Not so long ago Park Lane had been Tyburn Lane of dubious repute. There was not much of a view of Hyde Park, for the high wall which had been built to screen the residents from the condemned on their way to the scaffold was still there. One enterprising resident had had part of the wall removed and the entrance to his house made leading from Park Lane itself, but the rest still preferred to keep to Park Street, which was still the front entrance for the rest of the houses.

Up until that moment when he walked into his parents' house and made his way to the library,

Lord Andrew would have considered himself the most fortunate and happiest of men. Unlike most younger sons, he was very rich, having been given one of the minor ducal houses and estates as his own. By studying all the latest innovations in scientific farming, he had made it prosper. The money from his estates had been carefully invested. He could have afforded his own town house and could have lived completely independently from his family if he chose.

But the Duchess of Parkworth had managed to turn the large town house into a home. It had an air of ease and prettiness and elegance. Lord Andrew found it restful.

In his early years, he had not seen very much of his parents from one year's end to the other. He had an excellent tutor whose job it was to turn him into a gentleman. Lord Andrew had admired this tutor greatly. And so Lord Andrew went to Oxford University, and then on the Grand Tour with his tutor, and then into the army to "round him off."

When his tutor, Mr. Blackwell, died while he was away at the wars, Lord Andrew felt as if he had lost a father. Mr. Blackwell had orchestrated the forming of Lord Andrew's character, down to choosing his tailor. He had even seen to it that my lord had lost his virginity at a suitably early age at the hands of a lusty and bawdy housemaid. That last experience had caused Lord Andrew to acquire a certain distaste for the female sex. But on the whole, he was happy and carefree and interested in perfecting everything he turned his hand to, always trying to live up to the high standards of his now deceased tutor.

But as he sat down in the library and gazed at

the flickering flames of the fire, he felt, for the first time, uncomfortable inside his own skin.

Usually when he had done just as he ought, he could see in his mind's eye Mr. Blackwell's smile of approval. But all he could think of was that chilly kiss. What else did he expect? Marriage was one thing, lust another.

He usually looked forward to the Season as a break from the cares of agriculture. He enjoyed racing and fencing and dancing, the opera, plays, and parties. He did not have to attend the House of Lords. That chore fell to the eldest son, the Marquess of Bridgeworth, who enjoyed making long and boring speeches on the game laws.

But for the first time, Lord Andrew began to feel uneasily bored. He remembered when he had been very small, his nurse promising to take him to the servants' Christmas party. He had lain awake for nights before the great event, trembling with anticipation. But then his nurse had told him that his mother, the duchess, had learned of her plans, and he was not to attend.

He had not cried, for he knew even then that men of five years old did not cry. But life had seemed to lose color for quite a long time afterwards.

That was what he felt like now, as if he had just experienced a disappointment.

He shook himself and decided his spleen must be disordered from lack of exercise. He would go riding in the park.

He was just about to leave the library and go to his room and change into his riding dress when his father came in.

The duke was small, burly, and undistinguished.

He was wearing a banyan wrapped round his thick body and a turban on his head. The banyan was of peacock silk and the oriental turban was of cloth-of-gold, but he still looked more like a bad-tempered farmer than a duke.

"How do?" he grunted. "See the *Gentleman's Magazine* anywhere?"

"Yes, over on the table."

"Good, good," said the duke, shuffling forward to pick it up.

"I proposed to Miss Worthy, Father, and she accepted."

"Well, of course she would," said the duke, picking up the magazine and fishing in his bosom for his quizzing glass.

Lord Andrew smiled. "You think me a great catch, then?"

"Oh, no," said the duke, riffling through the pages. "The Worthys have been hanging out for a title this age. She's got a good dowry, Miss Worthy, and she could have married Mr. Benjamin Jepps this age, but they'd all set their hearts on a title."

"You did not tell me that," said Lord Andrew stiffly.

"Didn't I? Didn't seem important. She's good family, and you ain't exactly in the first blush of youth."

"Yet I am not in my dotage."

"Grrmph," said his father, settling himself down in a wing chair and studying an article in the magazine.

"When does Mother come to town?"

"Hey, what's that?"

"I asked when Mother was coming to town," said Lord Andrew patiently.

8

"Next week," said the duke, "with this Miss Whatsit she's bringing out."

"Mother sponsoring another debutante? Why was I not told of this?"

"Why should you be? Not your home. Got enough blunt of your own to buy your own house. Why don't you?"

"I would have thought my dear mother and father would have been glad of my company," said Lord Andrew acidly.

"That's common!" said the duke, much shocked. "You've been seeing too many plays. You'll be sitting on my knee next."

"Hardly," said the six-foot-tall Sir Andrew caustically. "Anyway, who is Miss Whatsit, and why is Mama bringing her out?"

"I don't know," said the duke tetchily. "Some parish waif. You know what your mother's like. Lame ducks underfoot the whole time. Poor relations, plain Janes who can't get a husband. Whoever this Miss Whatsit is, you can take it from me she'll be as ugly as sin and won't own a penny. Your mother will have her all puffed up with consequence and vanity, she won't take, and she'll be sent back to the country with a lot of useless airs and graces and marry the curate. Now, run along, do," he added, as if Lord Andrew were still in shortcoats.

Lord Andrew went off to exercise the blue devils out of his system. He rode hard that day, he fenced, he boxed, and then, feeling tired and slightly better, he made his way home again. But as he walked past a row of shops in South Molton Street just as the light was fading, he saw an interesting tableau in the upstairs window of an apartment above a butcher's shop.

9

The little shopkeeper's parlor was ablaze with candles. The butcher and his wife, dressed in their best, were facing a young couple, a pretty girl and a tall, honest-looking young man. The young man said something and took the girl's hand in his. The girl blushed and lowered her eyes. The young man put his hand on his heart. The butcher's wife began to cry happy tears, and the butcher raised his burly arms in a blessing.

Lord Andrew felt a queer little tug at his heart. Had he not been the son of a duke, had he been, say, the son of a shopkeeper, he would have been brought up close to his parents. His engagement would have been a celebration, thanks would have been given to God, and he would have received his father's blessing.

A cold wind blew an old newspaper against his legs, and he angrily kicked it away.

Among their many properties, the Duke and Duchess of Parkworth owned the Sussex village of Lower Bexham. The squire, Sir Hector Mortimer, had recently died, leaving a pile of debt to his one surviving child, Penelope.

The vicar of St. Magnus the Martyr, the church in Lower Bexham, had written to the duchess about young Penelope's plight.

The duchess wrote back immediately, promising to call on this Miss Mortimer. The Duchess of Parkworth had a soft heart, easily touched, but unfortunately, although she started off with enthusiasm to help her lame ducks, she could not sustain any interest in them for long. She was lame duckless for the moment. The previous charge had been a young footman who had confessed to a longing to be an army captain. The duchess had arranged everything and then had promptly forgotten about the footman. Even when she got a sad little letter from the footman saying he would have to resign his commission, for without any private income, he could not pay his mess bills, she had pettishly thrown it away, saying, "It is of no use to go on helping people who cannot help themselves."

Fortunately for him, the footman had the wit to then write to Lord Andrew, who investigated his capabilities as a soldier, sorted out his debts, and arranged an allowance for him. When the duchess learned that the ex-footman was still a captain, and when she had not heard further from him, she had gone about saying, "There you are! People must stand on their own two feet."

She descended on Penelope Mortimer suffused with all the warm glow of a Lady Bountiful.

Penelope Mortimer's appearance came as rather a shock. The duchess was used to forwarding the careers of plain girls. Penelope had blond, almost silver hair, with a natural curl. Her blue eyes were wide and well spaced and fringed with sooty lashes. Her figure was dainty. She was a trifle small in stature.

Miss Mortimer's one remaining servant introduced the duchess, who sailed in like a galleon. The duchess was almost as tall as Lord Andrew, but a liking for food had given her a massive figure, which she tried to reduce by wearing sturdy whalebone corsets. She had a small head and small hands and feet. Her massive figure did not seem to belong to her. It was as if she had poked her head through the cardboard cutout of a fat lady at the fairground.

11

The duchess was enchanted by Penelope's appearance and manner. She had not been in the house for ten minutes before she was already weaving dreams about what a sensation Penelope would be at the Season.

Penelope, bewildered by plans for her social debut, tried to explain where matters stood. Her mother had died some years previously, her father the year before. Penelope had sold up everything that could be sold, and most of the debts had been paid. She had put her home on the market and had already selected a comfortable little cottage in the village. She had not once considered coming out. In order to explain to this overwhelming duchess about the exact state of her financial straits, Penelope excused herself and then returned with a pile of accounts' ledgers, all written out in her neat hand. She popped a pair of steel spectacles on her nose and began to explain the figures to the duchess.

But the duchess was staring in horror at those spectacles. Penelope's dreaming expression had disappeared the minute she put those spectacles on, and her eyes gleamed with a most unbecomingly sharp intelligence.

"No, no, no!" said her grace, snatching the spectacles from Penelope's little nose. "You must never wear these dreadful things again!"

"But I must, Your Grace," said Penelope. "I am quite blind without them. How will I be able to read?"

"Books!" said the duchess with loathing. "Young ladies are better off without them, and although I am sure your accounts are correct, it is most unladylike of you to be able to do such things."

"Through lack of money," said Penelope firmly, "I am become used to doing quite a lot of things that young ladies are not supposed to do. I garden and I cook. I find useful occupation most entertaining."

"Horrors!" said the duchess, raising her little hands in the air.

"In fact, Your Grace, you must mot concern yourself with my future. Once I sell this house, I shall have enough to live on for quite some time. I have already put up a sign as a music teacher and have five pupils."

The duchess's mouth sagged in a disappointed droop. This gorgeous creature simply must come to London.

She pulled herself up to her full height. "You have no choice in the matter, Miss Mortimer. I command you to pack your things and come with me!"

There was nothing else Penelope could do. The duke and duchess owned the village. Ever practical, Penelope complied. She would try to enjoy herself at the Season and then return to the village.

A week later, she set out for London, a week during which she had asked and asked for her spectacles only to be told that the duchess "had them safe" but that they were too unbecoming. She presented Penelope with a tiny gold quizzing glass and told her to make the best of that.

At first Penelope tried to accept the loss of her spectacles philosophically. She knew that ladies did not wear them in public and that officers' wives were actually forbidden to wear them. The poor Duchess of Wellington dreaded going out in her carriage, for she was very shortsighted and could not recognize anyone, but even she had to abide by the social laws and leave her spectacles at home.

But on the road to London, Penelope began to think of ways to get them back, hoping the duchess had kept them by her. To this end, she passed most of the journey making friends with the duchess's lady's maid, Perkins, and finally discovering that Perkins herself had the spectacles in safekeeping.

By the time the carriage rolled along Park Street, Penelope had those spectacles back in her own reticule after many promises to Perkins that she would never let the duchess know she had them.

Their arrival was late at night, and so Penelope did not see any of the other occupants of the house. She drank a glass of hot wine and water given to her by Perkins, popped her glasses on her nose, fished a novel out of her luggage, and began to read, putting all this nonsense about the Season firmly out of her mind. On the journey to London, Penelope had become even firmer in her resolve to endure it all as best she could and then return to freedom.

She awoke early despite the fact she had been reading a good part of the night. The bedroom that had been assigned to her was much grander than any room Penelope had slept in before. The bed was luxuriously soft and had a canopy of white lace. There was white lace everywhere—bed hangings, curtains, laundry bag, and even the doilies on the toilet table.

Feeling rather gritty and dirty, Penelope rang the bell and shyly asked the chambermaid who answered it if she might have a bath. But no, that was not possible, was the reply. Water was pumped to the London houses three days a week, and today was not a water day.

Penelope stripped off and did the best she could with the cans of water on the toilet table.

She put on a pretty white muslin with a blue spot and then ventured downstairs. The great house was hushed and quiet. Penelope knew from reading the social news in the papers that the great of London often did not rise until two in the afternoon. But she was very hungry.

A footman was crossing the hall as she came down the stairs, and to her request, he replied that it would be served in the morning room as Lord Andrew liked an early breakfast.

The morning room, he said, was on the first floor on the left. Penelope retreated up the stairs and pushed open the door.

A pleasant smell of coffee and hot toast greeted her. There was a tall man already seated at a table by the window. Penelope could not see him very clearly, but she gained an impression he was black-haired and handsome.

He rose to his feet at her entrance, bowed, and pulled out a chair for her. "You must be Miss Mortimer," he said in a pleasant voice. "I am Childe."

Penelope blinked and then stifled a giggle. It was rather like meeting one of those savages portrayed in the romances she liked to read where a savage would say to the bewildered heroine stranded on some foreign shore, "Me man." Then she remembered Lord Andrew Childe was the duchess's younger son.

"What is amusing you?" asked Lord Andrew.

"It was a nervous giggle," said Penelope primly. "This is a ducal mansion. I am not used to such grandeur. It unnerves me."

"Indeed!" Lord Andrew thought little Miss Mortimer looked very composed. She was not his mama's usual choice of protégée, for there was no denying that Miss Mortimer was remarkably pretty. But there was a vacant, unseeing look in those beautiful eyes of hers which marked a lack of intelligence, thought Lord Andrew. Therefore, after he had helped her to toast and coffee, he was not at all surprised when Penelope asked him, "Do you read novels, Lord Andrew?"

"No," he said with the kind of indulgent smile he reserved for the weaker-brained. "I consider them a great waste of time."

"Life would be very boring without imagination and romance," said Penelope. "Reality can be fatiguing."

"Nonsense. Retreating into novels shows a sad lack of courage. What do you find in the real world so distressing, Miss Mortimer?"

Penelope held up one little hand, rough and reddened from her gardening and cooking, and ticked off the items on her fingers. "My father died last year. One. He left a monstrous pile of debt. Two. I thought I had solved my future and my financial problems when the Duchess of Parkworth arrived and told me I must have a Season. Three," she ended with a final flick of the third finger.

"I see. I am sorry to hear of your father's death and of your troubles. I agree with the first two items, but surely a Season is to be enjoyed!"

"But I didn't want a Season," said Penelope reasonably. "I wanted to be left alone."

"Then you have only to tell my mother that," he said stiffly.

"Oh, but I did!" said Penelope. "And she commanded me to come with her, and as your family owns our village, I could not very well refuse."

"Of course you could have refused. This is not the Middle Ages. Did you expect my mama to take some sort of revenge had you not complied with her wishes?"

"Something like that."

"Now, there we have a good example of the pernicious effect of novels," said Lord Andrew. "You have been imagining all sorts of Gothic nonsense."

"I have?" Penelope tried to bring his face into focus, but it remained a vaguely handsome blur. She had been warned that screwing up your eyes gave you premature wrinkles, and although she was not vain, she had no desire to look old before her time. So to Lord Andrew, her expression appeared vacant and rather stupid.

"Do not trouble yourself further," he said. "I shall speak to my mother today. You will find yourself returned to the country as quickly as possible."

"Thank you," said this irritating beauty meekly. "But you will find it will not serve."

Chapter Two

Knowing his mother would sleep late, Lord Andrew walked round to the Worthys' home in Cavendish Square. Miss Ann Worthy had often assured him she was up with the lark.

But although it was nearly ten in the morning, he was told that the whole family was still in bed. Unable to believe his love could be other than truthful, he commanded the butler to take up a message requesting Miss Worthy to come riding with him that afternoon at two.

Ann Worthy was not amused at being awoken at dawn, as she put it. She was further annoyed by Lord Andrew's invitation. She and her parents were to go that afternoon to visit relatives in Primrose Hill. The relatives included four unmarried misses in their teens. Ann was looking forward to putting their noses out of joint with the announcement of her engagement.

Besides, what was the point of going driving at two in the afternoon? Five was the fashionable hour. There was no one in London at two, thought Miss Worthy, carelessly dismissing the other ninety-eight percent of the town's population from her mind.

She was to see Lord Andrew at the opera that evening. It would do him no harm to learn early that she was not prepared to be at his beck and call. With a novel feeling of power, Miss Worthy sent back a note with the intelligence that she was not free that afternoon. She did not trouble to give any explanation.

Lord Andrew found himself becoming highly irritated. He did not believe Miss Worthy was in bed, for surely since she was not given to extravagances of speech and would not make claims to be an early riser were it not true, he felt she might at least have had the courtesy to receive him.

He did not know that a great deal of his irritation sprang from an unrealized desire to see her again as soon as possible to allay that nagging doubt at the back of his mind.

That he had any doubts about his engagement, he would not admit to himself. Miss Worthy was of good family, she was a lady, and he had made a careful choice. He had done the right thing—as usual—but unusually, doing the right thing had not brought its usual mild glow of satisfaction.

He went for a solitary ride in the park, where he remembered the plight of Miss Mortimer. He smiled indulgently as he recalled the silly little thing's fears about his mother taking revenge.

He rode home and strode up to the morning room. His mother was reading a newspaper, squinting horribly at the print.

"You need spectacles, Mama," he said.

"Nonsense! The light is bad here. Those trees quite take away the sun."

Lord Andrew glanced about the bright room, at the sunlight sparkling on the silver of the coffeepot, but decided argument would be useless.

"Put down that paper, Mama," he said. "I wish to talk about Miss Mortimer."

"Penelope," said the duchess with a fond smile. "Such a dear little thing, and so exquisitely pretty. I declare she will turn all heads."

"But it appears that Miss Mortimer does not wish a Season. She assures me she would be perfectly happy to return to the country. Although she is lacking in intelligence, she does appear to have a certain decided opinion of what she does want. I pointed out to her that she had only to tell you, and you would be happy to let her go."

The duchess's face took on a rather sulky look. "Fiddle. Girls of that age do not know their own minds. And what, pray, is a more pleasant way of occupying a girl's mind than parties and balls?"

"I assure you, that is not the case with Miss Mortimer."

"I know what is best for her," said the duchess. "She must be guided by me. Just wait until Maria Blenkinsop sees my charge! She is bringing out a plain little antidote who she has the gall to say will take the town by storm. When she sees my Penelope, she will change her tune."

"You leave me no alternative," said Lord Andrew. "It appears I must make arrangements myself to send Miss Mortimer back to the country."

The duchess's pale gray eyes hardened. "You may have forgot, my dear boy, that we own that village in which she resides. She has to sell her father, the squire's, house, and plans to buy that little cottage at the end of Glebe Street near the parsonage ground. She has hopes of securing a lease. But I am sure there are others who would be equally interested in that cottage. Quite a sound building, and in good repair."

Her son looked at her in horror. "Are you saying you would punish Miss Mortimer were she to return?"

"No, I did not say that," lied his mother. "What is all this to you, Andrew? You are engaged to exactly the sort of female I would expect you to propose to. . . ."

"Meaning?"

"Never mind. But this is not your house, and Miss Mortimer has nothing to do with you. Why do you not go about your own business and stop meddling in mine? I am sure your fiancée will be desirous of a visit from you."

"Miss Worthy is engaged elsewhere this afternoon."

"Splendid!" said the duchess. "You shall take Miss Mortimer on a drive. She cannot appear anywhere tonish until I have ordered her wardrobe."

"I shall do no such thing."

Lord Andrew had never crossed swords with his mother before. He had dealt with the matter of the footman-turned-captain without telling her about it. He had never before realized that her passion for her lame ducks was so very strong. He was horrified to see tears start to the duchess's eyes. Her whole massive body shook with sobs, and her small face above it pouted like a pug's.

"You never cared for me," hiccuped the duchess. "Never. You always were an unnatural and unfeeling boy. Oh! When I am on my deathbed, then you will wish you had tried to please me. Angels come and take me! My son spurns me. Ah, what is left?"

21

"I'll take the brat out," shouted Lord Andrew. "Where is she?"

"In the drawing room," said the duchess from behind the cover of her handkerchief.

Lord Andrew stormed out.

The morning room had two doors, one leading from the landing and another from the backstairs. The duke entered by the one from the backstairs, holding a cup of chocolate in one hand and a pile of letters in the other.

"What was all that screaming about?" he asked.

"Nothing, my dear," said the duchess placidly. "I was just having a little talk to Andrew."

Penelope looked up in surprise as the door of the drawing room crashed open. She had only a bare second in which to whip off her spectacles before Lord Andrew, still in his riding dress, marched into the room.

"You are coming driving with me," he said abruptly. "Get your bonnet."

"There is no need to shout," said Miss Penelope Mortimer primly. "I did warn you she would not be moved on the matter."

"What are you talking about?" roared Lord Andrew.

"I'll get my bonnet," said Penelope, scrambling from the room.

Lord Andrew looked down at his riding dress. He wondered whether to change and then reflected he could not be bothered going to the effort to please such as Miss Mortimer.

That was the first crack in his perfection, for Lord Andrew had hitherto always worn the correct dress for the occasion.

Penelope selected a gypsy straw bonnet embellished on the crown with marguerites, and tied it firmly under her chin by its gold silk ribbons. She put on her one, good pelisse, her last present from her father. It was of gold-embroidered silk and lined with fur. She had a longing to see what Lord Andrew really looked like, and so when she returned to the drawing room, she opened the door very quietly, raised her quizzing glass which was hanging round her neck, and studied him as he stood by the window looking out over the park.

Lord Andrew sprang into focus. He had thick, glossy black hair cut in the Windswept. He had a high-profiled, handsome face and a firm, uncompromising mouth. His black riding coat was tailored by the hand of a master. His white cravat was intricately pleated and folded. He was wearing breeches and top boots.

She dropped the glass quickly before he turned around, and was idiotically glad he had changed back into a comfortable blur instead of the disturbingly arrogant and handsome man she had seen through the quizzing glass.

"I am driving an open carriage," he said. "It is being brought round from the mews. It is quite correct for you to go out with me without a chaperone."

"I am glad you are at liberty, sir," said Penelope. "I would have thought your time would have been occupied in squiring Miss Worthy."

"Has my mother told you already of my engagement?"

"I did not know you were engaged," said Penelope. "Her Grace remarked on the journey to London that you were courting a Miss Ann Worthy and would no

23

doubt propose to her. May I offer my congratulations?"

"Thank you." He walked across the room and held open the door. They went down the stairs together and out into Park Street.

He helped her into a smart phaeton, seated himself beside her, and nodded to the groom to stand away from the horses' heads.

Soon they were bowling through the park. It was a sunny, brisk day, and the young leaves were just coming out on the trees. Penelope could see things at a distance quite well, and so she settled back to enjoy the prospect. It was only when she realized they were going round the ring for the second time that she ventured to say shyly, "I do not know London at all well. Would it inconvenience you too much to take me somewhere else?"

"Where would you like to go?"

"I would like to see the wild beasts at the Tower."

He was about to refuse, for he could not think of a more vulgar or tedious way of passing the afternoon, but his tutor had always instructed him to be gallant to the ladies. She was his mother's guest, and her wishes must come first.

"Then we shall go to the Tower," he said in a colorless voice.

He began to be amused as they drove along Oxford Street by Penelope's exclamations of delight at the goods in the shop windows. As the shop windows were just about the right distance from the carriage for her to make out things with her faulty vision, Penelope hung on to the side of the phaeton and watched everything and everyone.

"I wonder if the duchess will let me actually shop for a few things," she said wistfully. "I am a good needle-woman, and it is so much more economical, you know, to make one's own things. I have become used to being busy."

"You must ask her, for I cannot be the judge of what goes on in my mother's mind," he said stiffly.

"So she *did* say she would be displeased if I left—to the point of making life awkward for me?" said Penelope.

"That, too, you must find out for yourself."

"You do not appear to be well acquainted with your mother," remarked Penelope.

There was a trace of amusement in her voice, and he looked at her sharply, but her face under the pretty bonnet was demure.

"No, not very well," he agreed after a pause. "Naturally, I spent my youth with first my nurse and then my tutor. When I grew up, I was away a great deal. My father gave me Baxley Manor and estates in Shropshire, and it is there I made my home. This will be my second Season in London since returning from the wars. My parents are somewhat strangers to me."

"But even in a great household, the children are brought down in the evenings to join the family; is it not so?"

"Not always. Not in my case. Do not look so sad, Miss Mortimer; I had every comfort and a good upbringing. It is those novels you read which lead you to sentimental thoughts of a mother's love."

"It is mine own inclination, sir," said Penelope tartly, "which leads me to ideas of motherly love. I am convinced I should be quite a doting mother. But as I am not likely to put it to the test, I shall be unable to offer you any proof."

"Miss Mortimer, with your face and figure, not to

mention my mother's patronage, you will be married before the end of the Season."

"Not I," she said calmly. "My mind is quite made up. Her Grace wishes to produce me at the Season because she considers my looks of a high order. She wishes to compete with her friends."

"You are too harsh," said Lord Andrew. "You are not the first young miss my parent has sponsored. Certainly the prettiest, but by no means the first. She enjoys helping people in trouble."

"Highly commendable. Did Her Grace have a protégé last Season?"

"Yes."

"Tell me about her. Was she a success? Did she marry and live happily ever after?"

Again he looked at her sharply, for there had been, he was sure, a definite hint of mockery in her voice, but she turned her beautiful vague eyes to his and gave him a sweet smile.

"No," he said. "She was a Miss Thornton, a cousin of mine four times removed. Very little dowry and previously accustomed to a modest style of life. She was plain and rather silly. She did not 'take.'"

"Oh, poor Miss Thornton."

"I would not pity her. She had a great many airs and graces before the Season was over and bullied the Park Street servants quite dreadfully. Mother sent her packing."

"At the end of the Season?"

"No, before then. I do not wish to discuss the matter any further."

Lord Andrew remembered the obnoxious Miss Thornton, whose silly head had been quite turned by the duchess's favors. She was allowed to do as

26

she pleased, to eat chocolates and read novels most of the day, and to go to balls and parties for most of the night. But the unlovely creature had been an object of pity on the day the duchess became tired of her. He wondered how long it would be before his mother tired of Miss Mortimer.

It took longer to get to the Tower of London than he had expected, for no sooner had Miss Mortimer seen the bulk of St. Paul's than she demanded to be taken inside. He himself had privately long considered the famous cathedral a depressing barn of a place, but Miss Mortimer dutifully went over it all.

When they left, he suggested they should return home and see the Tower on another day, but Penelope apologized so prettily for having wasted so much time and said that the Tower was so very close that he finally capitulated.

The menagerie was as smelly and depressing as he remembered it to be. He walked away a little and left Penelope to examine the cages.

The cages were not very big, and so Penelope could only dimly make out the animal shapes inside. She was wildly disappointed. She had left her spectacles at home, but even if she had brought them, the stern social laws would have prevented her from putting them on. Then she remembered the quizzing glass the duchess had given her. She put it to one eye, and a lion sprang into view.

A careless keeper who had just fed the animals had left the door of the lion's cage open. Penelope walked closer and closer, assuming that the closeness of the animal was due to the strong magnification of the glass.

The lion opened its cavernous mouth and let out a warning rumble. But Penelope, with one eye

27

screwed shut and the glass at the other, did not realize she had walked into the cage, and thought herself still on the safe side of the bars.

And that was the interesting scene which met Lord Andrew's horrified gaze when he turned around.

There was dainty little Miss Mortimer standing over a large lion, holding a quizzing glass, and calmly looking down its throat.

The day had become hazy and golden. The little tableau looked unreal. But he hesitated only a moment.

He was frightened to make a sudden movement for fear of startling the animal, and frightened to call for the keeper, knowing the resultant shouts and screams might make the lion spring.

He walked slowly into the cage, inching toward Penelope.

"Miss Mortimer," he said in a quite voice, "do not move suddenly or scream, no matter what happens."

The lion gave a full-throated roar. Penelope dropped her quizzing glass in fright and realized the lion was right at her feet, for that animal blur of hair and teeth must be the lion.

Lord Andrew put a strong arm around her waist, lifted her up in his arms, and began to back away. The lion, made sleepy by food, began to follow them slowly.

"Good God," muttered Lord Andrew. "The beast is going to follow us across London."

A startled cry from the keeper at the other end of the row of cages nearly made him drop Penelope. He darted backwards to safety and slammed the door of the cage shut.

"What were you doin' of?" demanded the red-faced keeper, coming up to them. "Them hanimals ain't for playin' with. You Peep-o-Day boys is all the same."

"It is your own cursed carelessness in leaving the cage door open which has brought about this folly," said Lord Andrew.

He turned and marched away with Penelope still in his arms.

"You can put me down now," said Penelope.

He set her on her feet and glared down at her. "How could you be so stupid?" he raged. "What possessed you? Why walk straight into the lion's cage?"

It somehow did not dawn on him that Penelope was longsighted. Practically every member of the ton carried a quizzing glass. The use of it was an art in itself. Many of them were made of plain glass.

Penelope opened her mouth to confess to her longsightedness. But her mother and father had considered it a terrible defect in a lady and had trained her to conceal it on all occasions and never to be seen with spectacles on. She had not troubled to keep up their standards after her father died, but all the stories she had heard of gentlemen taking an acute dislike to longsighted ladies came back into her mind. Normally sensible, Penelope was made silly by a sudden desire not to appear ugly in Lord Andrew's eyes.

"I am sorry," she said, hanging her head. "I have never seen a lion before, and I was so fascinated, I just kept walking closer and closer."

"If you ladies would stop playing around with those silly quizzing glasses, you might see where you are going," said Lord Andrew, glaring at the top of her bent head.

"I *have* apologized," said Penelope huffily. "The least you can do is accept the apology."

"Very well," he said. "Now may I take you home before you get up to any more mischief?"

Penelope tried to start up a conversation on the road back, but Lord Andrew only replied in monosyllables, and at last she fell silent. Lord Andrew was rapidly coming to the conclusion that Miss Mortimer was a trifle simple. He wondered whether she was a result of inbreeding. The fright he had received on seeing her peering down the lion's throat was still with him, and he blamed her bitterly for that fright.

When they arrived in Park Street, he made Penelope a stiff bow and went in search of his mother. She was in the drawing room, studying fashion plates and swatches of cloth.

"Oh, Andrew, you are back," said the duchess amiably. "Tell me what you think of this pink muslin for Miss Mortimer. White is so insipid."

"Mama," he said patiently, "do not concern yourself further with choosing a wardrobe for Miss Mortimer. She is leaving." He crisply outlined the events of the afternoon. The duchess had deliberately put Penelope's longsightedness out of her mind. There should be no flaw in her latest interest.

"I am sure you exaggerate," she said mildly, and fell to studying the pages of the fashion magazine on her lap.

He took the magazine away from her and sat down opposite. "You must be guided by me," he said seriously. "I agree that Miss Mortimer is vastly pretty. But she is not of our rank. She is only the daughter of a country squire and cannot hope to marry above her station. She is alarmingly lacking in wit."

The duchess's well-corseted bosom swelled dangerously. "She is *not going anywhere*," she said harshly. "Go away, and do not trouble me on this matter again."

"Mama . . ."

"You don't love me," cried the duchess. "You never have! You never have had the least spark of feeling. You do not stay here out of any filial warmth but because it suits your pocket not to have an establishment of your own. Ah, your indifference strikes sharp knives into my maternal bosom!"

Lord Andrew turned red. "There has never been any closeness between us," he said. "I barely know my parents, and it is not of my doing."

The duchess held a vinaigrette to her nose and took a noisy sniff at its contents.

"It was all your own doing, not mine, Andrew. All your love was for that tutor of yours, Blackwell."

"May I point out that when Mr. Blackwell wrote to you from Oxford University and suggested I spend a year at home before going on the Grand Tour, you wrote in reply you could not be troubled."

"That's right, it's all *my* fault!" screamed the duchess. "You unnatural and unfeeling child. Oh, my heart." She slapped her hand somewhere in the region of her heart, and her corsets let out a creak of protest. She swayed in her chair. "Water," she whispered.

Thoroughly alarmed, Lord Andrew rang the bell,

and when Perkins, the maid, promptly answered it, he told her to see to her mistress.

"Tell him to go away," moaned the duchess faintly. Perkins looked helplessly at Lord Andrew, who hesitated only a moment before leaving the room.

When the door closed behind him, the duchess straightened up and said briskly, "Do not fuss, Perkins. Go and fetch Miss Mortimer. I wish to show her this vastly fetching creation of pink muslin with gold frogs."

Chapter Three

The sad fact was that Miss Ann Worthy was in the same state as a schoolboy who, having strained every brain cell to pass a difficult exam, and having succeeded, abandons all further academic effort.

For Miss Worthy had worked long and hard to bring Lord Andrew up to the mark. She had diligently studied reports of the war and of politics in the newspapers, although she was completely uninterested in either. She had paid several guineas of her pin money to a Latin scholar to write a little Latin poem for her and coach her in pronunciation so that she could startle the handsome lord with her erudition and wit. Although she preferred to wear all the latest extravagances of dress from damped and near-transparent muslin to head-dresses of fifteen feathers all dyed different colors, she had, on the advice of a top dressmaker, modified her dress to suit her years and status, although she felt sure it did not become her in the least. But Lord Andrew, she knew, was a martinet with very precise ideas of what ladies should wear and how ladies should behave. She had made a study of him before she had actually been introduced to him.

Now the "exams" were over. She had won her

lord. An engagement between two such well-bred members of society was just about as binding as a wedding.

Flushed with triumph and being possessed of a good deal of personal vanity, Miss Worthy quite forgot that she had not appeared to be very attractive to men before her engagement and became convinced she was a diamond of the first water.

The weather, which had turned fine just after Miss Mortimer's arrival in town, stayed that way. London was a pretty sight with all the fine clothes and jewelry on show and windows of ballrooms open to let in the balmy air.

While Penelope Mortimer endured being pinned and fitted for gown after gown, Lord Andrew squired his fiancée to various events. He considered her dress was becoming most unflattering but felt it impolite to say so. In the past, when a lady's attire or manner had displeased him, he had simply made a point of steering away from her. But he was engaged to Miss Worthy, and so he decided to indulge her odd tastes until they were married, by which time she would have promised before God and man to obey him.

It was the way she had begun to ogle other men and then claim that they were smitten with her that grated more than anything else.

At the opera ball or at Almack's Assembly rooms she would flash bold glances in the direction of some newcomer to society and then whisper to Lord Andrew, "Only see how that dreadful man stares at me! I wish he would not. I declare the gentlemen never realize how their bold looks terrify us weak females so!"

Had Lord Andrew had any high opinion of women,

then a week of this would have been enough to give him a violent disgust of his fiancée, but he rated the fair sex as low, weak-minded, clinging creatures who only needed a firm hand.

But no doubt had Miss Worthy gone on behaving in this way for much longer, then even Lord Andrew might have seriously begun to consider ways to break the engagement. Help was to come from an unexpected quarter. After a week, Penelope's new gowns, slaved over into the night by a row of seamstresses, were ready, and she made her debut. Penelope Mortimer was the one who was going to send Miss Worthy back to her studies.

Lord Andrew had considered removing himself from his parents' home, for his mother's odd behavior had given him a resentment of her which clung in his mind like a burr. But for all her faults, the duchess knew how to run a beautiful, charming home, and so he was reluctant to leave, particularly as accommodation was hard to find at any price once the Season had begun.

The duchess was expert at flower arrangements and at the clever use of colors and fabrics. Having no feeling for servants at all, she treated them like pieces of machinery and saw that they were well oiled with plenty of good food and were kept in tip-top running condition.

And so he continued to stay. He did not see Penelope at all during that week after the disastrous visit to the Tower of London.

Then his mother summoned him. He eyed her rather warily now, hoping she would not do any of those strange things like scream at him or faint.

"Andrew," said the duchess, "tonight is Penelope's debut."

He mentally checked his own social calendar. "The Dempseys' ball, I presume?"

"Yes. You attend, of course. Shall you be fetching Miss Worthy?"

"Not tonight. Miss Worthy said she might be late, and I agreed to meet her there."

"Good. In that case little Penelope and myself will be glad of your escort."

"So long as you do not expect me to dance attendance on Miss Mortimer once we are there."

"Well, you know, Andrew, I do think you might stand up with her for two dances. Your engagement has been announced in the newspapers, and so everyone knows you are shackled to Miss Worthy."

"Are you sure," said Lord Andrew, "that Miss Mortimer knows how to go on in society? Has she had any training?"

"She does not need any. She looks so beautiful."

Lord Andrew only remembered Penelope as being pretty.

"I hope," he said cautiously, "that you are not going to force me to entertain Miss Mortimer during the Season?"

"No. After tonight she will have beaux aplenty and will have no need of you."

Lord Andrew took particular pains over his dress that evening. He felt he was putting on armor to protect him from the social gaffes he felt sure Miss Mortimer was bound to commit. His black hair was brushed and pomaded until it shone with blue lights. The white sculpture of his cravat rose above the trim line of a green and gold striped waistcoat. His coat of raven black and his black silk knee breeches and white stockings with gold clocks all appeared molded to his tall, athletic body.

He dabbed some perfume behind his ears, picked up his bicorne, his gloves, and his fan, and made his way downstairs, grateful that the fashion for men carrying enormous muffs had been "exploded"—the cant for out of fashion.

He had drunk several glasses of wine before his mother creaked into the drawing room over an hour late, her little crumpled face flushed with a high color caused by the wicked constriction of her corsets. She looked like one of those nests of Russian wooden dolls where the head of one has been removed, leaving the thick outer body of the first doll with the smaller head of the second doll poking out of it.

He glanced pointedly at the clock on the mantel and asked, "Where is Miss Mortimer?"

"Penelope should just be descending the stairs. Let us go."

Mother and son went out into the hall. Lord Andrew looked up. Penelope was indeed just descending the staircase.

Her fair, silvery hair was crowned with a coronet of pink and white roses. Her gown was of rose pink, criss-crossed with threads of gold to make a diamond pattern. The neckline was low. The sleeves had been slashed like a Renaissance gown.

He thought in a dazed way that she looked like an illustration to one of the stories by the Brothers Grimm.

It was almost a relief when the new fairy-tale Penelope said in a practical voice, "I was dressed an hour ago, but I gather it is the fashion to be deliberately late and so make an appearance."

"You look so very beautiful, Miss Mortimer," he

said gallantly, "that you do not need to do anything to attract attention to yourself."

"Thank you," said Penelope. He took her cloak from her arm and put it about her shoulders.

The butler hurried to open the street door.

Lord Andrew frowned as he saw his mother's landau waiting outside. "An open carriage!" he exclaimed.

"Yes, an open carriage," said the duchess. "Everyone will see us."

"Are you not afraid the mob might spit on you?" asked Lord Andrew.

There had not been a revolution in England as there had been in France, but members of the proletariat often roamed the streets of the West End and would jeer and catcall at the aristocracy as they went out for the evening's amusements.

"We have two outriders," said the duchess placidly, "and you, dear Andrew, will protect us."

But Penelope's beauty, Lord Andrew discovered, was not the kind to excite envy in the bosom of the ordinary people. Rather it drew gasps of wonder and admiration. When their carriage stopped for a moment in the press of traffic, passersby stood on the pavement and stared open-mouthed with pleased smiles on their faces, rather like so many poor children looking at a beautiful doll in a toy shop window.

Penelope appeared very calm, but inside she was frightened to death. She was now appalled at the amount of money that had been spent on her clothes. What if she was not a success? The duchess would be furious. Oh, beautiful cottage in Lower Bexham, where she planned to improve the garden during the lazy summer days—where she could be her own mistress!

She gazed down unseeingly into the admiring eyes of the populace and wished she could spring down from the carriage and run away.

Lord and Lady Dempsey's house had a deceptively narrow frontage which led to enormous rooms once you were inside. It was all glittering and bewildering to Penelope as they passed between a line of footmen in red and gold livery with gold dress swords lining either side of the staircase which soared from the hall of black and gold tiles. The most enormous chandelier Penelope had ever seen blazed overhead—and she could see it, the chandelier being far enough away.

Miss Worthy had made a late arrival, but Penelope's entrance came half an hour after her own.

Until that moment, Miss Worthy had been feeling very well satisfied with her own appearance. She had not been asked to dance but had assumed that every man in the room longed for her company but respected the fact that she was now Lord Andrew's property. Her near-transparent white muslin was worn over an invisible petticoat. She was wearing fifteen multicolored plumes as a headdress.

Her eyes dropped from the tall figure of her fiancé to the smaller figure of Penelope at his side—Penelope, who was causing a ripple of admiring comment to run along the row of chaperones. Her dress was nothing out of the way, thought Miss Worthy, staring at the rose pink gown embroidered with gold. The duchess led Penelope over to where Mrs. Blenkinsop was seated. Lord Andrew looked about the room, saw Miss Worthy, and crossed the floor, bowed to her mother, who was seated next to her, and sat down on Miss Worthy's other side.

"Who is that odd female with the dyed hair who came in with you?" asked Miss Worthy.

"Miss Penelope Mortimer, a protégée of my mother. She is but lately come to town, and she does not dye her hair."

"Indeed!" said Miss Worthy. "Such an odd, unfashionable color. Do you not think so, Mama?"

And Mrs. Worthy, who on seeing Penelope had sent up a prayer of thanks that her daughter was engaged to Lord Andrew, and that there was therefore nothing to fear from this dazzler, said stoutly, "Yes, it looks false. Quite like spun glass."

"I am surprised the dear duchess could not persuade the chit to wear white," said Miss Worthy, waving a large fan of osprey feathers.

"The dress was my mother's choice," said Lord Andrew. "I think it a delightful creation, simple and modest."

"It is cut too low for such a young girl. She is showing too much neck," said Miss Worthy. Her fan tickled his nose, and he turned his head away in irritation. He looked across to where Penelope was now sitting with his mother. The neckline of her dress just exposed the tops of two firm white breasts.

"Perhaps," he said, for he was suddenly out of charity with Miss Mortimer for looking so seductive when his fiancée seemed hell-bent on appearing as the female of some barbaric tribe.

Miss Worthy smiled. "I am glad you are come, for that terrible rake, Mr. Barcourt, is here, and no woman is safe with him."

Lord Andrew looked across to where Mr. John Barcourt was standing with a group of friends. Barcourt was a fine figure of a man with hair almost as fair as Penelope's own. He had a dreamy, romantic expression. Lord Andrew did not think him a rake but only a highly susceptible man who fell violently in love at least three times during the Season.

"Has he been troubling you?" he asked.

"He has not dared come near, for all the world knows I am engaged to you," said Miss Worthy. "But such scorching looks as he has sent in this direction! Is that not so, Mama?"

"Yes, my love," said Mrs. Worthy dutifully.

Penelope was glad the ballroom was so large. Although the people near her were little more than a colored blur, she could clearly make out the faces and dress of the guests on the other side of the ballroom. Her wide blue gaze fell on Mr. Barcourt. She looked at the London Season's famous heartbreaker and thought he reminded her of that desperately handsome boy who worked in the butcher's shop in Lower Bexham: handsome but weak.

The duchess meanwhile was narrowly watching the progression of her friend, Mrs. Blenkinsop, round the ballroom. Mrs. Blenkinsop was gossiping busily, and eyes were turned in Penelope's direction.

Fiddle, thought the duchess angrily. She is out to sabotage me. She is telling them all that Penelope is merely another of my lame ducks and has no dowry whatsoever. Her gaze shifted to the young lady who sat next to her on the other side from Penelope. Miss Amy Tilney was Mrs. Blenkinsop's niece, a plain, shy wisp of a thing. But Maria Blenkinsop had already let it be known the girl was possessed of a comfortable dowry. Her eyes took on a hard, stubborn look. She would not be defeated by Mrs. Blenkinsop.

"Do change places with me, Miss Tilney," said the duchess, "and chat to Penelope. I am desirous to talk to Mrs. Partridge." Amy changed places and sat next to Penelope while the duchess smiled sweetly on Mrs. Partridge, London's biggest gossip.

"And how is the world with you?" asked Mrs. Partridge.

"The world goes very badly," sighed the duchess. "But I shall not live to see much more of it."

Mrs. Partridge nearly fell off her chair with excitement. "My dear duchess," she cried, "never tell me you are ill."

"Gravely ill," said the duchess. "I do not think I shall live much beyond the end of the Season. Do you know Mr. Anderson, the royal doctor? He tells me I have the Blasted Wasting."

"Gracious! What is that?" asked Mrs. Partridge, eyeing the duchess's well-upholstered figure.

"A rare disease brought from the Indies," said the duchess with a dismissive wave of her hand.

"Then you should be home in bed."

"My duty lies with little Penelope here. It must be well known that I am to leave my vast personal fortune to her, and I would see her safely launched and protected from adventurers before I . . . die."

"Is this your first Season?" Amy was asking Penelope timidly.

"Yes, and I hope my last," said Penelope gloomily.

"Oh, yes, it will be your last," said Amy simply. "You are so very pretty, you will be wed quite soon."

"I do not want to be wed at all," said Penelope, taking a liking to this girl although she could not quite see her, but warming to the friendly interest in her voice. "I want to be left alone."

"I know what you mean," said Amy in a low voice, "but it is not possible for such as we. We have no free will."

"Oh, yes we have," said Penelope. "No one can stop us thinking what we want to think. And it is always possible to plot and plan a way out of any predicament."

"Here is Mr. Barcourt approaching us," said Amy with a hint of longing in her voice. "He is so very handsome."

"May I have the pleasure of this dance?" said Mr. Barcourt, bowing low before Penelope. But as Penelope could not quite make him out and assumed somehow that he and Amy were acquainted, she also assumed he was asking Amy to dance. So she smiled and said to Amy, "There you are, and off you go, Miss Tilney. Your first dance of the evening."

Somehow there was nothing Mr. Barcourt could do but take Amy onto the floor. At his invitation, Penelope had not looked at him once but had immediately turned to Amy Tilney.

Then Penelope suddenly found herself being besieged on all sides to dance. She picked the first one who had asked her and went out to join a set being made up for a country dance.

She found that dance a great strain, for her weak eyesight put her constantly in danger of losing her partner. She hoped once the dance was over that she would be allowed to go back to her chair and sit quietly. But no sooner had it finished and no sooner had she dropped gracefully down into a curtsy than she was besieged again by a group of gentlemen.

In another part of the ballroom, Lord Andrew

was being hailed by his closest friend, a Scotsman called Mr. Ian Macdonald. Mr. Macdonald was as messy and careless as Lord Andrew was precise and correct. Where Lord Andrew's tailored clothes flattered his athletic figure, Mr. Macdonald's were either too tight or too loose. He had a huge, beefy face, small, clever brown eyes like a bear, and a mop of glossy brown curls.

"My good friend," Mr. Macdonald hailed Lord Andrew. "Why did you not tell me the dreadful news? Perhaps I could have been of some comfort."

"What terrible news?" demanded Lord Andrew acidly, for he feared his friend might be referring to his engagement. Lord Andrew glanced to where his fiancée was now dancing with a thin young army captain. One of her feathers was dropping down her back, and a good part of the revelation of her charms which should have been saved for the marriage bed was being displayed through damped muslin at a London ball. He felt, nonetheless, that his distaste at her appearance was overly severe. Many of the ladies were wearing just as little, and it was an age when they stopped posting guards at the opera to keep the prostitutes out, for the guards kept arresting ladies of the ton, not being able to tell the difference.

"Come over here and sit down," said Mr. Macdonald. He led the way behind a potted palm to where a sofa had been placed against the wall.

"I lost my own mother last year, as you know," began Mr. Macdonald in a low voice. "I cried for weeks, I can tell you. Still miss her." He gave a hiccuping sort of sob and pulled a large handkerchief from the pocket in his tails and dabbed his eyes.

"I know your grief must still bite deep, Ian," said

44

Lord Andrew, who had long envied his friend his closeness with his family. He rose and stepped behind the palms and told a footman to fetch them two glasses of wine, and then returned to his friend.

"Talk about your grief, Ian," said Lord Andrew. "I was supposed to dance attendance on my mother's new lame duck, but she is such a success, I cannot get near her. So I have plenty of time to listen to you."

"I'm not talking about my mother," said Ian Macdonald. "I'm talking about yours."

"Mine! There is nothing up with her."

"Oh, my dear friend. That I should be the first to tell you! The Duchess of Parkworth has"—his voice sank to a mournful whisper—"the Blasted Wasting."

"Never heard of it."

"A rare disease from the Indies."

"Dammit, man, does my mother look as if she's wasting away? Who is putting about such a farrago of lies?"

"Not lies. For that gossip Partridge had it direct from the duchess herself. And there is worse."

"Can there be?" demanded Lord Andrew cynically.

"She says she is going to leave her personal fortune to that chit, Penelope Mortimer."

The footman appeared with a bottle of wine and two glasses. Lord Andrew ordered him to leave the whole bottle. When he had poured out two glasses, handed one to Ian, drained his own in one gulp, and refilled it, he said, "Ian, the situation is this. My mother is competing with Mrs. Blenkinsop. Mrs. Blenkinsop is bringing out her niece,

Miss Tilney. Miss Tilney does not rate highly in the looks department but has a sizable fortune. Miss Mortimer has none. Mrs. Blenkinsop, I know, has already been gossiping to the effect that Miss Mortimer is one of Mother's lame ducks, of no fortune or breeding. But before that acid began to bite, I assume my mother told all those barefaced lies to Mrs. Partridge. Hence Penelope Mortimer's success."

"You are sure?"

"Oh, quite."

"But Miss Mortimer is divinely beautiful, is she not?"

"She is very well in her way," said Lord Andrew repressively. He stood up and peered through the palms. "Strange," he said over his shoulder. "She is nowhere in sight. You will keep this to yourself, Ian, but it is my belief that Miss Mortimer is a trifle simple. I hope she has not done anything silly. Perhaps I had better go to look for her. But make yourself easy on the matter of my mother's death. I am sure she will live a great many years longer. In a few weeks, the novelty of Miss Mortimer will have worn off, and that is the last anyone will hear of her."

Lord Andrew diligently searched the ballroom, the card room, and the supper room. There was no sign of Penelope. His mother appeared at his elbow looking agitated and whispered that Penelope had said she was going off to refresh her appearance, but servants sent to the dressing room for the ladies had reported she was not there.

"You had best not rouse an alarm," said Lord Andrew. "I shall find her, and later we must talk of my mother's so-called forthcoming death."

46

He went out onto the landing and looked over the banister and searched the hall with his eyes. No Penelope. The dressing rooms for the guests to repair their toilet were on the floor above the ballroom. He made his way up there quite forgetting he was engaged to dance the cotillion with Miss Worthy.

Penelope was standing in a small, weedy enclosed bit of garden at the back of the house, wondering what on earth to do. She had been reluctant to return to the hot ballroom and had wandered downstairs and through the hall to the back and then along a little passage to an open door at the end. She had walked through it and found herself in the little garden. The air was sweet and warm, and a full moon silvered the tall weeds, making them look like magical plants.

Then some servant had slammed the door shut, Penelope had found it locked. Above her head, the loud noise of the orchestra drowned out her frantic knockings.

She raised her skirts and took her precious spectacles out of a pocket in her petticoat and popped them on her nose.

She was now thoroughly terrified of what the duchess's rage would be like if she stayed missing for much longer. A long black drainpipe rose up the back of the building, and one of its arms shooting out at right angles was right under an open window on the second floor where Penelope remembered the dressing rooms to be.

She could easily climb that drainpipe, but her gown would be ruined, that gown which had cost so much money.

Penelope decided frantically that if she removed

her dress and slung it round her neck and climbed up in her petticoat, she could dive into the dressing room, pop on her gown, and run down to the ballroom. Shivering with nerves, she put her spectacles back in her petticoat pocket, untied the tapes of her gown and took it off, and then tied it around her neck.

Lord Andrew became convinced Penelope was in the ladies' dressing room, probably hidden behind a screen. This glittering social event had probably been too much for such a country-bred miss. There was surely no other logical place she could be. He sent one of the maids in to search thoroughly, but the maid returned and said there was no one there.

Lord Andrew handed her a crown and told her to stand guard outside while he looked himself.

He went in, glad that no ladies seemed to want to make repairs at that moment, and looked everywhere. But it was a fairly small room, and it was obvious there was nowhere Penelope could hide.

He was about to leave when he heard strange noises coming from outside the window. He leaned out of the open window and looked down, and then clutched the sill hard.

Pulling herself up the drainpipe, clad in a white petticoat, flesh-colored stockings, and the most frivolous pair of rose-embroidered garters Lord Andrew had ever seen, came Penelope Mortimer.

He darted to the dressing room door, locked it, ran back to the window, and leaned down to catch Penelope's arm as she came within reach.

She let out a cry of terror and lost her hold, but he had her safe. He pulled her up and then helped her in the window.

"Dress yourself," he said, turning his back on her.

Blushing furiously, Penelope slipped the gown over her head and then asked him in a trembling voice to help her tie her tapes.

He swung about and fastened the tapes and then put his hands on her shoulders. "We must get out of here before anyone comes," he whispered. "I shall talk to you later."

He straightened her headdress, seized a washcloth and roughly scrubbed a smudge of soot from her nose, and then scrubbed her dirty hands.

He unlocked the door and led her out. "Miss Mortimer had fainted," he said severely to the startled maid, "but here is a guinea for you, for you did your best."

He tucked Penelope's arm firmly in his own and led her down to the ballroom.

Miss Worthy saw them arrive. She was furious and frightened. An acid-tongued friend of her mother's had told Miss Worthy that she looked like a harlot and that if she was not careful, The Perfect Gentleman might decide to ditch her in favor of that Mortimer chit, thereby keeping his mother's money in the family.

So to Lord Andrew's relief, after he had delivered Penelope to his mother, he found a meek and ladylike fiancée who had reduced her feathered headdress by eight plumes and who had allowed her damped muslin to dry. To her questions, he replied tersely that Miss Mortimer had fainted and that he had had to rescue her and that Miss Mortimer was the most tiresome idiot it had ever been his ill luck to come across.

"Perhaps," ventured Miss Worthy, "I could set her an example as to manners. She has not had the social training of a member of the ton."

"If you could be a friend to her," said Lord Andrew, "that would indeed be very noble of you. Miss Mortimer needs to be guided by some lady nearer her years."

"Then I shall call on her tomorrow," said Miss Worthy, privately deciding it would be as well to get to know as much about this new enemy as possible.

"You are very good," said Lord Andrew. He gave her a sweet smile and led her to the floor.

Chapter Four

Lord Andrew meant to tackle his mother again on the subject of Miss Mortimer, but the duchess was so flushed with success over Penelope's triumph that he decided to leave it for the moment.

Penelope, on the other hand, must be spoken to immediately.

They settled down over the tea tray in the drawing room before going to bed. The duchess regaled her husband, who had not been present at the ball, with every detail from the sour look on Mrs. Blenkinsop's face to the name of every gentleman who had danced with Penelope.

"But why were you absent for so long?" demanded the duchess at last.

"As I told you, Your Grace," said Penelope, stifling a yawn, "I fainted." Penelope had decided the easiest course was to adopt Lord Andrew's lie.

"Fainted!" said the duchess awfully. "F-a-i-n-t-e-d," she added, drawling out the word. "I did not say anything when you told me at the ball, but I am convinced you did nothing of the sort, Penelope. This sensibility business is not the fashion it was, and I trust you have not begun to put on airs. You felt a trifle dizzy and exaggerated it into a faint, did you not?"

51

"Yes, Your Grace," said Penelope, too tired to argue.

"Just as I thought," said the duchess, who had no desire to sponsor a flawed beauty. "Now, you must go to bed and refresh yourself for the morrow, for, if I am not mistaken, we can expect many callers."

Lord Andrew cleared his throat. "I have asked Miss Worthy to call. I am sure her example would be beneficial to Miss Mortimer."

"Fiddlesticks. I do not want Penelope to learn how to dress like a Cyprian or to start parading about with a head full of feathers."

"Mama! Miss Worthy's dress this evening may have been a trifle unfortunate . . ."

"Very unfortunate."

"But Miss Mortimer stands in need of social training."

"All that will happen," said the duchess with relish, "is that Miss Worthy will have her nose put out of joint by all my Penelope's admirers."

"As Miss Worthy is engaged to me, she is in no need of admirers or to be jealous of any other woman."

"That must be just about the most pompous remark I have ever heard," said Penelope.

"Don't sit there glaring, Andrew," said his mother. "Penelope, off to your room."

Penelope gained her room with a sigh of relief. She had walked over to the toilet table to begin her preparations for bed when there was a knock at the door.

"Enter," she called, wondering why Perkins should knock at the door, a thing good servants never did.

Lord Andrew came in.

"Now, Miss Mortimer," he said, "explain what happened this evening."

The little French clock on the mantel chimed four in the morning. "Yesterday evening," corrected Penelope gloomily.

"Very well. Yesterday evening."

Penelope sat down wearily in front of the lace-draped toilet table, raised her arms, and unpinned her headdress.

"It was a chapter of accidents," she said. "I did go to the dressing room. Then I went back down past the ballroom to the hall. I wanted to walk about for bit. The ballroom was hot, and I was tired of the effort of dancing." Penelope meant she was tired of the effort of remembering her place in the sets when she could not see very well. "There was a door open at the back of the hall. I went through and found myself in a neglected bit of garden. The air was pleasant," she said dreamily. "Then some servant slammed the door and locked it. The orchestra in the ballroom struck up, and no one could hear my bangings and shoutings. I thought if I removed my gown so that it would not be soiled and climbed up the drainpipe to the dressing room, where the window was open, that I might be able to put on my dress and go down to the ballroom, and no one would be any the wiser. But all's well that ends well. I told your mother I had fainted. I am unhurt." She yawned and rubbed her eyes with her knuckles.

"For your own good, and for my mother's good, you cannot go on making social gaffes," said Lord Andrew. "I urge you to attend to Miss Worthy's advice."

Penelope had had a very good view of Miss Worthy when that lady had been dancing far enough away from her.

"I am not used to London ways," said Penelope primly, "nor can I adopt the extremes of dress. It is all very well for a lady of Miss Worthy's mature years, but in a young virgin, it would be damned as fast."

"Miss Worthy, like most ladies, is sometimes given to odd mistakes in dress," said Lord Andrew angrily—angry because the more he thought about his fiancée's gown, the more shocking it seemed. "But she is the epitome of elegance and social deportment most of the time."

"What Her Grace needs," said Penelope half to herself, "is another lame duck."

"I beg your pardon!"

"I wish your mother would find another interest," said Penelope in a stronger voice, "and preferably an interest who takes the same size in gown as I. Were it not for my horror at the amount of money that has already been spent on me, I would run off to the country and risk the duchess's wrath. What is my behavior to you, in any case, Lord Andrew? I am Her Grace's protégée, not yours."

"Then if you wish me to keep out of your affairs," said Lord Andrew angrily, "do not embroil me in them by walking into lions' dens or climbing up drainpipes half naked."

"I was not half naked. Believe me, my lord, in my petticoat, I still concealed more then your fiancée did with her ballgown."

"You are an impertinent little girl. How dare you speak to me so?"

"How dare *you* speak to *me* so!" retaliated Penelope. "Oh, *do* run along. I am so very tired."

"There is just one thing," he said, "before I leave you, which needs explanation. In order to compete with Mrs. Blenkinsop, my mother has seen fit to put it about that she had a deathly illness and she is going to leave her money to you. I trust you do not believe such rubbish."

"No," said Penelope. "Of course not. But there is one thing I have to say to you. It could be argued that neither Her Grace nor Miss Worthy appear to have behaved at the ball with ladylike decorum, the one telling rank lies and the other indecorously gowned, so I do not know why you are standing in the middle of my bedroom giving me a jaw-me-dead."

There was a scratching at the door, and Perkins walked into the room and stopped short at the sight of Lord Andrew.

"I am just going," he said crossly, suiting the action to the words.

A few minutes later his valet struggled to assist a master who kept muttering and cursing under his breath. His valet, Pomfret, was breathlessly saving up every curse and wild gesture to describe to the upper servants the next day. Pomfret had been hired as a valet to Lord Andrew just before the beginning of the previous Season. Hitherto, he had found the work boring. Lord Andrew's impeccable manners and impeccable dress gave Pomfret nothing to work on. His correct politeness with equals and servants gave the gossip-starved Pomfret nothing to talk about. Now it looked as if Lord Andrew was either drunk or about to suffer from a nervous breakdown. The valet handed his master his nightcap and his glass of warm wine and water and looked forward to a rosier future.

That lie, which had been so useful to the duchess the evening before, turned out to be the wreck of her plans for the following day.

She had quite forgotten about it and was mortified to find that the gentlemen who had danced with Penelope had not called in person. Mute witness to this was in the array of unbent cards in the silver tray in the hall. Gentlemen or ladies who had called in person always turned down one corner. Certainly one had sent a love poem—the duchess considered it her right to open Penelope's post—and another two, bunches of flowers.

It was only when Miss Worthy arrived and began to speak to the duchess in a hushed whisper, and occasionally pressing that lady's hand, that the duchess found out the truth of the matter.

"No callers at all," the duchess complained.

"I am here, dear Mama-in-law," mourned Miss Worthy.

"Stop calling me by that stupid name. You aren't married yet, and if you go about flaunting yourself in damped muslin for much longer, you won't be."

At that Miss Worthy began to cry. "No need to take on so," said the duchess impatiently. "Andrew's shackled to you, and there's an end of it."

Miss Worthy raised streaming eyes. Penelope, sitting a little way away from the couple, wrinkled her nose. There was an odd smell of onion in the drawing room.

"It is your courageous behavior which quite goes to my heart," said Miss Worthy, who had learned the story of the duchess's doom from her parents and had not yet had a chance to discuss it with Lord Andrew.

"Stop crying. *I'm* the one who should be crying. I have a weak heart," said the duchess crossly.

"I know. I know," wailed Miss Worthy. She flashed a look at Penelope, who was sitting looking out of the bow window at the trees in the park. "I am shocked at you, Miss Mortimer," said Miss Worthy. "Some show of distress, some sensibility, would be more becoming in you."

"I hope Penelope knows better than to cry and bawl because she hasn't any callers," said the duchess. "Where's Andrew? Was ever a woman so plagued."

"I am talking about the Blasted Wasting."

"The Blasted what? I distinctly heard you snigger, Penelope. Mind your manners."

"The Blasted Wasting," said Miss Worthy. "You know, that disease from the Indies."

"Oh, that," said the duchess. "Oh, fiddle. Oh, damme. So that's why no one has called! I have not got the blasted anything, Miss Worthy, so you may dry your eyes. It was some malice put about by Maria Blenkinsop because she's jealous of Penelope, only having a Friday-faced antidote to puff off herself."

"I thought Miss Tilney charming," said Penelope.

"And who asked your opinion, miss? I must make calls. I must scotch this rumor. Andrew!" she cried as her son's tall figure entered the room. "Do take Miss Worthy away somewhere . . . anywhere. I know, take her for a drive in the park, and take Miss Mortimer with you."

Miss Worthy was wearing an elegant carriage dress of gray alpaca with a black velvet collar. On her head was a stylish shako. Her appearance put Lord Andrew in a good humor.

"I must change," said Penelope. "I won't be long."

She reappeared a bare quarter of hour later in a carriage dress of green velvet piped with gold braid. A grass green velvet hat shaped like a man's beaver was tilted at a rakish angle on her curls. She looked breathtakingly lovely.

"You must speak to your mama about Miss Mortimer's dress," whispered Miss Worthy to Lord Andrew while Penelope was making her farewells to the duchess.

"Yes, I shall," he said curtly. "That dressmaker she found for Penelope is a genius."

So the three left together in a bad mood. Lord Andrew was cross because he felt Penelope had deliberately gone out of her way to outshine Miss Worthy, Penelope did not like Miss Worthy and had spent a long and tedious day waiting for those gentlemen callers who never came, and Miss Worthy was furious because Lord Andrew had refused to criticize Penelope's dress.

He drove them in his phaeton, Miss Worthy on his left and Penelope on his right. By the time they had driven a certain way into the park, Lord Andrew realized with a shock that he was behaving very badly indeed. It was not like him to indulge in a bout of bad temper and forget his social duty.

"You must forgive me, Miss Worthy," he said, "but I fear I have been put sadly out of temper by family problems."

Miss Worthy saw a way to score. "*Iris furorus brevis est,* is it not, Miss Mortimer?"

"I think you mean *Ira furor brevis est*—anger is short madness," said Penelope. "Do you read much Horace, Miss Worthy?"

"Yes, all the time," said Miss Worthy grimly.

"I prefer novels," said Penelope.

"That does not surprise me."

"Indeed, Miss Worthy. Why?"

"Most young ladies addle their minds with such rubbish."

"I would not call them all rubbish and dismiss them so. Have you read Miss Austen's *Sense and Sensibility*?"

"Of course not. Have I not just explained? I have no time for such frivolities."

"Oh, you should," said Penelope. "It would quite convert you."

Miss Worthy abandoned the subject of literature and then proceeded to try to score with art.

"Oh, stop!" she cried.

Lord Andrew reined in his horses. Miss Worthy raised her gloved hands and formed them into a square. "The perspective," she murmured. "See, over there where the guards have stationed their horses under that stand of trees. What symmetry!" She closed her eyes.

Penelope, who had excellent long sight, gazed interestedly across the park to see what had entranced Miss Worthy.

The guards on their horses ceased to be picturesque, for one of them, having drunk too long and too well, leaned over his saddle and "cascaded" into the bushes.

"How very moving," murmured Miss Worthy, her eyes still closed.

"I agree with you," said Penelope with a snort of laughter. "I should think that poor guardsman has *moved* most of his insides."

Miss Worthy's eyes flew open. The guards were

riding off. What on earth did Miss Mortimer mean? And why had Lord Andrew begun to laugh?

She decided not to ask but sat with her back ramrod straight and her face set in a disapproving look.

It was just as well. For Lord Andrew would have been hard put to explain why he found it all so funny. But it had touched a chord of the ridiculous in him which he had not known he possessed. He had never laughed at anything silly before and did not know why he could barely control himself.

Somehow the day had become sharp and crystal-bright. Everything was new and green and fresh, and he felt more alive than he had ever done in his life before.

Although he soon had his outburst of laughter well under control, the strange elation remained with him, bubbling and chuckling inside like a brook running over the pebbles.

He then began to wonder what really went on inside Miss Mortimer's beautiful head and lurked behind those vacant eyes. She could quote Horace, and she had made Miss Worthy's artistic posturing quite ridiculous. He gazed down at her with a new awareness in his eyes, but Penelope only saw a blur of his face turned in her direction and dutifully smiled.

The breeze lifted a tendril of her silver-fair hair, and her wide eyes were as blue and innocent as the sky above. He felt a queer little tug at his heart as he looked at her. She did not belong in London society, and he felt, were she to remain much longer, she might become spoiled. She would soon learn not to indulge in saying exactly what she thought. He decided the best thing he could do would be to try to help her to get her wish by returning her to the country.

This thought preoccupied him on the road back. He drove Miss Worthy to her home and then returned to Park Street with Penelope. She did not say anything as they drove through the streets but contented herself with staring off into the distance. Lord Andrew did not know that Penelope, as her long sight was good, was contenting herself by looking at all she could see.

"I would like a word with you, Miss Mortimer," he said as they entered the house.

"Another lecture," sighed Penelope.

"No," he said. "Perhaps I might be able to help you."

The duchess, he learned from the butler, was still out on her calls, and the duke had gone to his club.

He led her into the drawing room and asked if she would like tea. Penelope said she would, so he waited until the tea tray had been brought in, said yes, he took sugar, and then watched in amazement as Penelope proceeded to pour tea into the sugar bowl.

"I do not like my tea very sweet," he said.

"I have not yet given you any sugar, my lord."

"On the contrary, you have just filled the sugar bowl with tea."

"How silly of me," said Penelope. "Now what shall I do?"

He rang the bell, ordered another bowl of sugar, and then, when it had arrived, busied himself with the tea things.

"You puzzle me," he said. "How comes it that a lady who can quote Horace does quite mad things like filling up the sugar bowl with tea?"

Pride kept Penelope from telling the truth. Had not her parents always said that ladies who had to wear spectacles never attracted gentlemen and that it was best to conceal one's defect until one was married? *But you don't want to get married!* said a cross little voice in Penelope's head, but she ignored it and said aloud, "I am absent-minded, I fear. What did you wish to talk to me about?"

"I am persuaded you would really be much happier in the country. To that end, I am prepared to talk to my mother again."

Penelope took a delicate sip of tea. "All you will do is provoke the most dreadful scene. I am still a novelty, you know. Give it a few weeks and you will find Her Grace beginning to tire."

The door of the drawing room opened, the duke poked his head around it, saw them, and muttered something about going to the library.

"You are very cynical," said Lord Andrew. "Would you not like to wed? That is the whole purpose of a Season."

"No, I would not," said Penelope. "Your mother will have explained her lies away. Everyone will now know I have no money or any expectations of it. I cannot hope for a rich husband; therefore I should not have the comfort of being separated from him the way I would were I to command a large establishment. A rich husband is always on the hunting field, at his club, or in Parliament. One need not see much of him. A husband with modest means is always underfoot, or so I have observed. I am not prepared to spend the rest of my life with someone I do not like just for the sake of becoming married. Now, in your case, as you are, or so I learned, greatly interested in agriculture, Miss Worthy will not have to see much of you."

"What on earth, my impertinent Miss Mortimer, gives you the impression that my fiancée does not dote on my company?"

"She is not in love with you, nor you with her."

He sighed. "Those pernicious novels! I have seen respectable girls running off with footmen, and all for love. I have seen young men marrying portionless girls of little breeding, and all for love. Their marriages always end in disaster. Love is no basis for marriage. Equal breeding, similar tastes, and similar interests are the bedrock of any relationship."

"Perhaps for such as you," said Penelope. "But in my case, I shall marry for love or not at all, which probably means not at all. But I shall have my independence and hard work to keep me occupied. I have discovered a gift for gardening. I grow very fine vegetables, I assure you."

"What kind of soil do you have?"

"Clay soil. Very heavy."

"And what do you use?"

"Lime to break it down and sweeten it, and then I find that horse manure is a great fertilizer, and to be had for nothing. One simply goes out in the roads with a shovel."

Lord Andrew blinked at the idea of this fairylike creature searching the country roads with a brush and shovel. "What an undignified picture you conjure up!" he exclaimed.

"Ah, but as my own mistress, I do not have to care about dignity or the lack of it. There seems to be a great deal of toing and froing downstairs. Perhaps you have callers."

63

"Then no doubt someone will let me know if anyone wants to see me."

"More tea?" asked Penelope, picking up the pot.

"Yes, I thank you." Lord Andrew grabbed his cup and held it out in time to catch the stream of hot tea which had just been about to descend on his knee. "Are you longsighted by any chance, Miss Mortimer?"

"Not I," said Penelope quickly.

He leaned back in his chair and studied her thoughtfully. They were to go to the opera that evening. He would study Penelope's face as she watched the opera. He would ask her questions about the costume and the performers, for he was all at once sure she had difficulty in seeing.

The door burst open and the duchess came rushing in, her face mottled with excitement and every stay in her corsets creaking like the timbers of a four-master rounding Cape Horn.

"My dear!" she cried. "Such excitement. Mr. Barcourt is come to ask our leave to pay his addresses to Penelope. He called on Giles when I was out." Giles was her husband, the duke. "I came just in time to add my permission. Such a triumph. Barcourt! Ten thousand a year. Very comfortable and all, just as it ought to be."

"Barcourt cannot be serious," said Lord Andrew testily after a quick look at Penelope's stricken face. "He is always falling in love."

"But he has never proposed to anyone before," said the duchess. "Come quickly, Andrew."

Lord Andrew looked helplessly at Penelope, but she was now sitting sedately in front of the tea tray with her eyes lowered.

"Come, Andrew," repeated his mother in imperative tones.

He followed her reluctantly from the room.

Penelope waited until the door was closed behind them, opened her reticule, took our her ugly but efficient steel spectacles, and popped them on her nose. She took off her pretty bonnet, put it under her chair, and then combed her hair straight up on top of her head and wound it into a severe knot.

Then she folded her hands and waited.

The door opened and Mr. Barcourt walked in.

Chapter Five

Mr. Barcourt stopped short on the threshold. For one brief moment he hoped that the young lady facing him would prove to be Penelope's elder sister. The sunlight winked on her thick-lensed spectacles, and her hair was scraped painfully straight up on the top of her head.

To know the character of women was not at all necessary to engender the exquisite pangs of love in Mr. Barcourt's breast. Their looks and his vivid imagination did all that was necessary. He had, therefore, fallen in love with Penelope at the Dempseys' ball. Her vague, dreaming expression combined with her ethereal beauty had prompted him to propose for the first time in his life.

Underneath all his romanticism, there was a practical streak in Mr. Barcourt's nature which had held him back before popping the question. But the intelligence that the duchess was at death's door and about to leave her fortune to this goddess had brought him up to the mark.

His first shock had come when the duke had pooh-poohed the idea of his wife's imminent death. He said bluntly that Penelope was portionless. Mr. Barcourt might have then withdrawn his offer had not the duchess arrived on the scene to say that Penelope would have a dowry of three thousand pounds. It was not much, particularly in the inflationary days of the Regency, but to a man who had thought a moment before that he would have nothing at all, it seemed a splendid sum. He was accordingly given the ducal blessing and told he might have ten minutes alone with Penelope.

"Come in, Mr. Barcourt," said Penelope, "and sit down."

Her voice was rather harsh and had a distinct country burr.

He sat down opposite her. Her eyes seemed smaller than he had remembered behind those awful glasses, and they glittered with sharp intelligence.

He sat dumb, wishing this creature would go away to be replaced with the fairy-tale figure of the ball.

"Would you like tea, sir?" asked Penelope. She had pronounced the "sir" as "zurr," just like the lowest peasant. Mr. Barcourt's love received a death blow.

"Er, yes, Miss Mortimer," he said. "Hot in here," he added, running a finger round the inside of his starched collar.

"I'm sure I hadn't noticed, zurr," drawled Penelope with the dulcet tones of a corncrake. "You'll be wantin' milk and sugar, I s'pose?"

"Yes, I thank you. Do you know why I am come?"

"Oh, yus," said Penelope. "You be wanting to marry me. I'd loik that. I've always wanted childer. Lots and lots. Mrs. Barnes, down in the village, now she got twenty-one, and all hale and hearty."

"Twenty-one!" echoed Mr. Barcourt faintly. His hand holding the cup and saucer began to tremble.

"I was glad to find you had a place in the country," went on Penelope. "For I don't loik the town, and that's a fact. Nothing loik good country air and plain country cooking and hard work in the fields, I always say."

Mr. Barcourt, a perpetually absent landlord who loathed the country and did not even hunt, was terrified. Stark, raving fear animated his wits.

He put his cup and saucer carefully on the table and said in a dazed voice. "Where am I?"

"You're about to propose marriage to me."

"Who you?" demanded Mr. Barcourt in a thin, high voice.

"Me Penelope Mortimer," said Penelope with a huge grin—a peasant grin, thought Mr. Barcourt, and his fastidious soul recoiled.

"I have lost my memory!" cried Mr. Barcourt, jumping to his feet. " 'Sdeath! I do not know where I am or what I am doing. Beg pardon, whoever you are." He scrambled for the door. "Good-bye. Forgive. Not myself. Servant, ma'am." He tumbled out onto the landing and nearly collided with the duke and duchess, who had just approached the door.

"I do not know who I am," wailed Mr. Barcourt. "I have lost my memory."

Lord Andrew came up to join the group. "What is this nonsense, Barcourt?" he said. "You have just proposed marriage to Miss Penelope Mortimer."

"No I haven't," screamed Mr. Barcourt. "Not I. Never propose to anyone. Who are you anyway?"

"We are the Duke and Duchess of Parkworth," said the duchess awfully.

"I'm sick," cried Mr. Barcourt. "I don't know anyone. Don't know what I am saying."

He dived down the steps, and the ducal family

stood looking at one another as the street door slammed.

They went into the drawing room. Penelope, her glasses tucked safely back in her reticule, her hat on her loosened curls, sat looking vaguely into the middle distance.

"What on earth happened?" screamed the duchess.

In her usual pleasant voice, free from any accent, Penelope said in a bewildered way, "I do not know. He talked so wildly. I think he is quite mad."

"But did he propose?" shouted the duchess.

"Oh, no, I don't think so," said Penelope, wrinkling her brow. "Let me see; he asked for tea, and then he began to shake and said he did not know who he was. I am vastly cast down, Your Grace, and would like to retire."

"You are not going anywhere, miss, until I get to the bottom of this," howled the duchess. "Oh, to think how I planned to crow over Maria Blenkinsop at the opera tonight! Andrew, you must challenge Barcourt to a duel."

Penelope gave a pathetic little sob.

"Let her go to her room," said Lord Andrew angrily. "Do you not see she has had enough?"

"Very well," said the duchess, suddenly subdued as the full force of her own disappointment hit her.

For half an hour after Penelope had retired, the Parkworth family chewed over the strange behavior of Mr. Barcourt. Lord Andrew urged his mother to set Penelope free and let her go home. But the duchess gradually brightened. "If she can attract such a one as Barcourt," she said slowly, "even though he chose this unfortunate moment to have a brainstorm, then who knows who she might draw into the net."

In vain did Lord Andrew argue the wisdom of letting Penelope go. He finally left his parents and went upstairs to change for dinner.

As he passed Penelope's room, he heard stifled sounds coming from inside.

He was angry with his mother, and he was angry with Penelope for taking the rejection of such a one as Barcourt so hard. He walked a little way away and then went back, opened the door of her room, and walked inside.

She was lying facedown on the bed, her shoulders shaking.

He went over and sat on the edge of the bed and put a comforting hand on her shoulder. "Come now, Miss Mortimer," he said. "Must I remind you that you said you did not want to marry except for love? And you cannot be in love with Barcourt. You barely know him."

"But he has s-such n-nice legs," came Penelope's muffled voice.

He looked down at her in sudden suspicion, and his grip on her shoulder tightened. He pulled her over on her back.

"You're laughing!" he exclaimed.

"Oh, it w-was s-so funny," giggled Penelope. "All that where-am-I and who-am-I. I wish you could have seen him."

He took her by the shoulders and gave her a shake. "Barcourt showed all the signs of a man about to propose. It was you—you did something to scare him."

"I was myself, I assure you, a good country girl." Penelope let out a snort of laughter.

Lord Andrew became aware of the warmth of the shoulders through the thin muslin of her gown as he held her down on the bed, of her pink lips trembling with laughter, of the tumbled disarray of her glorious hair, and of the wide blue depths of her eyes.

The Perfect Gentlemen leaned down and pressed firm lips against that laughing mouth.

They both stayed very still, pressed against each other, both shocked rigid by the skyrocketing emotions surging through their bodies.

He drew back gently. Then he got to his feet and walked to the door. Penelope struggled up on one elbow and looked at him in a dazed way. She could see him perfectly, for he was just the right distance away.

She could clearly see that tall, athletic figure, the strong legs, the crisp curls of his black hair, and that firm mouth which so recently had been pressed against her own.

He ran a hand through his hair. "Miss Mortimer," he said, "pray accept my deepest apologies," and he walked from the room.

Penelope turned her face into the pillow. But this time, she began to cry.

"My lord," said Pomfret, fussing about his master, "our cravat will not do!"

"What's up with the damned thing?"

"It is the soiled one we just removed."

"Oh, give me a clean one, and stop saying we, we, we the whole time. It drives me mad!"

"Yes, my lord," said Pomfret, although his eyes gleamed with pleasure. The cracks in the facade of The Perfect Gentleman were growing wider.

71

"And stop humming under your breath."

"Yes, my lord," said Pomfret cheerfully.

It was a subdued dinner. Penelope picked at her food, Lord Andrew maintained a brooding silence, the duchess was wondering how to get her revenge on Mr. Barcourt, and the duke was reading a magazine.

Penelope was wearing an opera gown of soft pale green muslin. It had a square neckline and puffed sleeves, the high-waisted fashion being simply cut and the gown ending in several flounces at the hem. All very modest on the face of it. But, Lord Andrew reflected, even had he not been told, he would have recognized the hand of a French designer. The muslin was cunningly cut and draped across the front to emphasize the swell of a young bosom, and the filmy cloth clung to the line of her hips. She was wearing one of the duchess's tiaras, a delicate thing of amethysts, tiny emeralds, and silver. About her white neck was a thin chain of emeralds and amethysts, the jewels burning brightly as if fueled by the youth and beauty of the skin against which they lay.

She had rolled back her long gloves to eat, and her small hands were red, with short, square nails. He was obscurely pleased at the mess of her hands and tried to concentrate his attention on them while he wondered what had made him kiss her. He had never behaved so badly before.

He glanced at her face. Her lashes were lowered over her eyes, those ridiculously long black lashes. His gaze returned to her hands. She dropped her fork with a clatter and blushed.

He knew his steady gaze was embarrassing her.

He glared at his mother instead and was told testily to eat his food and stop gawping.

The duke was to accompany them to the opera, which meant a closed carriage, the duke considering travel in open carriages being responsible for all the ills in London. The duke sat facing the duchess, and Lord Andrew, beside his father, sat facing Penelope.

The carriage was old and the springs needed repair. As they lurched over the cobbles, Lord Andrew's knees were suddenly pressed against Penelope's. He felt as if an electric current from one of the new galvanizing machines had been shot through his body. He swung his knees sideways and looked unseeingly out of the window.

He had a longing for the undemanding company of his fiancée. He had been celibate for too long, he thought cynically. The best thing he could do would be to persuade Ann Worthy into an early marriage.

The Worthy family had been considering the same thing, but not because of any of the lusts of the flesh.

Miss Worthy's description of their drive had alarmed Mr. and Mrs. Worthy, for although their daughter only described how awful and peasantish the behavior of Penelope Mortimer had been, her parents, remembering only Penelope's dazzling beauty, were becoming worried at the thought of Lord Andrew being under the same roof as such a charmer. Miss Worthy had failed to tell them it had been the duchess's idea that Penelope accompany them on the drive, and so they understood Lord Andrew to have been the one who suggested that she join them.

Then late that afternoon, just before dinner, Mr.

Benjamin Jepps, Miss Worthy's rejected suitor, had called and demanded a few private moments with Ann Worthy.

It is a reassuring fact that in this world there is always someone for everyone, and Mr. Jepps was still very much in love with Miss Worthy.

He was a thin, clever gentleman of middle height, plainly and soberly dressed. He had large liquid brown eyes, a sharp nose, and a small fastidious mouth. His brown hair was a trifle thin, and he stiffened and thickened it with a mixture of sugar and water. He thought Miss Worthy supremely stupid and rejoiced in her vanities and her occasional lapses into the worst of fashion. He was one of those men who could not have tolerated a woman of any intelligence whatsoever, feeling he himself had enough at least for two. He adored red hair, and Miss Worthy was blessed with a large quantity of it.

While he felicitated her on her marriage, his agile brain was working out ways to put an end to her engagement. He regretted that his prosperous manufactories in the north, and the source of his wealth—although he kept that source well hidden—should have necessitated him being away for so long.

Miss Worthy, who was still smarting over that mysterious shared laughter between Lord Andrew and Penelope, found Mr. Jepps's continued admiration of her all that it should be. She even found herself regretting that he did not have a title. She added to her parents' worries by inviting Mr. Jepps to share their box at the opera.

Mr. Jepps rushed home to change into his evening clothes, anxious to meet Lord Andrew and to find out how best to confound this enemy.

So while the Worthy family watched the opera, Gluck's *Orpheus and Eurydice*, he raised his opera glasses and studied the Duke of Parkworth's box. His eyes lighted with glee on the dazzling vision that was Penelope Mortimer. He leaned toward Miss Worthy and whispered, "Who is that young lady with Lord Andrew?"

"A nobody," said Miss Worthy curtly. "Some undistinguished, impoverished miss from the country the duchess has seen fit to bring out."

"She resides, then, with the family?"

"Yes."

Mr. Jepps continued his study.

Lord Andrew had leaned his dark head close to Penelope's fair one. He was actually asking her about the costumes on the stage, and Penelope's replies were showing him that she could see very well. There was something in the way Lord Andrew's body leaned toward this Miss Mortimer and the way Miss Mortimer's cheeks had a becoming flush that spoke volumes to Mr. Jepps. With a satisfied little sigh, he put down his opera glasses and began to plot.

Lord Andrew was looking forward to a quiet tête-à-tête with his fiancée at the supper which was held afterwards before the opera ball. Miss Worthy was wearing an opera gown of old gold silk, which became her well. She was wearing a tiara of old gold and garnets, which was attractively set on the thick red tresses of her hair. Semiprecious stones were all the rage. No one who was anyone appeared in diamonds.

But somehow it appeared Mr. Jepps had managed to maneuver everyone into the one party at supper—himself and the Worthy's, and Penelope and the duke and duchess and Lord Andrew.

Mr. Jepps sat himself next to Penelope and set himself to please. He discovered she liked novels and immediately assumed her taste ran to Gothic romances.

"There is a vastly interesting pile on the borders of Hertfordshire," said Mr. Jepps, gazing into Penelope's eyes while signaling to a footman to replenish their glasses. Mr. Jepps knew that a well-lubricated Ann Worthy could always be manipulated, and although he was giving Penelope all his attention, he wanted to make sure his beloved was kept in a malleable mood.

"Indeed," said Penelope politely.

"It is Dalby Castle, former seat of the Earls of Dalby. It is said to be haunted."

"By the ghost of a young maiden, no doubt," said Penelope.

Mr. Jepps gave her a sharp look, but her blue eyes were vague. "Yes," he said. "By the ghost of Lady Emmeline, the third earl's daughter. It is a most romantic place. I have been thinking for some time of organizing an outing. Would you care to go, Miss Mortimer?"

"Yes, she would," said the duchess, who had been studying Mr. Jepps as he talked to Penelope, and thinking, Twenty thousand a year at least. More perhaps. Unmarried. Couldn't be more suitable.

"And to complete the party," said Mr. Jepps, "Miss Worthy and Lord Andrew!"

Piqued at Mr. Jepps's interest in Penelope, Miss Worthy said, "Yes, I should like that above all things." No one waited for Lord Andrew's approval.

"Splendid. Then if the weather holds fine, we could set out the day after tomorrow at seven in the morning."

Mrs. Blenkinsop and Miss Amy Tilney came up at that point, followed by Lord Andrew's friend, Mr. Ian Macdonald. Lord Andrew did not want to find himself in the undiluted company of his fiancée, her rejected lover, and the increasingly disturbing Miss Mortimer. He hailed the newcomers with relief. "We are just planning an outing to Dalby Castle in Herts," he said. "I am sure Miss Tilney would like to join us, and you too, Ian."

Ian Macdonald read an odd look of appeal in his friend's eyes and said heartily he would be honored to be of the party. Maria Blenkinsop, seeing the look of fury on the duchess's face engendered by Miss Tilney being included in the invitation, accepted on behalf of her charge, adding maliciously, "I am sure, dear duchess, that we will both be glad of a break from the fatigues of chaperonage. Neither of us is young enough to face such a long outing with equanimity."

And so it was all set, and the rest of the evening passed pleasantly enough on the surface. Lord Andrew did not ask Penelope to dance, but Mr. Jepps asked her twice and had the satisfaction of seeing his interest in the girl was causing Miss Worthy a certain amount of jealousy.

On the road home, the duchess lectured Penelope roundly on the merits of Mr. Jepps and ordered her to do her best to ensnare him. "Although," she added, "I must send for Mr. Barcourt tomorrow and ask him to explain himself."

"That will not be possible," said Lord Andrew, stretching his long legs in the carriage and then recoiling as from a snake when they brushed against Penelope's legs. "It was all the talk tonight. I wonder you did not hear it. Barcourt is claiming total loss of memory and has gone to the country until his brain has recovered."

"Pah!" said the duchess crossly. "Pah! Pooh!" And she was still pahing and poohing as they made their separate ways to bed.

Lord Andrew found himself praying for rain, but the day of Mr. Jepp's outing dawned fresh and fair. There was an hour's wait for Miss Worthy to put in an appearance, but Mr. Jepps had allowed for that, stating the time of departure as seven, but knowing they would be lucky if they got on the road by eight.

Lord Andrew led the way in his phaeton with Miss Worthy beside him, Mr. Jepps followed with Penelope, and Mr. Macdonald and Miss Tilney brought up the rear.

At one point on the journey, Penelope dropped her fan on the floor of the carriage. She leaned forward and groped about for it. Mr. Jepps bunched the reins in one hand and picked it up for her with the other. He wondered if she was very longsighted and, if so, if that defeat could be put to some use. His sharp eyes had already noticed the way Lord Andrew's eyes had kept studiously avoiding Penelope before they set out. And Penelope *was* worth looking at. Although Mr. Jepps's goal was Ann Worthy, he did admit to himself it was pleasurable to be sitting beside such a fair partner. Penelope was wearing a thin gown of transparent blue muslin over an underdress of blue silk. She wore a warm Paisley shawl about her shoulders, and her dashing little straw bonnet with a narrow brim was ideal for carriage wear as it did not flap about in the wind.

Mr. Jepps fell to questioning her about the duke's household and kept bringing up Lord Andrew's name and noticed that whenever he did so, Penelope became reserved.

The little party stopped at an inn for luncheon at eleven. Ian Macdonald was in high spirits and inclined to tease little Amy Tilney, who kept blushing with delight.

Mr. Jepps somehow had managed to sit beside Miss Worthy and keep her attention on himself. Lord Andrew asked Miss Worthy whether she would like to take a stroll with him in the inn garden, but she did not appear to hear. Quite out of charity with her, he forgot all his resolutions and, seeing that Penelope was already heading in the direction of the garden, followed her.

"What a lovely place," said Penelope, walking across the grass as he fell into step beside her. "Mr. Jepps appears to be a good organizer."

"Yes," said Lord Andrew curtly.

His feelings were mixed as he looked down at her. On the one hand, he was relieved she showed no sign of remembering that kiss. On the other, he had an obscure wish that she might somehow betray that the effect of it had startled her as much as it had him.

"Miss Worthy and Mr. Jepps appeared to be old friends," said Penelope.

"Yes, I believe their friendship to be of some years' standing."

"One never quite sees the attractions of one's own sex," ruminated Penelope. "Now, to quite a

79

number of women, Miss Worthy would not appear as a heartbreaker."

"I do not discuss my fiancée with anyone," said Lord Andrew in chilly accents.

"Then we shall discuss Miss Tilney. Your mother regards her as an antidote, and she is possibly trying her best to view her from a male point of view. Matchmakers always think they know what the gentlemen like. But Miss Tilney appears to me to have great charm."

"She has a neat figure, is well mannered, and would do or say nothing to put any gentleman to the blush," said Lord Andrew.

"Unlike me?"

"Unlike you, Miss Mortimer."

"Then perhaps she and Mr. Macdonald are well suited while you and I, my lord, are two of a kind."

"What can you mean?"

"Well, I may walk into lions' dens, but you, my lord, are engaged to one lady and yet bestow your kisses on another."

"If you were a lady," he said savagely, "you would forget that incident completely."

Penelope laughed. "Was it so very unpleasant?"

He turned on his heel and marched back into the inn and demanded to know if they were all going to hang around this cursed hostelry all day.

Chapter Six

Mr. Jepps pointed out that as the castle was quite near, it would be easier if they all traveled in his barouche. So forceful and energetic were his arguments that the rest found themselves agreeing, although as they all crammed in beside Mr. Jepps, they began to wonder why they had so readily agreed, particularly Lord Andrew, who was jammed against the delectable side of Miss Penelope Mortimer and suffering from various uncomfortable physical reactions which he had hitherto believed only courtesans were supposed to prompt in gentlemen.

The day had turned very warm and sultry, more like high summer than an English spring day. The young leaves hung motionless on the trees, and spring flowers in the cottage gardens stood to attention like serried ranks of gaudy guardsmen.

The remains of Dalby Castle soon rose into view above the trees. It had been destroyed by the Parliamentarians in the Civil War, and only the Dungeon Tower remained standing. The Dalbys were proud of their ruin, and the grass around the tower had been cropped close by sheep to a billiard-table smoothness and swans swam among the water lilies on the moat which surrounded the tower and the piles of fallen masonry which were all that remained of the rest of the castle.

The small party alighted, and Penelope immediately went to look at the moat. Mr. Jepps raced after her and caught her just as she was about to step over the edge. He pulled her back and noticed the long-sighted way she blinked in the sunlight.

The half-formed plan that had been burgeoning in Mr. Jepp's agile brain sprang into flower. He knew the ruin well and knew there was a dark cellarlike chamber in the basement of the ruin which had a lock on the door as gardening tools and other estate equipment were stored there.

For the moment, he decided, it suited his interests to pay court to Miss Mortimer.

Miss Worthy looked decidedly peeved. She had not made much effort to engage the interest of her fiancé on the outing because he had already been snared, so to speak. But she had expected Mr. Jepps to remain her devoted admirer.

Lord Andrew had made up his mind to devote the day to his fiancée and put Penelope out of his mind. The normally shy and diffident Miss Tilney was delighted with the easygoing, undemanding company of Ian Macdonald.

Seeing that everyone else was occupied in strolling around the edge of the moat, Mr. Jepps said to Penelope, "Come with me and I will show you the most dark and romantic room at the bottom of the tower."

"I do not find dark rooms very romantic," said the ever-practical Penelope. But at that moment, Miss Worthy, walking in the distance with Lord Andrew, stumbled, and he put an arm around her waist to support her.

Penelope felt a sharp pain somewhere about the region of her heart. The idea of getting away from the very sight of Lord Andrew became welcoming, so she added, "But if you care to show it to me, I shall be glad to go."

They walked sedately together out of the sunlight into the shadow of the tower. Mr. Jepps led the way inside and then down a crumbling flight of stairs to a stout door in the basement.

"And shall we find terrible instruments of torture?" asked Penelope sarcastically.

"Undoubtedly. I am anxious to see the room myself, for I have never been here before," lied Mr. Jepps. He turned the key in the lock and stood aside to let Penelope past. She walked into the cold, dark chamber lit faintly by light from a barred window well above her head. She looked about her blindly. "What is here, Mr. Jepps? It is so very dark. No rack or thumbscrew?"

"Excuse me!" called Mr. Jepps. "Forgot something. Back in a trice." He slammed the door.

Why leave me here? thought Penelope, half-amused, half-exasperated. And why is it that the gentlemen always believe we females will fall into Gothic raptures at the very sight of a dirty old room? From the sound of lapping water, she gathered the room was under the level of the moat outside.

She put on her glasses and looked about her. There were piles of gardening implements and empty sacks.

After some minutes, she began to feel cold and went to the door and turned the handle, only to find it firmly locked.

"Silly man!" she said to herself. "Oh, well, he will

be back soon enough." She stowed her spectacles safely away and began to walk up and down the room.

Mr. Jepps hurried across the turf to where Lord Andrew was walking with Miss Worthy. He could see from the expressions on their faces that they had been having a row, which in fact they had. Miss Worthy had called Penelope a bold minx and had said she was flirting shamelessly with poor Mr. Jepps, and Lord Andrew had remarked acidly that she, Miss Worthy, was the one who had been flirting shamelessly. So when Mr. Jepps asked for a word in private with Lord Andrew, Miss Worthy turned sulkily away.

"What is it?" asked Lord Andrew testily.

"It is Miss Mortimer. She is desirous to speak to you."

"I cannot think why. Where is she?"

"In a room in the basement of the tower."

Lord Andrew gave a click of exasperation. He was beginning to dislike Mr. Jepps. He thought him a poor, fussy sort of fellow.

"Very well. Lead the way."

Mr. Jepps ushered Lord Andrew down the stairs to the underground chamber. He unlocked the door, ignoring Lord Andrew's startled question as to why Miss Mortimer was locked in. Penelope swung round. "Thank goodness you are come," she said. "You locked me in, Mr. Jepps!"

"What is it you want to see me about?" asked Lord Andrew, striding forward. Mr. Jepps retreated swiftly and slammed and locked the door again. Ignoring the furious cries coming faintly from inside, he made his way upstairs and out into the warmth of the sunlight.

Now his biggest task lay ahead. He had to persuade the others to return to London, to persuade them that Lord Andrew and Penelope had already left. Clouds were rising up in the sky, and a blustery wind had rushed out of nowhere, hissing in the trees and ruffling the waters of the moat.

He was sure Ann Worthy, activated by jealousy, would readily believe him, but Ian Macdonald and Miss Tilney were going to be difficult.

He cocked his head to one side, but no shout or scream escaped from the thick walls of the underground room. If they could climb up to that barred window, they might make themselves heard. Better to move quickly.

He went straight to Ann Worthy.

"A most odd thing has happened," he cried. "Lord Andrew and Miss Mortimer have gone off—walked off—declaring their intention of going to the inn. I think it very strange behavior in a man who is affianced to you, Miss Worthy. Very odd, and so I told him. He told me to mind my own business, and Miss Mortimer giggled. If we leave now, we can catch them up on the road, and you may demand an explanation."

"And he shall give me one!" said Miss Worthy, quite beside herself with fury.

Ian Macdonald had already taken a strong dislike to Miss Worthy. He was also accustomed to his friend, The Perfect Gentleman, never putting a foot wrong. So if Lord Andrew had decided to walk back to the inn with Miss Mortimer, it followed he probably had some highly conventional and boring reason for doing so.

Mr. Jepps heaved a sigh of relief. It was all so much easier than he had imagined. He would send a messenger from London the following morning to let the couple out. By that time they would have spent the night together, and Lord Andrew would be obliged to marry Miss Mortimer. Mr. Jepps was sure that Lord Andrew would challenge him to a duel. But he was not afraid of that. He would accept the challenge and, since dueling was illegal, alert the authorities to arrest Lord Andrew.

Now one more obstacle lay ahead. Lord Andrew's phaeton.

As soon as they reached the inn, Mr. Jepps urged the party to go inside. Then he ran round to the stables. He was in luck. An unsavory-looking idler, the type who hangs around horse fairs, was leaning against a post, chewing a straw. In a hurried whisper, he agreed to pay the man ten pounds to drive Lord Andrew's horses and Phaeton to London and leave them in the Park Street mews. The fellow was paid five pounds in advance and was to call at Mr. Jepps's London address that evening for the other half.

Then Mr. Jepps strolled back into the inn. Miss Worthy was wondering aloud why they had not overtaken the couple on the road. Mr. Jepps went off to see the landlord and explained that Miss Worthy's fiancé had taken off with another lady. It would take time to break the news. The landlord was to wait an hour and then enter the coffee room and say someone had seen the couple driving off. As a matter of fact, Mr. Jepps said, handing over some guineas to the gratified landlord and drooping one eyelid in a vulgar wink, the couple were putting up with an accommodating friend in the vicinity and had sent their carriage back to London to throw dust in the eyes of the party. Flattered to be included in all this aristocratic intrigue, the landlord agreed to play his part.

Mr. Jepps had no fear of the repercussions that would arise from his machinations. He was a very wealthy man and was confident of bribing his way out of any situation. He might even have to travel abroad for a time but, without Lord Andrew, he was confident that Miss Worthy would wait for him. In fact, flight, rather than waiting around to be challenged to a duel, might be the wisest course.

Ian Macdonald began to assume long before the landlord put in an appearance that his friend, Lord Andrew, had finally come to his senses and decided to do something wrong for once in his life—namely, ditching a sour-faced fiancée for that blond charmer. He decided to play along, only remarking that the weather had changed and they had better set out before the rain came. But Miss Worthy hung on until the landlord finally removed any hope from her angry breast. She drove back to London with Mr. Jepps, breathing fire and vengeance and breaches of promise. Mr. Jepps listened sympathetically to this tirade and insisted on entering her house so he could support her as she told her parents of Lord Andrew's perfidy.

Mr. and Mrs. Worthy listened in horror. There was only one thing to be done. They called for their carriage and set out for Park Street to complain to the duchess about her son's behavior.

The duchess laughed at them. Lord Andrew had never behaved badly in his life, she said, and was not likely to start now. There would be some very conventional explanation. Much reassured, the Worthys left, not knowing that as soon as they were out of the ducal town house, the duchess went into a fit of hysterics, threatening to string Penelope Mortimer up by the thumbs should she ever see her again.

Meanwhile, in the underground chamber, Penelope Mortimer was standing on top of Lord Andrew's shoulders sawing desperately at the bars at the window with a saw they had found buried under the pile of gardening tools. "Cannot you try a little harder?" he called up.

"I am trying as hard as I can," said Penelope crossly. "You do it if you think you can do any better."

"Don't be silly. How can *I* stand on *your* shoulders? Keep sawing."

"I've done two bars already," sighed Penelope, squinting at the window. "It looks very dark outside."

"I do not care if there is a blizzard raging. That cur Jepps planned to make us spend the night together so that he could marry Miss Worthy. What a flat I was to be so taken in! But we must get out of here. I'm damned if I'll be made to marry you."

"Who would want to marry *you*, of all people?" said Penelope furiously.

"Shut up. Keep sawing and just shut up."

Penelope sawed and sawed. The bars were old and rusty, but she was exhausted when the last bar broke and fell into the moat.

"Don't come down," said Lord Andrew. "Do you know how to swim?"

"Yes."

"Then jump through the window and swim across the moat."

"Have you no feeling, sir? I shall be soaked to the skin. Furthermore, it has started to rain."

88

"If you do not go through that window of your own accord, then I shall throw you through," said Lord Andrew. "Get a move on; there's a good girl. My shoulders are aching, and you are not making things easier by jumping about on them and putting up missish arguments."

Penelope threw the white blur of his face a baleful look. She hauled herself up by the remaining stumps of the sawn bars, tore her gown dragging her body across them, and tumbled headlong into the moat. Something heavy underwater brushed against her body. Penelope immediately thought of large carp with large teeth and frantically swam to the surface and struck out for where she believed the far side of the moat to be.

"I declare you are as blind as a bat," said Lord Andrew's voice from somewhere above her head. "The other way, girl."

Penelope turned around and struck out away from the tower again and this time reached the opposite side of the moat. She clambered out, long trails of green, slimy weed hanging from her torn and soaking dress. Clouds were boiling black in the sky above, and cold, driving rain pounded down on her head. Her frivolous little bonnet floated on the surface of the moat.

The great wave resulting from Lord Andrew diving into the moat from the window submerged the bonnet, which disappeared completely from view. Penelope began to cry. All at once it seemed the most tragic thing in the world to lose that pretty bonnet.

Had the circumstances been more civilized, then Lord Andrew would have soothed Penelope and dried her tears. But the increasing storm raging above made him behave as if he were still in the army.

"Why are you crying?" he demanded harshly.

"I've lost my bonnet. You drowned it," said Penelope pathetically.

"Of all the idiotish girls. Pull yourself together this instant, Miss Mortimer!"

Penelope gave a defiant sob and looked down at the ruin of her dress. "There is not much left *to* pull together. It is so dark. What time is it?"

He pulled out his watch and looked at it. "I suppose it must have stopped when I hit the water. It is about nine in the evening."

"Nine!"

"It is all your fault, you know. You took hours sawing those bars."

"It may amaze you to know that bar sawing is not a ladylike accomplishment. But who knows? They may even begin to teach it in the seminaries and dame schools along with the art of lock picking."

"Come along. I do not suppose it is of any use looking for my carriage. I am sure Jepps found a way to get rid of it. What I fail to understand is why Ian Macdonald did not stay around to find us. Well, it is of no use standing here wondering. We must find shelter."

Had Lord Andrew turned right on the road outside the ruined castle instead of to the left, they would have found themselves back in the village where he had left his carriage, the landlord would have recognized them, and they would have been made welcome. But the blackness of the night as they scurried along under the trees was bewildering. They half ran, half stumbled along the road under the increasing ferocity of the storm.

They had been hurrying along like this for over an hour when the flickering lights of a village appeared out of the blackness.

At the edge of the village was a small inn called The Green Man, its sign swinging in the wind.

Lord Andrew strode up to the inn with Penelope tottering behind him, and pushed open the door.

He found himself in a small hall. He rang a brass bell on a side table. Penelope came in and stood, shivering.

"Shut the door behind you," snapped Lord Andrew. "Or are you not cold enough?"

A small, stocky landlord appeared from the tap and eyed the bedraggled couple warily.

"And what would you two be wanting?" he asked.

"I am Lord Andrew Childe," said Lord Andrew haughtily, "and, as you can see, we have been caught in the storm. We wish rooms where we can dry ourselves, and we need dinner, for I am sharp-set."

"It's a fine lord you make," said the landlord. "Where is your carriage? Your servants?"

"I went for an outing and was tricked. I do not know where my carriage is." Penelope gave a dismal sneeze.

The landlord's wife came out to join him, demanding to know what was up.

"This here gent," said the landlord, his voice laden with sarcasm, "says as how he's a lord and he's asking for rooms and dinner."

"This is a respectable inn. . . ." began the landlady. Penelope coughed and sneezed and shivered. The landlord's wife looked at her, and her face softened. "But the poor lady is mortal wet. We have only one room, and you're welcome to that if you pay your shot in advance. But only if you are married, mind."

Lord Andrew suddenly caught a glimpse of himself in an old, greenish mirror over the hall table. His black hair was plastered down on his forehead, his cravat to his coat. He looked at Penelope. She had not only lost her bonnet in the moat, but her shawl as well. Her filmy muslin gown clung to her shivering body.

"Yes, we are married," he said. He fished in the pocket in his tails, relieved to find a rouleau of guineas still there. He pulled it out and began to shake gold coins out into his hand. "How much?" he asked curtly. "We will need to hire a carriage after we have dined."

The landlord's jaw dropped when he saw the gold. "I don't know as there's a spare gig around here at this time of night, my lord. Why don't you and your lady go upstairs, and we'll call you when dinner is ready. There's a couple o' gents in the private parlor, but they're nigh finished."

"Good," said Lord Andrew. "How much?"

But the sight of that gold had worked wonders on the landlord. "You may pay your shot when you leave, my lord," he said, bowing low. "I am Mr. Carter, and this is my wife, Abigail. Mrs. Carter, do take my lord and my lady to their room."

"But I'm not—" Penelope began weakly, and then let out a scream as Lord Andrew stamped on her foot.

"I am so sorry, my love," said Lord Andrew, taking her arm in a firm grip. "An accident. Come along. You are in no fit state to talk," he added in a threatening tone of voice. "Mrs. Carter, we would be obliged if you could find us dressing gowns of some sort. We cannot dine in our wet clothes, and I fear we have no others."

"I'm sure I can find you something," said Mrs. Carter, made as cheerful and obsequious as her husband by the sight of that gold.

They followed the landlord's wife up a crooked staircase and along a short corridor. "It's our best bedroom," said Mrs. Carter proudly.

Lord Andrew and Penelope stood shivering while Mr. Carter and a waiter entered with a coal and logs and proceeded to build up a roaring fire. Mrs. Carter disappeared only to reappear shortly with flannel nightgowns and two dressing gowns, both men's and both made of coarse wool, and two red Kilmarnock nightcaps.

A maidservant came in with cans of hot water and rough huckaback towels. The landlord then delivered a tray with a bottle of white brandy and two glasses and a kettle of boiling water.

"We will leave you to change, my lord. My wife will take your wet clothes down to the kitchen to be cleaned and dried. The private parlor is next door to your room, so you may dine in your night rail without disturbing any of the other guests."

Lord Andrew wanted to say that they planned to set out for London as soon as their clothes were dried, but Penelope looked white and exhausted, and he felt he would tackle further explanations when they had dined.

Finally Penelope and Lord Andrew were left alone.

"If you will go out into the corridor, my lord," said Penelope weakly, "I will change my clothes."

"There is no need for that," he said. "I will draw the bed hangings to form a screen. You undress on this side in front of the fire, and I will change on the other. First, have something to drink."

"Later," said Penelope.

"No, now!"

He poured her a stiff glass of brandy and topped it up with hot water and stood over her until she had drunk it.

Then he picked up his nightclothes and went to the other side of the bed, drawing the chintz hangings closed to form a screen.

Penelope looked dizzily about her. The room had an odd way of moving up and down. It was like being on board ship, or rather, like the descriptions she had read about life on a sailing ship. She removed her thin, sopping clothes, those summer clothes which had been so beautiful earlier that day, and pulled on the nightgown, and then wrapped the man's dressing gown tightly around her. She was leaning over the fire, trying to dry her hair, when Lord Andrew came round to join her. He seized a towel and rubbed her hair with it and then opened her reticule to look for a comb.

"No," screamed Penelope, snatching the reticule from him. Ill and faint as she felt, she still did not want him to see those glasses.

She took out a tortoiseshell comb, drew the strings of her reticule tight, and then tried to comb her hair, but the comb kept getting caught in the tangles.

"Here, let me," said Lord Andrew. He tilted up her face and gently eased the comb through the tangled mess of her drying hair.

"Why did you say we were man and wife?" asked Penelope. "Are you trying to compromise me?"

"I am trying to stop us from both getting the ague," he said impatiently. "We could not possibly have gone further in our soaking state. We will set out for London as soon as possible."

A buffet of wind hurled rain against the windows. "I am so tired," said Penelope wretchedly.

"You will feel better when you have dined," he said. He looked at the pathetic little figure in front of him with a sharp stab of concern. Anger at the way he had been so easily tricked combined with the rigors of running through the storm to shelter had made him treat Penelope very badly indeed. He had always believed women to be delicate and frail creatures. What if she fell ill? He would never forgive himself. Why hadn't he left her in the shelter of that tower room and gone for help himself? She must be exhausted after sawing those bars. But he could not have done it himself. There had been nothing to stand on, and it had been difficult enough for him to clamber up the wall and out of that window.

The landlord appeared to announce dinner— "though it be more of a supper," he explained, "dinner being at four."

Penelope and Lord Andrew went through to the private parlor. Dinner consisted of salt fish, leg of mutton boiled with capers, roasted loin of beef, and plum and plain puddings. The landlord explained a wedding was to be held at the inn the next day, and the food was part of the preparations for it. Any other time, and my lord would have had to be content with a cold collation.

After they had finished eating in silence and the

95

cover had been withdrawn and the port and fruit and nuts set on the plain wood, the couple found themselves alone.

"Now, what am I to do with that fellow Jepps?" said Lord Andrew, half to himself. "If I challenge him to a duel, then ten to one he will accept but then alert the authorities. I think I will content myself with smashing his face in."

"He wants Miss Worthy," said Penelope sleepily. "He is very much in love."

"Nonsense."

"Why nonsense? He has gone to great lengths to prevent your marriage. He must know you could kill him, although you do not look very ferocious in that funny dressing gown and with that red night-cap on your head."

"You look pretty silly yourself," said Lord Andrew, although he privately thought she looked very endearing in the enormous dressing gown and with her silvery-fair hair drying in a cloud about her head.

"The thing is this," went on Lord Andrew, pouring a glass of port for Penelope and then one for himself. "We will now see if our clothes are dry enough and borrow a greatcoat for you to wear and then see if we can hire a gig. We shall set out for London. We shall say we escaped from the tower, hired a gig, and journeyed through the night. The fact that we were masquerading at this inn as man and wife, if only for dinner, must never come out. Do you understand?"

"Yes, my lord," yawned Penelope.

"You had better wear my ring until we are clear of this inn." He drew a heavy gold and sapphire ring from his finger and handed it over. Penelope slid it over her fourth finger. "It's too big," she said. "It wobbles."

"Then crook your finger round it. Now, go and lie down for half an hour while I make the arrangements."

When Penelope had left, he summoned the landlord and ordered him to find some sort of carriage and horses.

The landlord scratched his head in perplexity. "I don't know if I can do that at this time of night," he said. "My own gig's broke. Mayhap squire would have something, but he's an old man, and it won't do to rouse him this time of the night. Then there's Mr. Baxter over at Five Elms—"

"Do your best," said Lord Andrew. "But we must leave for London this night."

Mrs. Carter brought their clothes up from the kitchen. The mud had been sponged from them, but they were still damp. Lord Andrew spread them over two chairs in front of the bedroom fire to dry.

Then he walked over to the bed and looked down at Penelope. She was fast asleep, one small red hand bunched into a fist to hold his ring safe.

What a brute I am, he thought with remorse. If only I could allow this child to sleep. Mercy, but I am exhausted myself. Perhaps just half an hour . . .

He stretched out beside her. She moved in her sleep and, with an incoherent little murmur, snuggled against him.

He was filled with a great wave of tenderness. He put his arms about her and held her close and rested his chin on the top of her head. The bedroom was warm and comfortable. The sensations coursing through his body were languorous and sweet.

He kissed her hair and his heavy eyelids began

to droop. It would do no harm to kiss her goodnight. He moved his lips to her sleeping mouth and kissed her gently.

His head slid down to rest on her bosom, and with his arms still tightly about her, he fell asleep.

"Morning, my lord!"

Penelope and Lord Andrew slowly came awake. Sunlight was pouring into the room. Mrs. Carter was standing smiling down at them indulgently. Lord Andrew realized his arms were still about Penelope, and his legs appeared to have become tangled up with hers during the night. They were both still lying on top of the bedclothes.

"Why did you not call me when the carriage was ready?" he said, sitting up.

"To be sure, there was nothing we could do about getting you anything in the middle of such a storm," said Mrs. Carter. "Mr. Carter, he came up after supper to tell you so, but you was sleeping like babies, and so he left you. 'Tis six in the morning. Mr. Carter says I was to wake you as soon as we got a gig, which we did, and it's the smartest little turnout you ever did see. Mr. Baxter himself brought it over and is waiting to see your lordship."

"Thank you," said Lord Andrew, while his mind raced. Provided Penelope held her tongue, they could still be in London before anyone was awake— the fashionable world not stirring until two in the afternoon. He dismissed Mrs. Carter and stripped off his dressing gown and nightgown and began to wash himself. The angry jerk of the bed curtains as the startled Penelope shut off the interesting view of his naked body sounded behind him. He felt himself blush as he had not blushed since he was an

98

adolescent. How could he, who had been so perfect until so recently, have forgotten the simple proprieties?

After a rushed breakfast, they were both at last seated in a small gig pulled by a glossy little pony. Mr. Baxter had supplied them with greatcoats, for although the sun was shining once more, the morning was chilly.

Lord Andrew wondered whether to take this country gentlemen into his confidence and then decided against it. The explanations would prove too embarrassing. He thanked Mr. Baxter again, grimly introduced Penelope as his wife, and promised to send his servant back with the gig and pony the following day.

Penelope was glad of the greatcoat. Her gown had shrunk and was stretched indecently over her body. Lord Andrew, too, was glad of his covering. His clothes, although they had not shrunk, were wrinkled and shabby-looking. After various efforts with the mangled remains of his cravat, he had decided to wear his cambric shirt open at the neck.

He thought gloomily that he and Penelope looked like a couple of gypsies and could only hope some parish constable would not stop them and accuse them of stealing the gig.

Chapter Seven

A thin mist was rising from the fields as they journeyed along. Drifts of may blossom scented the sunny air. Busy birds hopped along the thickets, and smoke from cottage chimneys rose lazily into the air. Soon, apart from a few broken branches and twigs lying on the road, there was no sign of the terrible storm of the night before.

"I have never made so many mistakes in my life before," said Lord Andrew, breaking a silence that had lasted over an hour.

"Well, it was a bit silly, if you don't want to be compromised, to lie in bed hugging me," said Penelope practically.

"I was cold."

"Then next time put the blankets over you!"

"There won't be a next time."

"Oh, yes there will," said Penelope nastily. "Someone as easily gulled as you will no doubt end up in a brothel convinced he is staying at the most respectable posting house."

"I was wondering why I treated you with so little consideration yesterday," said Lord Andrew evenly, "but now I realize why. It is because you have no delicacy, no shame, no—"

"Shut up, do, you pompous ass!"

"How dare you speak to me thus, Miss Mortimer! How dare you!"

"That is exactly how you speak to me. It is amazing how people who are expert at dishing out the nastiest medicine do not know how to take it themselves."

Penelope, in her way, was as stubborn and arrogant as Lord Andrew. If one of them had said at that point, "I love you," then the row would have been at an end. But both were suffering badly from frustrated physical desire, neither would admit it to themselves, and so they traveled on, sniping at each other, each searching their tired brains for the most wounding things to say.

When the sun had risen high in the sky, Penelope had told Lord Andrew in a conversational tone of voice that he was, in fact, not at all handsome and lacked breeding and elegance, and Lord Andrew had told Miss Penelope Mortimer that there was something blowsy and peasantlike about her blond looks which must set up revulsion in the fastidious breast.

By the time the pair, made stiff and haughty by bad temper, sailed into a richly appointed posting house demanding refreshment, it came like a douche of cold water to both to find themselves turned off the premises with insults.

"Well!" said Penelope furiously as they climbed back into the gig. "What a dreadful man. He said you were a highwayman and I was your moll! He refused to serve us. He said we were dirty gallows birds! Why did you not thrash him for his insolence?"

"I took one look at you, my sweet, and saw the force of his argument."

"It was you he was addressing. And you do look remarkably slovenly."

The pony plodded on. Lord Andrew stared at its ears and wondered what it would be like to strangle Penelope Mortimer.

"I am very hungry," she said at last. "Are you going to find us some food or are you going to sulk all day?"

"I never sulk."

"Fiddle. You are in an arch sulk. Here is a village and there is a shop. Now, if we bought some bread and cheese and some wine, we could find a comfortable field and have a picnic."

He was about to tell her he now had no intention of stopping until they reached London, but he was very hungry and the pony needed a rest.

He reined in and, without a word, went off to buy various things, eventually coming back with them all packed up in a new wicker basket.

"Walk on," he said to the pony, and not looking at Penelope, he stared straight ahead.

"Truce," said Penelope in a small voice.

"What?"

"You heard. We can either decide to have a pleasurable picnic and make what we can of our journey or we can continue to be nasty to each other and get indigestion."

He began to laugh. For some reason, his bad temper evaporated like the morning mist. "Truce, Miss Mortimer," he cried, "and there is the place for our picnic." He pointed with his whip to a little stream which tumbled down through a wood of young oak and birch.

Soon the pony was unhitched and they were seated on a flat rock by the stream, drinking wine out of thick tumblers and eating ham and bread and cheese.

The sun glittered on the sapphire on Penelope's finger. She drew the ring off and handed it to him. "I unmarry you, Lord Andrew Childe," she said, "and with this ring I thee divorce."

He took it and tossed it up and down in his hand. Then he handed it back to her. "I want you to have it," he said.

"Why?"

"I think our adventures need a memento. When you are old and staid, you can look at it and say to your grandchildren, 'I remember the day I got locked in a castle dungeon with the terrible Lord Andrew.'"

"Then I shall keep it, but I shall remain a spinster, I assure you."

She had taken off her coat. Her gown was stretched across her figure. He lay on his back in the sun and half closed his eyes. Through his lashes he could see a strand of torn muslin on the front of her gown fluttering in the light breeze. It was as well the underdress had remained intact, he thought, although what she was wearing left little to the imagination.

"We must go soon," he said, but he did not move. "Duty waits."

"Duty?"

"Duty to my parents, duty to Miss Worthy, duty to my name. I cannot marry you, Miss Mortimer."

"I do not expect you to. I look for the impossible anyway. I look for a man who would marry me for love."

He opened his eyes and rolled over on his side,

propping his head on his hand to look up at her as she sat next to him.

"You will find such a one, Miss Mortimer," he said. "You are very lovable."

Penelope forced a laugh. "What! I? A blowsy peasant?"

"I did not mean a word of it. You are beautiful and courageous, and your hair is like the sun and your eyes like the blue sky."

"I liked you better when you cursed me," said Penelope. "You have no right to speak to me so. Let us leave."

He stood up and held down his hand and drew her to her feet. The river chuckled and bubbled, the pony lazily cropped the green grass, and the lightest of breezes rustled the leaves of the trees above and lifted the silken curls of her hair.

"Put on your coat," he said quietly.

"It is too hot."

"You are revealing too much."

"Oh!" Penelope blushed and stooped down to pick up her coat. He took it from her and held it out. She slipped her arms into the sleeves, her back to him. He drew her against him and they stood silent, listening to the river.

"Back to London," he said softly in her ear.

"Back to London," echoed Penelope on a sigh.

They collected the remains of their picnic and packed them in the basket, not looking at each other. They harnessed up the horse and climbed into the gig. The little pony gallantly plodded along the roads, which were now white with dust.

They did not speak again the whole journey home. As they trotted along Piccadilly to Park Street, Penelope could feel a dark weight pressing on her heart. There were explanations to be given, and then the life of the Season would go on. Lord Andrew would squire Miss Worthy to balls and parties, and she, Penelope Mortimer, would put up with a few more weeks of the Season before returning home. Penelope knew if she refused one more suitor, then the duchess would tire of her.

Lord Andrew and Penelope were told that the duchess was in the red saloon on the ground floor. The butler held open the door and announced them.

Penelope ducked just in time. A vase sailed over her head and smashed against the door jamb.

"Stop it immediately," said Lord Andrew, seizing his mother's arm as the duchess was about to follow the vase with a bowl of flowers.

"Scheming harlot!" raged the duchess. "Oh, God! Strike this poor wounded mother dead! What have I done that I should be cursed with a fool for a son?" She ducked under Lord Andrew's arm and flew at Penelope. Penelope darted off with the duchess after her, finally shaking her off by running over the sofa. The duchess tripped and fell on her face on the floor, where she lay sobbing and screaming and drumming her fists. Lord Andrew jerked his mother upright and forced her down into the depths of an armchair while she continued to scream, not out of fury but because the pressure was forcing the bones of her stays to dig into her back.

At his wits' end, Lord Andrew seized the bowl of flowers his mother had been trying to throw at Penelope and upended the contents on the duchess's head.

105

There was a deathly silence. The duchess stared at her son while hothouse roses and dahlias hung dripping from her muslin cap.

"Now, listen," said Lord Andrew quietly. "I am still engaged to Miss Worthy. Nothing happened. Miss Mortimer and I were victims of a cruel practical joke. Do you understand?"

"But where *were* you? You *must* have spent the night together."

"We traveled all night and most of today. We borrowed a gig and a little pony which could not travel fast. Is that not so, Miss Mortimer?"

"Oh, yes," said Penelope.

"Why did you not say so in the first place?" said the duchess, glaring round the room. Three liveried footmen who had been pretending to be busy about their duties exited sideways with their traditional sliding step like so many gold and scarlet crabs. Perkins, the lady's maid, who had been crouched in the corner while the scene was at its height, rushed forward to fuss about her mistress.

"So," went on the duchess brightly, pushing Perkins away, "we must prepare for the evening. Penelope, my love, put on the silver ballgown, I beseech you. There is a turtle supper followed by a masked ball at the Foxtons'."

"Miss Mortimer is in no fit state to go anywhere," said Lord Andrew.

But Penelope, relieved the dreadful scene was over, said, "I am quite recovered," and slipped quietly from the room.

Lord Andrew stayed only to tell his mother the full story of Mr. Jepps's trickery before going off to change. Pomfret, his valet, took one ecstatic look at the wreck of The Perfect Gentleman and burst into tears of gratitude, much to Lord Andrew's extreme annoyance.

Once more groomed and elegant, he drove straight to Mr. Jepps's town house. He was not very surprised to learn that Mr. Jepps had left for an unknown destination. He went on to the Worthys' house.

Miss Worthy and her parents were just sitting down to dinner. Lord Andrew was asked to join them. He was relieved that no one seemed inclined to shout or rail at him. His vastly edited story of his adventures was heard in attentive silence. Miss Worthy's green eyes began to glow with pleasure. Lord Andrew's tired, bored voice made his adventures, and the company of Penelope Mortimer, appear gratifyingly dull. Added to that, Miss Worthy found it extremely flattering that dear Mr. Jepps should have gone to such lengths to try to break her engagement. Although she outwardly expressed horror at his behavior and said, yes, Mr. Jepps must be found and punished, in her heart she wished the absent Mr. Jepps well. It was a pity he did not have a title.

After sympathizing with Lord Andrew's hardships, Mr. Worthy said, "You will, alas, be too fatigued to accompany us to the Foxtons'. There is to be a turtle supper, which is why we are dining so frugally at the moment." Mr. Worthy waved a deprecating hand to apologize for the mere five courses which had been set before them.

Lord Andrew opened his mouth to say that yes, he was too tired to attend. Life felt very stale, flat, and dull. Life was perfect again. He was engaged to a suitable lady, and he must forget he ever lay beside a stream with Penelope Mortimer at his side. But Penelope would be there. She would be so very tired. She would need someone to look after her. He

107

suddenly remembered reaching for her reticule to find her comb and how she had snatched it from him. What had she not wanted him to see? A letter from some country lover?

"The least I can do after my escapade is to escort my long-suffering fiancée," he said with a charming smile. "You must excuse me. I must return to find a mask. I have certain arrangements to make. I shall see you there."

When he reached Park Street, he made his way up to his room. He passed Penelope's bedroom door, then went back and pushed it open. Penelope was sitting in an armchair in front of the bedroom fire. She was dressed in a silver net ballgown. A delicate headdress of artificial flowers and silver wire was on her fashionably dressed head. She was fast asleep.

He saw the reticule she had carried on the adventures lying on a table beside the bed. He went over quietly, picked it up, and drew open the strings. It was empty.

He turned about and looked thoughtfully at the still-sleeping Penelope. There was a reticule at her feet, a frivolous little bag decorated with silver threadwork and pearls. He crossed the room and picked it up, and examined the contents. He slowly drew out an ugly pair of steel-framed spectacles.

He held them up to the light. The lenses were strongly magnified. "Longsighted," he murmured. "Poor little thing. Not much of a guilty secret." He put them back in the bag and quietly left the room.

He felt wretchedly tired during the turtle supper, and worse after the dancing had commenced. There were seemingly endless energetic country dances.

The full force of what she now regarded as her tremendous attraction for the opposite sex had gone to Miss Worthy's head. Her eyes glittered with excitement through the slits of her mask. Not knowing her initial attraction for Lord Andrew—apart from her birth and bank balance—was that she was quiet and restful, she chattered and flirted every time the movement of the dance brought them together. It was a relief to escape from her but not very pleasurable to stand and watch Penelope besieged by admirers. He noticed with a sinking heart that the middle-aged Duke of Harford—one of the few gentlemen who was not wearing a mask—whose wife had died two years ago, was unable to take his eyes off Penelope. Now, if *he* proposed, Lord Andrew felt sure his mother would lock Penelope up and keep her on bread and water until she agreed to marry the duke.

He turned and went into the room set aside for refreshments. Ian Macdonald hailed him and demanded to know the full story.

Loyalty to his fiancée stopped Lord Andrew from telling the truth. In a flat voice, he recounted the same story he had told the Worthys, adding that Jepps had fled.

"Well, I am sorry for you," said Ian. "I had the most prodigious good time. Little Miss Tilney made sweet company."

"Do not mislead her, my friend," cautioned Lord Andrew. "She is young and no doubt does not know you are a hardened bachelor."

"I am not hardened in the least. I had not met any lady before who interested me enough."

"And Miss Tilney does?"

"Greatly. I only saw her yesterday, and I miss her

dreadfully already." He looked through the door of the refreshment room, and his face lit up. "Why, there she is! And accompanied by her dragon."

Lord Andrew caught his friend's arm. "Stay a moment. Never say you mean to propose!"

"Not here and now," said Ian Macdonald. "I shall call on the Blenkinsop female tomorrow. What is it to you? You are going to be married yourself."

"Yes. Yes, of course." Lord Andrew released his arm and watched Ian Macdonald threading his way through the dancers to Miss Tilney's side. Miss Tilney was masked, and Lord Andrew would have been hard put to it to identify her. Love obviously sharpened the sight wonderfully. He would not have recognized Miss Worthy had she not accosted him first. If Ian proposed, he thought gloomily, then his mother would make sure Penelope became engaged to someone, anyone, as well. Where *was* Penelope? His eyes raked the ballroom. Now he knew how dreadfully longsighted she was, he feared she had wandered off into the garden, where there was a small ornamental pool.

He walked through the ballroom to the long windows overlooking the garden. One window was open onto a terrace. He walked out and stood with his hands on the balustrade, his eyes searching the garden.

Then he saw a glint of silver over in the far corner. He walked down the steps leading from the terrace and then round the little lake with its ornamental fountain and into the darkness of the shrubbery.

Penelope, wearing a silver mask to match her gown, sat on a marble bench under the drooping branches of a lilac tree. The sooty air was heavily scented with lilac blossom. She started in alarm as he came up to her, her eyes only seeing vaguely the black velvet of his mask.

He sat down beside her and said, "Do not be afraid."

"Oh, it's you," said Penelope in a flat voice.

"You do not know me, ma'am. I am a stranger to you."

Penelope let out a gurgle of laughter. "We can hardly be strangers. I think we must be two of the most exhausted people at the ball. Oh, if only I could go to bed and sleep and sleep."

"And who do you think I am?"

"Lord Andrew Childe."

"I cannot be Lord Andrew. Lord Andrew is engaged and would not dream of pursuing lovely beauties into the darkness of a town garden. Lord Andrew," he added bitterly, "never does anything wrong."

"What a terrible man he must be," said Penelope, her voice soft with laughter. "There must be so many things he is afraid of doing for fear of being less than perfect."

"Oh, yes. He could not, as I can, tell you how very beautiful you are and how you bewitch him."

"No, he could not," said Penelope sadly, the laughter gone from her voice, "and neither must you."

He took her gloved hand in his own and raised it to his lips. "And yet," he murmured. "perhaps the perfect Lord Andrew has a longing to kiss someone like you, just once, before he is leg-shackled for life."

The strain of a waltz drifted out in the evening air.

"Penelope!" came the duchess's voice from the terrace. "Are you there?"

Penelope opened her mouth to call back. He seized her roughly in his arms and silenced her with a kiss.

"Penelope!" called the duchess again.

But Penelope was deaf and blind to everything but the feel of hard lips moving sensuously against her own and of a hard-muscled chest pressed against her bosom. He lowered his mouth and kissed her neck, and she buried her fingers in his hair. He lifted her onto his knees and pulled her even more tightly against him. The wine both had drunk at supper combined with their fatigue had deafened them to the proprieties. Penelope felt her body becoming loose and wanton under his caressing hands and caressing mouth.

Their bodies seemed to be fused together with heat and passion. Silver net melted into the hard blackness of evening coat as they strained desperately against each other.

The sound of a twig snapping near them made them break apart, breathing raggedly.

"Miss Mortimer?" came Ian Macdonald's voice. "Is that you?"

"Are you alone, Ian?" called Lord Andrew.

"Yes."

"Then leave us a moment and tell no one you have found us."

"Very well."

His footsteps retreated.

Lord Andrew set Penelope on the bench beside him. "I am sorry Miss Mortimer," he said huskily, "and yet I am not sorry. I had to say good-bye to something very precious."

"There is nothing else you can do," said Penelope.

"No. She will sue me for breach of promise, and your name would be dragged through the courts. What a fool I am! Jepps was the best friend I ever had, and I did not know it!"

Penelope got to her feet. She was almost on the point of offering to be his mistress. She wondered if she could go on seeing him courting another. But being a mistress would be a dreadful life, a furtive, worrying life, a life of pain.

"We shall need to learn to live without each other," she said in her usual practical voice. "Stay here. It will look bad if we enter the ballroom together."

He stood and watched her go. She nearly walked blindly into a statue of Minerva beside the pool, but veered away from it just in time. The glint of her silver gown flashed in the moonlight as she gained the terrace. Then she slipped in through the French windows and was lost to view.

He stood for a long time in the garden, and then he, too, went back to join the laughter and music, looking about him blindly as if he had just come from another land.

When Penelope awoke the next day, it was to learn from Perkins that Lord Andrew had gone to his country home and would not be back for a fortnight. Her heart felt as heavy as lead. She rose and patiently submitted to Perkins's grooming.

As the maid was on the point of leaving the room, she gave an exclamation and said, "I had quite forgot, Miss Mortimer. Lord Andrew left this for you." Perkins picked up a flat parcel from a side table and carried it over to Penelope.

Seeing that the curious maid was waiting for her to open it, Penelope said quietly, "That will be all, Perkins," and waited until the maid had left the room.

With shaking fingers, she tore off the wrapping and looked down at a flat morocco box. Jewelry, thought Penelope sadly. He already thinks of me as a mistress. I shall not accept it. She opened the box and, to her surprise, found lying on a bed of white silk, a dainty lorgnette with a fine gold chain. The lorgnette itself was of solid gold. She raised it to her eyes, and the things on the toilet table sprang into sharp focus. There was a card in the box. She picked it up. "No need to wear such ugly glasses," Lord Andrew had written. "Carry these, and you will set the fashion. A."

Penelope's eyes blurred with tears. He knew about her glasses, and he had gone to the trouble to buy her this pretty and useful gadget. Unlike her glasses, she could carry the lorgnette anywhere.

Later that day the duchess said sharply, "Where did you get that?" and pointed her fan at the lorgnette, which was hanging by its chain round Penelope's neck.

"From Lord Andrew," said Penelope. "He knows I am longsighted."

"How clever of him!" said the duchess. "Take it off and let me have a look. Goodness, I can see very well, and one can wear this sort of toy with an air. I must get one myself. That's Andrew for you. Always knows the right thing to do."

Penelope turned her face away to hide her tears.

A week later, Mr. Jepps, staying at a comfortable inn in Sussex, threw down the morning papers in disgust. Still no news of his beloved's cancelled engagement. Somehow his plan had backfired. He dared not appear in London or Andrew would attack him. What on earth was he to do?

Another week went by. Lord Andrew was expected home. Ian Macdonald had proposed to Amy Tilney and had been accepted. He was possessed of a comfortable fortune and rated a catch. The duchess received the news, brought to her by a triumphant Maria Blenkinsop, with sweet calm. For while Mrs. Blenkinsop was crowing over her charge's success, the Duke of Harford was closeted with the Duke of Parkworth, and the duchess knew the Duke of Harford was asking permission to propose to Penelope. She said nothing to Mrs. Blenkinsop, however, preferring to wait for her own magnificent triumph to burst upon the polite world later that day.

As soon as Mrs. Blenkinsop had left, the duchess went to Penelope's bedchamber and told that young lady to be prepared to accept the Duke of Harford's offer of marriage.

Heavy-eyed, Penelope listened to the news. She knew if she told the duchess she had no intention of accepting the offer, then the duchess would start screaming and shouting. Best to see whether she could frighten the duke away as she had frightened Mr. Barcourt.

The Duke of Harford was standing in front of the fireplace in the drawing room when Penelope was propelled into the room with a sharp shove in the back from the duchess.

The duchess retired, and Penelope was left alone with the duke.

He was a squat, burly man wearing an old-fashioned wig. His coat was covered in snuff stains, and he obviously believed bathing new fangled nonsense, for he smelled very strongly of what Penelope's mother used to describe as Unmentionable Things.

"Well, Miss Mortimer," he said, "so we're to be wed."

"No, Your Grace," said Penelope firmly. "I must refuse your proposal."

"Yes, yes. Knew you'd be gratified."

"I'm *not* gratified," said Penelope. "I mean, I am highly sensible of the honor being paid to me, but I must decline."

"We'll rub along tolerably well," said the duke. "You may shake my hand." And he held out two fingers.

Penelope walked forward and shook the proferred fingers, saying clearly as she did so, "You misunderstand me, Your Grace. I am not going to marry you."

"What's that? A March wedding? If you like. But we ain't going to be married in a church. Nasty, drafty places."

"Your Grace!" screamed Penelope. "I AM NOT GOING TO MARRY YOU."

"Yes, yes. Quite overcome. Your face has gone all red." The duke rang the bell, and when the duchess promptly came into the room, he said, "That's all fixed. Got an appointment at m'club."

"Oh, my darling child," cried the duchess, pressing Penelope against her stays.

It was only too late that Penelope realized the Duke of Harford was as deaf as a post. And yet she shrank from having a scene with the duchess.

Since Lord Andrew had left, all her courage had gone and she felt tired and ill.

It was then that Penelope decided to say nothing and escape. She would go back to the country, buy that cottage, and lock and bar the doors against all comers. With any luck, the duchess would be so disgusted with her, she would put her out of her mind and not go ahead and take revenge. So she smiled weakly and said she was too overcome to honor any social engagements this day.

While the duchess went out in her carriage to broadcast the glad news, Penelope scraped enough of her own money together to buy a ticket on the roof of the stage. With only one bandbox containing her old clothes, she finally jogged out of London on a windy afternoon, feeling better than she had done since Lord Andrew had left. The empty fields of freedom stretched on either side. She was going home—home, where heartbreak would be more bearable.

Chapter Eight

Lord Andrew's first feeling on finding his family home in an uproar over the disappearance of Penelope was one of relief. He was glad she had escaped.

The duchess's scenes were ripping the town house from top to bottom. He went to his father's study to find the duke singularly unmoved by all the fuss. "That's what comes of taking little nobodies out of their stations," said the duke. "She'll come about in a day or two. Then we'll have another upstart foisted on us. She's sent for Harford to explain. That should be interesting because Harford has quite acute hearing when he really wants to understand anything."

"Well, let's hope Harford does understand," said Lord Andrew wearily. "For if the idiot shows the least sign of still wanting Penelope after this humiliation, then Mama is bound to go to the country to drag Penelope back. She would not take the cottage away from her, would she?"

"Oh, yes she would, and quite right, too," said the duke. "Little mushrooms like Penelope Mortimer should be taught not to bite the hand that feeds 'em."

"Mushrooms do not bite hands."

"You know what I mean. Anyway, that interfering vicar, Troubridge, went ahead and handled the sale of Miss Mortimer's home in her absence and secured the lease of the cottage for her. Can't get her that way. Went through her room here to see if we could pin theft on her, but she's left everything behind."

"Everything?" Lord Andrew thought of the ring he had given her.

"Yes, everything, down to the last bonnet."

"I am glad you found nothing to enable you to bring a charge of theft against her," said Lord Andrew, "for I would have been forced to appear in court and say my parents were lying."

The duke shot his son a nasty look. "No use you going spoony over the chit. If you want to get your leg in her lap, then set her up in a house in town."

Lord Andrew felt himself becoming very angry indeed. "If Miss Mortimer were as pushing and vulgar as you are trying to make out, then why did she not jump at the chance of being a duchess?"

"I don't know," said the duke waspishly. "I don't understand the little minds of mushrooms."

A footman came in to say that the Duke of Harford had arrived and that Her Grace requested the presence of the duke.

"Not I," said the little duke, picking up the newspaper and rattling the pages angrily. "You go, Andrew. It's all your fault."

Lord Andrew bit back the angry retort on his lips. He was suddenly curious to see this duke.

He found his mother, the Duke of Harford, and Miss Worthy in the drawing room.

He crossed to his fiancée's side. "You had better leave, Miss Worthy," he began.

"Oh, let her stay," moaned the duchess. "She is to be of the family anyway."

"What I want to know," said the Duke of Harford, "is where Miss Mortimer is?"

"She is in the country," said Lord Andrew clearly and distinctly.

"What's she doing there?" asked the duke.

"She does not want to marry you," said Lord Andrew.

"Wants to tarry a bit, does she? Fetch her back."

"SHE DOES NOT WANT TO MARRY YOU," shouted Lord Andrew.

A peculiarly mulish look crossed the duke's face. He turned his head away and looked out of the bay window to the trees in the park.

"Don't know what you are saying," he said. "The Duchess of Parkworth has agreed to this engagement, so as far as I'm concerned, it still stands."

A gleam of hope appeared in the duchess's eyes.

"My dear Harford," she cried. "Such understanding, such generosity."

"Pooh, pooh, ma'am," said the duke, waggling his fat fingers. "I can count on you to arrange matters."

Lord Andrew's eyes narrowed into angry slits. It was all too evident that the Duke of Harford was going to hear only what he wanted to hear.

"I take leave to tell you, Harford," he said, "that you are a pompous old fool!"

"Lord Andrew!" screamed Miss Worthy in alarm. "You must not speak to our poor Harford so. Miss Mortimer has behaved shamelessly. The least she can do is to come to her senses."

Lord Andrew rounded on his fiancée. "Please be quiet, Miss Worthy," he snapped. "You will soon be my wife, and I shall expect you to obey me in all respects. Is that clear?"

Miss Worthy burst into tears and was comforted by the Duke of Harford. "Don't cry," said the duke. "It's not our problem, Miss Worthy, it's theirs. What about coming for a stroll in the park with me, and leave 'em to arrange things, mmm?"

"That would be most kind of you," said Mis Worthy, throwing Lord Andrew a defiant look. "I can see I am not wanted here, and I was only doing my best to help."

"Yes, yes," said the duchess in an abstracted way. "Run along, do. This is most unfortunate. Maria Blenkinsop shall have the last word after all."

Casting a final reproachful look at Lord Andrew, Miss Worthy exited on the arm of the Duke of Harford.

No sooner had they left than the Duke of Parkworth shuffled in. "Well, my dear," he said, kissing the air somewhere near his wife's left cheek, "how goes it?"

"Better than we could have expected," said the duchess. "Harford still wants Penelope. All we have to do is bring her back. It will take a *leetle* coercion."

"Can't do anything about her cottage," said the duke. "That vicar, Troubridge, is an interfering cleric."

"Oh, there are other ways," laughed the duchess. She rang the bell, and when a footman answered it, said, "Henry, tell—let me see, I need some men with muscles—ah, tell Beedle, the groom, and James, the second footman, to make ready to come with me to the country. Have the traveling carriage brought round. Tell Perkins to get the maids to pack for me, oh, two days stay at least."

Lord Andrew looked at his mother in horror. "You are going to force her to come back. You are even prepared to kidnap her. Father . . ."

"No use looking at me, boy," said the duke grumpily. "I think your mother has been shamelessly tricked by Miss Mortimer." His face brightened. "Don't use force. Tell her we'll have her committed to the madhouse if she doesn't behave herself. Got no relatives. Best way of getting rid of unwanted people that I know of. Got the chaps who will sign the papers."

Lord Andrew stood up and looked down at them as they sat side by side on the sofa. Two pairs of hard, aristocratic eyes stared up at him—the eyes of the old aristocracy, as brutal and stubborn as any peasant. He began to wonder wildly if they really were his parents. He thought of appealing to his elder brother, the marquess, and then dismissed it. His brother would think they were behaving just as they ought. Then Lord Andrew conjured up the image of his beloved tutor, Mr. Blackwell. But that excellent man would no doubt tell him that arranged marriages happened all the time and that Penelope Mortimer would live to thank his parents. But then, Mr. Blackwell had always considered love a romantic invention of poets and women.

He turned on his heel and went up to his room. There was nothing he could do. He would need to dress for the evening and go on as if nothing happened.

"What shall we wear this evening?" asked his valet, Pomfret.

"Clothes, you fool," snapped Lord Andrew.

"Certainly, my lord," murmured Pomfret, delighted at having the choice of wear left in his expert hands for almost the first time. He busied himself laying out evening clothes. "We will wear the sapphire stickpin in our cravat," said Pomfret happily, standing back and narrowing his eyes as he surveyed the clothes laid out on the bed. "Ye-es. And your lordship's sapphire ring. Do you have it? I have not seen it in our jewel box this age."

"What?"

"The sapphire ring, my lord," said Pomfret patiently. "We have not got it."

"Wait," said Lord Andrew abruptly. He strode from his room and went to Penelope's bedchamber. He searched in the jewel box on the toilet table. There were all the jewels his mother had lent Penelope still there. He searched in closets and drawers, and then stood in the middle of the room, frowning. She had kept his ring. She had also kept the lorgnette. She had spurned everything else, but she had kept those.

He returned to his own room. "My riding clothes, Pomfret," he snapped. "Also a small imperial with a change of clothes for several nights. Hurry, man. And then run downstairs and tell them to get my traveling carriage ready—no, that won't do—get the racing curricle, and put the bays on it."

"May I ask where we are going?"

"We are not going anywhere. I am going to a prizefight. Bustle about, man, and do not stand there with your mouth open. And when you've done all that, send a footman round to Miss Worthy's with my apologies. I shall not be dining with them this evening."

123

"And what excuse shall we give?" asked Pomfret in a pained voice. "We cannot tell the lady we are going to a prizefight."

"Tell the lady I have some dread disease."

"What kind of disease, my lord?"

"The pox. No. Dammit, use your imagination. Say I have gone to Bath to take the waters."

So as Lord Andrew rode hell for leather out of London, crisscrossing the back streets so as not to be seen passing his mother's carriage, Miss Worthy was shocked to learn that Lord Andrew was suffering from a severe case of gout and had gone to Bath.

The Green Man, the inn where Lord Andrew and Penelope has spent the night, was in the village of Beechton.

Trade had been slack over the past few weeks, and so Mr. and Mrs. Carter were delighted to welcome a gentleman guest.

Mr. Jepps was that guest, and Mr. Jepps was bone-weary. He had scoured the countryside around Dalby Castle, trying to find evidence that Lord Andrew and Miss Mortimer had racked up somewhere for the night. They must have claimed to have traveled all night, but remembering that storm, Mr. Jepps hoped to find proof they had lied. He had gone from inn to posting house along the road he had traveled back himself, but without success. He had been thinking of giving up when he decided, as the weather was unusually fine and as he was still in hiding from Lord Andrew, that he might as well pass the time of his exile by trying in the opposite direction.

He told the Carters that the room they had assigned to him was very comfortable and that dinner had been excellent. He was just about to ask that all-important question—had a certain noble lord and a young miss resided at the inn—when Mrs. Carter, who had served his meal and who was predisposed to gossip, the inn being unusually quiet, said, "I'm glad you find your room to your liking, sir. There was a noble lord staying there not so long ago with his pretty wife, and he found it most comfortable."

"He did?" said Mr. Jepps idly, and then sat bolt upright in his chair. "He *did*?"

Flattered by his interest, Mrs. Carter leaned her hip against the table and went on. "Yes, ever so glad they were to get out of the storm. Don't know as you recall that storm. Fearsome, it were."

"Yes, yes," said Mr. Jepps.

"They was soaked to the skin. He up and says he's a lord, and Mr. Carter warn't about to believe him. All shabby and muddied he were, with no servants or carriage. But he produced gold and offered to pay all in advance. Well, when we seen that there gold, we knew right away we had the quality. And his poor lady was shivering fit to drop."

"He may be a friend of mine," said Mr. Jepps as casually as he could. "What was his name?"

"Lord Andrew Childe."

"Ah!" Mr. Jepps sighed with pure satisfaction. "And they spent the night together?"

"Why, to be sure, yes! Mind you, my lord, he was all for leaving in the middle of the night if we could have got a carriage, but we couldn't do anything till dawn, when the storm was over. Mr. Baxter, a gentleman who lives close by, lent them his pony and gig."

"And they share the same bed?"

Mrs. Carter looked at her visitor in sudden disapproval, beginning to suspect there was something prurient in his interest.

"What else should a man and wife do?" she said crossly. "Mr. Carter went up during the night to tell them that the storm was still bad and that he could do nothing for them till the morning, but he did not like to disturb them. They was lying like babies in each other's arms."

"Alas, Mrs. Carter," said Mr. Jepps, "you have committed a sin. You have been most grievously misled."

"Whatever do you mean, sir?"

"I mean that Lord Andrew Childe is not married, and the lady with him is an innocent protégée of his mother's whom he has appeared to have deflowered with your innocent connivance."

"Never!" Mrs. Carter turned quite pale, for Mr. Jepps looked threatening. She went to the door and called her husband.

When the landlord came in, Mrs. Carter repeated all that Mr. Jepps had said.

Mr. Carter scratched his head. "That there lord should be forced to marry the girl," he said roundly. "Sech goings-on! Mr. Baxter'll know what to do. Mortal clever is Mr. Baxter. You go along with me to Five Elms. Mr. Baxter keeps late hours."

So Mr. Jepps set off with the landlord, hoping that this Mr. Baxter would not prove to be some bluff member of the country gentry who would only turn out to be amused by the episode.

He was in luck. Mr. Baxter was a Puritan, a scholar, and a Whig. He considered the English aristocracy decadent. He felt their days were past. He

126

had been a staunch supporter in his youth of George Washington and then Napoleon. But George Washington had become too fashionable in Britain to excite the radical mind of Mr. Baxter. Instead of reviling the great general, the unaccountable British erected statues to him—long before there was even one statue to Washington in America—named clubs after him, and members of the military praised his acumen. Mr. Baxter had turned his allegiance to Napoleon, longing for the day when liberty, equality, and fraternity should come to the streets of Britain. But Napoleon had made himself emperor, and that had left Mr. Baxter without a hero. Although now older and staider than in the days of his enthusiasms, Mr. Baxter still retained all his loathing for the aristocracy, crediting them with wielding more power than they actually did. Had Mr. Baxter been born a gentleman, then he might have realized the aristocracy and landed gentry came in a mixture of good and bad like everyone else. But he had been born of working-class parents and had worked his way up to be a printer, amassing a comfortable fortune which had allowed him to buy Five Elms and retire to a life of pleasant isolation with his books.

He had been annoyed at the alacrity with which he had lent Lord Andrew his gig and pony. Mr. Baxter had found himself flattered at being able to be of service to a lord and his pretty lady. He looked back on his obsequious help to them now with a sort of loathing, the way someone else might look back on a night of debauch.

And so when he heard that Lord Andrew had passed the night in the arms of a hitherto innocent girl, his eyes began to gleam with a crusading fire.

He remembered Penelope's fresh beauty. In his mind's eye, Lord Andrew's features became those of a brutish satyr. If anyone had told Mr. Baxter that he was an extremely romantic man, he would have been quite furious. He did not realize he was weaving a vulgar Haymarket tragedy about Penelope and Lord Andrew—the innocent country girl deflowered by the wicked lord. He could see it all. Penelope walking along in the snow with a babe in her arms begging for crusts while this rake went on to ruin another virgin.

"I am sure the idea of making Lord Andrew see the folly of his ways is rather daunting. . . ." began Mr. Jepps after Mr. Carter had told his story.

"He has sinned, and he must make reparation," cried Mr. Baxter. He was a small man with black hair combed down in a fringe on his forehead. His black eyes gleamed with reforming zeal. "We will set out on the morrow and confront this Lord Andrew."

Mr. Jepps had no intention of confronting Lord Andrew himself, but he was confident that the puritanical Mr. Baxter could be safely left to do everything that was necessary.

"First of all," said Mr. Baxter, "let us pray."

Mr. Jepps looked helplessly about him, but the landlord had pulled off his hat and was already getting down on his knees. The prayer lasted over an hour. Stiff and sore, Mr. Jepps finally breathed "Amen" with such grateful fervor that Mr. Baxter looked at him approvingly.

While Mr. Baxter was praying for her redemption, Penelope Mortimer was down on her hands and knees in her new cottage garden, pulling out

128

weeds. It was a beautiful evening. The air was warm, the birds chirped sleepily in the branches of the trees above her head.

She had been almost unable to believe her good fortune when she had arrived back in Lower Bexham to find the cottage hers, and her few remaining bits and pieces had already been carried there. She felt she had no longer anything to fear from the Parkworth family but a most unpleasant scene. Of course, she could always have taken the money from the sale of her family home and moved to some village far away from the Parkworths'. But that would have entailed finding some female companion. It was all very well for a pretty young girl to live alone in the village of her birth, where everyone knew her, but to do so in a strange place would certainly have excited censure.

Penelope leaned forward to wrench at a particularly tough dandelion root, and Lord Andrew's ring, which she had transferred to a chain about her neck, bobbed against her breasts. She hoped he would not mind her keeping it. She hoped he would understand. She also hoped he would never realize how much his kisses and caresses had meant, and how longing for him dragged at her heart from morning till night. Her eyes filled with tears and she brushed them away with one earthy hand, leaving streaks of mud on her face.

She rose shakily to her feet and walked to the garden gate and looked along the winding road which led into the village. One or two candles were already gleaming behind the thick glass of the cottage windows. Families would be settling down by the fire before going to bed. Penelope felt a rush of loneliness. There had been so much to do since her father's death that she had not felt lonely before. But now she did, a great aching void of loneliness. She even began to wonder whether she had been a fool to turn down two eligible men. Marriage would have meant a home and children.

She heard Lord Andrew's carriage before she saw it. She heard the rattle of carriage wheels, the creaking of the joists, and the imperative clopping of horses' hooves. She was about to turn and flee, for she was sure it was the duchess, when the racing curricle came into view at the end of the road. With her good long sight, she recognized the driver and stayed where she was, her hand on the gate.

Lord Andrew reined in his team, tethered them to the garden fence, and strode forward and stood looking down at her.

"Your face is dirty," he said.

"Did you come all the way from London to tell me that?"

"No. We must leave immediately. My mother is on her way here. That idiot Harford expects the marriage to go ahead."

"Mercy! But what can Her Grace do? She cannot turn me out. The papers have been signed and witnessed. She cannot force me to marry the Duke of Harford either."

"Let us go inside and I will explain," said Lord Andrew. "But we must be quick."

Penelope led the way inside to her living room, picked up a taper, lit it from a candle, and pushed it through the bars of the fireplace, sitting back on her heels and waiting until the tinder had burst into flames, before rising to her feet and facing him.

"Now, my lord . . ."

"Now, Miss Mortimer," he said wearily, "the situation is this. My mother, with my father's backing, is coming here with two bullyboys to carry you off. If you do not wed Harford, then they are quite prepared to take their revenge by having you consigned to the madhouse."

"Ridiculous," laughed Penelope. "This is the nineteenth century!"

"And in this new century people are confined every day to madhouses against their will."

"But they are your parents! No one could believe such villainy possible," said Penelope, not knowing that a certain Mr. Baxter would be prepared to believe that this sort of behavior was commonplace in elevated circles.

"They do mean it. For the moment. Pack your bags. You are coming with me."

"Where?"

"I shall tell you on the road. For goodness' sake, wash your face."

Penelope stood her ground. "Isn't that so like you? You come to me with a tale of Gothic revenge and then complain about my dirty face. This is my home, and I am not dashing off anywhere. You may stay and take a glass of wine. Then we shall walk together to the vicarage and get Mr. Troubridge to find you a bed for the night."

"Miss Mortimer, believe me, you are in great danger."

"I am willing to believe Her Grace is capable of indulging petty spite . . . but kidnapping! Do not be ridiculous. I know your mother better than you do yourself."

"I know my mother *now*," he said sarcastically.

131

"Believe me, we have but recently become acquainted, but I do know she is capable of this."

"Sit down, my lord, and let us discuss this like two rational beings. I shall fetch you some wine."

Before he could protest, she had left the room. He paced angrily up and down. His mother could not be far behind. If Miss Mortimer continued as stubborn as this, he might be tempted to use force himself.

He looked around the little living room, at a few good bits of furniture, which obviously belonged in a grander setting. The ceiling was low and raftered, and he was in danger of banging his head on the beams.

Penelope came in with a decanter and two glasses on a tray.

"What is it?" asked Lord Andrew.

"Elderberry wine."

"No, thank you, Miss Mortimer. Now, listen to me—" He broke off. There was a steady rumble of a carriage approaching at a great pace.

"My mother is arrived," he said grimly.

"She will make the most dreadful scene," said Penelope, turning a little pale. "But then that will be the end of it."

"Stay where you are!" he commanded as she made for the door.

"Fiddle. It is best I meet her and get this distressing business over with as soon as possible."

"As you wish." Lord Andrew pulled a pistol out of his greatcoat and began to prime it.

Penelope laughed, amusement driving out fear. "You are being ridiculous. Your own mother! One would think you were preparing to meet Attila the Hun."

She walked to the door and held it open.

The duchess was sitting in the heavy traveling carriage. Two outriders in jockey caps and striped waistcoats and breeches sat on horseback on either side of the carriage. There was a thickset coachman up on the box.

A footman and groom came up the path at a run and seized Penelope by the arms and began to drag her towards the carriage.

"Get her quickly," shouted the duchess through the open carriage window, "and gag her if she starts screaming."

"Leave me," said Penelope, wriggling in her captors' grasp.

"Yes, leave her," came Lord Andrew's level voice from the doorway.

The footman and groom twisted about and found themselves looking down the barrel of Lord Andrew's pistol.

"Only taking orders, me lord," said the groom. They dropped Penelope's arms, and she ran back to Lord Andrew's side.

The carriage door crashed open, and the duchess jumped down onto the road.

"Unnatural boy!" she screamed. "How dare you interfere. I command you to go away and leave this matter to me."

"No, Mama," said Lord Andrew. "It is you who must leave. You have lost your wits. This is madness. This is folly."

"You are no son of mine," cried the duchess. "Go on. Shoot me. Kill your sainted mother and strike her down." She wrenched open the bosom of her gown. A black whaleboned corset of quite staggering dimensions was exposed to view.

"Cover yourself up," said Lord Andrew sharply. "You look ridiculous."

"Ah, do you hear his words?" shrieked the duchess. "I curse you. You are no son of mine. From this day hence, I renounce you."

"Good," said Lord Andrew coldly. "For you are become a most tiresome parent."

"Help me," said the duchess, beginning to sway, her round figure making her look like a spinning top on the point of running down.

Lord Andrew drew Penelope inside and shut and locked the door. "NOW will you pack your things?" he said.

Penelope threw him a scared look and darted up the ladder, which led to her little bedroom under the eaves. Lord Andrew crossed to the window and looked out. Without her audience, for the Duchess of Parkworth did not consider servants people, she had closed her gown and was being helped into the carriage. Lord Andrew stayed by the window until she had driven off.

He was sure Penelope now had nothing to fear. A part of him knew his mother had shot her bolt. But there was a little doubt left, and that little doubt was enough to spur him on to get Penelope into hiding.

Chapter Nine

"Where are you taking me?" asked Penelope in a small voice as Lord Andrew drove her through the village of Lower Bexham.

"I don't know," he said crossly. "Supper first, I think, and somewhere to rack up for the night."

"You are going to compromise me again," said Penelope.

"Not I. We shall have separate rooms at the first well-established posting house we come to."

"Where, no doubt, Her Grace is waiting."

"If you had your wits about you, you would notice we are not on the London road."

"There is nothing up with my long sight," said Penelope. It was hard to imagine, thought Penelope, that only so recently she had been yearning for him. Now they were engaged in their usual rancorous exchange like a married couple who should never have married in the first place. The shock of the duchess's visit had made her feel weak and shaky. She longed for comfort and caresses, and that longing sharpened her tongue.

"And how goes Miss Worthy?" she asked.

"Very well. All is forgotten and forgiven."

"Of course it is," said Penelope. "You are rich and have a title. That must cover a multitude of sins."

"I am not deformed and I am not old."

"But not young," said Penelope sweetly. "Nigh middle age, I should guess."

"If you have nothing pleasant to say, then hold your tongue, miss."

"You started it."

"Started what, for goodness' sake?"

"Sniping and complaining and saying my face was dirty."

"*Is*, my dear Miss Mortimer. *Is*."

"Ooh!" Penelope scrubbed at her face with a handkerchief. Then she took out a phial of rose water, moistened her handkerchief, tried again, and looked down gloomily at the resultant mess on the once-white cambric.

She decided to make a heroic effort to be pleasant and natural, as if it were quite normal for duchesses to appear on the doorstep on kidnapping expeditions. "The weather is very fine, is it not?" she ventured.

Her companion said something like "Grumph," and Penelope relapsed into silence.

Lord Andrew was wrestling with his conscience. Back in London lay stern Duty, that mistress who had controlled him for so long. He could turn about and take Miss Mortimer back to her cottage. He himself could put up at the vicarage and stay for a day or two to make sure there were no further attempts to take her away. There was no need to head off into the unknown with her.

But an air of irresponsibility and holiday was creeping over him. The greenish twilight turned the landscape into a gentle dream country where the trees stood out like black lace against the fading light. He did not need to rely on his parents for a single penny, he mused. He did not need to marry a woman with a dowry. How very simple it would be to marry Penelope Mortimer! There would, in all probability, be a nasty breach-of-promise case, but when all was over and Miss Worthy financially compensated for her loss, then he and Penelope would be together. His senses quickened at the thought.

Since he had lost his virginity at the clumsy hands of that housemaid, he had never really lost his head over any woman. Courtesans and prostitutes repelled him, and so he had taken his infrequent pleasures with a few of the ladies of cracked reputation, widows or divorcées who knew how to carry on a light affair and take their leave gracefully.

His whole body craved that of Penelope Mortimer. He glanced down at her. She looked so young and fresh and innocent that she made him feel hot and sweaty and lustful. Such a virginal creature as Penelope could never be racked with the same dark passions as a man.

Penelope looked vaguely over the dreaming landscape and wondered if her body was going to fall to bits. Every little cell seemed to be straining towards her companion. She had a sudden picture of what he had looked like naked, and blushed all over. Fiery, prickly heat made her clothes itch, and there was a nasty cramping feeling in the pit of her stomach. There was no cure for what ailed her. Or rather, no cure she could possibly have. The only relief for this sickness would be if it were possible to throw off all her clothes, claw his from his body, and lie with him naked. A moan nearly escaped her lips.

They were approaching a fairly sizable town. Lord Andrew drove into the courtyard of a posting house. This time, the respectably demure and bonneted Penelope and the exquisitely tailored Lord Andrew were treated to a warm welcome. Lord Andrew asked for a room for his ward, one for himself, and a private parlor for supper.

The posting house was modern, and the rooms were light and airy. There was no need for fires in the bedrooms. There was always a need for fires in Penelope's little cottage, which was built over an underground stream and therefore damp and cold even in the best of weather. Penelope brushed her hair till it shone and twisted it into a loose knot on the top of her head. She put on one of her own favorite gowns, a simple blue silk, hoping that the piece of new silk she had let in on the front to replace a piece that she had burned with the iron would not show.

They both drank a great deal at supper and talked little. Both were trying to damp down the fires of passion with quantities of wine.

Supper consisted of fish in oyster sauce, a piece of boiled beef, neck of pork roasted with apple sauce, hashed turkey, mutton steaks with salad, roasted wild duck, fried rabbits, plum pudding and tartlets, with olives, nuts, apples, raisins, and almonds to accompany the port.

"You seem to take all this fare for granted," said Penelope. "There is on this one table enough to last me for over a week at least."

"That is understandable. You are poor."

"Yes, I suppose I am," said Penelope. "But by next year, I shall have vegetables from the garden and will be able to set some snares in the parsonage land at the back."

"What do the villagers think of such as you living alone?"

"They have known me all my life and do not think it odd. Were I to live somewhere else, I would be obliged to have a companion, and that would be a great deal of unnecessary expense."

"I can send you some game from time to time," said Lord Andrew.

"Your wife will object to that, I should think."

"Any wife of mine, Miss Mortimer, will do exactly what I say."

"It is very hard to enforce laws and rules unless you plan to beat her."

"It is woman's duty to look pretty and obey her husband," he mocked.

"Then it is as well I am not to be married," sighed Penelope, "for I should prove rebellious. But it is only in very elevated circles that women have the luxury of being idle and decorative. I am glad I am quite finished with high society."

"If my mother has anything to do with the matter, then I fear she will have ruined your reputation."

"It does not matter. A female's reputation only matters in the Marriage Market."

Her independence irked him. He did not like to think of her going out of his life, free to do as she wished, free of him.

"What do you wear on that chain round your neck?" he asked abruptly.

Penelope blushed and tugged out his ring, which had been hanging inside her gown between her breasts. "I was merely keeping it safe," she said awkwardly.

"No, keep it," he said quickly, seeing she was about to detach it from the chain. "I told you it was yours. I would like you to have it."

He was looking at her intently, and Penelope's eyes fell beneath his own. She rose to her feet. "I am tired, my lord, and would retire. Where are we bound tomorrow?"

"We will discuss that in the morning." He rose as well. They walked in silence to Penelope's bed-chamber. He held open the door for her and then stood looking down at her.

"Goodnight," he said softly.

"Goodnight," echoed Penelope, and darting inside, she shut the door in his face.

He went to his room next door and slowly washed and changed into his nightgown. He could sense her through the walls. The longing and desire would not go away. He had drunk a great deal, but his brain seem to be clear and wide-awake. He went to the window and raised the sash. There was a full moon riding above the trees. A dog barked in the distance, someone laughed somewhere down in the courtyard, and then there was silence.

He turned and leaned his back against the window-sill and crossed his arms. What was he to do with Penelope Mortimer?

He crossed the room and, seizing his quilted dressing gown, shrugged himself into it and marched next door. Penelope was lying in bed, reading a book, her steel spectacles on the end of her small nose.

"Do you ever knock?" she asked, peering at him over the tops of her glasses, too startled at his sudden appearance to remember to take them off and hide them. Her lorgnette lay in the bottom of her luggage. She wished she had unpacked it, but then, she had not expected a night visit from him.

"My apologies," he said stiffly. "They have forgot to give me soap. May I take some of yours?"

"By all means," said Penelope, waving a hand in the direction of the toilet table.

He picked up a cake of Joppa soap and tossed it up and down in his hand. "Are you comfortable?"

"Yes, my lord. Thank you."

"Well . . . goodnight."

"Goodnight, Lord Andrew."

He went back to his own room and moodily threw the cake of soap on his toilet table, where it joined the three tablets already there.

Damn!

He sat down on the bed and rested his chin on his hand.

After a few moments he sighed and took off his dressing gown and got into bed, sulkily pulling his nightcap down over his ears.

There came a scratching at the door as he was leaning forward to blow out his bed candle.

"Enter," he called.

Penelope came in wearing a nightgown and wrapper and a frivolous lace nightcap on her head. She did not look at him. "I find I have forgot my tooth powder," she said.

"I have plenty. You are more than welcome to take it," he said eagerly, swinging his long legs out of bed. "See, here is an unused tin of Biddle's." He handed it to her. She was so close to him, he could feel the heat from her body, smell the rose water on her skin.

"Thank you," said Penelope. "Well ... er ... goodnight."

"Goodnight, Miss Mortimer."

Fetters of convention kept those arms of his, which wanted to seize her, firmly to his side.

He sadly watched her go. He jumped back into bed, blew out the candle, tore off his nightcap, and threw it across the room, and then lay flat on his back staring up into the darkness.

Then all of a sudden, he had a clear picture of her toilet table next door. Among a few scattered bottles of washes and creams there had been a new tin of tooth powder. Could Penelope possibly be suffering as much as he?

His heart hammering against his ribs, he slowly got out of bed, pulled on his dressing gown, and went next door.

She was standing by the window, looking out.

"You already have a can of tooth powder," he said softly.

Without turning round, Penelope answered, "And you, my lord, have cakes and cakes of soap."

"I want you," he said raggedly, and held open his arms.

Penelope rushed into them, and burning, aching body clung tight to burning, aching body. He kissed and caressed her, feeling his passion rise to fever heat. He carried her to the bed and laid her down and then stretched out beside her and gathered her close. There was so many places to kiss: her eyes, her hair, her mouth, her breasts, her mouth again.

"No," he began to mumble like a drunk. "No, no, *no*. Must marry me. *Now*."

"I can't. You can't. It's the middle of the night. Oh, Andrew, kiss me again."

"No," he said more firmly. "This is torture. I bed you as my wife or nothing else. We have to get away from here, where you are known as my ward. We must go and find a preacher."

"We need a special license."

"Nonsense. I shall bribe some cleric to do the necessary and then marry you again in London."

"But Miss Worthy."

"A pox on Miss Worthy."

"Your mother . . . ?"

"Her, too. Come along. Clothes on."

"I am so tired."

"Penelope, if I kiss you again, I cannot answer for the consequences. We cannot live apart. If I do not quench this fever in my blood soon, I shall strangle you."

"But what if we are not suited?"

"You must be mad!"

"What if it is only lust?"

"If it is, then I swear there's enough to last a lifetime. Why are you always arguing and quibbling?"

"I am not quibbling," said Penelope crossly.

"Either you dress yourself or I shall dress you."

"No, I shall manage."

Lord Andrew rushed next door and started to pull on his clothes. He was worried she might take fright and run away. But she was just fastening the lid of her imperial when he erupted into her room again.

The landlord was distressed and thought he must have displeased his noble guest in some way, for Lord Andrew woke him up to pay his shot and shout for his carriage.

Soon they were bumping along the country roads. After a time, Penelope fell asleep with her head

143

against his shoulder. He drove on as dawn rose over the fields and the sun began to climb up above the fields and woods.

The large, bustling county town of Ardglover was reached by nine o'clock. It boasted an even more luxurious posting inn. This time Lord Andrew, having woken the sleeping Penelope, took the ring from her chain and put it on her finger before booking one room for Lord and Lady Andrew Childe.

Leaving Penelope to enjoy a solitary breakfast, he went off to explore the churches. He talked to several vicars before making his choice. The Reverend James Ponsonby was vicar of a run-down backstreet church called St. Jude's. Even at that early hour of the day, he smelled strongly of spirits. He took Lord Andrew into the vestry and there enjoyed a pleasurable hour of haggling before settling on the price of a rushed wedding.

Penelope was asleep when he returned to the inn. He made a hasty breakfast, sent for the barber to shave him, and, attired in his best morning dress, went to rouse Penelope and tell her roughly she was about to be married. Still exhausted, Penelope struggled into a white muslin gown with a pink sprig.

The church was damp and smelly and cold, and Penelope shivered her way through the marriage service with the vicar's spinster sister as bridesmaid while Lord Andrew had the ancient sidesman as bridesman.

For a time it seemed as if the wedding ceremony would drag on forever, but the vicar, getting thirsty, brought his sermon to an abrupt end, and they found themselves outside the church again, this time as man and wife.

They walked along in silence. Penelope felt awful. She had drunk too much the night before, and her head ached. Flashes of memory began to dart through her brain. Village girls talking and giggling about their wedding nights. "I declare, it hurt so bad, I thought I was like to die." "They never tell you you'll have to put up with that." "There was blood all over the sheets."

Passion withered and died.

Lord Andrew wondered if there was madness in his family. Here he was after a squalid ceremony, married to a lady of whom he knew little apart from the tartness of her tongue and the independence of her mind. The wave of feverish passion that had consumed him all the night before receded, leaving him escorting this little stranger along the street of a market town. He looked down at Penelope's beauty, and all he could think of was how she had looked with her spectacles on the end of her nose. Her eyes had been too sharp and intelligent for a woman.

"What shall we do now?" asked Penelope in a little voice.

"Go back to the inn, I suppose," he said in dull, flat tones. "I need some sleep before my journey on."

"Journey where?"

"To my home, Baxley Manor, in Shropshire."

"Oh."

"Did you have other plans?" he asked sarcastically.

"No," said Penelope dismally. "I shall probably never see my little cottage again."

"You can see that hovel of yours any time you want."

"There is no need to be so rude about it. I think you are a bully and you have a very low opinion of women. Perhaps you should have married someone stupid."

"It appears I did."

Penelope looked at him, at the shadows under his eyes and the bitter, disappointed twist to his mouth. Something had to be done. Instead of shouting at him, she said candidly, "What on earth possessed us to get married? We are quarreling already, and you are wondering what came over you."

She linked her hands over his arm and looked anxiously up into his face. "Did you have to pay that vicar an awful lot of money?"

"No, not terribly much. Not as much as I expected."

Penelope's face cleared and she gave a little skip and jump. "There you are then. It is all very simple. All you have to do is go back and bribe him again and get the marriage lines torn up!"

"I said I would marry you, and I have married you, so let that be an end of it."

"No, I won't!" said Penelope, stopping in the middle of the busy main street and facing him. "I won't be married to someone who looks as if he has just received a prison sentence."

"My dear child, there is no need for these dramatics."

"Every need, my dear lummox. I do not hide behind social lies and correct social behavior. I am not going to be tied for life to someone who despises me and talks down to me!"

He passed a weary hand over his face. "I shall sleep first," he said, "and talk to you afterwards."

"But, Andrew, you must listen to sense!"

He took her arm and roughly hustled her along, lecturing her on her behavior as he went. He was still nagging as they went upstairs to their room, where he at last stopped railing at her. He threw himself facedown on the bed and, in a minute, he was asleep. Penelope glared at him. Then gradually her face softened. Poor Perfect Gentleman, used to being flattered and fawned on all his life. Loved for his money, loved for his title, loved by all except his own mother and father. Penelope leaned down and gently stroked the heavy black hair which was tumbled over his forehead. She loved him still, and she knew she could not bear to be married to him if he did not love her with equal force. His passion for her would return after he had rested, but she would know it was merely a transient lust without respect.

In the years to come, he would thank her for what she was about to do.

She knew he kept the bulk of his money in a drawer in his traveling toilet case. She gently slid a hand into his pocket and dew out his keys, trying one after the other until she found the one that fitted the money drawer. She extracted a thick wedge of five-pound notes and peeled off six. What monstrous great white things they were, thought Penelope, who, like most of the population, hardly ever saw a five-pound note. Like pocket handkerchiefs!

She put on her bonnet and pelisse and made her way back to the church. There was no sign of the vicar, but the verger, who was sweeping out the pews, told her she could find him at the vicarage, which was round the back.

Penelope picked her way along an unsavory lane

and round to a low door in a brick wall on which "Vicarage" had been chalked in a shaky hand. There was no bell or knocker. She banged on the door with her fists.

No reply.

She looked about her and found an empty gin bottle a little way away and proceeded to apply it energetically to the door until it shattered and nearly cut her. She was about to scream with frustration when the door opened and the vicar stood swaying in front of her.

"Ish the bride," he said. He executed a great leg with a long scrape, fell forward, and clutched at her for support.

"Come inside, Mr. Ponsonby," said Penelope sternly. "I have business with you."

It took her an hour of pleading and raging and threats of legal action to get Mr. Ponsonby to strike the record of the marriage off the parish books. Thrifty Penelope, satisfied that she had achieved her ends without paying a single penny of Lord Andrew's money to get them, returned to the inn and quietly entered the bedroom. The marriage lines were lying on the desk by the window. She tore them up, drew forward a letter, explained she had canceled the marriage, wished Lord Andrew well, and left both letter and torn marriage lines on the desk along with five of the five-pound notes.

She quietly packed her own case and, thankful it was a small one, picked it up and made her way out of the room and out of the inn. She asked directions to the nearest livery stable and, offering the five-pound note, hired a post chaise to take her back to Lower Bexham.

Triumph at having overcome all difficulties so

quickly buoyed her up for part of the journey, but all the aches and pains of love soon returned. She looked out at the countryside, eyes hot and dry with unshed tears. Then she took out her spectacles and put them on her nose.

Miss Penelope Mortimer had decided to renounce men for life.

Chapter Ten

The Duke of Parkworth read a very long and complicated notice in the newspaper which stated, as far as he could gather, that Miss Ann Worthy was engaged to the Duke of Harford and that her previous engagement to Lord Andrew Childe was to be considered null and void.

He scratched his head, took a sip of hot chocolate, and turned to more interesting news. His desire to aid his wife in her campaign against Penelope had withered and died. He was as fond of his duchess as he could be of anyone, but even he was beginning to find her scenes wearisome. He even found it in his heart to envy Lord Andrew, who was well away from the storms and upheavals. He assumed his son must have set that Mortimer girl up as his mistress by now and vaguely wished him well.

But when he eventually collected the morning papers and wandered into the morning, it was to find his wife looking much her old self. She appeared calm and rational and began to discuss the idea of turning one of the bedrooms into a bathroom with running water.

"Are you sure?" asked the duke. "All this washing all over is newfangled nonsense. Do you know some fanatics even soap themselves all over! It's a wonder their skin don't fall off."

"It's a matter of keeping up with the times," said the duchess practically. "The Dempseys have a very pretty one. The bath is shaped like a cockleshell, and it has a machine at one end to heat the water."

"Waste of money," said her husband. "Why keep a lot of servants who are perfectly well able to carry hot water up from the kitchens and then heat the stuff yourself?"

"It's a fashion," said the duchess patiently, "like Mr. Brummell's starched cravats."

"Oh." The duke's face cleared. "Well, so long as you don't expect me to use it. It's sweat, you know, that keeps a man clean."

"Good. I shall call in an architect and have the plans drawn up."

"Seem like your old self again," said the duke. "Forgotten about the Mortimer girl, hey?"

"Oh, yes. I feared, you know, that Andrew might be stupid enough to marry her. But he always does the right thing. He will simply set her up as his mistress until he tires of her. She teaches music, you know, so when he is wearied of her, he will be able to buy her a little seminary in Bath."

"All this matchmaking is a bore," yawned the duke, "whatever side of the blanket it's on. How on earth do you think Harford managed to propose to Miss Worthy, or do you think she proposed to him?"

"WHAT?" The duchess turned a dangerous color.

"It's in the paper," said her husband, who had not been looking at her and therefore did not see the danger signals. "She's finished with Andrew and is getting herself hitched to Harford."

"No she is not!" screamed the duchess. "No one

151

. . . do you hear me . . . *no one* jilts a member of my family."

"Come now. You said yourself you had brought down a mother's curse on Andrew's head and all that. You can't curse people," said the duke practically, "and then start ranting and raving if they have a bad time of it, though if you ask me, Andrew'll probably be glad to get free of that frosty-faced antidote. Never liked her."

"Miss Worthy is a perfect lady. Entirely suitable. Good family, good fortune. It's that Penelope Mortimer. She ruined everything with her blowsy blond looks. Oh, that I had never seen her!"

The butler came in. "There is a person to see Your Grace."

"Which Grace?" asked the duke.

"Both, Your Grace."

"And who is this person?"

"A Mr. Baxter."

"Send him packing."

The butler bowed and retreated.

"I shall go to Ann Worthy, and I shall tell her what I think of her," said the duchess. "She will be sorry she ever was born. To think how that Blenkinsop female must be crowing over me. It's past bearing."

The butler came in again. "Mr. Baxter will not go away. He says this can either be settled amicably or he will return with the Bow Street magistrate."

"What are you talking about?" screeched the duchess. "Don't stand there gawping." She threw a plate of toast in the butler's face and immediately felt much better.

"He says Lord Andrew seduced Miss Mortimer,

and he has witnesses to prove it," said the butler, picking bits of toast from his livery.

At that, Mr. Baxter himself walked into the room.

The duke took one horrified look at Mr. Baxter's somber black clothes, fringe, low collar, square-toed shoes, and said, "Damme, if it ain't a Methody. Throw him out."

Mr. Baxter raised his arms above his head. "God grant me strength to bring light into the black souls of these decadent people," he shouted.

"I said throw him out," snapped the duke.

Two large footmen came running up the stairs, alerted by the shouts. They picked up Mr. Baxter and carried him out. He went as stiff as a board, so they hoisted him up on their shoulders and carried him down the stairs as if bearing off a corpse.

"I didn't hear anything, did you?" said the duchess, dabbing her mouth with her napkin.

"No, my love," said the duke, who knew his wife well.

"And I shall never mention Miss Mortimer's name again. She does not exist."

"Quite."

"I must have Perkins to set out my best tenue, for as you know, that toad Blenkinsop gives a breakfast, and I intend to put her in her place."

"I don't know why they call these affairs, which begin at three in the afternoon and go on till all hours in the morning, breakfasts," said the duke. "I don't want to go."

"Never thought you did," said his wife. She half rose, and then sat down. "Tell me, was there a most odd man in here talking rubbish a moment ago?"

"I think we imagined him."

At that, the duchess did stand up and placed a kiss on top of her husband's head.

"You are quite right, Giles. You are always right," she said.

At Maria Blenkinsop's breakfast, the duchess resorted to the Duke of Harford's tactics by going stone-deaf when anyone asked her about her son's engagement. Miss Amy Tilney, who really wanted to be assured that Penelope was well, plucked up her courage and approached the duchess only to retreat trembling before a basilisk stare.

Tables had been set out in the gardens of Mrs. Blenkinsop's Kensington villa. Kensington was only a mile outside London, far enough away to give the benefits of fresh air, but not far enough away from town to be vulgar.

Everyone was chattering and exclaiming over the beauty of the weather and saying they could never remember England enjoying such idyllic sunshine.

Despite her envy of Maria Blenkinsop, the duchess began to enjoy herself. Her new gown of watered silk had, she knew, struck an arrow of jealousy into Mrs. Blenkinsop's breast. No longer plagued with questions about Lord Andrew, the duchess settled down to enjoy her food. On the terrace which ran along the outside of the house a little orchestra was playing. The famous diva, Madame Cuisemano, was shortly to entertain them.

Mrs. Blenkinsop waved the orchestra into silence. "My lords, ladies and gentlemen," she said. "May I present Madame Cuisemano!"

There was a ripple of applause and then silence as Mr. Baxter walked onto the stage.

He was burning up with rage and fury. He had

gone to Bow Street, where an alarmed magistrate, on hearing talk of perfidious dukes and duchesses, had told him he would be put in Bedlam if he did not leave. So Mr. Baxter had returned to Park Street, seen the duchess leaving, and had run all the way behind her carriage to Kensington. He had entered the villa by climbing over the back wall.

As he walked onto the terrace, he saw them all, sitting before him, the hated aristocracy. Their jewels winked and glittered in the sunlight, mounds of exotic dishes were laid out in front of them; he saw their haughty, hard, staring eyes and knew with all the passion of a martyr that he would gladly go to the gallows provided he could tell them exactly what he thought of them first.

"You have all sinned!" he cried, his eyes glittering. "You are useless, bejeweled worms. You stink of iniquity."

Two burly servants crept towards him.

The Duchess of Parkworth heaved a sigh of relief.

The Countess of Winterton, a great social leader, suddenly jumped to her feet and cried, "Let us hear this divine preacher. You are a wonder, Maria. Such originality!"

There was a spattering of appreciative applause, and then they all settled down and listened with great enjoyment as Mr. Baxter ripped them all to pieces. But when he began to outline the sad plight of Penelope Mortimer, he had them sitting, breathless, on the edge of their seats. "I can see her now," ended Mr. Baxter, "carrying her baby—"

"Jolly fast birth, what!" a young man cried, and was scolded into silence.

"Carrying her baby through the snow," Mr. Baxter went on "while Lord Andrew goes on to seduce yet another fair maid. They must marry!"

"Poor Lord Andrew, poor Penelope," whispered Amy Tilney to her fiancé, Ian Macdonald. "What are we to do?"

"Absolutely nothing," said Ian Macdonald cheerfully. "Let this madman have his say. Andrew will have him in prison for libel soon enough."

"They must marry," repeated Mr. Baxter passionately. "Justice must be done. Now, let us pray."

There was a shuffling and rustling and whispering as the delighted guests got down on their knees. When the prayer was finally over, Mr. Baxter solemnly blessed them all and urged them to see the folly of their ways. Then he stood in the sunlight and blinked as deafening applause sounded in his ears.

"For the poor," said the Countess of Winterton languidly. She unclasped a gold necklace and tossed it at Mr. Baxter's feet. Brooches, necklaces, bracelets, and all sorts of expensive baubles followed.

"I have never felt quite so exalted in my life," sighed Mrs. Partridge to the duchess.

The duchess rose to her feet. She walked straight up to Mr. Baxter and hissed, "Follow me!"

"Do not worry, dear sir," cooed Mrs. Blenkinsop. "My servants shall collect all the jewels for you."

The duchess marched into a music room which led off the terrace and sat down. Mr. Baxter stood in front of her.

"Hear this," said the duchess. "Penelope Mortimer is a heartless slut. She betrayed my trust. I am always helping the unfortunate. I took her out of poverty and took her into my home and gave her a Season, and this is how she repays me."

"But right must be done. She must be married."

The duchess ignored him. "For years I have been helping people, giving all my time and money. And what is my reward? To be humiliated in front of Maria Blenkinsop."

"But Your Grace," said Mr. Baxter eagerly, "there are more sound ways of helping people than giving them a Season. For example, there is one orphanage of genteel females in Highgate Village alone which is constantly in need of food and clothes. There must be two hundred girls at least."

The duchess was about to scream at him, but the impact of what he had just said entered her brain. Two hundred lame ducks! Two hundred! She felt quite breathless. Two hundred packages of gratitude just waiting to be unwrapped.

"Mr. Baxter," she said firmly, "when we find Penelope Mortimer, we shall see that justice is done. In the meantime, we must help these girls in Highgate. You have all that jewelry. It must be sold, and a trust must be set up."

"Oh, excellent woman," cried Mr. Baxter.

"So just get out there again and tell 'em I'll be running your charity," said the duchess.

Mr. Baxter strode out onto the terrace and held up his hands. The duchess stood by the side of the window and watched Maria Blenkinsop's face and saw it slowly assume a pinched and withered look.

The Duchess of Parkworth had never felt quite so happy in all her life.

Lord Andrew awoke about the middle of the afternoon. For one brief moment he did not know where he was, but then memory came flooding back—Penelope, the wedding, the row. He closed his eyes again. He wished now he had not been so angry with her. But somehow, he knew it now, he was bitterly ashamed of himself for having rushed her into that grubby wedding. What sort of man was he that he could not even wait for a special license? He should not have taken his self-disgust out on her.

He opened his eyes again and twisted over on his back and looked about the room. All sorts of facts tumbled into his brian. Her imperial was gone, her toilet things were gone, and there was a letter for him on the desk. He could just make out his name under that little pile of torn paper.

He got up and went over to the desk. He was about to brush aside the scraps of paper when he saw they were the remains of their marriage certificate. He slowly crackled open the letter. It was very simple and to the point. Penelope had prevailed on the preacher to cancel the marriage. He would, she had written, find out it was all for the best. She had borrowed five pounds and would return it to him as soon as she could. He would soon find the sort of woman he wanted, compliant and obedient. Their characters were not compatible. He was free.

Free! He stood looking blindly at the letter. He did not feel free. He felt weighted down with chains of misery and guilt.

He sat down on the edge of the bed, the letter in his hand. He sat there for quite a long time. The sun went down, the landlord announced dinner and then supper, and still he sat there, unmoving.

At last he decided it was all really very simple. He wanted Penelope Mortimer—for life.

He jumped to his feet, ran out of the bedroom, clattered down the inn stairs, and sprinted across the courtyard. Now, where was that church!

Penelope awoke to another splendid day. She almost wished it were raining. Rain would match her mood. She climbed out of bed and shivered. If the cottage was this cold in some of the best weather England had had in years, what on earth was it going to be like in the winter?

She washed and dressed and tried to eat breakfast, but the bread stuck in her throat and the tea tasted dusty and old. She decided hard work was the only cure for her miseries. She collected a spade and went out to the back garden. It was fairly large, consisting of some fruit bushes, badly in need of pruning, and an expanse of weedy lawn. "All this space going to waste," marveled Penelope. She may as well start digging a bed for vegetables.

The sun was hot and the work was hard. She finally stood upright to ease her back and looked ruefully at the beginnings of callouses on her hands. She should have worn gloves. What man would ever want to hold hands with her now?

Penelope reminded herself severely that she had forsworn all men.

Lord Andrew Childe, having found the front door open, had simply walked through the house and out into the garden at the back.

Penelope was wearing an old, much-washed blue cotton gown of old-fashioned cut, which meant the waist was where waists were supposed to be and not up under her armpits. He thought she had never looked more beautiful or more dear.

"Good day, madam wife," he said.

Penelope turned round. "You should not have come," she said quietly. "It would not answer. You must see that. We are not at all suited."

"If we are not suited," he said huskily, "then why do I feel so ill and wretched?"

"You will find it is not love," said Penelope, striving to keep her voice steady. "We should quarrel the whole time."

"And make up. I would rather quarrel with you, my sweet, then live placidly with anyone else in the whole wide world."

"Now look what you have done," wailed Penelope. "Y-you h-have m-made me cry."

He walked forward and put his arms about her and held her close.

Penelope pulled away, took a handkerchief out of her pocket, and blew her nose. "Someone will see us."

He looked around the garden, which was bordered by an impenetrable thorn hedge, and smiled. He put his hands on her waist. "No one will see us," he said, "and even if they did, what does it matter? We are man and wife."

"Not now. I told you I canceled the wedding."

"And I uncanceled it," he said, holding up a marriage certificate. "The unfortunate Mr. Ponsonby didn't know whether he was coming or going."

"But you hated being married. I saw it on your face as we left the church."

"I was disgusted with myself. I was greedy for you and rushed you into a sordid, hurried marriage. But I do not only want you in my bed, I want you at my side, I want you to argue with me and irritate me and love me."

"Oh, Andrew, I think that's about the most beautiful thing I have ever heard. But you must not take all the blame. I wanted you very badly as well."

"But we are not animals," he said, stroking her hair. "We can wait for a proper marriage."

"Oh, yes, I do want to be married to you," cried Penelope. "I am so miserable without you."

She turned her lips confidingly up to his. He kissed her very gently and with great tenderness and respect. He was so proud of the cool restraint of his emotions that he kissed her again. But this time her lips clung to his so sweetly that he felt that awful roaring black passion engulfing him again. Then Penelope began to strain against him and moan in the back of her throat. "Let me take my coat off," he panted. "Just my coat. It is so hot. There! Kiss me again."

But the next kiss had him shaking with desire. "Faith, the sun is scorching. Pray let me remove my waistcoat. It is so tight. And this cravat is devilishly starched." Garments flew about the grass. They sank down onto the ground clutching each other.

"But we will wait," he said, making a heroic effort to control himself. "Won't we, Penelope?"

"Oh, yes," sighed Penelope languorously. And then she bit the lobe of his ear.

If passion could be compared to the waves of the sea, then a whole Atlantic poured into that garden and swept them away. There was one brief moment when Penelope's eyes dilated, when she remembered the whispers of the village girls, but the instinctive knowledge that the pain of lack of fulfillment would be sharper than any pain he could administer drove her on.

Lord Andrew slowly came to his senses. The hot sun was caressing his naked back. The naked body under his lay lax and peaceful.

"Oh, Penelope," he said ruefully, "I did not mean it to be like this. I have had such a rigid control over my feelings for so long, I cannot understand why I cannot control them now."

"Perhaps this is love," said Penelope.

"Of course it is love. I love and respect you. It is not only your delectable body I want. . . . What are you doing?"

"I am only making myself comfortable," said Penelope, moving her limbs. "You are heavy."

"Then I shall rise," he said, without moving.

"Yes, we must be sensible and make plans," said Penelope. "But before we become sensible, you might at least kiss me again."

It was late afternoon by the time Penelope locked up her cottage and allowed her husband to help her into his curricle. The dazed look in her eyes had nothing to do with longsightedness, and her lips were swollen. Lord Andrew picked up the reins, leaned over to kiss her, and let out a yelp of pain.

"What is it?" asked Penelope.

"Sunburn," he said ruefully. "My poor back is blistered."

Penelope began to giggle, and she was still giggling as they drove off into the gathering dusk.

They took two weeks to reach London. They lingered at various pretty inns on the way. But as they approached the outskirts of London, Lord Andrew became possessed of a desire to have his parents' blessing. Penelope privately thought it most odd of him, but refrained from saying so. Evidently Lord Andrew had not yet come to the realization that he was better off without the duke and duchess anywhere in his life. He and Penelope had learned of Miss Worthy's forthcoming marriage on the road. Lord Andrew was relieved, but Penelope knew that the news must have driven the duchess into another passion.

She tried to remonstrate, suggesting they should at least put up at a London hotel, when Lord Andrew announced his intention of driving straight to Park Street.

"No, my love," he said with a certain mulishness he had inherited from his parents. "My clothes and valet are still there. I am puzzled by my parents, but not frightened of them."

"Well," said Penelope candidly, "*they* frighten *me* to death. After all, they did try to kidnap me."

"They don't like being crossed," he said, which Penelope thought was a singularly mild way of putting it, but she held her peace. She was so happy that most things did not seem to matter very much.

The duke was crossing the hall, wrapped in his banyan, as his son and new bride made their entrance. "Oh, it's you, Andrew," he said mildly. Then he flapped his newspaper in Penelope's direction. "Not the thing to bring her to the family home, dear boy. Little seminary in Bath is just the place to unload her."

"May I present my wife, Father."

"So that damned Methodist forced you into it," said the duke with a shrug. "How lily-livered you young people are. Now, if I had allowed every damned Methody to force me into marriage every time I'd had my bit of fun, I would have had a harem like the Grand Turk. If you want your mother, she's in the library with the black beetle."

"I insist you treat my wife with every courtesy," said Lord Andrew.

"Haven't I just?" said the duke, opening his eyes wide. "I'm breathing the same air as she, and that's about as much courtesy as she deserves."

He shuffled off, leaving Lord Andrew fuming.

"There you are," said Penelope cheerfully. "Now I have shared the same distinguished air as that which your father breathes, we can leave."

"No we can't. Come along." He pulled her towards the library.

The duchess and Mr. Baxter were studying a chart pinned on the wall. It carried the names of various charities with the sums due to be allotted to each written underneath.

"Oh, Andrew," said the duchess, catching sight of him. "How tedious! You would have to go and bring that creature here, and I have too much to do to arrange a wedding."

"Sinners!" cried Mr. Baxter.

"We *are* married," said Lord Andrew crossly.

"Well, that's a relief," said the duchess. "For you caused such an unnecessary scandal, you know. Mr. Baxter learned from Mr. Jepps of your carryings-on at some hedge tavern, and it hurt his sensitive conscience. But if you are married, then there's an end of it."

"The sinners have been brought to repentance," cried Mr. Baxter. "Let us pray."

Lord Andrew and Penelope looked in amazement as the duchess and Mr. Baxter fell on their knees.

He drew her out of the room. "I do not know what is going on here, Penelope," said Lord Andrew, "but your idea of lodgings in a hotel sounds perfectly sensible now. Ah, here is Pomfret. Pomfret, why is Her Grace in such a fit of religious fervor?"

"This Mr. Baxter was apprised by Mr. Jepps of your lordships' . . . er . . ."

"This is my wife, Pomfret."

"Ah, delighted to serve your ladyship with the same devotion as I serve the master. Well, Mr. Baxter is society's latest craze. The more he tells them they are infidels and worms, the more they love him. They claim they have not been so beautifully insulted since Mr. Brummell fled to France. Her Grace scored a victory over Mrs. Blenkinsop by electing to run several charities for Mr. Baxter. She has several hundred protégées in various workhouses and orphanages."

"Pomfret, my wife and I do not wish to reside here. We will walk in the park and take the air while you find a suitable hotel."

"Certainly, my lord," said Pomfret with heartfelt gratitude.

"And engage a lady's maid for my wife."

"Yes, my lord."

"And arrange a marriage. I want to get married again."

"My lord, I am honored you should entrust me with such responsibility."

Penelope was relieved when the door of the ducal home in Park Street closed behind her. Apart from saying mildly that he had a good mind to go to Mr. Jepp's lodgings, see if he was home, and punch his head, Lord Andrew did not appear in the least disturbed by the interviews with his unnatural parents.

They walked sedately in the park, arm in arm, still too much in love to notice the odd looks they were attracting from various members of society.

"How lucky I am," sighed Penelope. "Poor Miss Worthy. Imagine settling for a deaf duke when she could have had you."

"Miss Worthy is not a romantic," said Lord Andrew. "Nothing exciting will ever happen to her. She will continue to lead a dull and uneventful life with her dull duke."

Unknown to them, in another part of the park, Miss Worthy was walking along with her maid two paces behind her. Miss Worthy was not feeling very well. She had just spent an agonizing hour with her fiancé, and her throat was sore from shouting. Harford had announced his intention of settling permanently in the country, and the horrified Miss Worthy had protested vehemently, but the more she shouted, the deafer the duke seemed to become. Miss Worthy did not like the country. It was too full of disorganized trees, and grass, and animals who did not respect the conventions.

A traveling carriage drew up alongside her, and a gentleman poked his head out of the window and called to the driver to stop.

"Mr. Jepps!" screamed Miss Worthy.

"I must talk to you privately," he said, holding open the carriage door.

"Very well," said Miss Worthy curiously. She told her maid to wait and climbed into the carriage beside Mr. Jepps. To her surprise, he lifted the trap with his cane and told his coachman to "Spring 'em."

"What is the meaning of this, Mr. Jepps?" cried Miss Worthy. "Where are you taking me?"

"Gretna," said Mr. Jepps. "You are going to marry me and no one else, Miss Worthy."

She argued and pleaded at length to be put down. Mr. Jepps occasionally interrupted her to kiss her. Her protests gradually grew weaker, and as they rattled out of London, her head was sunk on his breast. It was so much easier to do what Mr. Jepps wanted. And what a scandal she would cause! First engaged to The Perfect Gentleman, then jilting him for a duke, and then rushing off to Gretna with Mr. Jepps. A satisfied smile curled Miss Worthy's thin mouth. All these men after her! It was proof of what she had always known about herself. She was irresistible!

Lord Andrew was content. Pomfret had engaged a suite of rooms in a luxurious hotel. Penelope had been shocked to find out that he had asked Pomfret to fetch all the clothes the duchess had given her from Park Street. But Lord Andrew had pointed out it would save her a great deal of time at the dressmakers and that he himself would pay his mother for the cost of them. He had followed that by saying that Penelope might wear her spectacles when they were alone as there was really nothing she could do now that would make him love her less. It was rather a backhanded way of putting it, but Penelope gratefully put on her glasses and had all the joy of being able to see her handsome husband clearly.

They had finished dinner and were lazily looking forward to bed when Lord Andrew said seriously, "It's odd, but I would have liked my parents' blessing. I fear I am old-fashioned. Still, they will come about in time, I am sure."

Penelope thought of his parents with a shudder. She was sure they would not.

"Especially when we make them into grandparents," he added dreamily.

"Neither your mother or your father is being allowed anywhere near a child of mine, Andrew."

"My child, too."

"Your crazy mother is not going to come within a mile of my children," said Penelope, her eyes flashing.

"My sweet, you will obey me. I am your husband."

"That does not give you the right to make stupid mistakes. Your parents would be a bad influence. My children might grow up as warped as you."

"You have no say in the matter. You are my wife."

"And you are a hidebound, Gothic, pompous fool. How dare you order me around?"

The couple glared at each other.

Penelope's face softened. "Oh, Andrew. Can you see your mother dandling a babe on her knee? She would most likely tire of it and drop it on its head."

He gave a reluctant laugh. "Are you always to have the best of it, Penelope? Are you ever going to say, 'Yes, Andrew'?"

"All you have to do is ask something reasonable."

"Penelope, my wife, will you come to bed with me and let me kiss you all night?"

Penelope dropped a curtsy. "Yes, my lord. Most certainly."

He swept her up in his arms and carried her through to the bedroom.

THE PAPER
PRINCESS

For Madeline Trezza,
with love.

Chapter One

"It won't happen to me. Never to me!" said Miss Felicity Channing fiercely.

"Why not?" demanded her governess, Miss Chubb. "It's happened to your three elder sisters. Why not you?"

"I am made of sterner stuff," said Felicity. Miss Chubb looked at her delicate charge's sensitive face and wide, vulnerable eyes and gave a cynical snort.

Both ladies were seated beside the fire in the nursery at the top of Tregarthan Castle in Cornwall. It had been an exhausting day, a day in which Felicity had watched her sister, Maria, sob her way to the altar to wed a man she barely knew.

Felicity had three elder sisters, and Maria was the last of the three to be forced by the girls' stepfather, Mr. Palfrey, into an arranged marriage. Not content with being married to one of the richest women in England, Mr. Palfrey was always on the look-out for more money to support his lavish tastes. He had married Lucy Channing, the girls' mother, when she was a pretty, young widow and the Channing girls were all still in the nursery. Felicity's mother, now Mrs. Palfrey, had been a permanent invalid for some years, allowing her husband full rein.

173

Mr. Palfrey was a thin exquisite of some forty years with a nasty waspish tongue and a determination to get his own way. His main ambition was to rid Tregarthan Castle of all his stepdauthers and then to modernize the place to suit his luxurious tastes. To that end, he had arranged marriages for each girl as she came of age. Penelope had been the first to go, wed to a baronet in Devon, then Emily to a rich merchant, and now Maria to a wealthy bishop. His aim in marrying the girls to rich men was to provide himself with the reassurance that they would make no claim on their mother's fortune. He had bullied his sick wife into making a will in which she left everything to him, having pointed out that her daughters were in no need of money. There was a "Scotch" clause in the history of the Channings that meant the estates and fortune did not automatically become the property of the husband and could be left to the daughters, if Mrs. Palfrey chose to do so. When Mrs. Palfrey protested weakly that there was still Felicity, Mr. Palfrey replied that Felicity had turned eighteen and would soon "be dealt with" like her sisters before her.

But Penelope, Emily, and Maria had inherited their mother's meek and biddable ways. The late Mr. Channing had been a member of the untitled aristocracy, a brave man, and a good soldier. He had also had a great zest for life, and a strong sense of humor. Out of the four, only Felicity had inherited her father's courageous spirit.

Her elder sisters had their mother's fashionable beauty: small, straight noses; small, rosebud mouths; and dark brown hair. Felicity's dainty, elfin figure; her large greenish-gold eyes in a delicate little face; and masses of dark red hair gave her a rare elusive beauty that was all her own. Looking at her, as she sat on the other side of the nursery fire, Miss Chubb reflected that it was extremely doubtful if Mr. Palfrey knew the strength of character of the last of his stepdaughters. For Felicity was fond of her mother and did everything she diplomatically could to be quiet and biddable and not cause any of the family scenes that made her mother turn paper-white and gasp for breath.

Miss Chubb was worried about her own future. After Felicity was wed, she was expected to find another post. She could not expect a pension from Mr. Palfrey, who was tightfisted about any money that was not to be spent on his own comfort.

She knew she had little hope of finding another position. She was fifty-two, a great age in these times when the mortality rate was high. She was a squat, stocky woman with a heavy face, and large, sad, brown eyes that made her look like some old family dog.

Felicity roused herself from her reverie. "After all, Miss Chubb," she said, "there is surely no one left of a marriageable age in the vicinity."

"I have heard talk," said Miss Chubb, "about Lord St. Dawdy."

"I know about him. He is in his fifties and has been married twice before. Also, he was not invited to the wedding, which shows a blessed lack of interest in him."

"He would have been invited had he not been on the Grand Tour."

"Indeed! I thought only very young men went on the Grand Tour."

"It is said that the baron has been several times," said Miss Chubb.

"My stepfather does not know me very well. He will find it difficult to force me into marriage with anyone."

Miss Chubb forbore from depressing her young friend by pointing out the obvious—that a woman did not have any say in the matter, never had, and never would.

"I would not be too nice in my choice of gentlemen," mused Felicity, her chin on her hand. "I must admit that neither Penelope nor Emily seems to have any complaints, and Penelope has those darling children. Children must be a great comfort."

"Do you not have romantic dreams?" asked Miss Chubb, who had a great many herself.

"Oh, no, not I," said Felicity with a laugh. "I am eminently practical. But I would have freedom of choice, you know, and not be treated like some slave. I mean to have a say; neither of my three sisters ever tried saying, 'No.'"

"Perhaps they knew it would not have been of much use," ventured Miss Chubb cautiously.

"Pooh! They are afraid of Mr. Palfrey. But I am not! It is early yet. Has he retired?"

"I do not think so," said Miss Chubb. "One of the guests at the wedding breakfast spilt wine on the dining room floor, and just before I came up to join you, he was screaming at the housemaids and saying that no one must rest until the floor was restored to its former glory."

Felicity sighed. Due to Mr. Palfrey's finicky tastes, Tregarthan Castle was like a museum. It was not a medieval castle, but a relatively modern one, a sort of folly built in the middle of the last century by her grandfather, who had had romantic tastes. It even had a moat with a drawbridge, turrets with arrow slits, and great metal cauldrons on the battlements for pouring boiling oil down on the invading troops who had lived only in her grandfather's active imagination.

Inside, everything was polished to a high shine. Precious objects lay embedded in silk in rows of glass cases, for Mr. Palfrey was a great collector of objets d'art. Not a cobweb, not a speck of dust was allowed to sully any surface. The servants were overworked and consequently surly. Only this nursery up under the leads had been spared Mr. Palfrey's collecting and cleaning zeal. It was cluttered with some of the furniture he considered too old-fashioned for the state rooms belowstairs, including two fine Chinese Chippendale chairs and a carved William & Mary chest.

"Let us dress up and go out," said Felicity suddenly. Miss Chubb looked scared.

Sometimes, she and Felicity would dress up in men's clothes and ride to the nearest tavern. It was a small adventure because they usually went out when Mr. Palfrey was visiting in London and there could be no chance of their absence being noticed. The only servant in on the secret was the head groom, John Tremayne, who detested Mr. Palfrey with a passion and who only stayed on out of loyalty to the remaining Channings.

Felicity was still too young to realize it was most odd for an old and, seemingly, conventional governess to agree to such mad escapades, and did not yet even guess how very romantic and starved for adventure was poor Miss Chubb.

"Mr. Palfrey might come looking for you," said Miss Chubb.

"To kiss me good night? You know he never pays me the slightest heed."

"Miss Felicity, he is a fussy and ambitious man—ambitious to have the castle to himself. He will be anxious to arrange a marriage for you as soon as possible and may call you downstairs to discuss the matter. You may remember that Maria was sent for just after Emily had gone off with her new husband."

"Yes, yes. But Maria's bishop had been selected for her some time before Emily's marriage. You must admit, there is no one left for me—thank goodness!"

"You forget Lord St. Dawdy."

"Now, my dear Miss Chubb, the baron is abroad and he is too old even for my wicked stepfather to consider asking him to marry me, so there is no question of him sending for me. He is probably down on his hands and knees at this moment polishing the dining room floor himself."

Miss Chubb hesitated. She thought she had overheard Mr. Palfrey saying something about the Lord St. Dawdy and Felicity. On the other hand, the baron was surely far too old. It would cause a scandal in the neighborhood if Felicity were forced to marry him, and Mr. Palfrey longed to be admired and respected by the tenants as Mr. Channing had been admired and respected. Also, she enjoyed these harmless adventures. In the last century, when Miss Chubb had been governess to a lively family of girls in Brighton, the girls had gone to assemblies dressed as men for a joke and nobody had seemed to find it shocking. But times had changed and society was more strait-laced in this second decade of the nineteenth century. But she longed to escape from the castle, just for a little.

"Perhaps it would not be noticed . . ." she started to say and was interrupted by Felicity.

"My best of governesses!" she cried. "Hurry up! A ride across the moors is just what we need."

Felicity and Miss Chubb had spent one wet afternoon two years before studying the old plans of the castle. They had found, to their delight, a priest's hole, albeit a fake one, the castle having been built well after the days of the Cavaliers and Roundheads, and a secret staircase. Their disguises were hidden in the priest's hole and the staircase enabled them to make their way out of the castle unobserved.

Soon, what looked to all appearances like a slim youth and a heavy, John Bull-type of gentleman slipped through the darkness of the grounds to the stables after having negotiated the moat by means of a long ladder laid across it—the one part of the adventure Miss Chubb never enjoyed because she was sure the ladder would break one dark night under her weight.

It was a November evening, but unusually balmy. It had been a warm autumn and the stunted trees on the moors were only just beginning to send the last of their scarlet and gold leaves flying down on the warm, sticky gales which blew in from the sea.

Miss Chubb was not a good horsewoman and the old, steady mare John Tremayne had found for her suited her needs, being as slow and cautious as she was herself. Felicity had a frisky little Arab mare, a dainty little creature that could fly like the wind.

Miss Chubb's mount could not keep up with it, so Felicity had to content herself by riding off on long gallops on her own and then turning back to join the governess, whose horse was steadily and surely plodding sedately along the cliff path.

These little adventures had never palled, never lost their feeling of excitement, although they never entailed any real fear of discovery.

Felicity and Miss Chubb would ride to The Green Dolphin tavern, a well-appointed inn that drew people from all over because of the excellence of its food. They would drink two glasses of wine each, staying about half an hour, and then ride back to the castle, having enjoyed their harmless masquerade as gentlemen. Felicity, like her sisters, was given a present of pin money by her mother every quarter day, and it was with that money that she had purchased disguises for both of them.

The advantage of the popularity of The Green Dolphin was that neither the landlord nor the serving maids had much time to wonder about the identity of the heavyset "gentleman" and his "nephew."

Felicity threw the ostler a coin and told him to stable their horses, for the rain had started to fall. In fine weather, they left them tethered outside.

Miss Chubb entered the taproom first and then drew back abruptly, bumping into Felicity who was behind her.

"What's the matter?" hissed Felicity.

"Come back outside," muttered Miss Chubb.

But the landlord, Mr. Saxon, had recognized them as the two pleasant gentlemen who infrequently patronized his hostelry.

"Enter!" he cried. "We have a deal of fine folk

180

with us tonight. But I have your usual table at the window."

"I don't know . . ." began Miss Chubb, but Felicity lowering her voice several registers, said heartily, "Splendid, Saxon," and, walking past Miss Chubb, she entered the tap.

A hum of voices rose to greet her. Apart from a few of the locals, there was a party of richly dressed men who had put two tables together in the middle of the room. Mr. Saxon guided Felicity over to the little table in the bay of one of the windows where she usually sat. With a feeling of apprehension, Miss Chubb lumbered after Felicity.

Usually, they had only the locals to contend with—locals who were interested in gossiping to one another and not bothering to pay too much attention to the two quiet gentlemen in the bay.

But these strangers were a different matter. When Mr. Saxon himself had served them with their usual glasses of claret, Miss Chubb whispered, "We should not stay long, Felicity. These strangers may become overcurious."

Felicity was not listening to her. She was studying the men at a table in the center of the room with interest.

They were all dressed in riding clothes, and, from their conversation, she gathered they had all been guests at a shooting party at an estate farther along the coast. There were six of them. Their riding clothes were all well-cut as the finest morning dress and each man wore an expensive jewel in his stock.

But it was the man at the head of the table who held Felicity's attention the most. Once she had seen him, she found it almost impossible to look away.

He was quite old, she decided, about thirty years, and that *was* old in Felicity's eighteen-year-old eyes. He had a strong face with a proud nose and a firm chin. His eyes were very black and sparkling and held a clever, restless, mocking look. His brown riding coat was fitted across a pair of powerful shoulders, and his long legs encased in top boots were stretched out under the table. A ruby glittered wickedly in his stock and a large ruby ring burned on the middle finger of his right hand. His hands were very white and his nails beautifully manicured and polished to a high shine with a chamois buffer. Felicity was fascinated. Effeminate and decadent men were laughable; decadent and powerful men, such as this one, frightening.

"Do not stare so," whispered Miss Chubb urgently.

But as if conscious of Felicity's curious gaze, the man looked across at her.

"Gentlemen!" he called. "If you are so interested in our conversation, pray join us."

A gentleman next to him, who had his back to Felicity and Miss Chubb, swung round and stared at them rudely through his quizzing glass.

"Never say they are gentlemen, Bessamy," he drawled. "Just look at the rustic cut of that lad's coat." The other four solemnly produced their quizzing glasses and raked Felicity and Miss Chubb up and down as if studying two new and curious insects.

Then, as if finding them lacking in any merit whatsoever, they dropped their glasses and continued to talk about sport.

Miss Chubb let out a slow breath of relief. Felicity's face flamed.

"Pay no attention, my dear uncle," she said in a clear, carrying voice. " 'Tis naught but some city mushrooms aping the rudeness and the churlishness of the Corinthian set."

There was a shocked silence. Miss Chubb muttered prayers under her breath. One of the gentlemen, the one next to the man called Bessamy, rose to his feet and slowly picked up his gloves.

"He's going to challenge you to a duel," squeaked Miss Chubb.

Then Bessamy rose to his feet and with one hand pushed his friend down into his chair.

"Do not squabble with the locals," he said calmly. "Too fatiguing for words, and I have been bored enough this evening. Down, James, down, boy." He picked up his glass and, to Miss Chubb's horror, crossed over to their table, pulled up a chair, and sat down.

Felicity turned her head away.

"Permit me to introduce myself," he said. "Bessamy. Lord Arthur Bessamy, at your service."

"Charmed," said Miss Chubb gruffly.

"And you are . . . ?" pursued Lord Arthur, his wicked black eyes fastened on Felicity's face.

Miss Chubb pulled her wide-awake hat down firmly over her eyes. "I am Mr. George Champion," she said, "and this, my lord, is my nephew, Mr. Freddy Channing."

Lord Bessamy swung his gold quizzing glass on its long, gold chain slowly back and forth, still looking at Felicity. Miss Chubb watched the pendulum swing of that quizzing glass with large, hypnotized eyes.

"And have *you* nothing to say for yourself, young fellow-me-lad?" asked Lord Arthur gently. "You have just sorely insulted my guests and me. An apology would not come amiss. Or do you like dueling so much?"

Felicity forced herself to look at him. "Your friends were very rude," she said. "But I admit I was rude, too, and for that I apologize."

"Gracefully said, Mr. . . . er . . . Channing. Hey, landlord, another bottle here."

"We must leave, my lord," said Felicity, trying to rise to her feet, but he pushed her back into her chair in the same autocratic manner as he had dealt with his offended friend.

"No, you must join me in a glass of wine. I insist."

Miss Chubb groaned inwardly. In these days of hard drinking, she and Felicity were very abstemious, both of them preferring the taste of lemonade to wine. They only drank wine as part of their adventure, part of their masquerade. Both had admitted in the past that two glasses were definitely their limit. They had once experimented with a third but had found themselves becoming dangerously tipsy and inclined to relapse into their normal, feminine voices, instead of maintaining their adopted masculine ones.

Miss Chubb watched miserably as the bottle of wine was brought to the table. She knew she must rescue Felicity. There must be some way she could create a diversion. She rose to her feet.

"By your leave, my lord," she said. "I beg to be excused."

"But we have not broached the bottle," said Lord Arthur.

"I shall return very shortly."

"But where do you go?"

"To the Jericho," replied Miss Chubb, an ugly flush mounting to her cheeks.

"My dear sir, it is raining like mad. There are plenty of chamberpots in the sideboard over there, and we are all men here. I suggest you avail yourself of one."

"But the serving maids . . ." put in Felicity quickly.

"Are not in the room at present," he pointed out amicably.

"I insist on going outside," barked Miss Chubb truculently.

She hurried off. Lord Arthur watched her departure with raised brows and then turned to Felicity.

"Do you belong to these parts, Mr. Channing?"

"Yes, my lord."

"Channing . . . let me see. Ah, I have it. I have heard of a Mr. Channing of Tregarthan Castle."

"Not him, nothing to do with him. Anyway, he's dead." Felicity took a great gulp of wine to cover her confusion.

"How odd to have two Channing families in the same neighborhood and yet not related. This room is warm. Do you not wish to remove your hat?"

But Felicity knew if she removed her curly-brimmed beaver it would reveal her long hair piled up on top of her head. It was the custom for gentlemen to keep their hats on if they only meant to stay somewhere for a short time.

"I must leave soon," she said. "I have pressing business."

"That being . . . ?" Felicity surveyed this hand-

185

some lord with great irritation. Why did he ask so many questions? Then a thought struck her. If he could be made to believe she belonged to the shop-keeping class, he would probably remove himself from her table and go back to his friends.

"I am in the tailoring business, my lord," she said. "Apprentice to a Mr. Weston."

"But not the great Weston, as I can see from the cut of your coat. A tailor's lad, hey? Your master spoils you. I have never before seen a tailor's boy with such white hands."

He filled her glass again.

"Tailoring is not hard labor," pointed out Felicity. "But now that you know I am well below your class, you will no doubt wish to remove to . . ."

"You do yourself an injustice, Mr. Channing. I find your company quite fascinating. What is it like being a tailor's apprentice?"

Felicity took a deep breath, another gulp of wine, and prepared to lie. Where on earth was Miss Chubb?

Miss Chubb had at first headed for the outside privy. The rain was falling hard. As soon as she was sure she was unobserved, she veered off in the direction of the stables. There had been no more arrivals since she and Felicity had come to the inn, so the stable boys were in the tack room, sitting around the fire. She put her head round the tack room door and said she would lead out their horses and the boys were not to trouble disturbing themselves—something they were glad to agree to, none of them wanting to go out into the rain when they did not have to. Miss Chubb then took her horse and Felicity's and tethered them to a post in the yard of the inn over by the gate into the yard, but well away from the inn door.

Now, for that diversion.

Fear for Felicity sharpened her wits and made her brave. She returned to the stables and took a bale of hay and a small oil lamp. She carried the hay to the ground under the bay window at the side of the inn, behind which Felicity sat with Lord Arthur. The diamond-shaped panes of the windows were so old, so warped, and so small, she had no fear of anyone inside the inn being able to look out and see her.

She poured the oil from the lamp over the hay, took out her tinder box and tried to set it alight. The trouble with using a tinder box was that you had to be very lucky to get a light the first time. Often it took half an hour. Miss Chubb groaned. This looked like it would be one of the half-an-hour times.

Inside the inn, apparently enthralled, Lord Arthur Bessamy listened to Mr. Channing's highly fanciful tale of life as a tailor's apprentice. Rather muzzy with wine, Felicity kept talking and talking, frightened that if she stopped, he might ask more questions. And so this Scheherazade of The Green Dolphin launched into a long and complicated story about a fat man who had insisted on trying on a coat made for a thinner gentleman, insisting it must be the one he had bespoke because it "fitted him like a glove."

She had just got to the interesting point when the tailor had challenged the fat man to a duel rather than let him take a coat made for another customer, when the room began to fill with black smoke.

Lord Arthur seemed unmoved. He kept his black eyes fastened on Felicity's expressive face. But his friends had jumped to their feet.

And then through the thick, rain-smeared glass of the windows came the red glow of fire.

Not knowing Miss Chubb was responsible for it, Felicity saw, all the same, a golden opportunity to escape from Lord Arthur.

"Fire!" she screamed. "The stables are on fire."

The tap room broke into an uproar, men fighting after Felicity to get out to rescue their precious horses.

Miss Chubb seized Felicity as she erupted out of the inn door.

"Straight to the gate," she whispered urgently. "The horses are there."

With remarkable speed for such a heavy woman, Miss Chubb darted off with Felicity speeding behind her.

Lord Arthur's friends rushed straight to the stables. Only Lord Arthur, sauntering lazily to the front of the bay window at the side of the inn, found out where the flames were coming from. Or had come from. For the pounding rain was quickly reducing the once-flaming hay to a blackened mess.

He looked down at the hay, and then swung about as the clatter of hooves fleeing off into the night reached his ears. Then he returned to the inn.

Soon his baffled friends came back, exclaiming that they could not find the fire anywhere.

"Probably our imaginations," drawled Lord Arthur. "More wine, gentlemen?"

Felicity and Miss Chubb reined in their mounts at the top of the cliff. The governess told Felicity of how she had set the fire to cause a diversion. "You are really very clever and bold, Miss Chubb," said Felicity. "I declare, I am proud of you."

Miss Chubb blushed with pleasure in the darkness. "I am glad I was able to be of help, Miss Felicity," she said. "Lord Arthur Bessamy is a most terrifying man."

"Indeed, yes," agreed Felicity with a shudder, thinking of those clever, searching black eyes. "At least we need not trouble about him anymore and need not bother our heads about him again . . . thanks to you."

But in her bed that night, as a fierce gale whipped round the castle and moaned in the arrow slits, Felicity lay awake, plagued by memories of Lord Arthur Bessamy. She had never met anyone like him before.

"And probably never will again," said a gloomy voice in her head. "Not the sort of gentleman to be pressed into marriage with anyone, and a cut above your stepfather's usual choice of husband."

A large tear ran down her nose, and she brushed it away. She had drunk far too much and become maudlin, she told herself severely. Who in her right mind would want the terrifying Lord Arthur Bessamy as a husband? She pulled the pillows round about her ears to drown out the crying of the wind, and plunged down into an uneasy dream where she was sitting cross-legged on the floor of a tailor's shop stitching a wedding coat for Lord Arthur Bessamy, who was to be married the next day to the Queen.

Before he set out the following morning, Lord Arthur Bessamy made inquiries in the village for a tailor's assistant called Freddy Channing, but did not look in the least surprised to find no one had ever heard of the boy.

Chapter Two

For the next two weeks, life at Tregarthan Castle returned to normal—that is, normal for Tregarthan Castle.

Mrs. Palfrey lay on a chaise longue in the drawing room during the day, sleeping or reading novels, or writing long letters to friends with whom she often corresponded, saying she was still too ill to receive visitors. The physician had diagnosed "a wasting illness," and had recommended quiet. In fact, Mrs. Palfrey would have been greatly cheered by a visit from some of her old friends, but Mr. Palfrey frowned on that idea, insisting that such excitement would be bad for her health, but privately thinking that his wife's friends were blessed with too many children—children who might chip the gloss on the legs of the furniture and make slides on the glassy surface of the floor.

Felicity stayed in the nursery wing with her governess, sharing all her meals with Miss Chubb as usual, rather than face formal dinners with her stepfather in the chilly, polished dining room where only a very small fire was allowed to battle with the winter cold, as a large fire might create more dust and ash to sully the pristine surfaces of tables and glass cases.

Although she should have been glad that no sign of an arranged marriage had reared its ugly head, she was bored. Very bored. The brief meeting with Lord Arthur had shown her a glimpse of a heady world of sophistication, a world where ladies could expect to be allowed one Season in London and have at least a chance of finding someone suitable out of a selection of gentlemen. But Mr. Palfrey would never countenance the expense of a Season.

The rain had fallen steadily since her visit to The Green Dolphin with Miss Chubb. Both ladies had been confined to the castle. But at the end of the second week since their "great adventure" as Miss Chubb called it, the wind shifted to the east and then died down. Frost glittered on the lawns on the other side of the frozen moat and icicles hung down in front of the nursery windows.

Felicity and Miss Chubb were just getting warmly dressed, preparatory to going for a walk, when a liveried footman appeared with a message from Mr. Palfrey. Miss Felicity was to present herself in the drawing room immediately.

"Marriage!" whispered Miss Chubb as soon as the footman had left.

"I do not think so," said Felicity. "No one has come to call." She giggled. "They might leave wet footprints on Mr. Palfrey's precious floors. I shall not be long. Meet me in the hall."

Mr. Palfrey was seated in a wing chair in front of the small fire in the drawing room. Lying on the chaise longue drawn up in front of the window was Mrs. Palfrey, her eyes closed, a piece of half-finished embroidery lying on her lap.

"Come in, Felicity," said Mr. Palfrey, "and sit opposite me. I have good news for you."

Felicity sat down in a tapestried chair opposite. The pair surveyed each other cautiously.

Mr. Palfrey decided again that Felicity could hardly be classed as a beauty. There was something so . . . *wayward* about her appearance, and always a hint of rebellion at the back of those wide, innocent eyes.

Felicity was always struck afresh each time she saw him by how petty, nasty, and ridiculous her stepfather looked.

His sparse, graying hair was teased and combed back on top of his head. His blue morning coat was padded on the shoulders, and his cravat was built up high to cover the lower part of his face. He had a long thin body and very short legs, legs that were encased in skintight, canary-yellow pantaloons. With his thin yellow legs and his crest of hair, he looked like Mr. Canary in a children's story book. He had a little beak of a nose and very pale blue eyes.

"What news, Mr. Palfrey?" asked Felicity. After his marriage to their mother, Mr. Palfrey had begged the little Channing girls to call him "Papa." But not even the biddable elder girls had been able to call him that. He was so fussy, prissy, and spiteful that not one of them could view him in the light of father, so all had continued to call him Mr. Palfrey.

The castle was very quiet. The servants were expected to remain unseen and unheard as they went about their duties. If Mr. Palfrey came across, say, a housemaid, who had not time to run and hide, she was expected to turn her face to the wall and try to look as invisible as possible until he had passed.

The clock on the mantelpiece ticked a rapid chattering tick-tock, and a flame spurted out of a log in the fire and died, while Mr. Palfrey considered his reply.

"I credit you with a natural modesty and humility, Felicity," said Mr. Palfrey. "So it may have occurred to you that you are not *exactly* pretty."

"Not in a fashionable way, no," said Felicity mildly.

"Not in *any way at all*," said Mr. Palfrey sharply. "I have therefore had some difficulty in finding you a suitable husband."

Felicity went very still and tense. Who? Who? Who have you found for me? chattered an anxious voice in her brain along with the restless chatter of the clock.

Mr. Palfrey made a steeple of his fingers and looked at Felicity over them. "There is, moreover, a shortage of young men. You cannot expect a *young* husband such as your more fortunate sisters have found."

"Maria married the Bishop of Exeter," said Felicity tartly, "and he is in his forties."

"Enough!" said Mr. Palfrey, holding up one hand. "But you will consider yourself fortunate when you hear that I have found a suitable gentleman for you. A titled gentleman."

"Who is?"

"Lord St. Dawdy."

A faint moan came from the direction of the window. Felicity looked anxiously at her mother, but that lady still lay with her eyes closed, apparently asleep.

"You are not going to marry me off to anyone," said Felicity in an urgent whisper, her eyes blazing, "least of all to an ancient gentleman who has been married twice before. Besides, he is abroad."

"You have no choice in the matter," said Mr. Palfrey. "The baron has returned and has honored me by accepting my proposal. You will marry him or be thrown out of here."

"You cannot throw me out of my own home! Mama would never allow it. You would be the laughingstock of the neighborhood."

"I weary of trying to cultivate the goodwill of the peasantry. They may think me hard-hearted, if they wish. Once you are safely married, they will come about."

Felicity looked at him, appalled. She had never really dreamed he would go this far.

"Let me tell you this, Mr. Palfrey," she said, leaning forward, her eyes flashing, "you have not yet taken my measure. I am not meek and quiet like my sisters. I shall not let you force me into marriage. *I shall not let you!*"

Her voice had risen. Mrs. Palfrey stirred and moaned again.

"Don't, Felicity," she said weakly.

Felicity ran to the window and knelt down by her mother and took one of Mrs. Palfrey's thin, wasted hands in her own. "Mama," she said, "he says I am to marry Lord St. Dawdy."

Mrs. Palfrey's eyes glittered with tears. "Mr. Palfrey," she started to say, "I do beg of you . . ." but the rest of what she had been going to say was lost in a bout of asthmatic wheezing.

"Now look what you have done!" exclaimed Mr. Palfrey, fussing forward. "Leave us immediately."

Felicity rose and stood looking mutinously at her stepfather, prepared to do battle. But her mother's weak plea of "Yes, my dear, do leave us" went straight to her heart.

"I am going for a walk on the grounds with Miss Chubb," said Felicity, "and when I return, Mr. Palfrey, and when Mama is not present, we shall discuss this matter further."

She turned and ran from the room.

When she had gone, Mrs. Palfrey tried to struggle up. "Do not do this to Felicity," she gasped. "You misjudge her. She has strength and spirit, very like her father."

"That spirit is unbecoming in a young miss," said Mr. Palfrey, extracting a Limoges snuffbox and taking a delicate pinch. "St. Dawdy will soon break her to harness. Now, do not distress yourself over the tiresome child. I am going to ride over to St. Dawdy's to discuss the marriage settlement."

After he had left, Mrs. Palfrey fumbled in her sleeve for her handkerchief and dried the tears that had begun to flow over her white cheeks. Then she rang a bell placed on a little table beside her.

"Giles," she said to the footman who answered it. "Has Mr. Palfrey left?"

"Yes, ma'am, just this second. Shall I call him back?"

"No, no. I want you to go out on the grounds or even beyond, to find Miss Felicity, who is out walking with Miss Chubb. Bring her back to my bedchamber. Send Benson to help me upstairs." Benson was the lady's maid.

Meanwhile, Felicity and Miss Chubb had retreated to the one uncultivated corner of the garden by the south wall where a curtain of creeper drooped over a tangled mass of wildflowers, their winter leaves yellow and brown—mallow, foxglove, borage, and rosebay willow-herb. The rest of the garden about the castle was as manicured and ordered as the inside of the great building. Grass, cut into geometric patterns, surrounded the rosebeds; the roses were never allowed to grow to any height but were always ruthlessly pruned so that only a few regimented flowers were allowed to bloom each summer.

This one corner had, so far, escaped Mr. Palfrey's notice, and Felicity found it a soothing place to go, a place mercifully free of his fussy, nagging perfectionism.

She had told Miss Chubb about the marriage that had been arranged for her, stoutly maintaining that she would not be forced into it, and Miss Chubb listened, her heavy face drooping and her doglike eyes sad, for she really did not think Felicity, as her stepfather had pointed out, had any choice in the matter at all.

Felicity looked up after her defiant statement of independence and saw the footman, Giles, hurrying toward her.

"He wants me back for a further argument," she said gloomily. But as soon as she heard it was her mother who wished to see her, she ran like the wind. Felicity had not seen her mother alone for some time, Mr. Palfrey having forestalled any efforts in that direction.

It had been many years since Mrs. Palfrey had shared a bedchamber with her husband. But her own bedchamber had not escaped her husband's reorganizing zeal. The floor was slippery with beeswax and ornamented with an Oriental rug placed with geometric precision exactly in the center of the floor. Her bed was of the newfangled kind that

Felicity detested, having neither posts nor curtains, but shell-shaped and draped with a cover of chilly white lace.

"Come in, my dear," said Mrs. Palfrey faintly. "I do not have much time."

Mrs. Palfrey was now sure she was dying, but Felicity thought her mother meant that she had not much time before her husband came back.

"Now, don't interrupt me," said Mrs. Palfrey feebly. "Sit down on the end of the bed and listen. I have not been a good mother. No! You must not interrupt. I allowed Mr. Palfrey to arrange marriages for my other girls. It seemed as if he had good sense, for Penelope and Emily appear to be content, and I can only pray that Maria will find the same happiness. But from what I have heard of the baron, he is not the man for you, or indeed for any woman. You must have your independence, Felicity. Mr. Palfrey does not, I believe, know of the Channing jewels. I did not tell him about them. I knew he loved beautiful things, and I had planned to dazzle him with a display of them after we were married. I did not then know how greedy he was—but I soon found out.

"Before I fell ill, I hid the box with the jewels. It may surprise you to know there is a priest's hole in this castle."

"But I do know," said Felicity, wondering. "I have been in it."

"There is a ledge up at the top of it. You probably never looked up there. It is hard to see in the blackness. You will find an iron box there. That is your dowry. I shall leave them to you in my will, and you must point out to Mr. Palfrey that with such an enormous dowry, you may marry whom you please. In the meantime, appear as if you have decided to accept the baron. I do not wish to die without having made some provision for you."

"Mama! You will live a long time. Perhaps another physician should be called."

"Perhaps I shall live longer than I expect," said Mrs. Palfrey with a weak smile, "but we shall try for a stay of execution. I shall tell Mr. Palfrey I do not wish you to be married until I am well enough to attend the ceremony. The Channing money is still mine, and at least I have that hold over him, though I have never used it before.

"Now, I wish to add a codicil to my will, leaving you the jewels. I need two servants to be witnesses, but I must have two who are trustworthy and who will not talk to Mr. Palfrey or to anyone else."

"There is John Tremayne, the head groom," said Felicity slowly, "and he will know of another who is as loyal to the Channings."

"Fetch him quickly. Now."

"But, Mama. You are making me afraid with this talk of death."

"I have no time at the moment to talk to you further, my child. Go!"

Felicity longed to take her mother into her arms, to try to beg her to leave the castle and perhaps go to London where a physician might be better qualified to diagnose her illness. But fright and agitation were making Mrs. Palfrey's breath come in ragged gasps. Felicity left to go in search of John Tremayne.

After a short time, John Tremayne appeared with a housemaid, Bessie Redhill. The head groom was half in love with Bessie, who was plump and motherly.

Mrs. Palfrey asked Bessie to help her over to her writing desk. She pulled forward a sheet of parchment and then hesitated. She was suddenly consumed with hatred for this husband of hers who had only pretended to love her and whose greed and spiteful bullying character had become evident right after the wedding. Up until this moment, she had kept such feelings at bay, thinking them sinful. She had sworn in church before God to love and obey her husband, and she had tried so very hard to abide by the promise. But the fear that time was running out for her sparked the first strong feeling of rebellion Mrs. Palfrey had ever had. Why not leave everything she possessed to Felicity? It would only mean writing a very short will. Felicity could be trusted to share the money with her sisters and look after any servants who might have to be pensioned off.

She began to write quickly, while John and Bessie stood by, trying to mask their curiosity. At last she was finished, and she asked them both to sign. John Tremayne was illiterate and made his mark. Bessie had been educated at a dame school, and her bold, quick eyes traveled rapidly down the page before she signed.

Then she helped Mrs. Palfrey back to bed and left the room with John Tremayne.

When the servants had reached the stair landing, John asked, "What was that all about, Bessie? Was it her will?"

Bessie hesitated. It was a great secret, that will; a rare secret. She decided to hug the knowledge to herself. The housekeeper, Mrs. Jessop, was always sneering at her. It would be nice after Madam died to startle the servants hall by saying that she,

Bessie, had been witness to the will that was driving Mr. Palfrey mad with rage.

"Dunno," she said laconically. "Warn't time. I just signed my name without reading it."

"Well, I hope there's something in there for Miss Felicity," said John. "Give us a kiss, Bessie. No one's around."

Bessie giggled and kissed him on the lips, privately thinking that John Tremayne was a bit of an old goat. Then the servants went downstairs together.

At the time the servants were signing the new will, Lord Arthur Bessamy was strolling into his club, Boodle's, in St. James's. Boodle's was not a club for the politically-minded, like White's, which favored the Tories, or Brooks's, which had a membership of Whigs. It was a more comfortable place with the convenience of a "dirty room" in which members who had failed to dress for dinner were segregated.

Lord Arthur made his way to the coffee room, and there, sitting by the fireplace under the Abraham Hondius painting, *Stag Hunt*, he recognized the wilting figure of his friend, Charles Godolphin.

"You look," said Lord Arthur pleasantly, "about the sickest thing in London, Dolph. There is an inn in Devon called The Green Dolphin that would suit your complexion perfectly."

"Been drinking Blue Ruin," groaned Mr. Godolphin. "Don't tower over me, there's a good chap. Sit down, do. Craning up at you makes my head ache."

Lord Arthur sat down and surveyed his friend. Dolph was a tubby man, so small that his plump legs, encased in black Inexpressibles, did not reach the floor. His starched cravat supported two chins, and his short-sighted green eyes were crisscrossed that day with little red veins. He had teased his thick head of fair hair into the Windswept that morning, only to see it spring back into its normal style which resembled the thatched roof of a Tudor cottage. In despair, he had told his man to set it by using a mixture of sugar and water. That had seemed to do the trick, although it had given his hair a rigid, stand-up appearance that made him look as if he had been struck by lightning. The sugar and water mixture had dried on the road to the club, and the little crystals of sugar now decorated the shoulders of his coat like some exotic type of dandruff. A pair of new corsets was playing merry hell with his swollen liver. In all, Dolph felt terrible.

"Did you mention The Green Dolphin?" he asked, as Lord Arthur sat down in a chair opposite him.

Lord Arthur nodded. "I was thinking of an inn of that name down in Cornwall, near Tregarthan Castle."

"I know it," said Dolph. "Deuced good food. I had to escape there from the claws of a grasping relative."

"Which one?"

"My Uncle Frank. He's Lord St. Dawdy. You know I'm always short of the ready, and I've been dipping deep. It occurred to me that the old boy might look at me in a kindly way in his declining years. He jaunters to the Continent a lot—had just got back when I arrived on his doorstep. We had an abominable supper, everything put in a pie, Cornish-style, but with great heaps of pastry to make up for the absence of meat.

"Still, I thought my digestion might be able to stand it—just. I asked tenderly after his health and said he must be curst lonely. Lives in a drafty, miserable place which looks as if it had been built by gnomes on an off-day—you know, low, low roofs, beams that bang even such a small chap as myself on the head, and sloping floors. He grinned and winked at me—he's a gross, vulgar, brutish man—and said he would not be alone for very much longer. 'Why not?' I asked, hoping he meant that he would soon be among heavenly company. He said he was getting married to a fine, lusty girl who would bear him sons. Well, after a rocket like that, there didn't seem much point in staying. I murmured something about urgent business and fled to the nearest hostelry—The Green Dolphin."

Lord Arthur took out a lace-edged cambric handkerchief and flicked a piece of dust from one glossy hessian boot. "When you were at The Green Dolphin," he said, "did you by any chance notice a weird couple of fellows in the tap—a big, heavyset man and a slim, pretty youth?"

"No one like that."

"And what is the name of the lady your uncle is going to inflict himself on?"

"Felicity Channing."

"Ah, that name again," murmured Lord Arthur. "Is this Felicity indeed a girl—or only a girl to someone of your uncle's age?"

"You may be sure I asked, hoping the marriage would not come to anything, you know. But it seems that even if Miss Channing does not want the baron, she will be forced to marry him nonetheless."

"I have heard of a Bartholomew Channing of

Tregarthan Castle, although that was when I was in short coats. My father said he was an admirable gentleman."

"Ah, but he died, and the widow married a Mr. Palfrey, a man-milliner sort of fellow, much despised by the locals. He arranged marriages for the elder three of the widow's daughters—not bad marriages as it turned out, but he has settled on my uncle for the youngest, and what he says goes."

"How very gothic. Do you attend the wedding?"

"Have to. He may yet leave me something."

Lord Arthur sighed and stretched. "Take me along with you, Dolph," he said finally. "I have a whim to see that part of England again."

Mr. Palfrey sat back in the carriage that was bearing him back to Tregarthan Castle and beamed with satisfaction. He had forced the baron to agree to only a very small dowry, explaining that Felicity's youth and beauty were dowry enough. He had had miniatures of all the girls painted as they reached the age of seventeen, but instead of showing the baron Felicity's miniature—for Mr. Palfrey privately thought Felicity a very poor sort of female in the looks department—he had shown him instead a miniature of Maria; Maria who had all the formal beauty of the Channings.

That had settled the matter, and the baron had almost drooled over that miniature and had agreed to the tiny dowry. Then Mr. Palfrey frowned. He did hope his wife was not going to make trouble over this marriage. But she had never made any trouble before. Still, she obviously doted on the odd little Felicity. Better to have a stern word with her.

But Mrs. Palfrey was beyond listening to any

stern words. When he arrived in her bedchamber, it was to find her lying serene and tranquil in the endless sleep of death.

Before summoning the servants, Mr. Palfrey sat down at her desk so that he could prepare himself to act the part of grief-stricken husband. It was all his now, he thought in a sort of wonder. Tregarthan Castle, the Channing fortune, and the Channing estates. All his. It was tiresome that Felicity's marriage would have to be delayed while a decent period of mourning was observed.

He half rose from the desk. And then he saw his wife's Last Will and Testament. He lit more candles and sat down to read it with a fast-beating heart.

The spasm of fury that consumed him was so intense that he thought his heart would burst through his chest. He looked at Bessie Redhill's signature and then at John Tremayne's mark. The head groom was illiterate, and perhaps the maid had not read what she was signing. And what was this about the Channing jewels? What jewels?

The earlier will, leaving everything to him, reposed downstairs in his desk in the library.

He must burn this one, and then see if he could quiet those servants. He picked up the will and carried it over to the fire. But the fire had burned very low. He threw on some coal and eagerly waited for it to burst into a blaze.

The door opened and Benson, the lady's maid, walked in.

Mr. Palfrey thrust the will into the pocket in his coattails.

Benson was staring in anguish at the still figure on the bed.

"My beloved wife is dead," said Mr. Palfrey. He

thought again of that will, and tears of rage spurted out of his eyes. Benson said afterward she had never until that moment realized how very much Mr. Palfrey had loved his wife.

Chapter Three

Felicity's courage appeared to vanish with the death of her mother. She was crushed down under a load of grief.

Her stepfather cried a great deal as well, but Felicity had noticed the strong smell of onion coming from his handkerchiefs and knew he was acting, but she did not even have the strength to become angry.

There was some comfort for her in the arrival of her sisters for the funeral. She was able to share her mourning and found a great deal of solace in noticing that not only Penelope and Emily appeared happy with their husbands, but that Maria was content with her bishop. He was a large man with a hectoring manner and a booming voice, but Maria appeared to hang on his every word. There was something to be said for arranged marriages after all, thought Felicity. Marriage to Lord St. Dawdy would at least mean having a home of her own.

Despite her grief, she could not help hoping the baron might ride over to attend the funeral, but Mr. Palfrey said Lord St. Dawdy detested funerals, and Felicity thought the baron must be a very odd man indeed to stay away from his intended bride's family mourning.

All too soon, Mr. Palfrey managed to fuss the sisters and their husbands out of the castle, which settled back into its usual deadly glacial quiet.

Felicity and Miss Chubb decided to go out riding the day after the Channing sisters had left, although the sky was darkening and there was a metallic smell of snow on the wind.

John Tremayne saw to the saddling of their horses himself. After he had helped Felicity up, he stood with his hand on her stirrup and looked up anxiously into her face.

"I do not wish to distress you, Miss Felicity," he said, "but has the will been read?"

"Yes," said Felicity curtly, putting a hand down to pat her little mare's neck, for the animal had sensed her sudden rush of anger and had begun to fidget. "It is as I expected. Everything goes to Mr. Palfrey."

"But, miss, you remember when you came for me the day Mrs. Palfrey died? You told me to find another loyal servant because Madam wanted two witnesses? I took the maid, Bessie Redhill, with me. Madam gave us a piece of paper with writing on it to sign. I can't read nor write and though Bessie can, she said she didn't have time to see what was on the paper."

"So, Mama did write that codicil," said Felicity slowly.

"What . . . what was it, that thing you just said?"

"Look, John. I shall tell you and Miss Chubb, but you must keep it to yourselves and not ever tell anyone, not even Bessie. Tell her only that the piece of paper was nothing important. You see, I believe my stepfather found that codicil which left Mama's jewels to me, and burned it. But I know where they are hidden, and I am not going to tell him!"

"I promise, miss. I'll never tell a soul, and if Bessie mentions that piece of paper, I'll deny it, that I will. It'll be her word against mine, and I think master'll be more inclined to believe an old servant."

At that moment, a groom came running up and said John was wanted in the castle by Mr. Palfrey.

"He probably wants to ask you where I am," said Felicity. "Stand clear, John. Come along, Miss Chubb. Off we go!"

John made his way slowly toward the castle.

Bessie, who had also been summoned, arrived outside the library before him. She had hugged the knowledge of that other will to herself. Surely Mr. Palfrey would pay, and pay well, to have it kept a secret.

Mr. Palfrey had an extensive wardrobe. He had changed into the coat he had been wearing on the day of his wife's death. It was the first time he had worn it since then. He was sitting down at his desk in the library when he heard the crackle of parchment from the pocket in his tails. He drew out his wife's last will, cursing that he had not destroyed it before this. When he found the coat that morning, it had been folded in a chest with some papers in his bedchamber, and he had forgotten why he had thrust it there. It was as well he had not put the coat with his others, or his valet would have found the will when he cleaned out the pockets. Why on earth had he been convinced he had already destroyed the will? He had drunk long and deep on the night of his wife's death. His memory of thrusting that plaguey will between the bars of the library fire must have been a drunken dream. It must be got rid of at once! He bent over the library fire.

Then he heard Bessie's heavy footsteps approaching across the hall and crammed the will back into his pocket.

He eyed Bessie carefully as she walked in. She seemed a pleasant, motherly woman. Probably there would be no difficulty in dealing with her.

"I am afraid I must give you your notice, Bessie," said Mr. Palfrey. "With the ladies married and my poor wife in her grave, there is no longer any need to maintain such a large staff."

"You're getting rid o' me because I know the missus wrote a last will leaving everything to Miss Felicity."

"Nonsense!" said Mr. Palfrey, turning a muddy color.

The door opened, and John Tremayne walked in.

Bessie looked at John triumphantly. "I was just telling Master that we signed a will that Mrs. Palfrey wrote—the day she died, it was."

John looked at her stolidly. "I never signed anything," he said.

"That you didn't," said Bessie scornfully, "you not being able to write. But you made your mark!"

Had Bessie told him that the will was one leaving everything to Felicity, John would have changed his tune. But he thought it was only that bit about the jewels he had witnessed, and Mr. Palfrey must never know about the jewels.

"I neither made my mark nor know anything about any will," said John firmly.

Color began to tinge Mr. Palfrey's cheeks. He had been about to fire John as well, never having liked the relic of the Channing dynasty who had come to the castle as a little stable boy when old Mr. Channing was still alive, but the fellow was obviously beautifully stupid, and just what he, Mr. Palfrey, needed.

"There you are," said Mr. Palfrey pompously, beginning to stride up and down. "You may pack your things and leave this day, Bessie."

Bessie looked from one to the other, appalled. Without John to back her, she had no proof there ever was a will.

John started. "I did not know you were getting rid of Bessie, Master," he said. "She is a good maid, and 'tis hard to find work hereabouts."

"That is not my concern," said Mr. Palfrey, fortifying himself with a pinch of snuff.

John hesitated, almost tempted to tell the truth, because the dismissal of Bessie had shocked him. But two things, apart from loyalty to Felicity, made him stay quiet.

The first was that he had overheard Bessie joking with one of the other maids only a week before. The maid had been teasing, Bessie, saying John Tremayne was sweet on her, and Bessie had tossed her head and replied that she could do better for herself and had done nothing to encourage the attention of an old and smelly groom like John Tremayne. John, a wiry man in his forties with a pleasant, weatherbeaten Celtic face, had been badly hurt by the insult.

Added to that, he now surprised a look of cunning and greed in Bessie's eyes that changed her appearance entirely, making her look almost sinister.

He did not know that Bessie had seen the will poking out of Mr. Palfrey's back pocket as he strutted up and down the library. She now wanted to find some way to get her hands on it before Mr. Palfrey managed to destroy it.

"You'd best come with me, Bessie," said John firmly. "If Master says you have to leave, then leave you must."

"Oh! Oh! *Oh!*" screamed Bessie, tearing her cap off and throwing it on the floor. "What will become of me? Please don't send me off." She threw herself into Mr. Palfrey's arms, nearly knocking him flat.

He tried to push her away, but Bessie clutched hold of him, and the ill-assorted couple did a macabre waltz over the polished floor.

With a great heave, Mr. Palfrey finally sent her flying. She stumbled backward and just managed to stop herself from falling.

But she had seized the will and had it hidden in the folds of her apron. Pretending to weep, she rushed from the room.

"You're a good man, John," said Mr. Palfrey. "You may go about your duties."

"Why did you send for me?" asked John, curiously.

"Because ... because I anticipated trouble with the maid and felt sure you would help to handle the situation. Where is Miss Felicity?"

"Out riding with Miss Chubb."

"She should be accompanied by a groom. Now that she is soon to be a baroness, she must begin to observe the conventions. See to it."

"Very good, sir," said John, touching his forelock and bowing his way out.

Outside the library, he scratched his head. Mr. Palfrey would normally have instructed the housekeeper to get rid of Bessie. He must be worried about those jewels. John gave a slow smile. Well, Miss Felicity had them safe. Mr. Palfrey would never get them. Pity about Bessie. She had seemed such a kind woman before. John shook his head dismally over the fickleness and cruelty of women and made his way back to the stables.

Felicity and Miss Chubb swung down from their mounts at the cliff's edge, some distance from the castle. They tethered their horses to a stunted tree and both looked down at the wrinkled gray sea far below them.

"I know he burned that bit about the jewels," said Felicity fiercely. "He is a liar and a thief. But he shall not have them!"

"You told me they were hidden in the priest's hole. Are there a great many jewels?" asked Miss Chubb.

"In truth, I never bothered to look inside the box. I have been too grief-stricken. I only checked to be sure it was there, where Mama said it was. Oh, poor Mama."

Felicity turned her head away and began to cry. Miss Chubb shuffled her large feet like an old horse. She could not share in Felicity's grief, for Miss Chubb had always considered Mrs. Palfrey to be a very poor mother indeed. "If Felicity were my daughter," Miss Chubb told herself, "then sick as I was, I would have yet found the strength to rid myself of such a nasty character as Mr. Palfrey."

She waited until Felicity had recovered and then said gruffly, "At least this period of mourning has put your marriage off. With any luck the baron might die before the year is out."

"Do you know, Miss Chubb," said Felicity, "this Lord St. Dawdy, though old, might be quite a pleasant sort of man."

"You said your mama did not think so," pointed out Miss Chubb. "And he is not liked in the county."

"People can be hard, particularly on absentee landlords," sighed Felicity. "And the baron has traveled a great deal. Besides, mama did not seem to be a great judge of people or she would not have married Mr. Palfrey. My sisters are content in their marriages. The arrangements worked out well for them. Penelope told me it was exceedingly pleasant to be mistress of one's own establishment and to have children. And I could take you with me."

Miss Chubb brightened, but then her face fell. "I cannot see any man countenancing the presence of an elderly governess."

"But if I were a baroness, surely I could elevate you to the rank of companion?"

"Perhaps," said Miss Chubb gloomily. "But I would not count on it."

"Look, the snow is beginning to fall," said Felicity with a shiver. "Perhaps when the weather is better, we can don our disguises and ride down to The Green Dolphin for another adventure."

"I was frightened last time," said Miss Chubb. "Lord Arthur was a very unsettling sort of man."

Felicity kicked a piece of turf. "Do you think there are many men like Lord Arthur in London, Miss Chubb?"

"He was very handsome and very grand," said Miss Chubb reflectively. "No, not many."

"It is of no use wondering about it," said Felicity, "for I shall probably never go to London. Or not as a single lady, anyway."

They rode together back to the castle to hear John's story of the sacking of Bessie.

"Poor woman," said Felicity. "I have some pin money left. She may have it."

When she and Miss Chubb entered the castle, the butler, Anderson, told them that Mr. Palfrey was searching everywhere for the blueprints to the castle and wondered if either of the ladies had seen them.

"No," lied Felicity quickly. Mr. Palfrey must never find those blueprints, or he would discover the priest's hole.

She and Miss Chubb hurried up to the nursery, took the blueprints out of a desk, took them to the priest's hole, and put them up on the high ledge with the box of jewels.

Mr. Palfrey had just learned that one of his tenant farmers, Ebeneezer Pulkton, had called and was demanding audience. Mr. Palfrey hesitated, half-tempted to send the man away, for in his search for the blueprints he had not burned the will. Also, he wanted to study it again in peace so that he might be sure that bit about the Channing jewels—unaccountably absent from the previous will—was indeed there. But Mr. Pulkton was a toady, and Mr. Palfrey loved toadies—they being a rare commodity in Cornwall, where the population were singularly independent-minded and did not have a correct respect for their betters.

He had received a bad shock over that will. He

longed to sit and drink a glass of port in congenial company. Mr. Palfrey had never felt lonely before. Now he did. In fact, he felt quite weak and helpless and wished his stern and domineering mother were still alive so that he could lay his weary pomaded head on her iron bosom.

"Show Mr. Pulkton in, Anderson," he said, "and bring us a couple of bottles of the best port."

Mr. Pulkton entered, hat in hand, his little piggy eyes darting here and there as if seeking something that he could turn into a profit. He was dressed in a holland drill smock, breeches, and ankle boots. His smock had three capes on the shoulders, denoting his status as farmer. In this age of elegance, even the farmers were dandies, and the front of Mr. Pulkton's snowy-white smock was embroidered with scarlet hearts.

"I din't like to come afore," said Mr. Pulkton slowly. "But I felt I must pay my respects, like. Terrible trajdy, Missus dying like that."

"Yes, yes," said Mr. Palfrey, giving his eyes a perfunctory dab with a wisp of handkerchief. "Sit down, man, and join me in a glass of port. Ah, Anderson. The table by the window, and we shall serve ourselves."

Mr. Pulkton looked suitably gratified.

As she sat on the edge of her bed in the room she shared with three other maids, Bessie heard the sound of approaching footsteps and thrust the will she had been studying under her mattress. She was alone, having been told to go and get her belongings, while the three more fortunate maids with whom she shared the room went about their duties.

Bessie started in surprise as Felicity walked in.

"I have heard of your dismissal, Bessie," said Felicity awkwardly. "Please take this money. It is not very much, but it will serve to keep you until you find another post."

"Thank you, miss," said Bessie. She had a sudden impulse to whip that will out from under the mattress and hand it to Felicity. Felicity had the same striking dark-red hair as her father, the same fascinating green-gold eyes. And Bessie remembered the late Mr. Channing very well. He used to throw open the castle once a year and entertain all the locals lavishly, a practice that Mr. Palfrey had not maintained.

But Miss Felicity was to marry a baron and would soon have all the money she wanted. Bessie knew that will could make her own fortune. She remained silent, and after giving the maid an embarrassed pat on the shoulder, Felicity left.

Bessie waited. She was to be allowed to stay the night before leaving in the morning. She must wait until she had guessed Mr. Palfrey had retired to his bedchamber and visit him there.

Mr. Palfrey climbed the stairs to his room after a euphoric drinking session with Mr. Pulkton.

His valet prepared him for bed, brushed out his sparse hair, gave him a glass of warm milk, and then left his master to sit by the fire.

Mr. Palfrey stared into the flames and sipped his milk. There was so much he could do now. He could fill the castle with the most beautiful treasures and become known around the world as a connoisseur of fine art. At last, he rose to his feet. Now for that will.

217

He was glad he had not burned it yet. There might be some hint, some clue, as to the whereabouts of the Channing jewels. He had told his valet to put his coat away without brushing it or emptying the pockets. He made his way to the wardrobe.

Behind him, the door opened.

Mr. Palfrey swung around.

Bessie Redhill stood there, smiling at him in a way he did not like at all.

"How dare you!" gasped Mr. Palfrey, one nervous manicured hand flying down to cover his private parts, although his nightgown was as thick as a bedsheet. With his other hand, he reached for the bellrope to summon help.

Bessie grinned broadly and held up the will.

With a squawk of outrage, Mr. Palfrey wrenched open the door of the wardrobe and scrabbled feverishly in the tail pockets of his coat.

Then he turned back to Bessie. His mind was working very quickly. The pleasant muzziness induced by his port-drinking session fled, leaving his brain sharp and clear.

He began to laugh. Bessie stared at him in surprise.

"You clever girl," said Mr. Palfrey. "So you've got the better of me after all!"

"Well," said Bessie, closing the door and moving into the center of the room. "I reckon we'll all be happy, sir, if we can do a deal."

"Of course, of course," said Mr. Palfrey, rubbing his hands. "Sit down by the fire; there's a good girl."

Bessie sat down gingerly, clutching the will.

"Now, a glass of brandy to warm us while we get down to business," said Mr. Palfrey cheerfully.

"Don't mind if I do," said Bessie with a broad smile. Mr. Palfrey looked so ridiculous with his little, spindly, hairy legs poking out from the bottom of his nightgown and with his red nightcap perched rakishly on the side of his head.

Mr. Palfrey went over to a cupboard in the corner and fiddled with bottles and glasses and came back with two bumpers of brandy.

He handed one to Bessie. "Now, how much?" he asked pleasantly.

Bessie took a deep breath, her eyes glittering in the candlelight.

"Five hundred pounds."

Mr. Palfrey stared. Five hundred pounds was a reasonable sum—very reasonable. But while he kept a smile on his face, his mind checked him by pointing out that Bessie would soon return for more. Like most of her class, she would probably drink to excess, drink would loosen her tongue, and before long the whole of the Duchy of Cornwall would know of his perfidy.

But just to make sure . . .

"And for five hundred pounds you will give me that will?"

"No," said Bessie, an unlovely look of cunning crossing her plump features. She folded the single sheet of paper into a small square and thrust it into her bosom. "Reckon I'll hang onto it for a bit."

"As you will," said Mr. Palfrey. "A toast to seal our bargain. And to seal a bargain you must drain it to the last drop. Probably too much for you," he said with a little laugh.

"Oh, I can take my drop," grinned Bessie. She

felt strong and powerful. She was now a lady of independent means. She would buy a silk dress and a carriage, and come calling on that housekeeper, Mrs. Jessop, and watch the old harridan's eyes pop out of her head.

She tilted the contents of her glass straight down her throat and then laughed and spluttered and gasped. Mr. Palfrey laughed as well and patted her on her plump shoulders.

"Now, wait here, Bessie," he said, "while I go to the strongbox and fetch you the money."

He darted from the room, but only as far as the other side of the door. He waited, his heart thudding against his ribs until he heard the sound of a heavy body hitting the floor.

His thin lips curled in satisfaction.

He opened the door again and went in.

Bessie Redhill lay with her head on the fender, as still as death. He bent over her and pried open one eye. "Still alive," he muttered. "Better move fast."

He had tipped enough laudanum into her brandy to kill anyone of a less robust stature.

He dressed himself in his traveling clothes, went downstairs, and roused his butler.

"Have my traveling carriage brought round to the front," he said. "I am going off on private business. I shall leave in about half an hour. I do not want any servant to be visible. Is that understood?"

Anderson bowed. He saw nothing odd in the request. Mr. Palfrey was always complaining about the servants. Unless actually serving him with something, he expected them to be invisible.

Mr. Palfrey went back upstairs, trying not to run. He took a large linen laundry sack out of a chest and with great difficulty, but with the strength of acute fear, managed to stuff Bessie's heavy body into it.

The carriage having been brought round, the servants kept well out of sight but listened in amazement to the crashes and bumps from the staircase.

Mr. Palfrey was not strong enough to lift Bessie on his back and so, piously thanking God for polished floors, he had slid his burden to the top of the stairs and proceeded to drag it down behind him.

Once outside, he almost gave up and called for help. He thought he would never be able to get Bessie inside the carriage. But at last, with one superhuman heave, he stuffed her inside and slammed the door.

He climbed up on the box and set off into the night. The snow had changed to sleet and drove into his face. But the madness of fear was on him, and he felt no discomfort.

He was grateful that the port of Falmouth was not many miles away.

In Falmouth, he went straight to a tavern he knew was frequented by sea captains and soon found the sort of character he wanted.

Captain Ferguson was only too pleased to have the "present" of a fine, strong housemaid whom he could sell in America as a bonded servant. When Mr. Palfrey also gave him one hundred guineas, the captain swore lifelong friendship.

He saw nothing very odd or criminal in receiving a drugged body on board. In these days, when press-ganged victims could arrive bound and gagged, it was nothing much to take on the body of a drugged maid.

Luck was with Mr. Palfrey. The wind was fair, the good ship *Mary Bess*, would set sail before the morning, and when Bessie came out of her stupor—*if* she came out of her stupor, for he might have broken her neck dragging her down the stairs—she would be well on the way to the New World.

Anxious to remove himself from the vicinity as soon as possible, Mr. Palfrey did not stay at the comfortable inn, but set out on the road home, singing snatches of song as he bowled along the Cornish roads.

Once back, his long-suffering valet prepared his master for bed again. Mr. Palfrey kept having fits of the giggles, for all he had drunk, both with Mr. Pulkton and the sea captain, had finally gone to his head.

The bed seemed to have a tendency to run about the room. He glared up at the canopy, willing the room to stop spinning.

All at once he was stark, staring sober.

The will!

The will was still somewhere in Bessie's capacious cleavage.

His mind raced and spun as the drunken room had done only a few moments before.

And then he gave a deep sigh. What could a bonded servant do about anything? If she survived the journey, which was unlikely, she would be sold. She would not be paid a groat until her seven years of slavery were over. Surely no American was going to listen to a mere housemaid's babbling about some will. Salt water, or rats, or sweat, or any of the hazards of the journey would probably destroy that paper before Bessie ever reached America.

* * *

Felicity was crossing the hall the next day when she saw a woman dressed in black bombazine standing with her face to the wall.

"It is I, Miss Felicity," she said impatiently.

"You may turn around, Mrs. Jessop." Felicity thought Mr. Palfrey's treatment of the servants was disgraceful.

The housekeeper bobbed a curtsey. "I heard the footsteps," she said, "and thought it was the master."

"Has Bessie left yet?" asked Felicity.

"Yes, but it's ever so strange. She did not take a thing with her, and she even left fifteen pounds on her bed."

"I gave her that money. I was sorry for her," said Felicity.

"You shall have your money back, miss. Mr. Anderson has it in safekeeping. I would not feel sorry for Bessie. She could be lazy and a bit cruel with some of her remarks."

"But if she left the money and her belongings, something may have happened to her," cried Felicity.

"That's what I thought. But Mr. Palfrey told me he saw her slipping out of the castle last night, and he says as how one of his silver snuffboxes has been taken."

"And did he inform the parish constable?"

"No, miss. He said he didn't want any scandal."

"Thank you, Mrs. Jessop." Felicity went up the stairs, wondering a little about Bessie's sudden turn to crime. Then her thoughts moved to her prospective marriage. She felt tired and beaten down, and weary with grief. She had not made any further protest about the marriage.

A little glowing image of Lord Arthur Bessamy's handsome face rose before her eyes.

She gave a resigned shrug. Dashing and handsome and tantalizing men were for more fortunate females. Best put him completely out of her mind. She had not really liked him very much, so it was odd how much the memory of him kept returning to plague her. She would, in all probability, never see him again.

But Felicity was wrong.

Chapter Four

"Got a letter from that old rascal in Devon," said Mr. Charles Godolphin to his friend Lord Arthur Bessamy.

Both men were strolling along the pebbly beach at Brighton, having followed the Prince Regent to that famous resort after the Season finished in June.

"Your uncle?"

"Yes, him. A most odd letter. He wants me to go there."

"Has he decided to leave you his moneybags after all?" asked Lord Arthur.

"No, he's going ahead with this marriage. Wants to marry the girl in September."

"Miss Felicity Channing is the lady, if I remember correctly. Is she proving difficult?"

"Well, this Felicity has, quite rightly I think, demanded a look at the goods first, or, to put it less vulgarly, she wants to see her intended."

Lord Arthur looked amused. "Do you mean they have never met?"

"Not even for a cup of tea. Whole thing was arranged by the girl's stepfather, Palfrey. The mother died last November and one would have thought

225

they'd have waited until a year of mourning was over."

"So why does Uncle Baron need Dolph?"

"He needs me because he says he's fallen madly in love with the chit."

"A chit whom he has never set eyes on?"

"He's got her miniature," said Dolph, "and gazes at it night and day. He says he feels like a lovesick schoolboy."

"Touching."

"It would be," said Dolph, stooping down, picking up a stone, and shying it out to sea. "Only trouble is he's a satyr, a lecher, and a boor. Nevertheless, he wants me there to hold his paw and put in a good word for him with Miss Channing. I am to present myself at Dawdy Manor in two weeks' time."

"My dear Dolph, if you intend to go, you had better set out now. It will take you all of that to get there—with your driving, that is."

"Hoping you would drive me," said Dolph.

Both men came to a stop. The sun was setting, and a sea gull called mournfully over their heads.

Lord Arthur gave a slight shrug. "Why not, my friend? Why not? Nothing at all amusing has happened to me since I was last in Cornwall."

Although it was quite cool within the thick walls of Tregarthan Castle, Mr. Palfrey was sweating profusely. He had just endured a terrible scene with his stepdaughter.

He had arranged a meeting for her with the baron, he had sent her measurements to London's finest dressmaker so that she might appear to advantage in the baron's eyes—and then he had commanded her to dye her hair brown, hoping to make her look as much like that miniature of Maria as possible.

And Felicity, who until that point had been meek, crushed, and biddable, with the one exception of demanding to meet her intended, had thrown back her head and let rip. She told him what she thought of him. She accused him of destroying her mother's health. The Holbein he had lately purchased would have repaired the tenants' cottages on the whole estate and have left plenty to spare, Felicity had raged.

The whole unsettling scene had brought all Mr. Palfrey's fears about Bessie rushing back. What if Bessie had shown that will to the captain or to anyone on board? The cunning captain would soon see the value of it. Why had he not killed her?

But Mr. Palfrey realized that, although he did not mind a rap if she died on board of cholera or typhoid, he could never bring himself to directly take away another's life.

And those jewels! He was weary with searching the castle from cellar to attic. There was a long portrait in the morning room of the late Mr. Channing's mother. She was in court dress and had a diamond tiara on her head and a fine diamond collar about her neck.

Where were the Channing jewels?

He was so upset, he decided he would have to brave the baron's possible fury. The marriage settlement had been signed. Surely the baron would not back out of the marriage just because Felicity had red hair and was not precisely handsome.

All his worries swirled about his head and settled down to focus on Felicity. With that redheaded jade out of the way, he could begin to lead an orderly and carefree life. He had not worried so much about Bessie for some time. It was Felicity's vulgar scene, which had rattled him so much, and brought all the fears rushing back.

Felicity, on the other hand, felt better than she had since her mother's death. That scene, that angry release, had brought all her confidence rushing back. She rode out with Miss Chubb, contemptuously dismissing the escort of a groom as "one of Mr. Palfrey's more harebrained ideas."

After they had gone a little way from the castle, Felicity slowed her pace to an easy amble and told Miss Chubb all about that splendid confrontation. "I know red hair is not fashionable," said Felicity, "but to ask me to dye it!"

"He is very anxious for this marriage to take place," said Miss Chubb.

"Pooh! It will not take place should I take this baron in dislike."

"Have you thought," said Miss Chubb cautiously, "that should you decide not to marry the baron, and tell Mr. Palfrey about those jewels, he might simply claim them. He has every legal right."

"John will swear to the codicil."

"John Tremayne cannot read or write and has already sworn he did not sign anything. And Bessie has disappeared."

Felicity frowned. Somehow, she had always regarded those jewels as an investment, as a dowry, as a trump card to slam down in front of her stepfather. How could she have been so naive?

Of course, she could take the jewels and run away. But what respectable jeweler was going to buy gems from a slip of a girl? And an unrespectable jeweler would belong to the criminal class and would no doubt pay her only a fraction of their worth.

"If I were a man!" she cried suddenly to the uncaring summer sky.

She thought of Lord Arthur Bessamy. He had probably never known what it was like to be pushed around in the whole of his pampered life. That was what gave him his great air of arrogance and command. That was why he chose friends of a lesser type of man, thought Felicity, her lip curling in contempt as she remembered the gentlemen who had stared at her through their quizzing glasses and had dismissed her as a bumpkin. Lord Arthur was no doubt as bad as Mr. Palfrey—only happy when in the company of toadies. She wished for a moment that she could see Lord Arthur again so that he might not go happily into his dotage without knowing how much she utterly detested him.

And yet . . . and yet, was he so very detestable?

He had kindly treated them to wine and had not turned a hair when she had said she was a tailor's apprentice. Damn Lord Arthur. Every time she thought of him, she became upset. Better to think of the baron.

Felicity, in her mind, had turned Lord Dawdy into a genial sort of fatherly man, a bluff, rough traveler who would no doubt be content to have her company during his declining years. Miss Chubb had, unwisely, done nothing to explode these dreams, thinking sadly that it was as well Felicity used her imagination to resign herself to her fate.

* * *

"Gad! Is this the place?" Lord Arthur slowed his team to a halt on a ridge and looked down in awe on Dawdy Manor.

It had started life as a single-storied Tudor dwelling. One hundred years later, a prosperous ancestor had tagged on a second story, much higher than the bottom one and with large windows ornamented with fussy stonework. It made the bottom of the building look as if it were slowly returning to the earth, an impression heightened by the vast quantity of ivy that clung to its walls.

"That's it," said Dolph. "Drive on, there's a good chap. I'm mortal sharp-set."

Lord Arthur began to wish he had not come. He sensed bad cooking and worse drains waiting at the end of the road. It was folly to indulge a whim, to run off to Cornwall because a certain Freddie Channing and his peculiar uncle had sparked his curiosity and imbued the whole of the duchy with an air of novelty, which he now thought it probably did not possess.

"If your uncle is as clutch-fisted as you say he is," said Lord Arthur, "and keeps country hours, then you will not have any dinner until four in the afternoon, and it's now only twelve noon."

It transpired that Lord Arthur was right. To Dolph's plaintive request for food, the baron replied sourly that they should have stopped for something to eat on the road. This business of luncheon was newfangled nonsense, and he would have nothing to do with it. But they would only have to wait a couple of hours to break their fast. Tea would be served at two o'clock when Miss Felicity arrived with her stepfather.

"It is as well I have arrived ahead of time," said Dolph. "Three days early, in fact."

"Decided I didn't need your help," said the baron. "Anyway, you don't like me, and you're only here because you hope I'll leave you something in my will."

"Yes," agreed Dolph with what his friend, Lord Arthur, considered a singular lack of tact.

But the baron seemed not in the slightest put out. He fished in his pocket and pulled out a miniature. "Here," he said, "cast your peepers on this beauty. That's my Felicity."

"Very beautiful," said Dolph. He glanced up at Lord Arthur to see his friend's reaction and was surprised by an odd sort of look of—could it be disappointment?—on that gentleman's face.

"Is it possible to have a tankard of something wet, baron?" asked Lord Arthur. "The roads were dusty, and I've a devilish thirst."

"There's water outside in the pump," said Lord St. Dawdy ungraciously. "My housekeeper will show you to your rooms, and I'll see you back here at two o'clock."

While they waited for the housekeeper, Lord Arthur studied his host. He was a wreck of a man. One swollen leg, encased in bandages, was propped up on a footstool. He wore a grubby stock and an old-fashioned chintz coat covered with wine stains and snuff stains. He had a large round head covered in a Ramillies wig, a relic of his youth that had not been powdered or barbered for some time and had lost a great deal of its curl. Wisps of it fell about his bloated face, which was covered in angry red pustules.

The housekeeper, a thin, old, bent woman, dressed

entirely in black except for an enormous starched cap, finally arrived and led them up a shallow flight of uneven stairs to their rooms.

Lord Arthur hoped the ceiling of his bedchamber would prove to be a little higher than those in the rest of the house, because he was tired of stooping, but it proved to be as low-ceilinged, sloping-floored, and dark as the rooms downstairs.

The air was stuffy and stale, and smelled of a mixture of bad drainage, damp, and woodsmoke. He walked over to the mullioned window and wrenched at the catch until he managed to open it. Warm, sweet air floated into the room on the slightest of summer breezes. He leaned his elbows on the sill and looked out.

The garden was a wilderness, but wild roses tangled and tumbled over everything in a riot of color. On a little rise to his left was a "ruin," one of those picturesque follies built in the last century when it was fashionable for the host to ask his guests, "Would you care to promenade to my ruin?" It had originally housed a hermit, one of the locals whom the late baron had paid with a lifetime's free ale to sit in it and look wise and ancient. The hermit had died of a liver complaint and had never been replaced.

It seemed that the baron did not have menservants, for when Lord Arthur, finding no bell, shouted out into the corridor for washing water, an old chambermaid eventually appeared, bowed down under the weight of two brass-bound cans. Lord Arthur relieved her of her burden and asked for towels. She looked frightened and puzzled and then said she would try to find some.

"What on earth does the baron use when he

washes?" demanded Lord Arthur, half-amused, half-exasperated.

"The master only washes at Michaelmas and Martinmas," said the maid slowly.

"But when he washes his face?"

"Well, most times, me lord, he jist uses the bed hangings."

She came back after about half an hour with two paper-thin towels and a bar of kitchen soap. Lord Arthur cursed himself for not having brought his own valet. His Gustav, an energetic Swiss, would at least have bustled about and seen to his master's comfort.

He made a leisurely toilet, changing into a blue morning coat with plaited buttons, buff skin-tight trousers, and hessian boots. His deft fingers molded a snowy cravat into the Oriental, and he brushed his thick black hair until it shone with blue lights.

He heard the sound of horses' hooves in the distance and went back to the window and looked out.

At first he could see nothing but a moving cloud of white dust on the sunny road. Then he could make out an open carriage with two occupants driven by a coachman with a liveried footman on the backstrap. He heard Dolph clattering down the stairs, but he stayed where he was, watching the carriage as it turned in through the gates and began to bowl up the drive. The gentleman passenger appeared, as it drew closer, to be a fussily dressed man with a petulant face. The lady held a parasol, so he could not see her face.

The carriage rolled to a stop beneath his window. The footman hopped down from the back, went round, and opened the carriage door and let down a small flight of steps and assisted the lady to alight. She held up the skirts of her flounced muslin gown, exposing one delicate ankle to Lord Arthur's gaze.

She furled her parasol, then stood and looked about her.

Lord Arthur caught his breath. For this young lady was not the fashionable beauty of the baron's miniature. She was slim, dainty, and very young—definitely under twenty, he thought. She was wearing the very latest thing in "transparent" hats—that is, a wide-brimmed frivolity of stiffened gauze through which her red hair gleamed like living fire.

With a feeling of excitement, Lord Arthur turned from the window and made his way downstairs.

"He is a bad landlord, this baron," said Felicity, stabbing the dry earth with the point of her parasol. "If he is as rich as you claim, why does he not put some money into his estates? He must be almost as clutch-fisted as you are yourself. But at least, Mr. Palfrey, it is only your tenants' houses you let go to rack and ruin. Lord St. Dawdy treats his tenants with equal unconcern, but also, unlike you, prefers to live in a slum."

Mr. Palfrey turned pink with outrage.

"Guard your tongue, miss. Oh, if only you had dyed your hair."

"My dear stepfather, is it not well over time that you told me why you wanted me to dye my hair brown?"

Mr. Palfrey looked sulky. "I sent the baron Maria's miniature."

Felicity started to laugh. "Choice," she said. "Very choice, Mr. Palfrey. You have indeed gone and shot yourself in the foot. Let us go in and get this charade over with. I am relieved I am not what the baron expects. For I would not be married to a miser."

"You will behave, d'ye hear," hissed Mr. Palfrey, "or I will have you whipped."

Felicity paled slightly before the venom in his eyes and face. Then with a toss of her head, she moved before him into the darkness of the house.

The old housekeeper held open the door of the drawing room. Felicity went inside. Two gentlemen rose to meet her. The third remained sitting.

Felicity recognized Lord Arthur immediately. Her eyes, a polite blank, her face guarded, she curtseyed and then looked hopefully at Dolph—for surely her fiancé could not be that disgusting old wreck by the table.

"My dear," said Mr. Palfrey unctuously after Lord Arthur and Dolph had introduced themselves, "here is the baron."

"What's this?" cried Lord St. Dawdy, glaring awfully at Felicity. "Who's this red-haired chit? Where's my beauty?" And he pulled out the miniature.

"You have been sent the wrong picture," said Felicity, striving for calm. Why did Lord Arthur have to be here? She could easily have extracted herself from this painful situation quite calmly had he not been looking at her with those amused eyes. "That is a portrait of my elder sister Maria, who married the Bishop of Exeter last year."

"Oh, it is, is it?" raged the baron. "Well, let me tell you, Palfrey, the wedding's off. You cheated me. You promised me a beauty, not . . . not this."

Long afterward, Lord Arthur was to wonder why he had not remained silent. As it was, he said in

235

glacial tones, "My dear baron, your wits must be wandering. Miss Felicity has a very rare beauty— quite out of the common way."

Mr. Palfrey brightened. All might yet be saved. "Perhaps, my lord," he said with a genteel cough, "you might consider marrying my stepdaughter yourself. Her dowry is . . ."

"You vulgar little man," said Lord Arthur in tones of contempt. "Why don't you take her to Smithfield Market and put her on the block? How dare you treat any gently-bred miss in this common manner?"

"Now you mention it," said the baron with a wicked gleam in his eyes, "she's quite a filly. Walk up and down a bit."

"I am not in the ring at Tattersall's," said Felicity, gritting her teeth. "No!"

"Suit yourself," said the baron. "Sit down. Sit down. Here's tea."

The little company arranged themselves round the table at which the baron was seated. It was not covered by a cloth, and because of the sloping floor it sloped as well so that guests and hosts were kept busy catching their teacups as they slithered to the edge of the table. The tea was weak and tasted dusty. The sandwiches looked as if they had been made some time ago, which indeed they had, the baron having entertained the vicar to tea two days before. He had ordered the housekeeper to keep the leftovers so that they might be served up again.

For once, Mr. Palfrey and his stepdaughter shared the same thought, but for different reasons—if only Lord Arthur Bessamy were not present!

Dolph began to chatter nervously about the Prince of Wales's recent appointment as Regent and of the splendid party he had given in Clarence House. The baron's brooding and lustful eyes fastened greedily on Felicity's rounded bosom.

Felicity began to feel faint. The room was close and warm, and the smell from the baron was something quite dreadful. Lord Arthur's exotic and unexpected presence upset her. If only he had kept quiet! Then the baron might have continued to be disappointed in her appearance.

But one thing sang in her head. She would not marry the baron, no matter what happened. She had dreamed of an old and fatherly man, not this horrible, gross creature. She longed for Miss Chubb's reassuring company.

While Dolph rattled on, Mr. Palfrey and the baron exchanged looks and then the baron winked and nodded his head. Mr. Palfrey heaved a sigh of relief.

There was a smash as Dolph's teacup hit the floor. The rest were managing the peculiar exercise of leaving their cups for a moment, then catching them just as they slid to the edge of the table.

"You'll pay me for that," said the baron. "Why don't you take Miss Felicity outside for a walk, Dolph?"

Dolph jumped to his feet. Glad to escape, Felicity rose and accepted his escort. Lord Arthur followed them out.

They walked in silence through the sunny, tangled grounds, Felicity in the middle, Dolph on her left hand, Lord Arthur on her right. It was so bright, warm, and rose-scented that Felicity wondered bleakly why some of the sunshine could not light up the darkness in her soul.

"The weather is very fine, is it not?" ventured

Dolph. Felicity lowered her parasol and withered him into silence with a look of contempt. Here she was, about to be forced into marriage with an old lecher, and this London fool was babbling on about the weather.

"Tell me," said Lord Arthur, "have you ever met a tailor's boy called Freddy Channing?"

"No, my lord," said Felicity loftily, as if such a person were definitely beneath her notice.

"Strange," he murmured, "in such a sparsely populated region, I felt sure you would know everyone hereabouts."

"I do not go about much," said Felicity repressively.

"Perhaps after your marriage . . ."

"You are in error. I shall not marry, and certainly not Lord St. Dawdy."

"But your stepfather seems very determined."

"So am I," said Felicity. "What brings you here, Lord Arthur?"

"I came with my friend, Mr. Godolphin. He is Lord St. Dawdy's nephew."

"And do you visit your uncle often, Mr. Godolphin?" asked Felicity.

"From time to time," said Dolph, struggling with his stock, which appeared to have become very tight. He thought this ferocious little girl was proving to be an uncomfortable companion.

"You do not seem to be enjoying our company," said Lord Arthur, a mocking note in his voice.

"No, I am enjoying none of this," said Felicity. "If you had not found it necessary to praise my appearance, Lord Arthur, then the baron might have cried off."

"I am sorry, but then, I do find you beautiful,

Miss Channing," said Lord Arthur, a caressing note in his voice.

Felicity's face flamed, and she rounded on him. "But you do not like me well enough to marry me," she said evenly. "Only to praise me in order to bait the baron."

"I say," bleated Dolph helplessly.

Lord Arthur looked down at Felicity with something approaching dislike. He had been toying with the idea of doing something in the way of knight-errantry. He had been considering proposing to Felicity himself, for she fascinated and intrigued him, and he was sorry for her.

But because of his wealth and his title, he was used to people toadying to him quite dreadfully. No one had dared to criticize him for years, except perhaps Dolph, but Dolph was a man. Men who were friends were allowed the occasional remark—but females, never!

"I should not for a moment consider marrying such a broad-spoken termagant as yourself," he said, and then wondered why he immediately felt like a coxcomb. "After all," he went on quickly, "I have no intention of marrying anyone. Dolph here will tell you I am a confirmed bachelor."

"Then, since you have damned me as broad-spoken," said Felicity, smarting with hurt, "I shall go further and tell you that I do not like you one little bit, Lord Arthur. You are making a bad day horrible by your sneering and indifferent presence. I wish . . . I wish you would go away."

He looked down into her furious eyes and saw all the pain and fear there. His heart gave a lurch. "Miss Felicity," he began, but another aged and bent maidservant of the baron's materialized at his elbow to say that Mr. Palfrey was ready to leave and would Miss join him immediately.

Felicity ran off in the direction of the house.

"Phew!" said Dolph. "I pity my uncle if he marries that shrew."

"I behaved badly . . . very badly," said Lord Arthur curtly. "We are going to ride over to Tregarthan Castle tomorrow so that I may make my apologies."

"But, I say . . ." said Dolph.

"There's going to be a storm," said Lord Arthur, beginning to walk back toward the house. "Clouds are piling up in the west."

Dolph looked over to the west and saw a mountain of great, fat purplish clouds climbing up the sky. Then he hurried to keep up with his friend's long strides. Lord Arthur was behaving in a most odd way. Dolph began to wish he had not brought him.

Felicity and her stepfather each kept an icy silence on the road home. A great crashing peal of thunder rolled about the turrets of the castle as they entered the polished gloom of the hall.

Felicity was about to stalk off up the stairs, but Mr. Palfrey seized her arm in a vicious grip and started to call for his servants.

The butler, the footmen, the maids, and the housekeeper came hurrying into the hall.

Mr. Palfrey addressed them, still keeping tight hold of Felicity. "My stepdaughter has disgraced me," he cried. "She is to be whipped!"

Felicity managed to pull free, and stood white-faced, looking at the servants.

Not one of them moved to obey the command.

They stood stolidly, in a circle, looking at their master.

"Whip her!" screamed Mr. Palfrey, beside himself with rage.

Anderson, the butler, cleared his throat. "No, sir," he said. "That we cannot do."

Another great peal of thunder rocked the castle.

Mr. Palfrey stood panting with rage. He could not fire them all. And he longed for their admiration and respect.

He forced a laugh. "I was a trifle overset," he said with a ghastly grin. "Get to your room, Felicity. I shall talk about this later."

Felicity flew up the stairs, straight to the nursery, where she threw herself against Miss Chubb's well-upholstered bosom, and cried her eyes out. At long last, she calmed down and gave Miss Chubb the whole story.

"I have no hope," said Felicity with a pathetic little sob. "No hope at all."

"I have been talking to John Tremayne in your absence," said Miss Chubb. "We have a plan. We are going to run away tonight—you, me and John."

Chapter Five

"This is mad. Quite mad," said Felicity Channing with a shiver. "How on earth did I agree to such a mad scheme?"

She stood on top of the cliffs, a little way away from the castle, while the wind howled and the thunder crashed and tumbled about the heavens. A blinding sheet of lightning showed a rope tied firmly to a rock. At the end of that rope hung John Tremayne, staging the "accident."

Miss Chubb's plan was being put into operation. The governess had been planning it for some time, never really thinking they would do it, until Felicity's distress forced her to turn the dream into reality. The terrible weather conditions were perfect, and they might never again have such a good chance.

Felicity had left a note to say she could not bear to marry the baron and was running away with Miss Chubb and John Tremayne. They had packed one trunk with their clothes and another trunk that John had hurled over the cliff after opening the lid and removing some of the clothes.

They had gone to a part of the cliff that had fallen into the sea, the land broken away by the force of the deluge. John had noticed this section of cliff before and knew it was only a matter of time before it gave way. Before he had let himself down over the cliff, he had dug deep gouges in the earth with his hands to make it look like someone had desperately tried to save themselves. Now he was leaving torn scraps of clothing caught in rocks and bushes on the way down, as well as some of the contents of the trunk.

As abruptly as it had started, the storm stopped, the huge black mass of clouds sailing away overhead on a high wind. The moon shone down.

"Oh, hurry," breathed Felicity.

But John's head was already appearing back over the cliff's edge. He clambered onto safe ground, untied the rope, and picking up the heavy jewel box, slung it up onto his shoulder. Felicity and Miss Chubb followed behind, carrying the trunk with their clothes between them.

Felicity and Miss Chubb were dressed in their men's disguises. The going over the soggy, uneven ground was rough, and Felicity was beginning to wish they had thrown this trunk over the cliff as well when they came to a carriage and horses, hidden behind a thick stand of trees.

"Where did you get this carriage, John?" whispered Felicity, trying to stop her teeth from chattering.

"I went over to Baxeter and bought the lot. I gave a false name, of course."

"But where did you get the money?"

"Miss Chubb's savings," said John.

"So, you had all this planned for some time," said Felicity.

"Don't talk," said John urgently. "Get in the carriage."

Felicity and Miss Chubb climbed in. The carriage dipped and swayed as John climbed up on the box.

"Where are we going?" asked Felicity as the carriage moved off.

"Falmouth," said Miss Chubb. "It is at Falmouth that you take up your new identity."

"New . . . ? Miss Chubb, you had better start at the beginning and tell me what you and John have planned."

"Well, it's like this," said Miss Chubb, her voice sounding oddly youthful and excited. "Although I hoped the baron might not prove to be too terrible, I heard no good of him at all. I remembered how you said we could escape with the jewels, but we would always be hunted and not be able to live openly, even though Mr. Palfrey did not know we had them. So John and I decided that if we could get you to London, and give you a new identity—one that would be grand enough, and would allow you to sell the jewels openly to the best jewelers—you could have a Season and find a gentleman to suit you."

"And who am I going to be?"

"Princess of Brasnia."

"That is ridiculous. There is no such place."

"There is now," said Miss Chubb cheerfully, "for I have just invented it. I used to attend the London Season in the old days with my charges, before I came here to work for the Channings. It always struck me as odd that English society was almost ignorant of geography. So, you are now Princess Felicity of Miadaslav, which everyone knows is the capital of Brasnia, and I am your companion, Madame Chubiski."

"We'll never get away with it," said Felicity, wondering whether to laugh or cry.

"Rich people can get away with anything," said Miss Chubb cynically. "I have enough of my life's savings left to make a good show of it in Falmouth. You see, in our disguises, we arrive at the best inn, The Pelican. We say we are the menservants of the princess. She has just arrived in the country, and we demand the best rooms and a private parlor. Once in our rooms, we take off our disguises and put on our best clothes, and you, my dear, drape yourself in some of the showiest of the jewels. We stay two nights and then begin our journey to London—a slow, triumphal progress. By the time we arrive, everyone will know of our coming. Also, everyone will know that the princess did not come with money but with a great quantity of jewels, which she will trade from time to time."

"I feel sick," said Felicity dismally. "What if I am exposed as a fraud? I shall leave my head on a chopping block at the Tower."

"Now, that is only for impersonating an English peer or pretending to be any member of the English aristocracy," said Miss Chubb comfortably. "The only way you could face prosecution is by using a fake title to get money out of people, which of course you will not do."

"I don't like it," murmured Felicity. "Good heavens! Lord Arthur Bessamy and his friend, Mr. Godolphin. What if I should meet them? They will recognize me."

"You just stare at them haughtily and ask them why they are insulting you by suggesting you might be some country girl. Besides, the whole country will know of our deaths tomorrow. By the time the Season has begun, everyone will have forgotten about us—even Lord Arthur."

"But Lord Arthur struck me as being clever. I am sure he will know there is no such place as Brasnia."

"Nonsense! I assure you the English aristocracy cannot even point out on the globe the places they visited during the Grand Tour."

"But what . . .?"

"Miss Felicity," interrupted Miss Chubb sternly. "Do you want to marry the baron?"

"Oh, no," said Felicity. She sat nervously biting her fingernails, a most unladylike habit, as she worried about her future. But even if the masquerade should only last a short time, what fun she might have. What independence!

In the darkness of the carriage, Felicity began to smile. "Madame Chubiski," she said, "you are a wonder!"

"I have a very vivid imagination," said Miss Chubb ruefully. "Anyway, let us try to get some sleep before we arrive at Falmouth."

Dawn was gilding cobbles of the town of Falmouth when John Tremayne brought the carriage to a halt outside The Pelican.

"Here we go," muttered Miss Chubb.

Felicity could only stand by and listen in amazement as Miss Chubb, a hat pulled down to conceal most of her face, began to show a previously hidden talent as an actress. In heavily accented English, she grandly set about turning The Pelican on its ears.

The landlord, dazed at this unexpected visit of foreign royalty, set his servants running hither and thither. After all the fuss had died down and the best rooms had been prepared, he positioned himself in the yard to await the arrival of the princess. He was taken aback when Miss Chubb appeared, still in her male disguise, to tell him that the princess had slipped quietly into the inn during all the fuss, but would be prepared to give the landlord an audience, and thank him personally for all his efforts.

The landlord, Mr. Jem Peters, was told to attend the princess in half an hour.

Upstairs, as Miss Chubb darted in and hurriedly began to change into clothes suitable for a royal companion, Felicity threw open the lid of the iron box and blinked as diamonds, rubies, emeralds, sapphires, and gold flashed up at her.

"Oh, my goodness," said Miss Chubb. "What jewels! But we can admire them later. Put on the most showy, Miss Felicity, and quickly. The landlord will be here very soon."

Mr. Peters eventually scratched timidly at the door. John Tremayne answered it, hoping the landlord would not notice that the princess's attendant was wearing outdoor livery.

But the dazed landlord had eyes only for the little figure who sat on a chair by the window.

She was wearing a white silk gown. A diamond tiara blazed in her red hair, and a collar of huge diamonds was clasped about her neck. A rope of real pearls hung down to her waist and a yellow silk sash across her bosom was decorated with a large diamond and ruby brooch in the shape of a cross, which looked very much like an order.

"We are pleased to thank you," said Felicity in what she hoped was a foreign accent. "It ees varry comfortable here."

"Your Royal Highness," stammered Mr. Peters. "My humble inn is entirely at your service."

Felicity smiled and gave a stately little nod, and John Treymayne held the door open again to indicate that the brief audience was over.

Mr. Peters shot down the stairs, pausing only to grab his hat. The mayor must know of this, and the aldermen.

The beauty of this little princess spread like wildfire. All the long day, Felicity gave audiences, and feeling very guilty, received presents of flowers, fans, trinkets, bales of cloth, gloves, and even baskets of delicacies. She felt even more guilty when the mayor, in his full dress of office, bowed low before her and begged her to let the town of Falmouth have the honor of paying her stay at the inn.

But no one seemed to have the least interest in this mysterious country called Brasnia. No one even wanted to know on which ship the royal party had arrived. Felicity bowed and smiled, and accepted more presents, wondering what on earth was happening back at Tregarthan Castle, and if the infuriating Lord Arthur Bessamy ever even thought of her.

Lord Arthur Bessamy had slept badly. He had a nagging ache inside, which he put down to indigestion. The food at dinner had been abominable. The noise of the storm had been horrible. He found himself hoping Miss Felicity's boldness and courage ran to coping with storms, and the next minute damned her under his breath.

The ancient chambermaid creaked in and placed a small tray with a cup of weak chocolate beside the bed, and then drew back the curtains at the windows. Sunlight flooded the room. A fine day, thought Lord Arthur, clasping his hands behind his head and staring up at the frayed canopy. A good day for a ride to Tregarthan Castle. It was only decent, he told himself, to make every effort to dissuade Mr. Palfrey from forcing his young stepdaughter into marriage.

A flash of light on the canopy above his head caught his eye. He was just looking curiously at it and wondering what it could be, when the canopy gave way and a flood of water cascaded down all over his body.

He leapt from the bed with a yell. The roof had been leaking during the night, and the rainwater had formed a sort of lake on top of the canopy. Enough was enough. Dolph could stay if he liked, but he, Lord Arthur, was going to go straight to The Green Dolphin, after visiting Tregarthan Castle, and book a room.

Dolph, it transpired, had also suffered a similar disaster during the night, except that the flood had been in the closet where his clothes were hung. They had been dried in the kitchen at a scorching fire and most of them had shrunk.

He was a tubby pathetic figure at the breakfast table, with his waistcoat somewhere up about his chest, and his breeches strained to the point of indecency over his fat thighs.

He gloomily agreed to leave with Lord Arthur, although he tried to protest over the proposed visit to Tregarthan Castle. Miss Channing, pointed out Dolph, had seemed well able to look after herself, and it was folly to interfere in another family's affairs.

But the glory of the day when they finally set out

on the road, after leaving a note for the still-sleeping baron, restored both men's spirits. The air was full of lark song, and clouds of little blue butterflies performed their erratic ballet over the strips of fields.

"I didn't really want his money all that much," said Dolph.

"He may still leave it to you."

"Not if you succeed in putting an end to this proposed marriage, he won't," pointed out Dolph.

"I hadn't thought of that," said Lord Arthur, nodding as a laborer at the side of the road saluted them. "Better write and tell him it was nothing to do with you."

"On a sunny day like this, it all seems rather grimy—waiting for someone to pop off to get their moneybags."

Lord Arthur smiled but did not reply. He slowed as they approached a farmer driving a cart and asked the man if they were on the right road to Tregarthan Castle. It turned out they only had a mile to go.

Soon the fantastic turrets of the castle rose above the moorland.

"What a place!" exclaimed Dolph. "Like something out of one of those romances. I wonder if they have ghosts."

"If they have, they must be very modern ones. The castle is a folly, I believe, and quite new."

They bowled across the drawbridge under the portcullis, which glittered wickedly above their heads in the bright sunlight. "I wonder if it works," said Dolph, staring up at it. "I wouldn't want that thing to come crashing down on my head."

The inner courtyard was empty. No servant came

running to hold the horses or to announce their arrival.

Lord Arthur and Dolph got down and tethered the horses to a post and then rang the huge bell that stood beside the brass-bound door.

After some time, the door creaked open. Anderson, the butler, stood looking at them sorrowfully.

"Lord Arthur Bessamy and Mr. Godolphin present their compliments to Mr. Palfrey and wish to speak to him," said Lord Arthur.

The butler bowed, turned, and walked away. After some hesitation, the two men walked into the hall.

The butler disappeared into a room at the end of the hall. There came the murmur of voices, and then they could hear Mr. Palfrey's voice suddenly sharp and querulous, saying, "Get rid of them. The disgrace of it all. They must not know."

Lord Arthur raised his thin black brows. "Now, what is it that we must not know? Come, Dolph." And with Dolph following at his heels, he walked straight into the room from which they had heard Mr. Palfrey's voice emerging.

Mr. Palfrey let out an outraged squawk at the sight of them.

"Gentlemen," he said, shredding a handkerchief between his fingers, "normally I would be delighted to entertain you, but I am not well, not well at all."

"We are in fact come to call on Miss Channing."

"Sleeping," said Mr. Palfrey. "Can't be disturbed."

And then they heard cries from the courtyard and the sound of many feet.

All of them stood stock still, waiting. A group of

251

servants entered with a man in gamekeeper's dress heading them.

"It's terrible, Mr. Palfrey," said the gamekeeper. "Just terrible."

"Let me just see these gentlemen off the premises," began Mr. Palfrey, but one of the servants behind the gamekeeper cried out, "They be dead. All of them. Miss Felicity, Miss Chubb, and John Tremayne."

Like a puppet with its strings cut, Mr. Palfrey dropped into a chair. "You must be mistaken," he gasped. "Where? How?"

The gamekeeper took over. "We went to look for them like you told us to, seeing as how Miss Felicity had run away, her not wanting to marry the baron." Mr. Palfrey waved his hands in a despairing way, and turned a ghastly smile on Lord Arthur as if to imply that the gamekeeper was talking nonsense.

"We come to a bit o' the cliff along to the north," went on the gamekeeper, "and where the cliff had fallen into the sea during the storm, we found where they'd fallen over."

"I must see this. I cannot believe it," babbled Mr. Palfrey, now too overset to worry about Lord Arthur.

They parted to let Mr. Palfrey through, and Lord Arthur and Dolph followed close behind.

As they walked along the cliff, Dolph found himself muttering prayers. If only it were not true. Lord Arthur was clay-white, and his face was set in stern lines.

It was too beautiful a day for tragedy, thought Dolph, in a sort of dazed wonder. The sun still shone, the birds still sang, and the air was sweet with the smell of salt and wildflowers. Tufts of sea pinks grew along the top of the cliff, looking almost shocking in the gaiety of their summer display.

Finally the party came to a halt.

"Look," said the gamekeeper.

Mr. Palfrey, Lord Arthur, and Dolph looked at the jagged, broken cliff, and the pathetic marks of hands that had clawed into the mud.

"And look down!" cried the gamekeeper. They edged to the broken lip of the cliff. There was a dry bit of turf to the side of the mud. The three men lay down and looked over.

A piece of blue muslin, as blue as the sky above, was caught on a jagged rock halfway down above the foaming sea.

"That was the dress she was wearing," said Lord Arthur in a bleak voice. "She was wearing a blue gown when we saw her."

As they watched, a boat nosed round an outcrop of rock far below. The men in it were scanning the water. One of them cried out, and they put their grappling irons over the side.

"Oh, no," muttered Dolph. "I'm going to be sick."

But they watched as the grappling irons took hold. A black thing was being pulled up out of the water. It was a trunk with limp, soaking clothes dangling over the side. The men hauled it on board and continued their search.

Still they lay there and watched and watched as the men below searched the restless waves.

At last Mr. Palfrey got shakily to his feet. "It had nothing to do with me!" he cried. "It was not my fault."

A crowd of locals had gathered. As Dolph and Lord Arthur got to their feet as well, one of the yeoman farmers, a free man whose lands did not depend on Mr. Palfrey, bent down and picked up a clod of earth and threw it straight at Mr. Palfrey.

"Murderer!" he cried.

"Stop them," shouted Mr. Palfrey to his servants, as more missiles followed.

But his servants stood in a circle, staring at him with accusing eyes.

With a frightened little cry, Mr. Palfrey set off running, as stones and turf whistled about his ears.

Dolph reached up and put a plump hand on his friend's shoulder. "Come away, Arthur," he said. "There is nothing we can do for the girl now."

While Mr. Palfrey was fleeing back to the castle, it was still early morning in Williamsburg, Virginia, and Bessie Redhill was at last up for sale. It had been a nightmare of a voyage, as they were driven off their course time after time by storms and gales. Then the good ship *Mary Bess* had limped into Bermuda for repairs and to take on fresh water before finally setting off south for Virginia.

For a good part of the journey, Bessie had hung between life and death. She had been suffering from severe concussion, as well as from the overdose of laudanum; she had been violently seasick and then had contracted a fever. She sometimes thought that the only thing keeping her alive was her burning thirst for revenge. Before she had come down with the fever, she had begged a scrap of oilskin from one of the crew and had sewn that precious will up in it. She had not confided in the captain. The captain was an accomplice of Mr. Palfrey's in her eyes.

Virginia was about the worst place where she could have been sold. The decline of white servitude had begun some twenty years earlier because of the vast numbers of black slaves. Why buy a white, who must be granted his or her freedom and paid wages in seven years' time, when a black worked for nothing for life? White servants were rated cheap, and their masters often tried by various ruses to prolong their servitude. In other states, Connecticut, for instance, there were no laws under which a runaway could be recovered. But there were such laws in Virginia and a recaptured servant could have years added onto that seven-year term.

At least Williamsburg was far better than anything Bessie had expected. She had imagined with dread a wild and barren land. A former governor, Francis Nicholson, had planned "a green country town." Williamsburg was divided into half-acre lots on which dwellings were set back, by law, six feet from the street. The impression was one of prettiness, elegance, and cleanliness.

Bessie, standing on the auction block, envied the Scottish servants. Provided they had a clan name like Macleod or Macdonald, one of their American clansmen would buy them on the spot and set them free.

She was too tired and dazed to really know what was happening. The fierce heat on her uncovered head was making the colorful scene swim before her eyes.

"Get down, Redhill. You're took," barked the auctioneer. Numbly, Bessie stepped down.

A black manservant in neat livery said, "Follow me. Mistress is waiting in the carriage."

Bessie stumbled after him through the crowd.

A lady was sitting in an open carriage. "This servant shall travel with me, Peter," she said to the servant.

The manservant opened the carriage door and, catching the eye of his mistress, helped Bessie in.

"I am Mrs. Harrington," said the lady, unfurling her parasol. "Walk on, Peter." The carriage moved off.

"I must make one thing clear . . . Bessie, is it not? I am the wife of the Reverend Hereward Harrington. We do not believe in slavery. You will commence your duties as a kitchen maid until you are trained in our ways and may rise to a better position. You will be paid wages and you may, as from this moment, consider yourself a free woman."

"Thank you," whispered Bessie, tears of weakness and relief beginning to roll down her cheeks.

"You poor woman. You will be nursed back to health before you start your duties. Now, do not try to talk. Here, take this parasol, and keep the sun from your head."

Bessie looked into Mrs. Harrington's kind eyes and then at the saucy silk parasol with the ivory handle that she was holding out to her, and for the first time in her life, Bessie Redhill began to believe in the existence of a merciful God.

Dolph had felt more cheerful the next day after a good dinner and an excellent night's sleep on a comfortable bed at The Green Dolphin. But his feeling of well-being did not last long. It transpired that Lord Arthur had rented a rowing boat and expected his friend to accompany him to help in the grim search for the bodies.

The sea was mercifully calm, but the landswell was enough to make Dolph begin to wish he had not dined so well. Hatless and in his shirt-sleeves, Lord Arthur rested on the oars for a moment.

"One of the fishermen told me, Dolph, that bodies are often swept out to sea. I fear they may end up in France."

"In that case . . ." said Dolph hopefully.

"But we shall continue our search. Perhaps a little farther out." Lord Arthur began to pull away from the cliffs with powerful strokes.

Lord Arthur was the youngest son of the Duke of Pentshire. He was very rich. All of which, thought Dolph queasily, should have made the noble lord remember what was due his position. He should have hired men to search and men to row.

"There's something white in the water," shouted Lord Arthur suddenly, making Dolph jump. "Over on the port side."

Dolph looked over to his left and saw a white shape bobbing on the water. "Oh, dear," he moaned.

"Get the grappling iron," ordered Lord Arthur, shipping the oars.

Dolph closed his eyes while Lord Arthur fished in the water. When he opened them again, Lord Arthur was standing in the rocking boat, looking thoughtfully at a sopping white dress on the end of the iron. "More clothes," he murmured.

He took the dress off the iron and then sat down in the boat, shook it, and held it up. It had been a pretty little dress with a flounced yoke and a flounced hem.

"How tall would you say Miss Channing was?" asked Lord Arthur.

"Little under my height," said Dolph, surprised. " 'Bout five foot four inches, I would guess."

Lord Arthur studied the dress again, and then looked thoughtfully at the cliff.

"You know what puzzles me, Dolph," he said. "Clothes have been found. But you would have expected trinkets to have been lying down on the cliff, or floating about—fans and ribbons, shoes and laces." He picked up the oars and began to row powerfully back in the direction of the little harbor below the village.

"Where are we going?" asked Dolph.

"Back to Tregarthan Castle. I want a look at that trunk that was recovered."

"Why?"

"Oh, just an idea."

When they got to the castle, it was to find that the portcullis was indeed a working one, for it was firmly down at the end of the drawbridge.

"Mr. Palfrey must be frightened of a hanging," said Lord Arthur.

There was a bell beside the portcullis of the same size as the one beside the front door. He gave it an energetic peal and waited until a servant ran out to answer its summons.

"I was to let no one through, my lord," said the servant, "and Mr. Palfrey is lying down, having taken a sleeping draft."

"I merely want to examine the trunk of clothes that was found yesterday," said Lord Arthur. "Raise this silly contraption immediately."

He and Dolph waited while the servant ran to fetch three of his fellows, and it took the combined efforts of the four to winch up the portcullis.

Anderson, on hearing their strange request,

turned them over to the housekeeper, Mrs. Jessop, who took them up to Felicity's bedchamber.

"I had not the heart to take the clothes out and wash them," said Mrs. Jessop, beginning to cry.

"Do not distress yourself," said Lord Arthur. "Leave us for a little. We shall take our leave shortly."

Watched by Dolph, Lord Arthur carefully took items out of the trunk and studied them. Two strangely small dresses, an old pair of shoes, an ugly tartan scarf, four old bonnets—not the sort of styles one would expect the modish Miss Channing to wear.

A slow smile curled Lord Arthur's lips. Then he began to laugh.

Dolph looked at his friend in shock and outrage.

"Have you gone mad?" he cried.

"No, no, my friend," said Lord Arthur. "I fear the tragedy has overset my nerves." He put the clothes back in the trunk, slammed down the lid and left the room, with Dolph trotting at his heels. Grief took people in very strange ways, thought Dolph.

Princess Felicity of Brasnia made a triumphal exit from the town of Falmouth. The mayor bowed and a military band played a brisk march. Felicity waved graciously until the people and the town were left behind.

"Thank goodness that is over," said Felicity, leaning back with her head against the squabs. "It is amazing, this business of being a princess. No one will let us pay for anything. I feel such a fraud."

"They all enjoyed themselves," said Miss Chubb. "But the one thing now troubling me is our lack of servants. It will look odd if we do not hire some.

You have only John. And, oh, how difficult it will be with a retinue of servants. We shall have to play our parts even in our sleep.

"Perhaps our John will think of something," continued Miss Chubb. "He is proving to be amazingly clever."

"Well, at least I can take this heavy tiara and collar off for a little," sighed Felicity. "Do you really think Mr. Palfrey will believe us dead?"

"Bound to," said Miss Chubb bracingly. "It all went off splendidly."

Felicity frowned. "I am a little worried about the things we left in that trunk that went over the cliff. I put in some of my gowns that I had not worn since I was about thirteen. But I could not bear to throw away my lovely new clothes—you know, the ones Mr. Palfrey ordered from London to make me look attractive to the baron."

"But you did sacrifice the nicest one, the blue one that John tore a piece from and left on that rock."

"So I did," said Felicity cheerfully, "and no one would think for a moment that I would deliberately destroy such a lovely gown as that.

"As far as Mr. Palfrey is concerned, I must be as dead as mutton. I am glad I wrote to my sisters from Falmouth to tell them the truth—only not the bit about my going to London as a princess—only that I am alive and will soon be in touch with them. They will not betray me to Mr. Palfrey."

Now it was Miss Chubb's turn to look worried. "Even when they do not find the bodies, there will be some sort of service, and your sisters, bless them, are none of them actresses. Mr. Palfrey may notice their lack of grief."

"Not he," said Felicity. "He will be so busy covering up his own lack of grief that he will not notice how anyone else is behaving!"

Chapter Six

They were waiting in the wings, waiting to go on stage, waiting for the Season to begin.

London's curiosity about this new princess had not yet been satisfied. Princess Felicity's servants had announced to all callers that Her Majesty had no intentions of meeting any social engagements until the start of the Season.

Felicity wanted to be well prepared and to have her servants thoroughly coached. For very few of them were real servants. On their journey to London, John Tremayne had sought out the local candidates for the "royal" household. All, except the butler, had been found guilty of minor crimes, usually caused by near-starvation. The promise of a good home, wages, and an escape from prison had bound them all to secrecy. But they had to be trained. Housemaids and chambermaids were easily dealt with. The cook, a motherly widow whose only crime had been to steal a loaf of bread, had to have time to learn to produce large banquets, and she, in turn, had to train the kitchen staff. The butler, an ex-burglar turned religious maniac, had been chosen by John, who had found him emerging from prison after having served his sentence. That he had not been hanged was a miracle. It was his appearance that had struck John immediately. He was fat and pompous and had a cold and quelling eye. Apart from the fact that the new butler, Mr. Spinks, was apt to treat John Tremayne as if he were an angel specially sent down from heaven to rescue him, Spinks studied his new duties assiduously and soon showed a talent for running the household. He was apt to fall to his knees and pray loudly when upset, but so very little upset him these days that Felicity felt they could well put up with this little eccentricity.

They had been very lucky. They had not even had to search for a town house. On their journey toward London, a lord who had heard of their arrival in his area had promptly offered them the hospitality of his country mansion, and, on their departure, had insisted they take the keys to his town house in Chesterfield Gardens, Mayfair, saying that he did not intend to visit London during the next Season, and the house would otherwise be standing empty.

John Tremayne found illiteracy an increasing disadvantage and so, with Felicity's permission, he visited the Fleet Prison until he found a suitable schoolmaster, paid his debts, brought him back to Chesterfield Gardens, and set him up as resident tutor. The schoolmaster's name was Mr. Paul Silver. He was a thin, scholastic gentleman in his fifties with a head of beautifully fine, silver hair to match his name.

Felicity and Miss Chubb often donned their men's disguises and went out to walk about London and stare in awe at all the marvelous goods in the shop windows. After the quiet of the Cornish coast, London was a bewildering kaleidoscope of movement and color and noise. Light curricles and phaetons darted here and there like elegant boats surmounting the rapids of the London streets. Heavy stagecoaches rumbled along Piccadilly, but even their majestic sound was almost drowned out by the grumbling roar of the brewers' sledges and the government lottery sledges, grating over the cobbled streets. Carts piled high with fruit and vegetables from the nurseries of Kensington headed through the West End on their way to Covent Garden market.

Then there were so many varieties of street performers. Felicity saw, after walking along only a very short stretch of Oxford Street, a man with a dancing bear and a drum; an organ grinder with his monkey perched on his shoulder; a man with a trumpet announcing in a hoarse voice between fanfares that a six-headed cow could be seen for only two pennies; a pretty girl in a spangled dress who danced to a tambourine; and three acrobats throwing one another about.

It was all this whirling excitement of being in the capital that eased Felicity's guilty conscience. The boredom of those long, empty days in Mr. Palfrey's scrubbed and polished castle seemed even more horrible in retrospect than even Mr. Palfrey himself. She had not read the newspapers but had gathered from Mr. Silver, the tutor, who read most of them, that the story of her "death" had even reached the London papers, with a subsequent short paragraph saying that a memorial service had been held, during which Mr. Palfrey had been seen to weep copiously. "More onions," thought Felicity cynically.

The famous London jewelers, Rundell and Bridge, had heard of Princess Felicity. Not only had they bought some of the jewels for a fair sum, but had embarrassed Felicity dreadfully by sending her a present of an exquisite turquoise and gold necklace. She had had a dressmaker's dummy made of her figure and sent to the top dressmakers. Felicity did not want them to call at Chesterfield Gardens and gossip about herself and her staff until she felt they were all coached and ready for closer scrutiny.

But as the novelty of London began to die down, Felicity would often find herself thinking of Lord Arthur. He was thirty-one, she discovered, and had never married. Although he had the reputation of being a hardened bachelor, it evidently did not deter the debutantes and their mamas from hoping that one day he would drop the handkerchief. She knew she was bound to meet him during the forthcoming Season, and that thought sent little shivers of anticipation through her body.

It was Mr. Silver's job, apart from his teaching duties, to study the social columns and compile a list for Felicity of all the people she ought to entertain, along with a list of eligible bachelors.

She was looking down the latest list he had compiled one day when she said with a little laugh, "I see a Mr. Charles Godolphin here. I have met him and I hope to goodness he does not recognize me and only thinks the similarity in looks between the princess and a certain Miss Channing is extraordinary. But I see no mention of his friend, Lord Arthur Bessamy."

"Ah, no," said Mr. Silver, reaching for a pair of steel-rimmed spectacles and popping them on his nose. "Let me see ... I have my old lists somewhere about. I struck him off about a month ago. Yes. Here we are. Lord Arthur Bessamy became engaged to Miss Martha Barchester of Hapsmere Manor in Suffolk."

"I would have thought," said Felicity in a voice that to her own surprise trembled a little, "that Lord Arthur would never marry."

"So did everyone else," said Mr. Silver. "There is a piece about him here. I find the more scandalous newspapers a great source of information. He bought a place near Hapsmere Manor last winter. You see, as the younger son of a duke, he has money but no responsibilities or lands, and heretofore evidently lived only in town. But he appears to have decided to settle in the country. The Barchesters are his neighbors. A very suitable marriage. The Barchesters are a very old family—Norman, I believe." He broke off and looked up in surprise. Felicity had gone.

Felicity went quickly to her room and put on her male disguise. Then she slipped out of the house and walked rapidly in the direction of Hyde Park. A pale sun was shining, and the air was sweet with the heavy smell of hawthorn blossom. It was the fashionable hour, and carriages flew past round the ring with their elegant occupants, the ladies wearing the thinnest of muslins despite the chill of the spring day.

She stood watching them, thinking she did not really belong anywhere. She would never return to Tregarthan Castle, and yet she felt she did not belong in this world of giggling, overly sensitive ladies who practiced how to faint with as much assiduity as they practiced the pianoforte. And the men, with their flicking handkerchiefs and their fussy mannerisms, their rouged faces and cynical assessing eyes, repelled her.

And then a thought struck Felicity, a thought

that seemed to lighten her depression. "I do not need to marry. I can enjoy one Season, go to all the balls and parties, and perhaps even see the Prince Regent. And then I can sell some more jewels, and dear Miss Chubb and I can retire somewhere quiet in the country and settle down." It was a very comforting thought, and only a little nagging wonder about this Miss Barchester came into her mind to diffuse that comfort. What was she like, this paragon, who had succeeded where so many others had failed?

Miss Martha Barchester was like a Byzantine ivory. She had a long, thin, calm face and a long, thin, flat-chested body. Her thick brown hair was parted at the center and combed back into two wings to frame her white face. She was twenty-nine years old. Even her parents wondered what it was about this rather terrifying daughter of theirs that had attracted Lord Arthur.

It had taken a magic potion to make Titania wake from her sleep and fall in love with an ass. But at a certain stage in their lives, even the most hardened rakes and confirmed bachelors need no magic to make them fall in love with the first woman they see. All at once, they are simply hit with an overwhelming desire to get married. The period is usually brief and violent, and they usually emerge from it to find themselves married to a woman they do not know the first thing about.

And so it was with Lord Arthur. First had come the desire for a home and lands. Those being acquired, it followed that he must have a hostess for his home, and a mother for his heirs.

He had to confess to himself that he thought very

267

often about Felicity Channing. He felt he had escaped from the folly that can often lead gentlemen of mature years to propose to chits barely out of the schoolroom. Perhaps the attraction Miss Barchester held for him was that she was everything Felicity was not. She was cool and poised, and never made a sudden or hurried movement or appeared to be swayed by any vulgar emotion whatsoever.

Farming was Lord Arthur's new interest and consuming passion. He felt it would be wonderful to return in the evenings to such a calm and stately creature as Miss Barchester. Their wedding was to take place the following year in the local church. On the acceptance of his proposal, Lord Arthur had taken Miss Barchester in his arms and kissed her. Her kiss had been cool, and her lips had been tightly compressed. But because his physical outdoors activities had taken care of his more earthy feelings, Lord Arthur saw nothing wrong in her virginal response. Ladies were not expected to be passionate anyway.

Dolph, calling on a visit a week before the Season was due to begin, thought his friend looked remarkably well—healthy, happy, and a trifle pompous. Lord Arthur drove him out round the estates and the village, and everywhere forelocks were tugged by men, and women curtsied.

"Quite feudal down here," remarked Dolph, privately thinking that all this adulation was not doing his rather arrogant friend one little bit of good. "Don't know but what I don't prefer that independent lot down in Cornwall."

"Cornwall!" said Lord Arthur sharply. "Have you been there recently?"

"No, never been back," said Dolph, casting Lord

268

Arthur a sideways glance. "M'uncle wrote to say he was crushed down with that girl, Felicity Channing's death, although I suppose it's only the gout as usual. Seems Mr. Palfrey has restored his reputation. Of late he's had whole fleets of boats dragging all around the coast for a sign of the bodies."

"Dear me," said Lord Arthur. "Left it a bit late, hasn't he?"

"Well, he says he won't rest until Felicity has had a Christian burial. The locals say he must have been fond of her after all."

"I wonder," said Lord Arthur.

"Talking of Miss Felicity, I had the most awful shock t'other week."

"See a ghost?"

"Yes, how did you guess! Have you heard of the Princess Felicity of Brasnia?"

"Of where? My dear Dolph, there is no such country."

"There is. Everyone's heard of it. Somewhere around Russia." Dolph waved a chubby hand to the east. "As I was saying, all London has been abuzz with talk of this princess. You know, her beauty is said to be rare and her jewels magnificent. She has been in residence all winter, but no one had seen her. But last week, she went out driving for the first time. What a sensation! People fighting and screaming to get a look at her. At first, I didn't see her face, I was so knocked back with the idea of someone wearing a diamond tiara in the middle of Hyde Park during the day. Then I looked at her properly and nearly dropped down in a faint. I could swear I was looking at Miss Felicity Channing."

Lord Arthur let the reins drop, and the horses slowed to an amble. "And . . . ?" he prompted.

"I rode straight up to her carriage and, like a fool, I cried, 'Miss Felicity! You are alive!' She had one of those double glasses, and she raised it at me and looked at me with such hauteur that I nearly sank. 'You were saying somezink?' she asked, and of course, I realized all at once it was not Miss Felicity at all. How could it be? I stammered out my apologies, and she bowed her beautiful little head with those fantastic diamonds flashing and burning, and she said, 'We are giffink a rout on the tenth. You come?' I gave her my card and swore that nothing would keep me away. I'm the envy of all the fellows. Everyone desperately fighting to see if they can get an invite, sending presents and poems, and lying in wait outside her door. Duffy Gordon-Pomfret even slept on her doorstep, but her butler, a most odd man, came out, shook him awake, read him the parable of the talents, then told him if he had nothing better to do with his time, he might be better employed in finding a job of work. Work!" said Dolph, shaking his head in amazement.

"I would like to attend that rout," said Lord Arthur slowly.

"I'm sure you would," said Dolph gleefully. "But you can't. All of London wants to get through her door."

"When did you plan to return to London?"

"Well, unless you're going to throw me out, I meant to get back around the eighth to collect a new suit of evening clothes from the tailor."

"Call on Princess Felicity," said Lord Arthur, "and tell her your friend, Lord Arthur Bessamy, wishes to meet her, and see what she says. I shall take you back to London myself."

Dolph looked huffy. It was not often he was invited to a rout from which his rich and elegant friend was excluded. Then his face lightened. "I'll ask," he said cheerfully. "But she's bound to refuse. Now, when am I to meet your beloved?"

"If you mean Miss Barchester, then say so," said Lord Arthur curtly. "This afternoon, at four, for tea."

Dolph could not believe his eyes when he was introduced to Miss Barchester. He thought she looked as if one of the marble statues on the terrace of her home had come to life. She even had thick white eyelids and a small thin-lipped curved smile.

Lord Arthur, teacup in hand, was standing by the fireplace talking to Mr. Barchester. Mr. Barchester was a plump, rounded man with a jolly face, and his wife, dressed in chintz, looked like an overstuffed sofa. How two such cheerful individuals could have produced the pale and chilly Martha Barchester was beyond Dolph. He found that lady was eyeing him with a gray, cold look. Her gaze dropped from his face and fastened on the area of shirt that was bulging out from under his waistcoat. Dolph always felt his clothes took on a nasty life of their own the minute they left the hands of his valet. His waistcoats tried to move up to his chin, his shirts separated themselves from his breeches, the strings at the knees of his breeches untied themselves, and the starch left all his cravats a bare half an hour after he had put them on.

His teacup rattled in the saucer as Miss Barchester began to speak. "Our fashions become more extreme, do you not think, Mr. Godolphin?"

"I . . . I . . ." bleated Dolph.

"Yes, it is bad enough when the ladies adopt styles of semi-nudity and wear their waistlines up around their armpits. Now, *I* have my waistline in the right place. I never follow fashion. Fashion follows *me*."

"Indeed," said Dolph. "I fear London fashion cannot have had a chance to see you, Miss Barchester, for all the ladies adopt the high waistline."

"Are you contradicting me by any chance, Mr. Godolphin?"

"No, no. I . . ."

"Good. Male fashions are every bit as ridiculous. Why do you think so many men aspire to be Beau Brummells when they do not possess either his air or figure?" Her pale eyes fastened again on Dolph's area of shirt.

"Blessed if I know," said Dolph crossly.

"London fashions," pursued Miss Barchester, "are distasteful to me."

"Then, it's as well you ain't in London," pointed out Dolph. He took a swig of tepid tea and eyed her over the rim of his cup.

"But I shall be. I am thinking of persuading Mama and Papa to take me for a few weeks. I aim to . . . how do the vulgar put it? . . . *cut a dash*."

Dolph looked at her curiously. Could she be funning? Or was her vanity so great that she really thought she could impress society?

But she was his best friend's fiancée. He forced himself to be gallant. "Well, by Jove, Miss Barchester, the ladies of London will be agog to see the fair charmer who has stolen the heart of such a hardened bachelor as Lord Arthur."

"Exactly," said Miss Barchester sweetly.

Dolph blinked in amazement. This engagement to one of the most eligible men in the country had quite gone to Miss Barchester's head. What on earth did Arthur see in the creature?

At that moment Lord Arthur strolled over to join them. "You are making me jealous, the pair of you," he teased. "I saw you, rattling away there like old friends."

Miss Barchester at his arrival on the scene became quiet and submissive. The wings of her brown hair shone softly in the candlelight, and the smooth drapery of her old-fashioned gown fell in straight lines from her waist to the floor like a medieval garment. She kept her eyes demurely lowered.

"By George!" thought Dolph, alarmed. "Arthur thinks he's got himself a meek, old-fashioned wife."

At least Lord Arthur could be counted on not to ask his friend's opinion of Miss Barchester or discuss her in any way. And that was a mercy. For Dolph knew he would be hard put to it to think of anything good to say about her.

On the road home, he remembered the princess's rout and at the same time decided to do his uttermost to secure Lord Arthur an invitation. Anyone who saw the fairy-tale princess could never look with any complacency on such an antidote as Martha Barchester.

Mr. Palfrey told his butler, Anderson, to tell the boatmen to be ready to set off at dawn the next day. The search must go on.

Anderson bowed and then went off to confide in Mrs. Jessop, not for the first time, that they had been mistaken in Mr. Palfrey. He must have loved

Miss Felicity very much the way he searched and searched for her poor body.

Once he had gone, Mr. Palfrey darted to the door of the library and turned the key in the lock. Lovingly, he spread the castle blueprints out on the table before him.

In her haste, Miss Chubb had forgotten to shut the door of the priest's hole properly. Some months after Felicity's "death," Mr. Palfrey, in one of his feverish hunts for the jewels, had noticed the crack in the wall and had discovered the hiding place. And that is how he had found the plans. He had searched the priest's hole thoroughly and had found the high ledge and the clean square in the dust that showed that a large box had recently rested on it.

From there he had deduced Felicity must have had the jewels in hiding and had taken them with her. It stood to reason that she would not have dared run away without any money. So the Channing jewels must have gone to the bottom of the ocean and, at least they, unlike the bodies, could not have been carried out to sea.

That was the reason he had the sea under the part of the cliff where they had gone over, searched each day so thoroughly.

He rolled up the plans and decided there were really no more undiscovered hiding places outside the priest's hole and the hidden staircase.

He would go to sleep early so as to be ready to continue the search early in the morning.

As soon as a red stormy dawn lit the heaving gray sea, Mr. Palfrey was there in an open boat piloted by the yeoman who had shied a piece of turf at him, but who now respected this man who had proved his love for the lost girl. Mr. Palfrey had grappling irons and various contrivances for hooking down into the water. It was the lowest tide they had had for some months, and Mr. Palfrey saw with rising excitement that there was an almost uncovered stretch of sand at the base of the rock. "Over there!" he cried to the yeoman, Mr. Godfrey.

"Better be careful," shouted Mr. Godfrey as the open boat scraped its keel on the sand. "Won't be much time."

"The spade! The spade!" shrieked Mr. Palfrey excitedly to one of the other men. "No, no. Give it to me. I shall dig myself."

"Look the way he do dig!" exclaimed Mr. Godfrey. "He'll cut any corpse in half, spearing down like that."

They waited patiently, watching Mr. Palfrey's feverish efforts, half-amused, half-touched.

Then Mr. Palfrey felt his spade clink against something. He threw the spade aside, and, kneeling down on the watery strip of sand, began to scrape at it with his fingers.

With a triumphant cry, he held up a necklace. The fierce red sun shone on it and it burned with all the fire of priceless rubies.

Mr. Palfrey gave a hysterical laugh. "The Channing jewels!" he shouted. "I have found them. Oh, God, at last. After all these weary days of searching."

The men in the boat watched him, stricken. "You mean," said Mr. Godfrey at last, "that that's what you was looking for all along? You didn't give a rap for Miss Felicity."

But Mr. Palfrey, ecstatic with delight, turned the flashing stones this way and that.

Then a cloud covered the red sun. It took all the light out of the day. It took all the fire from the sea.

And the necklace in Mr. Palfrey's hand turned into cheap glass, as if the Cornish pixies had played some hellish trick on him.

He had betrayed himself. The men in the boat looked at him with eyes of stone.

Mr. Godfrey seized the oars and shoved off.

"You can't leave me," shouted Mr. Palfrey. "The tide has turned."

"Then, swim, you liddle ferret," shouted back Mr. Godfrey.

Mr. Palfrey stood there until the boat had disappeared round the point. Then, shivering and whimpering and cursing Felicity under his breath, he began to swim.

It was as well he remembered the secret staircase—for the castle was under siege by angry locals at the front. It would be a long time before he dared poke his nose out of doors again.

On the eighth of April, Mr. Godolphin had a very odd audience with Princess Felicity of Brasnia. For he did not see her.

He was ushered into a stately drawing room by an unnerving sort of butler who fixed Dolph's tubby figure with a haughty look, and said, "Make not provision for the flesh to fulfill the lusts thereof," before bowing and stalking out.

A terrifyingly massive woman, with a hand outstretched, came down the room toward him. She was dressed from head to foot in black velvet. "I am Madame Chubiski," she announced.

Dolph bowed. "I am come to see Her Royal Highness."

"Vot is eet you vish?" said Madame Chubiski.

"I wish to speak to Princess Felicity about it, if I may."

"What is it?" came a light young voice from behind a carved screen in the corner. Madame Chubiski waved an imperious hand, and Dolph approached the screen cautiously.

"I am come to beg a favor, ma'am," he said timidly. Then he thought of Martha Barchester, and his voice strengthened. "My friend, Lord Arthur Bessamy, would be deeply honored if you could manage to issue him an invitation to your rout."

There was a long silence, and Dolph felt almost as if the temperature in the room had dropped by several degrees. He turned about and smiled winningly at Madame Chubiski, who glowered back.

At last, the princess's voice came to him very faintly from behind the screen. "Yes," it said on a little sigh. "He may come."

"Thank you," said Dolph, bowing to the screen.

"You've got what you want, young man, so take your leave," growled a robust English accent behind him. Dolph started. But there was still only Madame Chubiski in the room—who had sounded so foreign only a moment before.

But he felt he had better leave quickly before the princess changed her mind.

When he had gone, Miss Chubb said ruefully, "Did you really have to give him an invitation?"

"Yes, this way Lord Arthur will not suspect anything," said Felicity, emerging from behind the screen. "Besides, there will be such a crush, the poor man will have difficulty in seeing me at all! And I am supposed to be dead, remember? You know, Miss Chubb, I am so tired of this silly accent

I have to affect, and your own is beginning to come and go alarmingly. Why do we not start to speak proper English—and praise our good Mr. Silver for effecting the transformation?"

"Good idea," sighed Miss Chubb. "Do you know. I live in terror of being confronted by some fool who claims to speak Brasnian!"

Chapter Seven

"I speak excellent Brasnian, Your Royal Highness," said Lord Arthur Bessamy.

Felicity carefully concealed all the dismay she felt. Miss Chubb had made a dreadful mistake. There must be a wretched place called Brasnia after all. Around them, the glittering cream of London society ebbed and flowed in the pink and gold saloon at Chesterfield Gardens.

With a thin little smile, Felicity said, "I do not wish to speak Brasnian. It would shame my tutor, who has been at such pains to teach me excellent English."

"You are a credit to him, ma'am," said Lord Arthur, smiling down into her eyes. "One would suppose, to listen to you, that you had been speaking English all of your life."

Felicity glanced nervously sideways, looking for help. But Lord Arthur was a leader of society and so was being allowed a few moments alone with her, a courtesy afforded to very few. Miss Chubb's tall, feathered headdress could be seen at the far end of the room. "She should not have left me alone for a minute," thought Felicity, irritation now mixing with her fear.

She took a deep breath. "May I congratulate you on your forthcoming marriage, Lord Arthur?"

"Thank you," he said stiffly. "You are well-informed."

"I make it my business to be so."

"Tell me, do you know much of our country?"

"No, not much."

"You have never been to Cornwall, for example?"

"I believe I have."

Lord Arthur leaned closer to her and murmured, "Where in Cornwall exactly?"

"Why, I arrived at Falmouth."

"His Royal Highness, the Prince of Wales, the Prince Regent," cried Spinks loudly.

Silence fell on the room. The guests parted to form two lines.

Lord Arthur bowed and moved away. Felicity began to shake. This was flying too high! She had not invited the Prince, would not have dreamed of doing so. But Prinny went anywhere in society he wanted to go, invited or not.

How very fat he is, was Felicity's dazed thought as the corpulent royal figure moved toward her.

Miss Chubb tried to edge around the outside of the room to get to Felicity. Why had the Prince come this evening of all evenings? wondered Miss Chubb frantically. It had all been going so splendidly, and there had been no flash of recognition on Lord Arthur's face when he had first seen Felicity. And she looked so young and regal, standing in a white silk gown embroidered with tiny diamonds and seed pearls and with the Channing diamonds glittering and flashing.

Felicity sank into a deep curtsey before the

Prince Regent. "This is a very great honor," she said.

"On the contrary," said the Prince, "it is you who do England honor. We have never been to Brasnia."

"No, sire?" said Felicity in a shaky voice.

"Can't go anywhere with Boney strangling Europe. Brasnia, now let me see . . . ?"

The color flew from Felicity's cheeks. She was about to be found out.

The Prince shook his heavy head so that the curls of his nut-brown wig bounced and shook. "We have never heard of the place. Where is it?"

"On th-the R-Russian b-border," stammered Felicity.

"And your father, King . . . ?"

Felicity closed her eyes in despair. She tried to think up some lie, something to say—anything! But it was as if terror had frozen her brain.

"I fear Princess Felicity is overcome with the heat of the rooms," came Lord Arthur's voice. "Let me explain, sire. Brasnia is a small principality, not a kingdom. It is a very small country, about the size of Luxembourg. Princess Felicity's brother, Prince Georgi, is the ruler." His voice dropped to a boring monotone. "It is mainly an agricultural country, growing maize-corn, wheat, and oats in the fertile plains surrounding the River Zorg. The river itself produces excellent fish, one of which is the curpa, a local delicacy that has to be cleaned by experts because it contains a deadly poison. Anyone who is unlucky enough to take this poison endures severe fits of vomiting and the flux prior to death. What is even more peculiar is that the vomit is bright green in color . . ."

"Gad's Oonds!" cried the Prince, holding his fat

281

stomach. "Enough! Enough! We do not wish to hear another word."

He nodded curtly to Felicity and hurried away. His voice carried back to Felicity and Lord Arthur. "What on earth is up with that fellow, Bessamy? Used to be a wit. Now about the biggest bore in Christendom. We are bored. We wish to leave . . ."

The Prince's petulant voice faded away as he disappeared out the door of the saloon with Lord Alvanley at his heels.

Felicity looked up nervously at Lord Arthur. Either he had gone raving mad or he had mistaken Brasnia for another country—or he knew the truth about her. And Felicity was very much afraid he knew the truth.

But he merely smiled, a charming smile that lit up his eyes. "You must have accepted many social engagements for the weeks to come, ma'am."

"N-no," said Felicity breathlessly. "I mean, I have not accepted any invitations as yet. Madame Chubb . . . iski is going to look through them all and choose which ones we should attend."

"So, you had not planned to go to the balloon ascension at the Belvedere Tea Gardens in Pentonville tomorrow afternoon?"

"No, my lord."

"Then, you and . . . er . . . Madame Chubiski must allow me and Mr. Godolphin the pleasure of escorting you there tomorrow at three o'clock."

"S-so soon? I had planned to stay quietly at home for a few days."

"Why not, Your Highness? Such poor creatures as myself and Dolph will not be able to come near you once you start the social round. Besides, we could talk about that fascinating country, Brasnia."

"Yes, we could, couldn't we," said Felicity miserably. She felt he was teasing her, playing with her. Well, she might as well accept his invitation and learn whether he planned to expose her.

"We shall be pleased to go with you," she said.

He looked down at the downcast little face under the flashing tiara. "Then, I shall go and tell Dolph the good news." He stepped back from her, bowing as he went, but before other guests could close in round Felicity, he suddenly said, "My goodness. How I have misled our Regent. I was thinking of another country altogether. I fear I had forgotten that I do not know Brasnia at all."

Felicity looked at him sharply, but could see no guile or mockery on his face.

He bowed again.

At that moment, Miss Chubb finally reached Felicity's side. She hoped nothing had gone wrong. But Felicity was already talking to some of the other guests. She looked relaxed and happy—happier than she had looked all evening. Miss Chubb smiled with relief. For one moment, she had thought Lord Arthur must have said something to upset Felicity, but it was obvious from Felicity's manner that nothing had gone wrong at all.

"No, I shall not wear that wretched tiara again during the day," said Felicity the following afternoon as she and Miss Chubb made ready for their outing. "It makes my head ache."

"But you are supposed to be a princess," protested Miss Chubb.

"I am sure princesses do not go about encrusted with jewels. Hand me that rope of pearls. They are magnificent enough on their own. And see, I have

283

this pretty straw bonnet ornamented with silk flowers. Surely that is smart enough for an afternoon occasion? Besides, the *Times* has been quite critical over the flamboyance of my dress." Felicity picked up the newspaper and read, "PRINCESS FELICITY, DESPITE HER BEAUTY, PORTRAYS A CERTAIN EASTERN EUROPEAN BARBARISM IN HER DRESS. TOO MANY JEWELS CAN ONLY BE CONSIDERED *NOT TASTY*. You see?"

"I suppose so," said Miss Chubb. "You seem to have been accepted by everyone. Lord Arthur worries me, however. All that nonsense he told the Prince Regent about Brasnia . . ."

"But I told you, he said he had made a mistake. I thought he might be mocking me, but there was no mockery or teasing in his face. All the same, it is as well to make sure, which is why I have not cried off."

"Do not waste too much time with Lord Arthur," said Miss Chubb anxiously. "He is engaged, or had you forgot?"

"I am not interested in him. He is too old and sophisticated and makes me feel uncomfortable. I have not told you, my dear Miss Chubb, but I have decided I do not wish to be married *at all!*"

Miss Chubb looked bewildered. "Then, what is all this agony about? All our preparations, not to mention the horrendous expense of that rout?"

"Well, I thought, you know, that after a few weeks of the Season, we should both retire somewhere in the country and be quiet and comfortable. But it would be pleasant to have a little fun first."

"Fun?" echoed Miss Chubb in a hollow voice. She remembered her own stark terror when the Prince Regent had been announced, the worry and fret over the preparations, the skeleton of exposure as an impostor always standing in the closet waiting to leap out.

"Yes, *fun*," said Felicity firmly. "Now let us finish dressing, or we shall be late. It is nearly three o'clock already.

But at three o'clock exactly, she and Miss Chubb descended the stairs just as Lord Arthur and Dolph arrived.

Felicity was wearing a blue muslin gown embroidered with little sprays of golden corn under a pelisse of gold silk. The Channing pearls glowed around her neck, and her jaunty straw hat was worn at a rakish angle on her red curls.

Miss Chubb, hoping to make up for Felicity's lack of display, was wearing a black velvet gown on which blazed an indeterminate number of jeweled brooches and pins. She was wearing a black velvet slouch hat that made her look like a highwayman.

She looked so worried and gloomy that Dolph, surveying the acres of black velvet, asked her whether she was in mourning.

"No, I am not," said Miss Chubb sharply, "and do not make personal remarks, young man." Dolph was crushed into silence. He bowed his way out of the house backward toward the carriage, tripped on the top step, and somersaulted onto the pavement. Spinks, the butler, picked him up, and said gloomily, "Pride goeth before destruction, and a haughty spirit before a fall."

"Where on earth did you find such a biblical butler, Princess Felicity?" asked Lord Arthur as he drove off.

"I hired him in London," said Felicity, and added primly, "I am fortunate in having such a God-fearing staff."

"What is the religion of Brasnia?"

Miss Chubb surveyed Lord Arthur with dislike. "Orthodox Brasnian," she said repressively.

"Oh, don't let's talk about Brasnia," said Felicity hurriedly, "or you will quite spoil my day. My poor country. So much turmoil. So many revolutions."

Miss Chubb emitted something that sounded suspiciously like a groan.

"By George," said Dolph. "Got the Jacobites over there as well?"

"You were not listening, Dolph," came Lord Arthur's amused voice. "Princess Felicity does not want to talk about Brasnia!"

While Felicity was on her way to the balloon ascension, a portly gentleman called Mr. Guy Clough, a Virginian tobacco planter, was landing at Bristol. After a decent bottle of port at a good inn, he began to feel much recovered from the rigors of the voyage. He fished in his pocket and drew out a small oilskin packet and looked at it thoughtfully. A minister, the Reverend Hereward Harrington, had given him the packet before he sailed and had told him the strange story of the repentant kitchen maid, Bessie Redhill. Mr. Clough debated riding over to this Tregarthan Castle and confronting this Mr. Palfrey with the evidence of his crime. But a man who could half kill a servant and have her transported might not hesitate to shoot any bringer of bad news. Also in his capacious pockets, Mr. Clough carried several letters of introduction to people in court circles. The Prince Regent was also Prince of Wales and Duke of Cornwall. Tregarthan Castle was in Cornwall. Then it would be better to get word to the Prince of the evil that had taken place in his duchy and let him cope with it. Mr. Clough was a lazy man and preferred to put any action off to the last minute. He returned the will to his pocket and proceeded to forget about the whole thing.

And, also on that afternoon Mr. Palfrey was arriving in London. Life had been too uncomfortable of late, hounded as he was by the locals and reviled by the servants. He had decided to take himself off to London. Time was a great healer. He would visit the opera, see some plays, and generally enjoy himself. By the time he returned to Cornwall, he was sure the whole business would have died down.

The Belvedere Tea Gardens were crowded to overflowing. Felicity was glad of the crowd and the noise. Lord Arthur had talked generally about ballooning, plays, operas, and the balls to be held during the Season. He had not mentioned Brasnia. But there was a feeling of waiting about him, and every time his eyes fell on Felicity, they lit up with amusement.

When they had set out, the weather had been fine. But now a thin veil of clouds was covering the sun and a chill wind had sprung up. Lord Arthur solicitously produced bearskin carriage rugs for the ladies.

The great balloon had been already filled before their arrival, and its huge red-and-yellow-striped shape rose well above the crowd. The pilot balloon was sent off, then two carrier pigeons. The crowd, who had become bored with the long wait—for it had taken over two hours to inflate the balloon—

cheered the pilot balloon and the pigeons wildly, glad to see some action at last.

Another cheer went up as the balloonist, a Mr. Peter Green, was escorted through the crowd. And another cheer rose as the cords were cut away and the gas-filled balloon began to rise.

Felicity's eyes filled with tears as she watched it. Lord Arthur's overwhelming masculine presence was making her extremely uncomfortable. She felt she would like to float away, like Mr. Green, far away from the troubles and worries of her masquerade, far up into the clouds, far away from staring, curious eyes. Lord Arthur silently handed her his handkerchief, and she stifled a sob and blew her nose. Silence fell on the crowd as the balloon began to climb and climb. When sand fell down from it like white smoke, the wind caught it, and it began to bear away steadily to the east. Felicity, like the crowd, watched and watched until the balloon grew smaller and smaller in the distance, until it finally disappeared into a bank of cloud.

And then all chaos broke loose. A crowd of people had been sitting on the wall of a house that bordered the tea gardens. As they swayed and shuffled to get down, the wall broke. There were terrific screams, and the crowd went mad. They pushed this way and that against the carriages. Lord Arthur's light curricle tilted wildly. Miss Chubb was thrown out, and Dolph leapt down after her to try to rescue her from the stampeding crowd.

Lord Arthur's groom was holding the horses' reins and brandishing his whip as he tried to keep the crowd clear of the terrified horses.

"We're going to be crushed with the carriage," cried Lord Arthur. He jumped down and lifted Felicity into his arms and began to force a way through the crowd, booting, kicking, and cursing as he cleared a path. He looked back over his shoulder. His groom had cut the horses free and was leading them safely away—just in time, for the curricle had been upended.

"Nearly safe," said Lord Arthur in Felicity's ear. His arms were tightly around her, and above one hand he could feel the swell of her bosom. Her light body seemed a throbbing, pulsating thing. The effect of holding her so close was making his head swim. He looked down at her. She had her arms tightly around his neck, but her eyes were downcast.

He carried her clear of the crowd and stood for a moment, filled with an overwhelming reluctance to free her.

"Look at me, my princess," he said softly. Felicity turned bewildered eyes up to his face and saw a light burning in those black eyes that made her tremble. He suddenly held her very tightly against him, smelling the light scent she wore, and feeling the trembling of her body.

Then he set her down, and, turning a little away from her, he said in a rough voice, "There is a posting house quite near here. If you can walk that far, I shall hire some sort of carriage to take you home. You had better hold my hand. There are a great many unsavory people about."

It would be all right to hold her hand, he thought. Any man, holding a beautiful young girl in his arms would have felt the way he did. But mere hand-holding was safe enough. He took her hand without looking at her. But a burning sensation seemed to run up his arm.

By the time they had reached the inn, he realized he wanted Felicity more than he had wanted any woman in the whole of his life. And he was engaged to be married.

"You are holding my hand very tightly," said Felicity in a small voice, "and we are well clear of the crowd."

He released her hand. He had meant to ask for a private parlor so that she might be able to have some refreshment before he escorted her home. But he knew he could no longer be alone with her without wanting to touch her.

In a loud voice, he demanded a carriage, any carriage, brushed aside the landlord's apologies that there was only a gig, said he would take it, and drove Felicity home, only breaking his silence once to assure her that Dolph could be trusted to protect her companion.

She was in such a nervous turmoil that she should have been glad to see him go, but when he swept off his hat and bent over her hand to kiss it, she found herself saying, "Shall we meet again?"

"Alas, I do not think so," he said. "I shall return to the country within the next few days." He half turned away and then swung round again. "But should you need any assistance, ma'am, tell Dolph, and he will know where to find me."

Felicity trailed into the house and stood for a moment in the hall, dwarfed by all the rented magnificence of tiled floor, soaring double staircase, and oil paintings in heavy gilt frames.

Mr. Silver, a book in his hand, came out of the library at the far corner of the hall.

"Good afternoon, ma'am," he said formally. Mr. Silver, like the rest of Felicity's employees, was well aware she was not a princess but always addressed her as if she were royal.

"Oh, Mr. Silver," cried Felicity. "Is Madame Chubiski returned?"

"Not as far as I know."

"She was with me at the balloon ascension when a wall collapsed. There was rioting, and we became separated. Lord Arthur's friend, Mr. Godolphin, was with her."

"Would you like me to go to Pentonville to look for her?" asked Mr. Silver anxiously.

"No, I am sure she is unharmed. But join me in the drawing room for some tea, and tell me how John Tremayne's education progresses."

They drank tea and Mr. Silver reported that John was progressing favorably, but both strained their ears for a sound of the return of Miss Chubb. When a footman came in to light candles, Mr. Silver rose to his feet. "With your permission, ma'am," he said, "I would like to go to Pentonville. I cannot feel easy in my mind. Madame Chubiski is rather shy and unused to London."

"Shy? Unused to London, perhaps, but I would hardly call Madame Chub . . . iski *shy*."

"I can assure you she is too gently bred a lady to be wandering about with a young boy of whom we know very little."

"Then, by all means go," cried Felicity.

Evening settled down over London. The parish lamps in the street outside were lit, and still Miss Chubb did not return.

At last Felicity heard the sound of a carriage stopping outside the house and ran out onto the front steps. But it was only Mr. Silver returning alone.

291

"I found no trace of her, ma'am," he said, his lined face anxious. "There were two people killed when that wall collapsed, and many more were injured in the rioting."

"Oh, what shall I do?" cried Felicity. "I cannot just wait here any longer, doing nothing. I know . . ."

She ran into the house and called for Spinks.

"Tell me," she said to the butler, "do you know the address of Lord Arthur Bessamy?"

"Yes, ma'am. When you told me to invite him to your rout, I made it my business to find out," said Spinks. "Lord Arthur lives in Curzon Street at Number 137."

"That is only around the corner," said Felicity, going into the drawing room and picking up her hat. Mr. Silver followed her in.

"You cannot go to Lord Arthur's house," he said severely. "That will not do at all."

"Abstain from fleshy lusts, which war against the soul," intoned the butler from the doorway, making them both jump.

"Oh, *Spinks!*" said Felicity crossly. "Do behave yourself. I am only going to call on Lord Arthur to enlist his help in finding Madame Chubiski."

"Then, I shall go," said Mr. Silver quickly. "For you to call at a gentleman's town house for any reason at all is just not done."

Mr. Silver departed quickly, and once more Felicity was left to wait.

In ten minutes' time the tutor returned with Lord Arthur. "You are fortunate, Princess," said Lord Arthur. "I was just leaving for my club when I received your message. I am sure you have nothing to worry about. Dolph is much more competent than he looks."

"But you do not understand," wailed Felicity.

"This is not like my companion at all. She may have been struck on the head; she may have been abducted. Dear God, she was simply covered in jewels . . ."

Lord Arthur studied her distressed face and then said gently, "I see you would feel better if you took some action. Your carriage is outside. Would you like to go back to the Belvedere Tea Gardens yourself and make inquiries? I am prepared to accompany you."

"Thank you," said Felicity.

"Then, I shall accompany you as well," said the tutor firmly. "You cannot go off alone with milord in a closed carriage."

Lord Arthur nodded, and the three went out into the carriage and set off again in the direction of Pentonville.

"Tell me, Mr. Silver," said Lord Arthur, "when you were making inquiries for Madame Chubiski, how did you describe her?"

In the light of the carriage lamps, Mr. Silver's scholarly face registered surprise. "Why, my lord, I gave a fair description. I asked if anyone had seen a handsome woman of regal bearing dressed in black velvet."

Felicity felt she could sense Lord Arthur's amusement. What was there in Mr. Silver's innocent description that he could possibly find funny?

They traveled the rest of the way to Pentonville in silence. When they arrived at the tea gardens, Lord Arthur put a restraining hand on Mr. Silver's sleeve. "Let me try by myself," he said. "You have already tried. I might have more success."

Before the tutor could protest, Lord Arthur swung open the carriage door, stepped down, and strolled into the tea gardens. Waiters were still clearing up the mess left by the crowd. He went up to the nearest one and said, "Hey, fellow, I am looking for a missing lady."

"Better have a good description," said the waiter sulkily. "All the world and his wife were here today."

Lord Arthur held up a guinea. "Now, think," he commanded, "and this guinea will be for you. I seek a squat, somewhat elderly lady wearing a slouch hat like a highwayman, dressed in black velvet, and covered in jeweled brooches and pins. She is accompanied by a tubby, cheerful man."

"Oh, them," said the waiter.

"You know them?"

"I seen 'em with me own eyes," said the waiter gleefully, reaching for the coin. "I was over at The Black Dog—over there—for a pint of shrub, and there they were, singing their heads off."

"And when was that?"

" 'Bout ten minutes ago."

Lord Arthur returned to the carriage. "I gather Dolph and Madame Chubiski are in the pub."

He turned and walked off in the direction of The Black Dog. Felicity and Mr. Silver scrambled out of the carriage and ran after him. They caught up with Lord Arthur just as he opened the door of the tap.

Felicity peered over his arm and let out a gasp. Miss Chubb was standing on a table in the middle of the room, belting out the third verse of "The Gay Hussar." She had a tankard in her hand and was being accompanied on the fiddle by a ragged Highlander. Dolph was sitting down at the table on which he was standing, looking up at her with rapt attention.

"Disgraceful!" cried Mr. Silver.

"Wait!" commanded Lord Arthur.

Miss Chubb finished her song to wild cheers and shouts and was helped down from the table by Dolph, who gave her a smacking kiss on the cheek.

"Well, Dolph," said Lord Arthur, strolling forward. "Having fun?"

"Oh, the bestest ever," said Dolph, peering at them blearily. "Let's have another chorus. Oh, with a tow, row, tow, row . . ."

"Silence!" roared Mr. Silver. "What have you done to this respectable lady, you . . . you rake? You have debased her. You have made a spectacle of her. By God, you shall answer me."

"I . . . I . . . I," babbled Dolph, goggling at the enraged tutor.

"No one is going to call anyone out," said Lord Arthur soothingly. "All outside. All home. Come along, Madame Chubiski. Your mistress has been very worried about you."

"Don't w-want to go home," hiccupped Miss Chubb. "Less have 'nother song."

"We'll sing all you want," said Felicity gently, "when we get home—you, me, and Mr. Silver. Come along; there's a dear."

Miss Chubb allowed herself to be led out, grumbling under her breath, "You said I was to have fun. Said everybody mush have fun."

"Yes, yes," said Felicity, throwing Lord Arthur an anguished look. What if the drunken Miss Chubb forgot she was companion to a princess?"

But as soon as the carriage moved off, both Miss Chubb and Dolph fell asleep, both snoring loudly, their heads rolling to the motion of the carriage. Felicity had Miss Chubb's full weight pressed against her, which in turn forced her to press against Lord Arthur. He smiled down at her and slid an arm about her shoulders. "There, have you more room now?" he asked, as his pulse leapt at the feel of her body.

"Yes," whispered Felicity dizzily.

Mr. Silver snorted, folded his arms, and glared grimly out the window.

As the carriage rattled through Berkeley Square, Lord Arthur found himself saying, "I have decided to stay a little longer in town. Would you care to come driving with me—say on Friday—in three days' time? I shall call for you at five."

He was not only a danger to this masquerade of hers, thought Felicity, he was a danger to her body, which seemed to be fusing hotly against the side of his own. When he smiled down into her eyes in that lazy, caressing way, as he was doing at that moment, he was a danger to her very soul. She must tell him she would never see him again. She must . . .

"Yes," said Felicity weakly. "I should like that very much."

It took the efforts of three strong footmen to carry Miss Chubb upstairs to her bedchamber and four maids to undress her and put her to bed.

Felicity sat by the bed and held her unconscious companion's hand and looked down at her face. "Oh, Miss Chubb," she whispered. "Why am I so very happy when it can all lead to disaster?"

Two days later Miss Barchester slowly lowered a copy of the *Morning Post*. It was a day old but carried a long description of the balloon ascension. The deaths of two people and the injuries of many only rated a small piece tagged on at the end. But the paragraph that riveted her attention went: THE AS-CENSION WAS GRACED BY THE PRESENCE OF THE DIVINELY FAIR PRINCESS FELICITY OF BRASNIA. LORD ARTHUR BESSAMY IS THE ENVY OF ALL MEN, AS IT WAS HE WHO HAD THE HONOR TO RESCUE HIS FAIR COMPANION FROM THE VULGAR AND RIOTING POPULACE, BEARING HER BOLDLY FROM THE SCENE IN HIS ARMS.

"Papa," said Miss Barchester. "Would it not be splendid to travel to London this weekend? Poor Lord Arthur must be pining away without me."

"Don't like London," grumbled Mr. Barchester. "And if Lord Arthur is pining that bad, he's only got to come home."

"Papa," said Miss Barchester, a steely note in her voice. "I have said I wish to go to London."

"Eh, what? Oh, very well, m'dear," sighed Mr. Barchester, who had long ago given up arguing with his strong-willed daughter.

Chapter Eight

It was the fashionable hour in Hyde Park. Spanking carriages darted along in the hazy spring sunlight. Dust rose from under hundreds of painted wheels. A carriage, particularly a lady's carriage, was not so much a means of transport as a sort of moving platform for the display of wealth. The more expensive the horses and carriage, the less used. No first-rate carriage horse was expected to travel more than fourteen miles a day at a maximum speed of ten miles per hour. In the wealthiest establishments, a large, expensive retinue of coachmen, grooms, and stable boys was maintained so that milady or milord could drive out in grand style for one and a half hours a day, six days a week. Some of the ladies, beautifully attired in the most expensive fashions of the day, drove themselves with a liveried groom sitting on the rumble seat behind, or, occasionally, following on horseback at a distance that was great enough to appear respectful but not so great that he could not afford immediate assistance with horse or carriage in an emergency.

All of the servants were dressed in colorful livery with gay vertically-striped waistcoats, though the footmen wore horizontal stripes indoors. Their coats were ornamented with silver or gilt livery buttons. The stable staff wore highly polished top boots, while the footmen wore white silk stockings that were usually padded out with false calves if their legs were thin. The coats of arms on the carriages were miniature works of art, and the whole display had an air of idle opulence.

But underneath all this atmosphere of languid elegance, each member of society was in deadly earnest. Mamas studied the faces of the eligibles for signs of interest while their daughters giggled and fluttered, and used fans and eyes to the best effect. Parvenus cut their country relatives dead as they fawned on the notables.

And Lord Arthur Bessamy was discovering, to his amazement, that one could make love to a lady with one's whole body without touching her or moving an inch. His eyes caressed the smooth pearl of her cheeks, his arms, correctly holding his cane and his gloves, were, in his mind's eye, clasped tightly about the slimness of her waist. His lips burned against hers in his imagination.

Felicity sensed a wave of sensuality emanating from him without quite knowing what it was, without knowing why her whole body seemed drawn to him, why her lips felt hot and swollen, and her breasts strained against the thinness of demure muslin.

Dolph was in good spirits, cheerfully waving to everyone he knew. Miss Chubb was downcast, her eyes red. Felicity had overheard Miss Chubb having the most terrible row with the tutor, but when asked about it, Miss Chubb had only sniveled dismally and refused to explain.

Felicity grew more uncomfortably aware of her own reddening cheeks and treacherously throbbing body. Lord Arthur was engaged to be married, she told herself firmly, and then wondered why that thought made her feel so depressed. When they stopped as a carriage full of Lord Arthur's relatives pulled up beside them, Felicity was glad of their company, glad to have Lord Arthur's disturbing attention taken away from her. But her peace of mind did not last long. One faded aunt with a long, drooping nose and pale, inquisitive eyes, said, "Bessamy, you have forgot your manners. Introduce us immediately to Miss Barchester—or do you mean to keep her away from us until the wedding?"

"This is not Miss Barchester," said Lord Arthur equably. "Allow me to present Princess Felicity of Brasnia." He then introduced his relatives to his party. Two aunts, two uncles, and two small female cousins bowed to Felicity and stared at her in open curiosity. "Charmed," said the inquisitive aunt who had been introduced as Mrs. Chester-Vyne. "Do you mean to reside in London for long, Your Highness?"

"Only for a few weeks of the Season, Mrs. Chester-Vyne."

"I am very good at geography and have a knowledge of the globes," piped up a small cousin with a face like a ferret. "I have never heard of Brasnia."

"Nor I," said Mr. Chester-Vyne, who looked remarkably like his long-nosed wife.

"Dear me," said Lord Arthur. "Never heard of Brasnia? I am ashamed of you all. It is quite lovely this time of year. They have the Festival of Manhood about now. All the young men in the villages are stripped quite naked and lashed . . ."

"Here, now!" protested Mr. Chester-Vyne. "Ladies present."

"Stripped naked and lashed," went on Lord Ar-

300

thur firmly, "until the blood runs. They are then sponged clean by the village maidens who are bare to the waist. A most touching ceremony, and quite colorful."

"Bessamy!" said Mrs. Chester-Vyne awfully. "We have no wish to have our sensibilities bruised by macabre tales of a barbaric race. Walk on, John."

The coachman raised his whip, and the relatives drove off with many a backward offended glance.

"By Jove!" said Dolph. "You have found out a lot about Brasnia."

"Not I," said Lord Arthur cheerfully. "I merely wanted to be shot of them. You must tell me the truth about Brasnia someday, Princess."

"Yes, I must, mustn't I," said Felicity in a small voice. She took little consolation from the fact that the encounter with Lord Arthur's relatives had had the same effect as a bucket of cold water being poured over her.

"Going to the opera tonight?" she realized Dolph was asking.

"We have no plans for this evening," said Felicity.

"Then, you must come with us!" cried Dolph. "Lord Arthur has a box, and you would be delighted to take the ladies along, now wouldn't you, Arthur?"

A vision of his fiancée's pale, cold face rose before Lord Arthur's eyes.

"You simply must come," he said. "Catalini is singing. We shall call for you at eight."

"I don't think I should attend," sniffed Miss Chubb. "I know Mr. Silver will be quite furious with me."

Felicity looked at her in surprise. "What on earth has our tutor to do with where we go?"

"Mr. Silver," said Miss Chubb heavily, "thinks I behaved in a most unladylike way after the balloon ascension."

"Then, I suggest you put Mr. Silver firmly in his place," said Dolph.

"Then, you will come?" asked Lord Arthur, saying to himself, just one more evening and then I shall behave myself.

Just one more time, thought Felicity.

"Yes," she said. "And do not look so worried, Madame Chubiski. I shall talk to Mr. Silver most sternly if he makes any trouble."

Mr. Palfrey was sitting at the toilet table in a room in Limmer's in Conduit Street, arranging his hair with the curling tongs, when a hotel servant arrived to say he had managed to secure Mr. Palfrey a seat in the pit at the opera.

Mr. Palfrey tipped him generously. His heart lifted. He was glad he had come to London. It was wonderful to be away from accusing Cornish eyes. Let the fuss die down, and then he could return to his search for the jewels. Somewhere at the bottom of the ocean, flashing fire in the green depths, lay the Channing diamonds. He had studied them minutely in that portrait at the castle until he felt he knew every stone.

As usual, he fussed a great deal over his appearance. Then he realized his cumbersome traveling coach was not suitable for a short journey, and besides, it was round in the mews and would take an age for the horses to be harnessed up. He debated whether to walk, but fear of arriving at the opera with muddied heels and possibly dirty stockings made him ring the bell and request a hack.

It was nine o'clock before Mr. Palfrey reached the opera house. The seats in the pit were simply long wooden benches, and they were already packed to capacity by lounging bucks and bloods by the time he arrived. He retreated from the pit and tipped an usher, who told him that a certain Sir Jeffrey Dawes would not be using his box that evening, and Mr. Palfrey would be able to use it.

Comfortably ensconced in a side box, Mr. Palfrey immediately raised his glass to his eye and scanned the house. He let out a slow breath of pleasure. This was where he belonged, not hidden away in some castle in Cornwall. Fans fluttered and jewels glittered on men and women alike.

His eye, magnified by the glass, traveled along the row of boxes opposite—and then he let it drop with a squawk and turned quite white under his paint.

"Shhh," hissed a dowager venomously from the box next to his.

Mr. Palfrey sat trembling. Surely that had been Felicity Channing in the box opposite!

Catalini's lovely voice soared and fell. She had the power to make all these society members look at her and listen to her—a rare feat, as most attended the opera because it was fashionable to do so and were usually not in the slightest interested in what was taking place on the stage.

Mr. Palfrey took a deep breath and raised his glass again.

It *was* Felicity! And a Felicity blazing and flashing with diamonds, the Channing diamonds that he had come to know so well from studying that portrait at Tregarthan Castle.

Now he shook with rage. Just wait until those servants and yokels in Cornwall heard about this!

He could barely contain himself until the opera was over. Two people had left Felicity's box, but she was still there herself with a male companion. Mr. Palfrey did not recognize Lord Arthur. What if they did not stay for the farce? It would be hard to reach them.

He rose to his feet and scurried along the corridor behind the boxes, shaking off the clutching hands of the prostitutes.

In his rage and confusion, he opened the doors of several wrong boxes before he hit the right one.

"Well, Felicity Channing," he said in a voice squeaky with outrage. "And what have you to say for yourself?"

The little figure with her back to him remained absolutely still. The man beside Felicity rose to his feet. Now Mr. Palfrey recognized Lord Arthur.

"What the deuce do you mean by this outrage?" demanded Lord Arthur, towering over Mr. Palfrey. "This lady is the Princess Felicity of Brasnia."

"Princess, my foot!" screeched Mr. Palfrey. "that's my stepdaughter, the minx. And those are my jewels."

He made a move forward to grasp Felicity's shoulder and then gasped as Lord Arthur pushed him back.

"Leave immediately," said Lord Arthur, "or I shall call you out."

"But that is my stepdaughter," cried Mr. Palfrey. "She pretended to die in order to trick me."

"Your Royal Highness," said Lord Arthur, "before I throw this fellow downstairs, do you wish to take a look at him? Perhaps he is a former servant of yours whose mind has become deranged."

"Servant!" shouted Mr. Palfrey. "Do I look like a servant?"

Felicity stood up and turned about.

She looked coldly at Mr. Palfrey. "I have never seen this man before in my life," she said steadily.

Her eyes were cold, and her expression haughty. All in that moment, Mr. Palfrey began to fear he had made a terrible mistake. The diamonds on her head and at her throat blazed with such a light that he could no longer be sure they were the Channing jewels, for their prismatic fire nearly prevented him from seeing the individual stones. But it was the beauty of the girl in front of him that took him aback. For Mr. Palfrey had convinced himself that Felicity was plain. In his memory, she was a drab little thing with carroty hair, not a regal goddess like the lady facing him.

He became aware that everyone in the house had begun to stare at Lord Arthur's box. Lord Arthur looked on the point of suggesting a duel.

"Pray accept my apologies," babbled Mr. Palfrey. "The resemblance is astonishing. You remember me, do you not, Lord Arthur? You were there when my poor Felicity was found missing."

Lord Arthur continued to regard him as if he were something that had crept out from under a stone, but Felicity spoke again, her voice strangely accented. "No doubt," she said, "grief over the death of your stepdaughter has sadly turned your brain." Then she sat down again with her back to him.

Stammering apologies, Mr. Palfrey bowed his way out.

"I have the headache," said Felicity. "I wish to go home."

"First Madame Chubiski with a headache, and now you," said Lord Arthur. "Come along. You are looking very white. Did that silly little man upset you?"

"Yes. What is all this about his stepdaughter, my lord? And do you know him?" Felicity trembled as she waited for his reply. For if he had not known she was an impostor before, surely he knew now.

"I met him once," said Lord Arthur in a bored voice. "His stepdaughter, also called Felicity, was running away from him. She fell over a cliff in a storm."

"How terrible!"

"Indeed, yes. I trust you do not have such dreadful happenings in Brasnia."

Felicity wanted to cry out to him that she was sure he had not believed one word of her nonsense, but there was still a little element of doubt, still a little hope that he believed her. She did not know why it was, but she felt uneasy and breathless and uncomfortable with him, and wretchedly lonely and afraid the minute he went away.

In the carriage ride home, with Lord Arthur riding on the box—for it was a closed carriage and she would have been compromised had he traveled inside with her—Felicity wondered desperately what to do. Thank goodness Miss Chubb had felt ill and had left with Dolph. Those two would surely have made up Mr. Palfrey's mind for him. She would need to leave London. She would need to get away, for she was sure that if Mr. Palfrey saw her with Miss Chubb, then the game would be up. And it would be folly to continue to see Lord Arthur. He was engaged to another woman.

To her dismay, Lord Arthur followed her into the house in Chesterfield Street.

She turned in the hall to tell him he must leave and then her eye fell on the enormous gold-crested card. She picked it up. It was an invitation to the Queen's drawing room in two weeks' time.

"The royal summons, eh?" said Lord Arthur, reading it over her shoulder.

"Do I have to go?" asked Felicity.

"It would certainly look most odd if you did not."

Felicity thought rapidly. Two weeks. She would leave town in the morning and return just for the Queen's drawing room, and then Princess Felicity of Brasnia would disappear forever.

"Will you come driving with me tomorrow?" Lord Arthur asked.

"N-no," said Felicity. "I am unwell and need country air. We shall be leaving in the morning."

He went very still, and then he said lightly, "And where are you bound?"

"I had not decided."

"May I suggest Brighton? It is quite near London, and it is possible to find comfortable accommodation out of Season."

"Perhaps. Perhaps that would be best." Felicity held out her hand. "Good-bye, Lord Arthur," she said firmly. "I doubt if we shall meet again."

He took her hand in his and smiled down into her eyes. She looked up at him with a dazed, drowned look. He dropped her hand and then placed his own hands lightly on her shoulders. His mouth began to descend toward her own. He kissed her very lightly on the lips, and then raised his head and looked at her in a sort of wonder. His arms slid from her shoulders to settle at her waist, and then he jerked her tightly against him and kissed her again, and both went whirling off into a warm sensual blackness while the clock in the hall ticked away the seconds, and then the minutes, as his mouth moved languorously against her own and passion sang in his veins.

"Is that you, Felicity?" came Miss Chubb's voice. And then her heavy tread sounded in the corridor upstairs.

They broke apart, breathing heavily as if they had been running.

"You shouldn't have . . ." whispered Felicity.

"Brighton," he said firmly. "Go to Brighton."

He turned on his heel, and then he was gone, leaving Felicity standing in the hall, her hand to her lips.

The council of war went on long into the night. John Tremayne was to ride ahead to Brighton and rent a house and then ride out to the first posting house on the road outside Brighton to give them the address. Felicity's dressmaker's dummy was to be sent to the dressmaker with the promise of double money if a court dress were made and ready in time for the Queen's drawing room.

"Brighton is certainly an excellent place to choose," said Mr. Silver. "What made you choose Brighton, ma'am?"

"Oh, I don't know," said Felicity vaguely. For she was sure there would be protests if she said the suggestion had come from Lord Arthur. Mr. Silver considered Lord Arthur and his friend, Dolph, to be corrupt and evil men who encouraged ladies like

Miss Chubiski to drink to excess, and Miss Chubb herself had become more and more worried about Felicity and Lord Arthur. Felicity had not told her about the embrace. Miss Chubb, she knew, would be deeply shocked.

Lord Arthur made ready to go out in search of Dolph the next day to see if that young man would fancy a trip to Brighton. But the fact that he was engaged to be married to Miss Martha Barchester was forcibly brought home to him when his footman handed him a letter. With a sinking heart, he recognized the seal. He crackled open the parchment. The letter was from Miss Barchester, saying that she and her parents were staying at the Crillon Hotel. Lord Arthur would no doubt be delighted and amazed to see her so soon. His presence was expected at the earliest moment.

He took a deep breath. He must disengage himself from Miss Barchester at the earliest opportunity. But what excuse did he have? That he had never been in love before? That he had never believed in such an emotion? That his heart was not in London, it was on the road to Brighton?

But did poor Miss Barchester deserve to be jilted because she no longer held any magic for him? That calmness and stillness of hers that had so attracted him now seemed dull. He felt like a cad.

He took himself off to the Crillon Hotel, preferring to walk, and so absorbed in his worries that he did not notice he was being followed.

Mr. Palfrey had had a quite dreadful night. He had dreamed of Felicity, and on waking, the dream face and the face of Princess Felicity merged in his mind and became one. He had to see her again, just to make sure. By diligently questioning the hotel staff, he obtained the princess's address in Chesterfield Gardens and set out there at eleven in the morning while the streets of the West End were still quiet. But after half an hour of surveying the house from the opposite side of the street, he had an uneasy feeling there was no one at home.

At last, summoning up his courage, he crossed over and hammered on the knocker. He could hear the sound of his knocking echoing away into emptiness inside. A butler came out of the house next door and stood on the step and looked up and down the street.

"Tell me, my good man," called Mr. Palfrey, "is the princess in residence?"

"Her Royal Highness and all her staff left early this morning," said the butler.

Mr. Palfrey stood, baffled. He had been all set to take some sort of action to ease his mind. There must be something he could do.

"Do you know where they have gone?" he asked.

The butler shook his powdered wig.

Mr. Palfrey paced restlessly up and down. Then his face cleared. She had been with Lord Arthur Bessamy. If he could find Lord Arthur, then that gentleman might lead him to the whereabouts of the mysterious princess. "Do you know where a certain Lord Arthur Bessamy resides?" he asked.

The butler turned his head away in disdain. Mr. Palfrey took two gold sovereigns out of his pocket and clinked them in his hands. The butler's head jerked round. "Just around the corner, sir," he said with an ingratiating smile. "Number 137."

"Thank you, fellow," said Mr. Palfrey cockily and, returning the sovereigns to his pocket, strolled off down the street and then flinched as a lump of dried horse manure flew past his ear and the outraged butler's screech of "Skinflint!" followed him around the corner into Curzon Street.

Then he stopped. Lord Arthur was emerging from his house. He was too formidable a man to be approached. Mr. Palfrey set out to follow.

He had to scurry to keep up with Lord Arthur's long legs. Soon he saw his quarry walking into the Crillon Hotel. He followed at a discreet distance, saw the hotel manager bowing and scraping, and then saw Lord Arthur mounting the stairs.

He waited a few moments and then strolled into the hotel and approached the manager. "I am desirous to know who it is Lord Arthur is meeting," he said, holding out the two sovereigns he had failed to give to the butler. The manager took the money, put it in the pocket of his tails, dabbed his mouth fastidiously with a handkerchief, and said, "Get out. We do not discuss anything to do with our guests or noble visitors."

"Then, give me my money back this instant."

"What money?" said the manager. "Here! Jeremy, Peter, throw this fellow out."

Mr. Palfrey cast a scared look at the approaching waiters and ran out into the street. He stood for a moment and then crossed the road and skulked in a doorway.

When Lord Arthur entered the Barchesters' hotel drawing room, he was relieved to see only Mr. Barchester. He did not yet feel ready to face his soon-to-be disengaged fiancée.

"Martha's putting on her pretties," said Mr.

Barchester. "Sit down, sit down, Bessamy. Help yourself to wine."

Lord Arthur poured himself a glass of burgundy and sat down opposite Mr. Barchester. "I fear you will not be pleased to see me when you learn the reason for my visit."

Mr. Barchester's shrewd little eyes twinkled in the pads of fat that were his cheeks. "I'll try to bear up," he said. "What's to do?"

"What would you say, sir, were I to tell you that I have fallen in love for the first time in my life, and, alas, not with your daughter?"

There was a long silence. Then Mr. Barchester tilted his glass of port to his mouth and took a gulp. "That's better," he said. "Oh, well, as to your question, I would say I have been planning new stables this past age."

Lord Arthur looked in amazement at Mr. Barchester. One of Mr. Barchester's fat eyelids drooped in a wink. "Come on, Bessamy," he said. "You always struck me as being a knowing cove."

"So," said Lord Arthur slowly, "am I to take it that if I build new stables for you, the Barchester family will not sue me for breach of promise?"

"That's right," said Mr. Barchester cheerfully.

"You do not seem in the least surprised. I feel a cad and a charlatan for treating your daughter so."

"She's used to it," said Mr. Barchester heartlessly. "See that new wing at Hapsmere Manor? That was when Sir Henry Carruthers cried off. And the fine tiled roof? That was . . . let me see . . . ah, that was Mr. Tommy Bradshaw. The staircase was the Honorable Peter Chambers, but then he didn't have too much of the ready . . ."

"How many times has Miss Barchester been engaged?"

" 'Bout four or five. M'wife'll put you straight."

"But don't you see," said Lord Arthur, appalled, "I cannot possibly bring myself to break the engagement now! After all these disappointments . . . I would feel like a monster."

"Take Martha out for a little walk and have a talk to her," said Mr. Barchester. "Martha's little talks always do the trick. You'll be back here like a rat up a spout, begging to give me those new stables."

Lord Arthur was not able to say any more, for at that moment the door opened and Miss Barchester walked in, accompanied by her mother. She was wearing a severe walking dress of old-fashioned cut and a poke bonnet. She treated Lord Arthur to a cool smile.

"Off you go, Martha," said her father heartily. "Bessamy here's come to take you for a little walk."

As they made their way to Hyde Park, Lord Arthur had an odd feeling he was being followed. He turned around sharply several times, but the streets were very busy and no one appeared to be paying him any particular interest.

Martha was talking steadily in a level voice and at last he was able to take in what she was saying.

"When we are married, I should like to spend most of the year in town," said Miss Barchester. "The ladies' fashions are sadly skimpy, and fashion would have a new leader."

"In yourself?" asked Lord Arthur, glancing down at her walking dress and wondering how she had managed to find material that was so drab, so mud-colored.

313

"Of course! And I am sure you will agree with me that marriages in which men spend all their time at their clubs end in disaster."

"On the contrary, it might be the saving of many."

"You are funning, of course. I have not told you before, Lord Arthur, but there is a certain levity about you which must be curbed."

Lord Arthur stopped listening to her, saving all his energies for the scene he knew must surely break about his head when he told her he no longer wished to marry her.

How could he have ever for a moment thought she might make a suitable wife? Well, she had seemed so calm, so docile, so biddable.

He led her to an iron bench by the Serpentine and dusted it before they sat down. There was a crackling and a rustling in the bushes behind him, and Miss Barchester looked around nervously.

"Probably a dog," said Lord Arthur.

Mr. Palfrey scrunched down in the bushes and strained his ears.

In a flat voice, Lord Arthur proceeded to tell Miss Barchester that he wished to terminate their engagement.

She heard him in silence and then said, "You will soon come to your senses. In any case, I refuse to release you."

"Even when you know this marriage would now make me unhappy?"

"Although you are not a young man," said Miss Barchester coyly, "I fear the company of a certain princess has turned your head. Now, do be sensible. I am sure you do not want a scandal. Gentlemen are like little boys. They never seem to know their own minds—which is why we ladies must make the decisions for them. Don't be silly, Lord Arthur. We are going to be married, and you have nothing to say in the matter."

"Madam! You have just persuaded me to go to any lengths to be free of you. Come, I shall escort you back to your parents."

"I prefer to stay here. It is pleasant."

"Then, stay by yourself," said Lord Arthur wrathfully, and, getting to his feet, he strode off.

He went straight back to the Crillon, up the stairs, and into the drawing room.

Mr. Barchester rubbed his chubby hands when he saw his face. "Have some more wine, dear boy!" he cried. "And let us discuss the new stables."

Miss Barchester screamed as a dandified, middle-aged man crashed out of the bushes behind her.

"Hush, dear lady," he said. "I am here to help you. Lord Arthur Bessamy was at the opera t'other night with a young lady calling herself Princess Felicity of Brasnia."

The scream for help died stillborn on Miss Barchester's thin lips.

"Who are you?" she demanded sharply.

Mr. Palfrey came around and sat down beside her. "Let me explain . . ." he began.

Chapter Nine

"Do you know," said Dolph, as he and Lord Arthur bowled along the Brighton Road, "I met an old tutor of mine from Oxford. Asked him about Brasnia and he said he had never heard of it."

"Odd, the ignorance of some of those Oxford dons," said Lord Arthur. "Come to think of it, it's quite disgraceful."

"But he's a clever chap. Everybody says so. Now, *you* tell me. Where's Brasnia?"

"It is up near the Arctic Circle," said Lord Arthur. "Quite a small country, very savage, full of polar bears and . . ."

"What kind of bears?"

"White. All over. So that they can hide themselves in the snow. As I was saying before I was so rudely interrupted, the inhabitants live in mansions carved out of ice in the winter, and, in the summer they live in tents made out of reindeer skin."

"But don't they have cities . . . towns? I mean doesn't the princess have a castle?"

"Of course she does. A white castle with long, glittering icicles hanging from the towers. It was built in the thirteenth century by Georgi the Horrible. He kept four maidens locked up at one time, which is why the castle has four tall towers. When he had ... er ... had his way with them, he fed them to his pet bears."

"The white ones?" said Dolph suspiciously.

"Except when they fed on the maidens. Then they turned a delicate, rosy pink."

"They must be very well-educated people. I mean, Miss Chubiski speaks English very well."

"Yes, she does, doesn't she. Alas, it is only the aristocracy who can enjoy the benefits of education. There is no middle class—only aristocracy and peasants. The peasants are illiterate to a man."

"Look here, don't tell me the shopkeepers are all aristocrats. How do they keep the books?"

"They don't. The price of each article is indicated by so many stamps of the foot, rather like that educated pig at Bartholomew Fair."

"What if something cost a hundred guineas? The shopkeeper would have a sore foot before he got the price out. And what about pounds, shillings, and pence?"

"My dear, dear Dolph, Nothing so complicated. It is a very poor country, so they don't have anything at all that costs over the equivalent of one pound. They have only a small coin called a secrudo, made of tin."

"Why do I get the feeling you're talking rubbish?" said Dolph. "Go on. Tell me about the ruler."

"The king is ..."

"Now, wait a minute, you told Prinny that Brasnia was a principality."

"So I did, and I made the whole thing up then. Now you are hearing the real truth. King Georgi the Fourth, is Princess Felicity's uncle. He poisoned his queen because he wanted to keep up the family

317

tradition of incarcerating maidens in the four towers and subsequently feeding them to the bears. He ... Dolph, this is all very interesting, and you keep twisting your head about."

"Well, it's a funny thing, but I was getting a nasty, prickling feeling in the back of my neck. I thought it was because you were prosing on about maidens being fed to bears. But I turned about and took a glance down the road behind. There's a traveling carriage, and as I looked, a head popped out the window and the passenger yelled something to the driver. I only caught a glimpse, but it looked horribly like that Mr. Palfrey."

"More than likely. I was unfortunate enough to meet him at the opera last night. We'll shake him loose. Long roundabout journey to Brighton, I am afraid."

Lord Arthur turned off the Brighton road and drove some ten miles to where Lord Achesham, a friend of his father's, had a mansion. His lordship was not at home, but his butler was delighted to receive a hefty tip to show them the back way out of the estate, and then to tell anyone asking for them that they were guests of Lord Achesham and would be staying for some time. And if an impertinent fellow should inquire after a certain Princess Felicity, the butler was to say that she, too, was in residence. If he insisted on seeing the princess, he was to be shown out.

Felicity had told John Tremayne not to use her fake title when he rented a house. She had no wish to be brought to the attention of the worthies of Brighton. It had proved remarkably easy for John to find a suitable residence large enough for Felicity and her staff. Until the end of the Season, Brighton was a quiet place. In June, when the Prince arrived with his court and followers, it would spring into life.

It was wonderful to settle down into relative anonymity. She often thought of Lord Arthur, but distance from him had given her courage. A man who was engaged to one lady, and yet could kiss another, was not a gentleman.

A few callers had tried to leave cards with Miss Chubb—Felicity having made the governess take the house in her name—as a certain interest had been provoked in the lady who had taken one of the largest houses in Brighton. But gloomy Spinks had told them all that Miss Chubb did not wish to see anyone. The advantage of renting a house complete with furniture and arriving with a highly trained staff meant Felicity had been able to settle in almost immediately.

No callers to Spinks also included Lord Arthur Bessamy and Mr. Charles Godolphin, who arrived on the doorstep three days after Felicity's arrival, it having taken them the whole of the previous day to track her down.

Lord Arthur, however, insisted on leaving his card, and that was to cause ructions. Felicity, determined to be good, might not have decided to see him had not both Miss Chubb and Mr. Silver cried out against the very idea. Now Mr. Silver, that assiduous reader of newspapers, could have told his young mistress that an announcement of the termination of Lord Arthur's engagement had just appeared in the *Times*. But it was not Lord Arthur he distrusted so much as Dolph, and so he deliberately did not tell her. Felicity herself rarely read the newspapers, finding the long tales of war in the Spanish peninsula frightening and depressing, and the social gossip a mixture of malice and trivia. But Miss Chubb and Mr. Silver's orders that she must not have anything more to do with Lord Arthur set up a spirit of perversity in Felicity. The memory of that kiss was achingly sweet. She was frightened at the idea of the approaching visit to the Queen's drawing room and craved the reassurance of Lord Arthur's presence.

Accordingly, when Lord Arthur and Dolph called the following day, Felicity had been watching for them and commanded Spinks to allow them to enter.

Lord Arthur promptly suggested that Felicity should accompany him on a drive, and Dolph, taking his cue, said he would be happy to stay and keep Miss Chubb company. Mr. Silver muttered something rude under his breath, and went out for a long walk.

The day was sparkling and brisk as Lord Arthur drove Felicity up over the downs. He laughed at her fears over her forthcoming presentation to the Queen. "It is not a terrifying occasion," he said. "People push and shove to get into the drawing room. They bow or curtsey, as the case may be. Her Majesty takes snuff and looks bored. And then they shove and fight back downstairs, usually to find that their disposables, such as shawls, hats, tippets, and cloaks, have been stolen."

"But surely there are some people who fall ill, who are unable to attend," said Felicity. "I could be one of them."

"It would be considered very odd in a . . . visiting royalty?"

His voice ended on a question, and Felicity blushed. "Why are you in Brighton, my lord?" she asked, as he stopped his team on a grassy hill above the sea.

"Now, I should have thought that was obvious. I came in pursuit of you, my princess."

Felicity turned her head away and fiddled with the long blue satin ribbons of her gown. "My lord, I must remind you that you are engaged to Miss Barchester."

"No longer. I disengaged myself."

Felicity suddenly felt ridiculously happy. But his next words took all that happiness away. "Now, Princess Felicity," he said, "do you not think it is time you told me all about Brasnia?"

She hung her head. She longed to tell him the truth, but would he believe her? I took the jewels and ran. But what proof had she that the jewels were really hers? And how could their relationship deepen unless she did tell him the truth?

"Don't look so miserable," he said gently. "We will have all our married life before us to talk about the wretched place."

Felicity's wide eyes flew to meet his. "You wish to marry me?"

"Of course. I do not kiss gently bred ladies unless my intentions are serious, and they have never before been as serious as this."

"I cannot marry you," said Felicity miserably. He jumped lightly down from the carriage and led his team of horses to a stunted tree and tethered them. Then he helped Felicity to alight.

"Now, why can't you marry me?" he said.

"My family would forbid it."

"Ah, back to Brasnia again. Perhaps I should go there and ask whoever I need to ask."

"That would not answer. I am already betrothed."

"To whom?"

"Prince Ivan, my first cousin."

"Here. You cannot go around marrying first cousins. You'll have a nursery full of imbeciles. My dearest, is it not time you told me the truth?"

Felicity walked a little head of him in silence.

"You see, you are going to marry me," he said, catching up with her. "And I then must go and see my family to tell them the good news, and then I must find a special license because I do not want to wait. Are you afraid of me?"

Felicity turned to face him. "Oh, yes," she whispered. "Very afraid."

He looked at her ruefully. "I must do something to end this farce. I never thought to use force, but . . ."

He deftly kicked Felicity's legs from under her, and as she fell backward on the springy turf, he crouched down beside her and pinioned her arms above her head.

"Now," he said, "let's kiss some of that Brasnian nonsense out of you."

"You are stronger than I am," said Felicity with pathetic dignity. "I can only appeal to your honor, if you do have any."

He smiled down at her wickedly. "Not a scrap," he said softly, and then his mouth descended on hers.

As he kissed her softly, he released her wrists, only to pull her body into his arms. Felicity planned to lie cold and unresisting in order to bring him to his senses. But her lips had a will of their own, and her body refused to listen to frantic messages from her brain and arched against his. As he felt her response he freed her mouth and kissed her neck. "Brasnia," he whispered against her skin. "Come along now. Tell me about Brasnia or I shall forget myself and leave you with no choice but to marry me. Brasnia!"

"No!" said Felicity.

Her dress was high-waisted and stiffened, to push her breasts up against the low neckline. He kissed the top of each breast and then rolled on top of her, pressing her into the ground with the weight of his body and began caressing her mouth again with his lips, soft stroking kisses that were more devastating than any savage assault.

Felicity let out a sort of gurgling moan, and he raised his head. Her hat had tumbled off onto the grass, and her red hair had come free of its pins and lay in a fiery cloud about her face.

"Oh, I shall tell you," she sighed, "and then you will go away and forget about me."

"I doubt it, Mr. Freddy Channing, Miss Felicity Channing and Your Royal Highness. I doubt it very much."

"You knew," said Felicity. "You knew all along."

"Of course I did, my widgeon! But I wanted you to trust me, to tell me. I hope I can recognize a pretty girl even when dressed in men's clothes. And I was there, you know, when Palfrey thought you had plunged to your death. It was when I fished a little girl's dress out of the sea that I realized you had only pretended to die. You might have left behind a more convincing wardrobe, you idiot."

"I can't think with you lying on top of me in this disgraceful way," said Felicity.

He rolled to one side, only to gather her in his arms again. "Now, go on," he said. "Where did you get the money to buy all those jewels?"

"They are mine," said Felicity. "Mama left a codicil the day she died, but Mr. Palfrey did not mention it. I think he found it and burned it. I knew where the jewels were hidden. It was on the day after I had seen the baron that Miss Chubb and John Tremayne told me they had been hatching a plot. It seems outrageous now, dangerous and silly. But I had to escape."

"So you had," he said, smoothing her hair. "So you will make a last grand appearance as the princess at the drawing room, and then we shall be married. The princess will disappear, and Miss Felicity Channing will take her place in time for the wedding."

"But Mr. Palfrey . . . ?"

"Mr. Palfrey will do nothing to cross swords with me. As my wife, no one will be able to harm you."

"Do you love me?"

Lord Arthur began to laugh. "I break my engagement, I chase you to Brighton, I make love to you on this drafty hilltop, and I ask you to marry me. Of course I love you. I think I loved you from the moment I saw you in that silly disguise at The Green Dolphin."

"Then, why did you become engaged to Miss Barchester?"

"I did not know then I loved you. I thought you a wild, ferocious little girl who had run away and would probably never be seen again." He gave her a little shake. "Do you love me, Felicity?"

"Yes."

"Then, prove it. Kiss me!"

Felicity wound her arms about his neck and kissed him with all her heart. He kissed her back and kept on kissing her until the sun went down and a chill wind began to blow in from the sea.

Mr. Palfrey had been billeted at an inferior inn near Lord Achesham's house for a week. Every day he went out and walked up and down outside the main gates leading to the mansion, and every evening he returned feeling defeated. He had written to Miss Barchester to tell her of his lack of progress. She wrote back to say that the list of guests to attend the Queen's drawing room included the name of Princess Felicity of Brasnia. She herself was to attend, and if Mr. Palfrey had not been invited, he had only to bribe a certain chancellor, pointed out Mr. Barchester's daughter.

Reading this welcome letter over a dinner of stringy mutton and watery beans washed down with acid claret, Mr. Palfrey heaved a sigh of relief. All he had to do was to return to London and wait. Miss Barchester was a woman after his own heart. She had encouraged him that first day they had met by saying she was sure there was no such place as Brasnia and that poor Lord Arthur had been tricked by a scheming adventuress. Should that adventuress turn out to be Felicity Channing, then she would be unmasked in front of the Queen. Mr. Palfrey had quailed before the drama of this idea, suggesting a quieter exposure of the impostor, but Miss Barchester had overridden his protests.

Miss Barchester thirsted to take her place on the center stage of society, a place she felt had been snatched from her by Felicity. Never before had the

cancellation of an engagement filled her with such
fury. She had initially persisted in believing that
Lord Arthur had not meant a word of it. All those
previous jiltings had not even dented her superb
vanity. But when she had returned to the hotel to
find her father gleefully poring over plans for the
new stables, she knew the engagement was definitely off. She had promptly sent a message to Mr.
Palfrey, summoning him back, and had said she
would help him in every way she could.

Mr. Barchester had grumbled most horribly over
the amount of money it was taking to send his
daughter to see the Queen. For he had had to pay
a hefty bribe to get her invited and then there was
the horrible cost of the court gown. He decided
Lord Arthur should be made to pay for this extra
expense. Besides, his daughter appeared to have a
new beau in the shape of that fussy little man, Palfrey. Palfrey owned Tregarthan Castle. Mr. Barchester began to dream about an ornamental lake.

Miss Chubb cried with relief when Lord Arthur
and Felicity returned to announce their engagement. Only Dolph was startled and disappointed to
find that Brasnia did not exist. All the long day
they had waited for the return of the couple while
Miss Chubb had told Dolph long and fanciful stories about the bears of Brasnia, feeling it politic to
expand on Lord Arthur's strange lies. Dolph felt
cheated. Brasnia had sounded like a marvelous
place, and he had more or less made up his mind to
go there.

So there was one last hurdle, the Queen's drawing room, and then they could all settle down to

plan Felicity's wedding and discuss the future of their servants.

Lord Arthur left the next day with Dolph. Felicity passed her remaining days in Brighton in a daze of happiness. She almost forgot that Mr. Palfrey was probably still in London.

But once she was back in Chesterfield Gardens, the full terror of meeting the Queen drove everything else, apart from Lord Arthur, out of her mind.

Dressing for the occasion took hours of work. The minimum amount of large feathers allowed on the headdress was seven. Carberry's, the plumassier, had sent round twenty-four, deeming that the correct amount for royalty, but Felicity refused to wear so many and settled at last for ten standing up from a garland of roses resting on a circlet of white pearls. The mixture of jewels, flowers, and feathers required for court dress seemed odd to Felicity, who was used to wearing the simple Grecian fashions of the Regency.

She was strapped into a tight bodice, and then an enormous hooped skirt, three ells long, was laced to her waist. The skirt was made of waxed calico stretched upon whalebone, which made it very wide in the front and behind, and very narrow at the sides. Over that went a satin skirt, and over that, a skirt of tulle, ornamented with a large furbelow of silver lace. Another shorter skirt, also of tulle, with silver spangles ornamented by a garland of flowers, went on top of all that and was tucked up at the hem, the opening of each tuck being ornamented with silver lace and surmounted with a large bouquet of flowers. Then a lady attending court was also expected to wear as many jewels as possible. Felicity had the Channing diamonds as well as the pearls about her neck, her headdress was finished at the back with a diamond comb, and diamond buckles were attached to her shoes.

Miss Chubb, also attired in court dress, was so huge that she had to turn sideways to shuffle out through the front door. Two carriages had been hired to take them to Buckingham House, for their enormous skirts would not allow them to travel together. So Felicity had no one to talk to as she waited and waited in the long line of carriages that crawled toward Buckingham House.

At last she and Miss Chubb entered the great hall of the Queen's residence. A double staircase rose up to the drawing room above. Those waiting to be presented went up by the left-hand staircase, and those who had been presented descended on the right.

Above the chatter of voices came the booming of the guns firing a salute in St. James's Park outside. At first Felicity and Miss Chubb had eyes only for the splendor of the display. Feathers of all colors were worn on headdresses. Jewels flashed and blazed. Ladies fidgeted and fretted, trying to protect their enormous gowns from getting crushed, and gentlemen in knee breeches and evening coats fiddled nervously with their dress swords.

As she began to ascend the staircase, Felicity sensed a malignant presence behind her. She wanted to turn around, but the great hoop of her gown prevented her from doing so. Then a familiar, tall figure ahead of her on the staircase turned and smiled, and she felt a great flood of delight and relief. For it was Lord Arthur, very grand in a dark blue silk coat and knee breeches. His black hair was powdered, and he carried a bicorne under his arm. His delight in the beauty of Felicity's appearance stopped him from noticing Mr. Palfrey and Miss Barchester close behind her.

All Felicity's fears left her. The masquerade was nearly over. One curtsey to the Queen among so many, and then she would be free to marry Lord Arthur.

By the time she and Miss Chubb had ascended the staircase, inch by inch, both were heartily tired of the long wait. And when it came their turn to be introduced, neither felt any nervousness at all as they sank down into low curtseys before Queen Charlotte, who surveyed them with great indifference and helped herself to a pinch of snuff.

Felicity was just backing away from the royal presence when a voice behind her cried, "Impostor!"

One look at the so-called Miss Chubiski had been enough to convince Mr. Palfrey.

There was a hushed silence.

Then Mr. Palfrey said, "Your Royal Majesty, my lords, my ladies, and gentlemen. This is not the Princess Felicity of Brasnia. This is Felicity Channing, my stepdaughter, who stole my jewels and ran away."

Miss Barchester laughed. "She is nothing but a paper princess," she said.

A paper princess! A great hissing and whispering set the feathers nodding and dipping. Queen Charlotte looked at the stricken Felicity with mild curiosity. Then she raised her hand. Two Yeomen of the Guard stepped from behind her throne.

Lord Arthur came to stand beside Felicity and held her hand firmly in his own.

"This is indeed Felicity Channing," he said, "who

is to be my wife. Your Royal Highness, let me tell you her story."

"Better let me tell it," said a portly man, waddling forward. "I am Mr. Guy Clough, tobacco planter. I carry on me the late Mrs. Palfrey's last will, which this man"—he pointed at Mr. Palfrey—"tried to destroy."

"Pray go on," said the Queen. "We have become interested."

There were screams and yells from the staircase outside, where the guests who had not yet gained the drawing room, but who had begun to hear garbled whispers of an attempted assassination by a Turk, were beginning to push and shove.

So Mr. Clough told Bessie's story and handed the will to Felicity.

As everyone pressed forward to look over Felicity's shoulder, Mr. Palfrey backed away. The down staircase outside was empty; no one wanted to leave until they had learned every bit of the drama. He darted down it and disappeared into the night.

"Quite like a gothic romance," sighed one sentimental lady. Ushers moved in to keep the guests in line. But Miss Barchester stood where she was, unable to believe the turn of events in Felicity's favor.

Queen Charlotte looked across at Miss Barchester, and her little monkey face creased in a frown. "That woman," she said. "Have her removed."

"It was nothing to do with me," said Miss Barchester, turning white.

"You are only wearing six feathers," said the little Queen. "It is an insult to us. We suggest you do not aspire to social circles until you learn to dress."

Despite her bewilderment and distress, Felicity

could find it in her heart to be sorry for the ex-fiancée of Lord Arthur.

Tears of humiliation were running down Miss Barchester's cheeks as she made her way down the grand staircase.

"Let us go," said Lord Arthur in Felicity's ear.

Clutching her mother's will, Felicity let him escort her down the stairs, past the goggling guests, who were still demanding to know if anyone had seen this murdering Turk.

At his hotel, Mr. Palfrey packed feverishly. He knew that the minute the initial shock of all the revelations had died down, a warrant would be out for his arrest. He was bending over his largest trunk, stuffing in shirts and small-clothes, when he heard the door behind him swing open. His heart gave a jump. But when he turned around, it was only Miss Barchester standing there, still in her court dress and with the despised six feathers, standing up on her head.

"You have ruined me," said Miss Barchester.

"It was you who had the silly idea of challenging her in the middle of the Queen's drawing room," pointed out Mr. Palfrey acidly. "You had better leave, or they might arrest you as well."

"I am ashamed. I shall never dare show my face in polite circles again," said Miss Barchester. "I shall go with you."

"Charmed, dear lady," said Mr. Palfrey, still packing. "But may I point out that I have only enough money on me to take me out of the country. What I shall do when I get to the Low Countries to survive is beyond me."

"Marry me," said Miss Barchester, "and Papa will give you my dowry."

"How much?"

"Five thousand pounds."

"Nearly enough, but not quite."

"You still hold the Channing estates. Go to the bank in the morning and draw out as much as you can."

"But the banker will have learned of all the fuss from the newspapers."

"Then, you must trust to the fact that men of business rarely have time to read their newspapers first thing in the morning. I shall go with you. Perhaps this Channing creature will not want any more fuss and scandal and will not prosecute. So, do not draw out all the money, only enough to keep us comfortably."

"I must leave this hotel immediately. Where shall I stay the night?"

"With my parents."

"They will think it most odd."

"Not them," said Miss Barchester bitterly, thinking that her father would only see Mr. Palfrey as a further extension to his estate. "Come, I shall help you pack."

There was something about Miss Barchester's stern, cold face that reminded Mr. Palfrey of his mother. With a weak little smile, he moved over and let her help him.

Chapter Ten

Felicity was roused early the next morning by Spinks, the butler.

"An urgent message from Lord Arthur Bessamy," he said sonorously. "We are to bar the door, close the shutters, and lock the windows."

"Good heavens! What has happened? Has Napoleon invaded?"

"Vengeance is mine, sayeth the lord."

"Pull yourself together, Spinks. Did not my lord explain the reason for his warning?"

"No, Your Royal Highness. But the end is nigh."

"Don't be silly. Rouse Miss Chubb immediately, and bring me the morning papers."

"I do not think that is a very good idea."

"Do as you are told, Spinks," said Felicity sharply. "And you may now address me as Miss Channing. The masquerade is over."

"Everything is over," said Spinks in a hollow voice.

The minute he had left, Felicity jumped from her bed and made a hasty toilet. Miss Chubb came in just as Felicity was finishing dressing.

"What is all this?" asked the governess. "Has Spinks gone mad?"

"Something awful is about to happen or Lord Arthur would not have sent a message."

There came a scratching at the door, and the tutor, Mr. Silver, came in, carrying the morning papers and with an expression on his face as gloomy as that of the butler.

"Is it war?" asked Felicity nervously. "Have the French come?"

"Worse than that," said the tutor. He silently handed Felicity the newspapers and told her to look at the social columns.

Each paper carried a full account of the Queen's drawing room, and each damned this upstart, Felicity Channing, who had dared to masquerade as a royal princess and play a trick on "our beloved Queen Charlotte." There was not a word of Mr. Palfrey's perfidy. Tricking her out of her inheritance and nearly murdering a maid was small beer in the eyes of the press compared to Felicity's audacity in tricking London society. "We had long noted," said the *Morning Post*, "a sad want of any royal traits in this paper princess."

PAPER PRINCESS screamed all the other journals. Miss Barchester had had her revenge after all.

"He will not want to marry me after this disgrace," whispered Felicity. "Lord Arthur's father, the duke, is very powerful and will stop the marriage."

"Listen!" said Mr. Silver. There were howls and cries outside, growing closer.

They sat staring at one another. Soon an angry mob was below the windows.

"You wouldn't think they would be able to read the newspapers," said Felicity.

"They don't need to," said Mr. Silver. A stone rat-

334

tled against the shutters. "I am afraid, dear lady, that lampoons of you will be in all the print shops by now. The speed of the satirical artists of Grub Street never fails to amaze me."

More stones began to strike the house and the roaring outside grew louder.

"If Lord Arthur guessed this was about to happen," said Mr. Silver impatiently, "then he should have arranged to protect us."

"Listen!" said Miss Chubb. "Someone is shouting something."

Despite anguished cries from Miss Chubb to be careful, Felicity opened the shutters and looked down.

Lord Arthur Bessamy stood facing the mob. He was making a speech. They listened to him in silence, and then a great roar went up.

"Come away from the window," shouted Miss Chubb. "They have seen you."

"No," said Felicity slowly. "Lord Arthur is below. He made a speech, they all listened and cheered, and now they are going away as quietly as lambs."

She turned from the window and ran out of the room and down the stairs to where John Tremayne was stationed by the door, holding a shotgun.

"Open the door," cried Felicity. "It is Lord Arthur."

John drew back the bolts and bars and opened the door. Felicity flew into Lord Arthur's arms, crying, "They are calling me the paper princess. Your father, the duke, he will never let you marry me."

"Don't clutch my cravat," said Lord Arthur amiably. "Quite spoils the shape. My dearest, by next week they will all have forgotten you exist."

"How did you get rid of them?"

"I told them about Palfrey. I told them I was going to marry you. But I think it was when I told them that I had arranged for free beer at the pub in Shepherd Market, for them to drink to your health, that started them cheering."

"I was so afraid you would not want to marry me."

"Idiot. But remember: It is to be our wedding, and only ours."

"I do understand."

"Miss Chubb and Mr. Silver may marry when they please, but not at the same time as us."

Felicity laughed. "Poor Miss Chubb. Of course she is not going to marry Mr. Silver."

"I fear you are blind to love," said Lord Arthur. "Why do you think Mr. Silver was so angry with poor Dolph? Now, do you want that wretch, Palfrey, arrested? After I left you last night, I went to call on Mr. Clough. He told me that Bessie is quite reformed and never wants to leave America."

"No, I would rather let all the scandal die down."

"Do you know the name of the bank where the Channing money is lodged?"

"It is Coutts in the Strand, I believe."

"Then, I had better go there directly or Palfrey will flee the country with all the Channing money."

He bowed and left, and Felicity went back upstairs to look at Miss Chubb and Mr. Silver with new eyes.

Lord Arthur was too late. He could only be glad that Mr. Palfrey had only drawn out ten thousand pounds. The estates, properly managed, would soon recover the loss.

Chapter Eleven

The Duke of Pentshire's home, Pent House, was
a palace in the middle of rich green countryside.
Felicity felt she had been hurtled down there out of
the chaos of London and then left stranded with a
great number of chilly people who did not approve
of her one little bit. The duke and duchess, Lord
Arthur's parents, were a handsome, formal couple
whose exquisite manners barely concealed the wish
that their youngest son had chosen someone else
for a bride.

The couple were to be married in the private
chapel. Felicity had made no suggestions of her
own as to preparations for the wedding. There had
been so much to do. John Tremayne had been par-
celed off to Lord Arthur's home to study estate
management under the tuition of the steward.
Dolph had volunteered to travel to Tregarthan Castle right after the wedding to take charge until
such time as Lord Arthur could manage to join him
and decide what was necessary to bring the
Channing estates into good order.

Felicity's servants had either been pensioned off
or found other jobs, according to their wishes.
Dolph had taken a fancy to Spinks, who he claimed

was an original, and had said he would take the biblical butler with him as a sort of aide when he went to Cornwall. Mr. Silver and Miss Chubb were to be married and were to live at Tregarthan Castle until a home of their own could be found for them.

Contrary to Lord Arthur's hopes, society had not forgotten or forgiven the paper princess, and news of her masquerade had reached the august ears of Lord Arthur's father. Felicity had not been present during the long family arguments in which Lord Arthur's parents had tried to talk their son out of marrying her. But she felt their disapproval keenly.

There could be no reassuring hugs and kisses from Lord Arthur. If he took her out on the grounds for a walk, a footman was always in attendance, as the duke and duchess held strictly to the rules of society, which decreed that no couple should be left alone for a minute until after they were married.

Lord Arthur was beginning to become furious with his parents. He had been left a fortune by a distant relative and was economically independent of them, so they could not forbid the marriage, much as they wanted to. But he could not help feeling they might have put a better face on things.

If he had brought home some actress, they could not have been more shocked.

The arrival of Felicity's sisters and their husbands did more to remove her from him, because she took refuge in her family's company in the guest wing, keeping as far away from his parents' aloof disapproval as she possibly could.

Felicity was feeling the strain even more than he guessed. In the stern lines of his face she began to read that he had begun to share his parents' distaste. Miss Barchester had seemed an odd sort of female for him to have ever proposed to. She could only be glad the duke and duchess had never met Miss Barchester. Her cold looks and old-fashioned dress would probably have pleased them. Felicity overheard the duchess saying one day with regret in her voice that it was a pity Arthur's previous engagement had come to nothing, for the Barchesters were a very old family. So were the Channings, the duchess had admitted, but Cornish! One never knew what went on in those castles and mansions down there, but it was well-known the Cornish were strange.

More of Lord Arthur's relatives continued to arrive, and the long formal dinners were an agony for Felicity. Miss Chubb was too wrapped up in her newfound happiness to be of much help. Lord Arthur, never allowed to sit next to her, was looking grimmer each day, and when Felicity retired with her ladies, she and her sisters were isolated in a corner of the drawing room as if they had the plague.

They were to spend their honeymoon in Brighton, Felicity having formed an affection for the place. While still in London, Felicity had looked forward to the honeymoon. Now she wondered if she would find she was tied for life to a man who bitterly regretted having proposed to her. It began to cross her mind that she might do him a great favor by running away. But to do so would spoil not only Miss Chubb and Mr. Silver's future, but John Tremayne's as well, who was so delighted and excited at the prospect of his new and important career. And then there was poor old Spinks. If she ran away, Dolph would have to drop the idea of taking Spinks to Tregarthan Castle, and Spinks had seen in Dolph's adoption of him the gracious hand of a benign God.

There was also all the great machinery of a ducal wedding that had been put into action. All tenants had been invited to a grand party on the grounds. Everyone appeared to have bought new clothes especially for the occasion. And if she ran away, the duke and the duchess would have the satisfaction of telling their youngest son that that was just the sort of disgraceful behavior he might have expected from an adventuress and impostor like Felicity Channing.

So her wedding morn finally arrived. She was dressed in white silk and pearls while the rain fell steadily on the formal gardens outside and ran down the panes of the windows like fat tears.

How she was beginning to hate jewelry—hate the cold feel of pearls and the clumsy weight of diamonds. How she loathed the long corset that for some mad reason she was supposed to wear. It was so long and tight, she could only take tiny little steps. How she hated the cold, slippery feel of her white silk petticoat.

It was a gloomy, depressed couple who finally made their vows to one another in the family chapel. It was a grim silent couple who sat side by side at the wedding breakfast and listened to the interminable speeches. Dolph, elated with wine, and blissfully unaware of the prevailing chilly atmosphere, made a speech about how he had actually believed there was a country called Brasnia, told them about the bears, hiccupped and laughed immoderately, toasted the "happy" bride and groom, and then sat down, heartily pleased with himself, not knowing that everyone who might have begun to forget about Princess Felicity of Brasnia was now remembering the disgraceful masquerade all over again.

Then Felicity was led upstairs to be changed into her carriage clothes. She looked desperately at Miss Chubb, dying to cry out for help, but that lady was smiling all over her large face and saying she was sure Felicity must be the happiest lady in the land.

Felicity's sisters hugged her and begged her to call on them when the honeymoon was over. Her clothes had been chosen for her by the duchess. A fussy carriage dress of brown velvet was put on over that constricting corset. The carriage gown was fussily tucked and gored and flounced. It was topped up by a navy straw bonnet shaped like a coal scuttle.

Lord Arthur was waiting inside the carriage when she made her way out. Felicity hugged her sisters, hugged Miss Chubb, and hugged Dolph, who was still laughing drunkenly about the bears, climbed in the carriage, and sat down primly on the seat beside her husband.

The carriage moved off.

Silence.

The rain drummed on the carriage roof, and the wheels whizzed through the puddles on the drive.

"Well, that's that," said Lord Arthur at last.

Felicity said nothing.

"Do you know," said her husband, "I think you are wearing quite the most horrible hat I have ever seen."

Felicity tore it off, threw it on the floor of the carriage, drummed her heels on it and burst into tears.

"Here now . . . now." He pulled her into his arms. "What's all this? Tears on our wedding day."

"Oh, it's awful . . . awful," sobbed Felicity. "Your parents hate me, you hate me . . ."

"I don't hate you, you stupid little wretch," he said crossly. "I love you to distraction. I've had to watch your gloomy face and torture myself wondering if you no longer loved me and yet at the same time being frightened to ask you."

"Oh, Arthur," Felicity dried her eyes. "I have been worrying about exactly the same thing."

"We are both fools. Come and kiss me."

He crushed her against him, and Felicity let out a yelp of pain.

"What is the matter?"

"It's this corset," wailed Felicity. "It has the bones of a whole whale in it, that I'll swear. I am laced so tight, I feel faint."

Lord Arthur released her and jerked down the blinds. "Take it off," he said.

"What!"

"I said, take the damned thing off. We are married. We can do what we like. No relatives, no parents. I have not felt so free since I came into my inheritance and left Pent House to set up my own establishment in town. Take it off."

Felicity giggled. "You had best help me with your mother's choice of dress. Her maid lashed the tapes so tightly, I think she had instructions to make sure I kept it on for life."

"More than likely." He dealt with the tapes expertly and began to slide the dress from her shoulders.

"You do that as if you were accustomed to it," said Felicity sharply.

"I was always good at untying knots," he said blandly. "Goodness, what a monster that corset is. You'll need to lie on your face on this seat."

Felicity lay down on her face while he struggled with the lacing of her corset, which had been lashed into a double knot at the back. Then he turned her gently over and began to unlace it at the front.

"Oh, what a relief," sighed Felicity as he at last slid the corset from under her and chucked it on the seat opposite.

"Felicity," he said hoarsely, looking down at the slim figure in the white silk petticoat.

"Arthur! You can't do anything yet. Not here! Not now!"

But his mouth silenced her, and his clever hands sent the rest of the world spinning away.

They were to spend the night at a posting house a comfortable distance away from Pent House.

Two tall footman jumped down and helped milord and milady to alight. The coachman and outriders took the horses and grand ducal carriage round to the stables.

"See if they've left anything in the carriage," called the coachman to one of the grooms. "Ladies are always leaving fans and reticules."

The groom poked his head in the carriage and then reached in an arm. He then slowly backed out and mutely held up the corset.

"Well, my stars," said the coachman, filled with admiration. "Couldn't even wait. Ah, well, that's the Quality for you!"

* * *

Felicity awoke during the night with a frightened cry, and her husband hugged her close.

"I had a nightmare," said Felicity. "I dreamt I was back at Tregarthan Castle, and Mr. Palfrey was having me whipped."

"Shhh. He cannot trouble you any longer. He has fled the country. I told you, Mr. Barchester said he had gone off and taken Martha with him."

"It seems unfair that such a wicked man should go unpunished."

"He's got Martha Barchester with him, and that is a fate worse than transportation. Besides, he will have to live in exile for the rest of his days. But now you are awake, I may as well take up where I left off . . ."

Discover love and romance with

MARION CHESNEY.

Published by Fawcett Books.
Available in your local bookstore.